PROWLERS

Eugene Izzi

BANTAM BOOKS
NEW YORK • TORONTO • LONDON • SYDNEY • AUCKLAND

PROWLERS

A Bantam Book

PUBLISHING HISTORY
Bantam hardcover edition published July 1991
Bantam paperback edition / April 1993

ISBN 0-553-29675-2

Published simultaneously in the United States and Canada

Bantam Books are published by Bantam Books, a division of Bantam Doubleday
Dell Publishing Group, Inc. Its trademark, consisting of the words "Bantam Books"
and the portrayal of a rooster, is Registered in U.S. Patent and Trademark Office
and in other countries. Marca Registrada. Bantam Books, 666 Fifth Avenue, New
York, New York 10103.

PRINTED IN THE UNITED STATES OF AMERICA

RAD   0 9 8 7 6 5 4 3 2 1

FOR KATE

PROWLERS

Chapter
1

They didn't even let Catfeet draw breath as a free man.
They were waiting for him at the bottom of the wide long stone staircase of the Criminal Courts Building at 26th & California, Mickey and another guy, what was his name? Larry, that was it. Fat strong bastard with a thick mustache who liked to be called Lar, the two of them drivers and bodyguards for Darrin Favore, who was the reason Catfeet had done this jail bit in the first place.

He walked down the stairs, fear strong inside him, trying to hide it as they noticed him and put on their tough guy glares. Catfeet did a little dance step down the last few steps, the way Cagney did at the end of *Yankee Doodle Dandy*, and was smiling as he stopped in front of them.

"Got a smoke?" He spoke to Mickey, who had a cigarette dangling out of his lips, the cold fall wind whipping the smoke away from his face. "I been smoking those damn Bull Durham roll-your-owns for a couple of years now, a Pall Mall would taste real fine."

They were going to see how far he wanted to take it,

where he wanted to go. Catfeet knew this because Lar stepped back and crossed his arms and Mickey didn't say anything, just reached inside his heavy black chauffeur's coat, into his shirt pocket and pulled out a pack of Marlboros, shook one out past the edge of the pack and offered it to Catfeet who took it, ripped the filter off and stuck the other end into his mouth.

"How about a light?"

He felt a sense of power as Mickey put the smokes away and brought out his Zippo, some of the old self-confidence coming back to him. He'd go a little further, see how far he could push. He accepted the light with a grunt of thanks.

"You guys bring me a present? A fat envelope filled with thousand-dollar bills? I did twenty-eight months in there for your boss, never said a word to anyone."

Larry shook his head, made a spitting sound. Mickey said, "We come to escort you home, to get the envelope from *you*."

"What envelope?"

"The one with the three and a half million inside it."

"That's what he thinks I owe him now?" Catfeet kept the fear out of his voice, but it was work. Favore could call it that way and make it stick, he had that kind of pull.

Catfeet took stock of the two sides of beef standing there in the cold, giving him the fisheye. Larry was stroking his mustache and sneering outright, a dummy who'd do as he was told and enjoy it. Mickey he knew pretty well from before, for years now. A jerk, or he wouldn't be able to put up with Favore for long, but a standup guy who knew how things worked.

So when he spoke he edged around so he could keep half an eye on Larry, but could look directly into Mickey's eyes, make this conversation one on one.

"You telling me he kept the meter running on the juice when I was inside? That what you're saying to me? I stand up and do time for Favore and he's not gonna forgive the juice?"

"It don't seem right to me, either, Feet, but that's the way it is."

"I ain't got that kind of money."

Catfeet heard Lar snort again and he ignored the man, kept his eyes locked with Mickey's.

"We're supposed to tell you—"

"Shit, let's tell him in the car, I'm freezing my balls off out here."

"What balls?" Catfeet said, and turned to face Lar, knowing now that he was safe. He knew where this conversation was heading, what they'd want him to do, and he wouldn't be able to do it if his head was busted or his fingers broken.

"You just better watch it, Millard. I don't take a lot of shit from the headbreakers and I sure ain't gonna take none from some punk of a thief."

To Mickey, Catfeet said, "Where's the car?"

It was a nice one. A black Mercedes with a car phone in the front and another one mounted behind him on the rear window ledge. The seats were leather and the floors were carpeted, and it was warm in here, smelled of some car wash perfume spray, liberally applied. Mickey drove it down the expressway fast and it had a good ride; if Catfeet closed his eyes, he could believe that they were standing still.

Catfeet sat in the back, alone, the two heavies in the front, leaving him alone for the most part, talking quietly to each other. He couldn't hear what they were saying and he didn't much care. He knew that when they did address him, it wouldn't be to bear good news.

He felt his belt digging into his belly, a tightness in the cloth around his shoulders. He'd worn jumpsuits inside, this was the first time he'd had his street clothes on since he'd gone before the grand jury two years ago and he must have packed on a few pounds. The shoes fit well though, except that he could feel a blister forming on the inside of his right foot; leather shoes were forbidden in jail, he'd only worn soft laceless tennis shoes.

" 'Ey, 'teef," Lar said, making no secret of how he felt about thieves. "Here's how it's gonna be. You work for us now, for Mr. Favore, but he don't want nothin' to do with no punk like you, so me and Mick, we run you. You owe the man three million, six hundred thousand. He'll forgive the change, something like sixty grand. And the meter's still ticking. You either start paying off the three-six this week, or by next week you owe another seven hundred grand."

"Six for five a month, is that what he charged me?"

"Loan that high, we usually cut a few points off, but for you, the boss said take it all. At least he didn't do it by the week."

They got off the expressway and were now driving down Clark, the two men knowing where he'd want to go, or thinking they did. To the rooms above the 909 Club, where he'd lived before he'd been arrested, when he wasn't staying with his woman.

They'd released Catfeet during the 6 A.M. morning movement, and he'd had the option of staying for breakfast and collecting his buck fifty when the gate opened at nine, but he'd passed. On his first day there, when he was being moved to his section, he'd passed through a long underground tunnel where the stench of urine was enough to make you sick. The floors and walls were concrete, painted and spotless, and there was a hack at either end of the tunnel. Out of curiosity, nervous, he'd asked the female hack who'd been escorting him, "Where did someone hide to piss?" and she'd laughed, told him that wasn't piss, that smell came in from the air ducts, from the kitchen, where dinner was being prepared . . .

It was still before seven and traffic was light, none of the businesses opened yet and few people heading to work. The few blue collar workers who were on the street were waiting for buses.

"We cut the juice off after the first big score, and from

there on you owe the principal only. When you work that
off, you're a free man."

Levinson's Jewelers was coming up, on the right,
Catfeet could see the sign maybe a block away. He said,
"That's how it is, Larry?"

"You call me Lar, or better, Mr. Dorbino."

"And what if I tell you to go fuck yourself?"

Lar turned in the seat, grinning.

"We got instructions about that, too. I wish you would,
honest to God, Millard, please, tell me to go fuck myself."

To Mickey, Catfeet said, "Pull over, right here.
There's something I want you to see."

They were maybe three doors down from Levinson's,
in front of a pawnshop. Catfeet got out and Lar was right
there with him, in case he was going to try and make a
run for it. The thought had crossed Catfeet's mind, but it
would only delay the inevitable.

He stepped into the alcove of the pawnshop and decided to try a little reality therapy.

He turned up the collar of his suit jacket and stuffed
his hands in his pockets, stamped his feet until Mickey
got the car alarm turned on and joined them, walking up
with a quizzical expression on his big dumb face. Lar was
right there in front of him, cutting off any hope of escape
from the alcove. Around him, all Catfeet could see were
guitars, typewriters behind the shop's glass . . .

When they were all standing on the concrete together
Catfeet said, "Levinson's is right there, a couple doors
down. Got a few mill in inventory in the safe in back. I
can't do a job that size alone, though. Let's go get it, the
three of us, get me off the hook right now."

Catfeet stepped around Lar, walked the few yards
down the sidewalk with the two of them right there beside him, stunned to silence. Into the alcove of Levinson's, where he took his hands out of his pockets and ran
them around the top of the door.

"Two alarms that I can see, but they sometimes put
them there to throw you off, figure you'll disarm them and

feel safe, then the silent infrared bastard gets you when you're not looking."

He turned to them, nodding his head.

"If there isn't a third alarm, we just might make it, in and out, before ten. Mickey, you got a tire iron in that Mercedes?"

"I ain't going in, forget that shit, I don't play that shit." Mickey was scared, was falling for it, and even Lar looked alarmed, wary and cautious if not frightened.

"It's not the same as busting someone's head, when you know goddamn well he can't go to the cops." Catfeet was speaking to Lar now, staring at him. "No baseball bat's gonna give you power in there. See, Larry, you're in there and if they catch you it's three to seven, mandatory, Class Two felony, and you know they're coming, have to figure they are. It's not like picking your own time and place to break someone's head, you go when you can and hope for the best and if they catch you there's always the chance that they'll want you off the street and they'll just come in blasting, or you'll catch a rookie, wants to impress his boss, sees shadows in a jewelry store and doesn't call for backup, charges in and gets scared when you jump 'cause he scared the shit out of you, and he empties his service piece in your ass.

"You go in with your asshole tight and your belly in your mouth, tasting copper. Your hands are shaking and you're scared to death but what's in that safe is worth it, Lar, so you take the shot and crawl on your belly like a snake to the safe because you have to assume that infrared alarm is blinking in there somewhere.

"Sometimes even with inside information you get screwed up because they might know the make of the safe but if they're off on the year it was made by even one year it can foul you up because they're always working to make those things harder to bust. I've spent eleven hours banging a box and was going through the alley door with the take while the manager was opening the store from the front, and that's cutting it close."

Catfeet stuck his hands inside his pockets but didn't take his eyes off Lar's. He didn't know it, but his eyes were glowing with intensity, laser-like. He was licking his lips and half-smiling as the memories of a score, the physical sensations of being inside a place you had no place being, flooded through him.

"These days you need a wire man with you because a good prowler doesn't work the sophisticated alarms, he's not an electrician. And you need a punk to carry and hold and hand you the tools because you can't waste time once you're in there, you just bust it, grab what's there and take off. You need a guy outside too, watching the street and listening to a portable police radio. And while all that other shit is happening to your emotions, you got to keep asking yourself if you can trust the guys you're with, because these days your partners rat you out in a minute—even if you get away free you got to think about it. Some chump gets caught with some cocaine and he bargains you away for a walk, it happens every day."

Catfeet smiled. "Go get the pry bar, Mick, and let me have a last smoke before we go in."

"I ain't going in nothing," Lar said, and Catfeet asked him if he was sure.

"I told you I ain't going in nowhere."

"What we got here is a chance to do this thing together, to share all the risks and if we score we walk away from each other, no problem, no hard feelings, everybody's happy. I'm not gonna offer again, so Larry, I got to ask you, you gonna go in with me, get these diamonds?"

"Fuck you, you're the prowler, not me."

"Then, Larry, you have to understand something. I am never, ever, in my goddamn fucking life, gonna take down a score then hand the money over to somebody ain't got the balls to take the risk with me, so you can just go and fuck yourself. You don't run me, you don't run my crew, you don't run shit."

For a second it was tense, Lar glaring and flexing his

muscles and Catfeet got ready to jump. Then Mickey put his hand on Lar's shoulder, gently coaxed him away.

"We'll give Mr. Favore your message."

"You do that, Mick," Catfeet said, then turned and walked away from them, stopped at the pay phone on the corner and waited for the big black car to pass him before he pulled his quarters out of his pocket.

And dropped three of them into the gutter because his hands were shaking so damn bad from the fear that he no longer had to hide.

Chapter 2

Charlie Lane was sitting behind his desk in his office, listening to the woman across from him complain and being kind about it, not saying anything about the lateness of the hour, not looking at his watch or doing anything else to give her the impression that she was wasting his time.

It was the way he was, a thinker, a listener. He paid attention and kept his mouth shut and was sometimes amazed at the things people would tell him.

Take now, for instance. This poor woman across from him, had to scale in at two hundred and fifty pounds, had gotten Charlie's wife's name and had run her down at the family business, gone to all that trouble and now Lina wouldn't even take the time to hear her out.

Charlie took the time, though, and was glad that he had. He was learning, too, why Lina hadn't.

"Look at this," the woman now shoving a picture of a younger Lina across the table, a pregnant Lina. "She lectured at our dieters' group and told us she'd lost fifty-five pounds in four weeks using her special diet plan and vitamins." The woman was wearing ski pants, for Christ's sake, the stretch kind with the little straps that went around your heels. Her round lower belly stuck far out of the pants, giving the impression that she had a watermelon stuck down the front there. Her breasts had to be size fifty. Long dark hair that could use a shampoo. Not very bright, and she'd been desperate.

"I fasted, didn't eat anything for a week like she told me, after that only salads, took the vitamins every day and blended the nutrients with skim milk, like she said to do, paid her a total of three hundred and seventy dollars for a month's supply and guess what?"

"It didn't work?" Charlie said.

She sat back a little, embarrassed but not wanting to pass up the opportunity. She waved her hand down the front of her body. "It look like it worked?"

Good God. Could Lina have been so dumb? Would she risk the integrity of her family name, even legally jeopardize the business just to make a few dollars on the side? Stealing the dreams of a neurotic mess like this for personal profit was sick. Not to mention cruel.

The worst part of it was, he could see Lina doing it.

Charlie reached into the inside jacket pocket of his tailor-cut suit, removed his personal checkbook.

He said, "Mrs. Williams?" She looked at his checkbook, shut her mouth as he scribbled, speaking to her as he wrote. "We run a legitimate vitamin-nutrient wholesaler here. We plan to run GNC out of business in five years." He finished writing the check, tore it out of the book and held it in his hand as inducement as he continued.

"My wife isn't in the room, so I won't speak for her or presume to understand what happened or why." She was staring at the check, her eyes narrowed, trying to make out how much it was for.

"But if you're willing to sign a release right now, I'll hand this four-hundred-dollar check over to you, your money back and an extra thirty for your time."

She had to play it cute and it didn't surprise him. Charlie was used to being subtle, it was part of his personality. Rarely speaking up and when he did speak, doing so in a quiet voice without a hint of threat in his tone. A lot of people, even smart ones, took this as weakness, which was fine with him. He didn't care one way or the other how people saw him, and it was always a thrill, a kick for him when they found out how tough he could be when he had to.

"I don't know . . ." the woman said. "Maybe I should talk to my lawyer before signing anything . . ." Whining now like Roseanne Barr. Going from grateful for having his ear to greedy with the stroke of a pen.

Charlie stood.

"Fine, Ma'am. We have lawyers who are overpaid for doing next to nothing on our payroll, and it'll be good to give them some work for a change." He smiled, took the check in both hands and she jumped on it before he could tear it up.

"Well, if you think I should . . ." Whine.

"*I* don't think any such thing. I just wanted to make things right with you. My lawyers, though, will tell the jury about other cases just like yours, have experts testify to how difficult it is to lose weight, how easy it would be for someone to sneak candy bars and not tell anyone . . . I'm really just trying to save you a lot of trouble." He didn't want to tell her that he figured she'd had enough to last her simply by looking the way she did. He dropped the check to the desk and walked to the door. "Should I tell my lawyers to expect your call?"

She had turned in her seat to watch him, maybe wondering if she could scam him out of more money, or if he was willing to negotiate, or if this was really the final offer.

"Mr. Lane?" the woman said, "where do I sign?"

This was about the last straw.

Charlie sat behind his desk, looking out at South Chicago Avenue, trying to calm down before he said or did something he might be sorry for.

Married less than a year, and the bloom had come off the rose in a hurry. Working now for the wife's father, John, a drunk who'd let the business go to hell, working mostly mail orders before Charlie came in and turned things around. Yet still getting the same pay since day one. Was that fair? Hell no.

Charlie flipped the morning paper over on his desk, so the sports page faced him. The headlines were too depressing. Some kid at the local high school had shot and killed some other kid in a gang war, right in the classroom, in front of the students and teacher, and hell, he was depressed enough already, what with what he was married to.

They'd met in college, Charlie a twenty-five-year-old freshman and Lina a thirty-five-year-old graduate student, and it hadn't taken him long to find out that she was looking for more on campus than her master's degree. She'd been the first long-term sexual encounter he'd had in half a decade, and he'd thought he'd been in love. He hadn't rushed into the marriage but was now sure regretting it. Finding out more about the woman every day and liking little of what he learned.

And maybe it was a two-way street.

She'd been attracted to his quiet attitude, his maturity and self-confidence. Had called him her "mystery man," and had made it her destiny to figure out his secrets. Six years later she saw him as surly, mistook his silence for hostility, was always carping on him about how he never shared things with her, how he opened up more with her kid than he did with his wife.

What kind of woman was jealous of her own son?

The same kind of person who would take snapshots of herself pregnant and use them as a marketing tool to break the hearts and wallets of fat people.

In Lina's worst day, she didn't go an ounce over 120 pounds. Short woman with small bones, her frailty being one of the things that attracted him to her. Divorced with a child? No problem. Charlie liked kids, they were honest, and there was no competition with Lina's ex-husband. The man didn't come around to the house, sent a car over to get the boy, Lance, every Friday evening, the same vehicle dropping Lance off Sunday night. Charlie had thought that the father just couldn't stand seeing his ex-wife and son in the presence of another man, thought that was why he had never met the man. These days, Charlie knew the real reason the ex kept his distance. He couldn't blame the man much, either.

So the marriage had probably been a mistake. No problem, he'd made them before, and on a much grander scale. The real problem would be in leaving the boy, in telling Lance that a second man was walking out of his life, getting that across to the kid without badmouthing the boy's mother.

Maybe he should wait. Give it a little time. The idea of counseling would never pass through the mind of a man like Charlie, nor through Lina's, although for different reasons. As far as Charlie could tell, she didn't see where there was a problem. She was in charge, the boss, and Charlie and Lance and her father and everyone else had been born to worship her. Let her think what she wanted, did it matter? Not to him. He hadn't rushed into the marriage and didn't want to rush out of it. Wait a few weeks, give it serious thought, then make his decision.

What did matter, however, was the fact that he had raised the company's gross to six times what it had been a year ago, and hadn't received any of the financial benefits. That problem, he could solve right now.

There was a single tentative knock on his door and then Lina walked in, shy for a change, smiling bashfully as she walked over to him, her beauty still enough to fill his heart at her sight.

Lina was lovely. Ten years older than he was, forty-one and looking twenty, her black hair in a pixie cut, her makeup light, highlighting her prominent cheekbones.

Lina who saw herself as the fashion model, the woman who'd taken time out of her non-career to save the family business. Probably couldn't stand to think about giving up the help which had mostly raised her, the maid, the butler at the family residence. People she said were like family to her but whom she treated like dirt whenever they were there.

Lina walked over to him and Charlie turned in his chair, tracking her, his face blank. Lina looking like nine-year-old Lance when the kid got caught reading comic books under the covers after bedtime.

"That horrible woman!" Lina spoke, being cagy, watching him. "How dare she come here? If Doddy found out—"

"He'd congratulate you on your business sense."

She took it personally, turned to the window and crossed her arms, giving him the patient adult treatment.

"They need that, you know," Lina explaining now, giving him her analysis. "Need hope in their lives, and nothing's cheap, is it?"

"We'll discuss it later."

"If we must." She turned to see him almost to the door, Charlie could feel her eyes on his back, the woman shocked that he was leaving before she dismissed him.

"And where are you going?"

"I have to have a little talk with your father."

"Not about the Williams woman!" Lina spat it out in surprise but he didn't answer her because he was already out the door.

What he had to say to the old man had nothing at all to do with Lina or Mrs. Williams. But Lina didn't have to know that. Let her think what she wanted, what did it matter? She would, anyway.

From behind him he heard her holler, "Chaz?!" He could hear his secretary and the order-takers giggling as he passed them, the workers putting on their coats, going home for the day. He didn't acknowledge their smirks, didn't bother to even smile. He wasn't sure if they were laughing at him or at Lina, and, again, he didn't care either way.

He'd learned the hard way the importance of staying in emotional control, when he'd lived in a place where if you failed the test, the instructor sentenced you to death.

John Lofgren's office had windows that looked out onto 84th Street, not that there was much out there to see. Dilapidated houses on this side of the building, falling apart right under John's nose. It probably made him feel good, knowing he wasn't the only neighborhood landmark that was rapidly going to hell.

Not that he didn't try to keep up appearances. John wore good clothes, expensive shoes handmade for him in Italy. The suits built to hide his deterioration, the damage he'd done to his body over the years with alcohol. John looked up as Charlie came into his office, catching his father-in-law half-dozing in his judge's leather chair, snapping to attention and shaking his head, glancing quickly at his watch as he swiveled to face Charlie.

"Charlie! Come in, son, come in!" John took a longer, official look at his watch, smiled.

"Well, I'd say the sun's past the yardarm!" He pushed back, took a fresh bottle of bourbon off the shelf, uncapped it and poured himself a stiff one. "Care to join me?"

Charlie wondered how many he'd had before the sun had passed the halfway mark. Judging from the glassiness of his eyes, the smell in the room, he'd had a few already.

"No, thanks, John."

"Suit yourself." His father-in-law took a polite sip of the booze, his pinky extended, lowered the glass a fraction then shot it up again, half-draining it. "Ahh . . . the first one's always the best," John said.

"That's what they tell me."

John poured himself another and exercised his will by pushing back and replacing the bottle, coming back to the desk and staring at Charlie without even once glancing at the alcohol. Showing Charlie or maybe himself something, how he had it under control.

"Good to see you, Charlie. Was just speaking of you at lunch, what an asset you've been to the company." Most likely laughing about it, how he had a guy who'd made the company millions and was working for pennies. Bragging to his cronies about what a good businessman he was. "Told half the club how the best move Lina's ever made was marrying you." Charlie could see John saying it in a different way, telling them how Charlie was pussy-whipped, would do whatever Lina wanted. Which was fine with Charlie, it would mean the man was off guard right now, unprepared for what he had to say.

"So you're happy with my performance?"

Now the man took a drink. Sixty-three and he looked eighty, fat and out of shape, red-faced, cheeks pitted. He put the glass down carefully on his desk blotter and nodded, coughing wetly deep in his chest, hardly any sound coming out of his tight-pressed lips. A drunk's cough.

John lit a cigarette. "How couldn't I be happy? Son, you've given this business new life." Then, "Didn't your quarterly bonus show you how grateful I am?" Lofgren had his problems, but he could still scheme.

"Not commensurate with what I've done, John." There, lay it out and see if the man had enough class to pick up on it. It was Charlie's way, letting others say what he wanted to hear, leading them to it with a few well-chosen words.

"Not commensurate . . . ?" John sipped his whiskey, never taking his eyes off Charlie's. "Hmm." Then, being cute, "Is it com*men*surate with the big money you were making—what—seven to twelve years ago, to the high-class job you had before college?"

John should count his blessings that Charlie was no longer that man. Back in those days, he would have climbed the desk and choked the man over an insult. Today, however, he was mature enough, patient enough to ignore a statement like that. He said, "I was thinking more of profit participation, of a higher salary, of a partnership."

Now John grunted. Were he and Lina alike? Like twins, having the same mannerisms, the same grating, shallow superiority because they came from old money. When John spoke this time, it was in a condescending, patronizing tone, laid on so thick that Charlie nearly lost his poker face.

"Charlie, there're people who've been with me since before you were born who aren't partners with me and who don't share in profits. I pay you well, son, and let's keep in mind, I was doing pretty good before you came on board."

"You had a failing vitamin mail order business that advertised in the *National Enquirer*. Now you've got ten Chicago wholesale stores, net profit up over five hundred percent—"

"No one earns a partnership in a year—"

"Stores going up in seven suburbs, and you've got all day to sit around in this office, drinking, while I earn you all your money."

That stopped him for a minute, John sitting forward in his chair and glaring, about to maybe start something before he remembered that Charlie was over thirty years younger than he and in better shape than John had ever been.

"I won't take that from you, Charlie." Said in half-threat.

"I don't blame you. I wouldn't either." He paused, enjoying it when the old man sat back, like he'd scored. Charlie wondered if he were particularly smart or if most of the people he interacted with were just plain dumb.

"Which is why this argument stops, right now. I want a raise, John, no two ways about it. Double the salary, effective immediately, or I'm history." He rose to his feet as John rocked back in his chair. Charlie smiled.

"Sleep on it, John, and I'll see you in the morning."

"You're leaving already?"

"Why should my last day be sixteen hours? Yeah, I think I'll go over to the club, work out, take a steam."

"The club membership was one of your perks, don't forget."

"Yeah, and the car and the cellular phones. All things I can pretty much live without, while I build my own vitamin-nutrition business. Take maybe six months to put you out of business."

"You wouldn't dare, I gave you your start!"

But John was yelling at an empty doorframe.

Chapter 3

Robert (Catfeet) Millard watched the fat guy eating, wondering how any of these mobsters ever managed to live past forty. The guy, he was disgusting, had to have put away three pounds of spaghetti, ravioli, lasagna, and bread rolls in the past two hours, stuffing it in his mouth before he was done chewing the last bite, washing it all down with vino.

Mrs. Luchessa, the mob guy's wife, could have passed for his brother if she hadn't been wearing a dress. They weighed about the same, were both short and fat, in their early sixties, the major difference being that the mob guy, Sal, didn't have a mustache. The woman was bringing the wooden serving bowls of food in from the kitchen and filling the plates as fast as Sal could empty them, smiling with glee as her husband smacked his lips, sucked his teeth, burped, or gave any other sign of enjoyment. Catfeet figured she was mostly happy just to have her man home for a change after dark; he usually took his meals in joints where the tables were covered with red and white checked cloths, had wine bottles that had candles stuck down the neck, the wax spilling onto the straw coverings, stuck in the middle of the table. Usually, too, Sal Luchessa would have some bimbo with him, about forty years younger than his beloved. A walking pair of tits, interchangeable, none of them able to cook more than coffee, which was all right with Sal. Anytime he wanted a good meal, he could go home.

Feet was uncomfortable. He'd been associated with Sal for nearly twenty years, and this was the first time he'd been invited into the mobster's house for dinner. On the street, in a restaurant or tavern, he could show the man the respect due him, run his business down for him and pay him his due, no problem. Here, he felt like a stranger, a student invited to the disciplinarian's house for supper, not knowing how the rules changed from the outside or if they changed at all.

Still, what Sal had always told him was that he admired the way Feet handled himself, his balls. That was good, because it was going to take a lot of balls for Catfeet to speak the words he'd come here to say.

Catfeet ate slowly and sparingly and smiled, getting full quickly and sipping on the wine often to give the impression that he wasn't giving up. The two-man party was in his honor, and he didn't want to do anything that would offend this man. Offending Sal could get you into the trunk of a car left in the long-term parking lot at O'Hare, so it wasn't a smart thing to do at any given time, but tonight Catfeet needed a favor, and he needed this man in a good mood.

Which he seemed to be in. Food did that to Sal. And Christmas, that always put him in a good mood.

"No, Mrs. Luchessa, honest to Christ, I can't eat another—" She'd snuck up on him, was shoveling some more macaroni onto his plate, now giving him the evil eye.

"What's the matter, you no like my cooking?"

"It's wonderful . . ." He shot a quick glance at Sal, saw the man frowning at him.

"And no use the Lord's name in vain in my house!"
She shoveled and Catfeet let her, figuring it would put
him in good with Sal.

"What's wrong, the jailhouse make you forget your
manners?"

Sal spoke softly and Feet looked at him quickly, relaxing when he saw the man was smiling. Even after all
these years, he still couldn't figure him out, his moods.
One second he'd be smiling at you, the next, he'd tear
your eyes out of your head and suck them into his mouth
right off the vein, like grapes on the vine. Or spaghetti off
the fork, Jesus. Feet was used to dealing with thieves,
with standup guys he picked himself, men he could for
the most part trust. Sal was the only man in this line of
work he dealt with, and the main reason for those dealings
was that in Chicago, if you were a professional prowler,
you always paid, one way or another. Some of the ones
who were adverse to negotiations even paid with their
lives, and right across the table from Feet was the guy
who gave all such orders. So even though Sal was smiling,
his eyes were hard and Feet didn't know if the hard act
was for his benefit or if Sal was only showing off for his
wife. Sal would see either scenario as equally important.

Feet mumbled something apologetic, waved his fork
as explanation for his mistake, tore into the lasagna, following Sal's lead, drinking down a big gulp of the wine
while his mouth was still full of noodles.

Sal seemed to accept it. Maybe he was mellowing in
his old age.

Or maybe it was the season.

Sal loved Christmas, was known to be more generous
to his men during the holiday season, let them off the
hook for things that would have cost them a beating from
January thru mid-November. Which was when Sal began
celebrating.

Feet had been a little embarrassed, walking up to the
big house in River Forest, some of the trees still having
leaves on them and here Sal was, with the Christmas dec-

orations up already, tons of them, a couple grand worth of lights and mangers with electrically operated Jesuses and Marys and Josephs, their heads bobbing in time to the choir blaring religious Christmas hymns from some artfully hidden speakers. There was a Santa on the roof, and eight tiny reindeer—tiny in this case meaning maybe only twenty feet tall in comparison to Santa's fifty feet—Rudolph's nose lit with what looked like a spotlight.

Inside the house it was more of the same. The tree was up, put together in front of the picture window, with tinsel and lights and a praying angel on top, a dozen or so brightly packaged presents under it, all a week before Thanksgiving.

Mrs. Luchessa came back in, this time with what looked like a mountain of some kind of pastry on a tray, poor little woman, bending under its weight.

"Need a hand, Mrs. Luchessa?" Sal said, not bothering to look up. Speaking with his mouth full. She didn't bother to answer him, put the cake down on the table, began slicing at it with a bayonet, gouging out huge slices and putting them on plates.

Sal always referred to his wife formally in front of people, and there were always people around. Somewhere in the house there would be four or five guys whose only reason for existence was to keep Sal safe and alive, the men hidden in this mansion every bit as well as the speakers were hidden out in the front yard. Feet wondered if that's what he called her in bed, back in the days when he'd still been snaking her. Feet could hear the man: Mrs. Luchessa, care to swish off the pantaloons and have a go at it?

"Something funny?" Sal said the words but sure didn't seem to think so, staring at Feet in a way that made Feet's skin crawl. It was another thing he always did in front of his wife; talk to the help like garbage, letting her see what a powerful man this fat little guinea used to work in the railroad yards was these days. Well, Feet had news for him if Sal hadn't already figured it out; he wasn't one of the help. Still, he calmed himself. He had agreed to come to dinner because he needed help that only the don could give.

"Just wondering where I'm gonna put all this food, Sal," Feet said, which caused Mrs. Luchessa to jump into the conversation.

"Do like Sally do, put it inna wooden leg!" She spoke as she placed his strawberry cheesecake down in front of him, giving him a good whiff of garlic breath, her mustache jiggling as she cackled at her wit.

"That's a good one, Mrs. Luchessa," Feet said, almost wishing he was back in the county jail.

Almost.

"Dig in," Sal said, smiling. "After we're done with the dessert, Mrs. Luchessa, if you'll excuse us, we'll be retiring to the den for an hour or so."

"Sure, sure." The woman smiled. She appreciated being asked if it was all right, her husband giving the guest the illusion that her opinion mattered. She waddled out of the room and Sal looked at Feet, stuck about three ounces of cheesecake in his mouth and spoke around it.

"You got to find yourself a good woman one of these days, Bobby." Sal never called him Catfeet or any of the derivatives, Cat or Feet or Foot or even Sole, like some of the boys did. Sal didn't play that nickname stuff. The closest he'd come would be his own personal Italian familiarization of Robert, Bobbeet. When Sal called him that, Feet knew the man was in a good mood.

"The best one in the world's already been taken," Feet said, nodding toward the kitchen, making Sal smile.

He dug into the cheesecake, wanting to get it done, hoping Sal would be satisfied with one helping. He wanted to get into the den as soon as he could, say what he had to say and get the hell out—he had some living to catch up on.

"You need anything in there?" The woman was standing in the doorway, compulsively rubbing her hands, looking solicitous. Like everyone else in his life, serving

Sal. Sal said something to her but Feet didn't hear what it was, he was too busy wondering when he'd stopped thinking of Mrs. Luchessa as old. Hadn't seen her that way since he'd walked in the door.

Maybe twenty-eight months in the county jail had made him feel older than she'd ever be.

"Uncle Darrin, I don't *want* to come home, shit it's *cold* up there." Merle Como spoke into the phone in the bedroom of the mansion on Singer Island in Palm Beach, Florida, wishing his uncle was there in front of him instead of back home in Chicago. He always could get his way with the man when he argued his case face to face, man to man, the way he liked to do business.

But Darrin Favore wasn't playing games this time, telling him to bring his ass home before Friday, come see him as soon as he landed. Merle listened and didn't talk back. His mother's brother-in-law was not a man to argue with, even long distance.

"I'll be there, Friday," Merle told him, and his uncle —who did he think he was?—hung up on him. Merle put the phone back on the nightstand and thought about it.

Merle knew who his uncle was, and what he was, and wanted no part of either side of the man. Every time he did business with that pud he wound up going to jail.

Friday, though, shouldn't be too bad, give him four more days to play around here, wrap things up, milk this beauty here next to him for whatever more he could get.

She was lying naked next to him in her king-sized bed, the widow of an ex-radical hippy who'd made good writing a series of books about the 60s revolution. Some idiot had bought the rights and made a TV show out of the story line, and the show had been in the top twenty for seven years, these days was in syndication, the widow getting a fat check for each time of the four it was shown weekly on cable.

Moonbeam was doing all right for herself.

Merle had guessed a month ago that she'd either screwed the sucker to death or poisoned him for his money, one, this tall thing who couldn't get enough in the sack and who couldn't cook none, either. They had to go out to eat all the time and it was a pain in the ass, getting all dressed up and going to places that didn't have any of the stuff he liked to eat, no rare steaks and fries, no eggs fried in bacon fat. Bacon was *out* in Palm Beach, had too much cholesterol or something. As for Moonbeam, she'd try and be creative, whipping up vegetable dishes mixed with fruit; pineapples and carrots, lightly steamed. Meat was out of her life; the preservation of animals and their civil rights being her latest cause.

The other thing, though, he had no problem with. Merle could never get enough sex, either.

Moonbeam spoke without turning her head.

"Where you going?"

The light was on in the bathroom, casting the bedroom in a ghostly glow, a strip of radiance falling across her bare backside, showing him her smooth roundness. She had to have planned it that way, her ass being the part of her he liked best—Moonbeam up on her knees, her chin buried in a pillow, her eyes riveted on the mirror built into the headboard, taking him the way he wanted to give it to her.

"Gotta head back into Chi-town for a few days." There was no sense in letting her know he probably wouldn't be coming back for a while.

She rolled over onto her back, tossed her long black and gray hair out of her eyes.

"No," she said, simply. Giving an order.

Merle knew how to be reasonable and didn't want to spend his last few days in town in some hotel, or, worse, down the road a ways, across the bridge in the poor section of Palm County, in his daddy's shack. "Honey, I told you before, I got business dealings up there—"

"With your uncle? He a big businessman, is he?"

He'd never seen her like this. What had happened to

do your own thing, or even better, the philosophy she claimed from the title of her favorite song: We'll sing in the sunshine? Moonbeam was maybe twenty years older than he was, about fifty or fifty-one or two, happy to have a young good-looking guy like Merle to show off around town and who had the guts to help her meet her radical agenda. But now she was glaring, making him mad. He didn't take kindly to rich bitches thinking they owned him. It could be done, but she hadn't offered enough yet by a long shot.

"What's he in, the catfish business? Or do you trap coons, make hats out of their fur?" She grinned, being what she probably thought was superior. "Or do you run your Mexican friends in from south of the border?" She was messing with him now, making fun of his humble upbringing across the bridge, still in Palm Beach County, but a million miles away from the riches that was *this* Palm Beach. Besides, there was only one Mexican Merle dealt with and he was back in Chicago, Moonbeam had never met him. The ones she was referring to were Peruvians, and the last thing Moonbeam wanted to do in this life was to let them know she took them lightly. Besides, when he was out with his friends was the only time he could eat some real food, instead of crap like fried bananas and artichoke hearts.

If she kept this up, he might have to give her The Punch.

Still and all, he didn't reply, just rolled out of bed and walked naked over to the window, looked out at the plush grounds, the close-shaved grass, the fountain in the middle spouting water high into the air, colored by the fans of rotating lights underneath, Merle feeling Moonbeam's eyes on his back.

He knew what she was seeing and he tightened his muscles, giving her a show, her thrills.

Merle was tall, slender, going six-two and one-seventy-five, with a body that was all planes and angles. He had a small pot belly now, the product of too much beer and too many steaks this past month or so that he'd been back home in Florida, but he held his shoulders back when he walked, stuck the belly out with pride, the way his uncle Calvin did, and who in Palm Beach County was fool enough to mess with Merle's uncle Calvin?

When they'd first met Moonbeam had told him that he looked like a young Christopher Walken, and he hadn't known how to take it, presumed it to be a compliment. He had high cheekbones and deepset eyes, a haunted, sad, lonely baby face that lit up to a thousand watts when he smiled. He could charm anybody with that smile, with his air of boyish vulnerability. It sure worked well with the Chicago judges. He combed his brown hair straight back, and wasn't ashamed to admit there was Indian in his blood.

He heard her get out of bed and slog through the thick white shag carpeting toward him; she put her arms around his waist just as the air conditioning clicked in. Eighty-five degrees down here, and in Chicago it was probably snowing.

Moonbeam rubbed her cheek on his back, squeezed his belly. "I'm sorry baby," Moonbeam said.

Merle turned around and held her, stiffening up and wanting to get right to it, but having to straighten her out first so that she'd stay on her toes. He smiled, bright and childlike, Merle having a face that was easy to love.

"Just for a few days, 'Beam."

"My old man left me two million dollars he earned and three times that from his family's fortune he inherited." She stuck her face into the light hairs of his chest, licked around his right nipple. "You don't need Chicago, Merle. There's to much to do here, too much work left."

Right, wait for winter and spray orange paint on the fur stoles that the old Jew broads wore, or maybe there was even heavier stuff planned. Stuff she and her buddies thought was militant and dangerous, but which to Merle was just a little harmless fun that passed the time until something better came along. Although he had to admit, he was good at this zealot stuff.

He ran his hands up her back, to her neck, caressed her hair, then the back of her neck, running his hands around to her throat. She moaned as he pressed slightly, maybe thinking he was having his pleasure with her; she liked the rough stuff, and he'd known some like that before, but she was the first woman who'd ever shown him how to cut off her oxygen so she could get a bigger come.

She licked harder, nibbling at his nipple now, and he squeezed a little more, pushed her head back so he could look at her, so she could see him.

Merle wasn't smiling now. His dark eyes were malevolent, on fire as his fingers closed on her throat.

Moonbeam began to panic, to flail at him, and he ducked his head, hunched his shoulders so her little bitty girl's fists wouldn't touch his face. He didn't care if they marked his chest. He twisted his legs so she couldn't knee him in the balls, waited until she stopped fighting and began to sag in his arms before he eased up on the pressure.

He led her gently to the bed and laid her across her side, covered her with the sheet and turned his back on her, hearing her gasp for breath, the sound intermingling with the forced air coming out of the air conditioning vents.

He began to dress, quickly, knowing she was watching, giving her a chance to get at the gun she kept on the nightstand on her side of the bed. If he heard the drawer slide open, he'd jump on that bed and whale the tar out of her, but she didn't have to know that, he wanted her to think that he just didn't care either way.

The fact was that he didn't. He thought he had her number but if she took this the wrong way he'd still be just fine. Hotels beat jail cells. And he could always show up in Chi-town early.

"Mer—" Her voice was a hoarse whisper. She was still breathing raggedly.

Merle pulled on his pants, shoved his feet into his shoes, sat on the bed and began to lace them.

"Merle . . ." A little better, still pretty much sounding like she'd been gargling with thumbtacks, but better than before. "Where're you going?" There was panic in her tone. Good.

"I'm gone, lady." Merle spat the words in his nasal South Florida drawl. "You think you own me, or what, ordering me around, making fun of me, the way I am, all the time fussing about my friends, like you're better than they are."

"Merle!" She threw herself across the bed and grabbed him from behind and he sat up straight, didn't pull her arms away but didn't comfort her, either.

"Please," Moonbeam whispered. She was sobbing now. "I thought you loved me."

He could feel her fingers unlocking around his waist, working their way south. Fumbling at his belt.

He still didn't move.

"I'm sorry, Merle, I'm a bitch."

There you go.

Merle said, "Say it again," and felt her fingers hesitate, Moonbeam now knowing that everything was all right, that she had a way back into his good graces.

Softly, with shame, she said, "I'm a bitch."

Merle turned to her. "Sure, you are," he said, then said, "And what can you do to stop being a bitch."

Her eyes were cast downward. She shook her head. "Whatever you want me to do." Still sounded rough, but sincere.

Sometimes, Merle knew, you had to treat them this way in order to keep them humble.

Chapter
4

Charlie was pumping iron, the only way he ever really let off steam. He didn't drink or smoke, never yelled or fought with anyone, stated his case calmly at all times and never allowed anyone to ever see him upset.

If they know they can make you mad, Cat used to say to him, then they've won.

He pushed it, bench pressing 250 pounds of free weights without a spotter, going for his fourth rep and not sure if he was going to make it, his fear at the prospect of not being able to do so driving him on, giving him the strength to get it up there into its stand. He dropped the weights gratefully, rolled out from under the bar and got to his feet, walked around the room blowing deep breaths, his hands on his hips.

He'd worked the gut hard, the same as he did every day, and today he was working the back, chest and triceps. Yesterday he'd done his biceps and legs, and it was a good idea to take a day of rest between working each muscle group. He rested, on his feet though and moving, grateful that in this part of the gym he was usually left to

himself, the trendy types who frequented the joint prefer-
ring the sleek machines to the ugly, heavy free weights.
It's a lot easier to move a pin in one of those contraptions
than it is to stack plates on a bar, especially when you're
trying to look macho and cute for the females on the other
machines.

Still in all, this room was as bad as the others, with the
mirrors pasted to the wall, hell, what kind of man liked to
see himself lifting weights? The kind who was posing as
well as lifting, Charlie knew. There were a lot of that type
hanging around in the place.

He stared at himself in the mirror, at his red face, at
the pumped-up muscles, his arms larger than normal because he'd been working them. Seeing a young man of
average height but with a powerful build, a full head of
blond hair over a face that a generous person might call
handsome. He'd built those muscles the hard way, using
free weights in a yard that had no mirrors, no carpet, only
gray cold concrete and a wall that went far up into the
sky. Back then, working out had been his only link to
sanity, the only thing that kept him from killing things.

He wondered if that were still true today, then decided that it didn't matter. As long as he never let them
see him as weak, they couldn't push the buttons, couldn't
set off the time bomb ticking inside.

Charlie turned away from the mirror before someone
came along and caught him looking at himself. It would
ruin his image.

He grunted a laugh at the thought, knowing that some
of the people who worked out here took his silence for
arrogance while others saw it as an invitation, saw him as
an egg to be cracked, were intrigued by his presence. One
woman had even given him a psychological workup after
knowing him ten minutes, telling him he acted the way he
did because he was young and insecure and was afraid
that if he opened his mouth he'd make a fool of himself.

He wondered where they got it, the need to have to know everyone in their company fully within the first hour of meeting, he wondered where it came from.

He wasn't arrogant, nor was he insecure. He said what he had to say, always said hello to everyone here and at the country club where he played poker two nights a week. Could talk on the phone for hours, making the sale or trying to convince a wholesaler why they should jump onto his ship.

It was just that in his personal life he didn't feel the desire to be one of the boys, to tell jokes, to slap backs or jump up for high fives after a round of tennis. The people in this circle were strangers to him, even Lina now, and he didn't think you should try to impress strangers. It was better if they always saw you as dumb, as if you were just there. You learned more that way.

Charlie loosened the bolts on the weight bar sleeves, put them on the bench and added 20 pounds. He replaced the sleeves, tightened them, and slid under the bar.

270 pounds. He'd see if he could lift it three times. Maybe shoot for four. If he couldn't, the thing would collapse on his chest, crush him, but there was no sense in doing it if there wasn't an element of danger involved.

Feet sat in the den, listening to Sinatra sing "Have Yourself a Merry Little Christmas" on the stereo, sipping the Gran Marnier that Sal had poured for him. He could smell the logs burning away somewhere behind him in a fireplace, the den being about the same size of most of the luxury apartments Feet had rented in his time.

Sal sat behind his desk, happy, burping a lot and rubbing his stomach. "Jesus," Sal said, "I got some case of heartburn tonight."

Was this supposed to be a shock? The way the man ate, he was a living Pepto Bismol commercial. "Good food, Sal, best I had in a while."

Sal burped, rubbed his belly, laughed.

Now it was like Feet remembered it, Sal being Sal, none of the stern business now that the wife was not around to be impressed. Why would a man of real weight want anyone to be impressed with him anyway? Feet didn't know. He had stopped trying to figure out the Italians a long time ago.

Sal said, "You was locked up, what, twenty-four months?"

"Twenty-eight, Sal." Twenty-eight months and three days and six hours, but there was no sense in splitting hairs.

"Well, you had a home-cooked meal." Sal opened a desk drawer and took out an envelope, tossed it toward Feet, who caught it and let it sit right there on his lap. "Something for you, for doing the right thing," Sal said. "So, here you are, you're having a drink, you got money," he nodded at the envelope, "and now all you got to do is get laid." He barked for a while, his idea of a laugh, then reached into a humidor and took out a cigar.

It took him a while to get it going and Feet appreciated the break in the conversation. It gave him time to readjust.

Things had changed the second the den doors had closed behind them, Sal lightening up and treating him more like an equal than a toady, which he appreciated but couldn't figure out. Sal was the boss; not Catfeet's boss, because Feet wasn't in the mob, rather, Sal was the boss of Chicago, the head man in charge. They'd done a lot of business over the years because a man like Feet could not survive without the blessing of the mob, and he paid them a percentage off the top of all his business as his street tax. Still, though, he wasn't of them, and so had been shocked after calling for a sit-down this morning after his problem with Mickey and Lar and winding up getting invited for dinner.

Shocked even more to have been treated so shabbily

after he arrived, like a retarded relative who had to be put up with because of the holidays.

So what was going on now? Why was he being treated like a loyal mob underling all of a sudden? All he'd wanted to do was to ask the man for a favor, and it was turning into an all-night thing.

Sal said, "You know that wine? I get it made for me, special. I think the guy who stomped it didn't wash his feet this time." Bark, bark.

Feet let him laugh. He was forty-three years old and felt sixty, overweight now because of the high starch jail diet and the lack of exercise. On the outside, Feet would swim every day at a health club. What was he supposed to do in the county jail, play basketball with the colored guys? He could scare himself, thinking of what would happen to a white guy who tried to join the game. He'd been in the county before, years ago awaiting trial before the fix was put in and he'd skated. It had been bad then, and had gone downhill from there. He was out of shape, unused to being in civilian clothes and eating good food, and the blister on his foot was beginning to throb.

"Jesus, my gut's *killing* me." Sal got up and left the room, leaving the door open behind him. Feet had to fight the urge to get up and take a look around, maybe scope out the inside of the desk. This guy, he probably had hidden cameras watching every move, or had one of his boys hidden behind a false spot in the wall, watching through a knothole in the mahogany paneling. In the relative quiet he could hear the fire roaring and crackling behind him in a fireplace that was bigger than some beds Feet had slept in, could see the shadows jumping across the walls as the fire blazed skyward.

Since Sal had lit a cigar Feet felt free to smoke a cigarette; there had been no ashtrays in the living room or dining room, and he hadn't dared earlier. He was dying for a smoke. He fumbled one out, lit it and sat there puffing, opened the envelope Sal had thrown him, just to have something to do.

There was twenty-eight grand in there, in hundreds. A grand for each month he'd been away. Welcome home, Catfeet. Good old Sal, pretending he hadn't known how long Feet had been away. The song faded as Frank crooned the last note, holding it, playing it like he used to be able to do, then a short silence, the only sound the fire, then Frank was back, this time doing "Silent Night."

What the hell was it for? He wasn't on the payroll, didn't get a stipend when he was away. Feet shoved the envelope into his inner jacket pocket and could see the bulge through his jacket when he looked down. A lot of money, there, and he was in no position to refuse it. In the first place, he needed it, and in the second place you didn't say no to Sal. He might get it in his head to have you shoved into the fireplace, then he and the boys would gather around and toast marshmallows on your melting flesh, sing along with old Francis Albert while they strung popcorn for the tree.

Feet got up, walked over to the ashtray and tapped his ash into the sculpted crystal, heard Sal walking down the hallway, grumbling something in Italian, and got back to his seat before the guy came in, maybe figured him to be prowling the room.

He heard Mrs. Luchessa speaking rapidly in dago, her voice betraying her discomfort, her worry. Had she cooked a bad meal? Feet wondered if these old country women punished themselves when they did, if they committed suicide.

Then Sal was in the doorway, backing through it, mumbling at his wife, who stood there still dry-washing her hands, a look of abject failure on her face.

A sight Sal closed the door on.

He was carrying a bottle of Maalox-plus in his right hand, shaking it up and down, the cigar in his left. He opened the bottle, poured some down his throat, capped it, took a deep puff on the cigar and sat down again in his high-backed leather chair, putting the medicine on the desk, replacing it with his Gran Marnier. He burped, said, "Ahhh," dragging it out, then smiled.

"Jesus," Sal said.

In the den, you could obviously take the Lord's name in vain without getting your ass chewed out.

"You check out your Christmas present?" Sal said.

Feet said, "Yeah, while you were gone." He hesitated. "You okay? You don't look so good."

Sal shrugged. "I ain't been feeling so hot lately. I think my gall-bladder's ready to go, having trouble making bile, Bobby. Get heartburn a lot lately. Don't worry about it."

"Sal? What's this for."

"For you, my friend, a homecoming gift, Christmas gift, whatever you want to call it. You think I don't reward loyalty? You did time for us, Bobbeet."

Feet wasn't about to push it.

"That's what I called about, Sal."

"I figured as much; I heard from Darrin."

"You think he's right?"

Sal took a sip of his liqueur, puffed at his cigar and sat back in the chair. "I think it ain't my problem."

"I just did better than two years so Favore wouldn't have a problem. You, Sal, you *never* had a problem. Grand jury says your name to me, I go away for life before I admit to them I even know you.

"But Favore now, that's another story. When was the last time a gambler went to jail in this town? Shit, I bet he had the outcome wrapped before the grand jury was called. Greylord or no Greylord. They call me in, ask me about his activities, I clam. They give me immunity, I stay clammed. They lock me up for the life of the grand jury, send some dipshit in a fifty-dollar suit around a couple times a week, tell me I hold the key to my own cell, do I want to leave?"

"And you kept your mouth shut." Sal sat forward and crossed his arms on the desk, staring at Feet. "Listen, Bobby. You got any idea how many guys in my outfit would cut off their fingers to get a chance to eat in this house, to drink in this den? The grand jury was showboating, it was election time and the politicians knew that Favore was *out* of favor with me at the time, so they figured they'd be doing *me* a favor by calling a grand jury to investigate him. I let it go for a while for two reasons: To put the fear of God into Darrin Favore and to see who might do any talking the second they got called in. Talk's cheap; I wanted to see how some of these tough guys stood up to heat. Soon as it got serious, when it looked like someone might rat and Favore'd wind up indicted, I got it squashed. I got no use for that son of a bitch, but still, he's of the blood, and he knows too much. We need guys like him, get us legit in the business world."

"And I was still in the county."

"You walk before the grand jury is dissolved, you know where it would be? Front page of the *Tribune,* that's where it'd be."

"Still . . ."

Sal grabbed the bottle of Maalox-plus and gave it some hearty masturbation, drank some of the stuff then leaned back again, rocking back and forth slightly in the chair. He kept rubbing his stomach. "That money in your pocket's my way of paying you back for the time you did for us."

"I did it for Favore, and the way I see it, he owes me. I go in owing him twenty-two dimes, I get out and find out he kept the meter running. It ain't fair, Sal, a man shouldn't have to pay juice when he's locked up because he wouldn't rat out the guy he owes the money to."

"Darrin doesn't see it that way."

"Your nephew call the shots now, Sal?" Feet spoke the words knowing what a risk it was, knowing that if Sal took it the wrong way he could get killed tonight, rather than tomorrow or the next night or next week or whenever Darrin Favore came around looking for his twelve million or whatever stupid amount he claimed Feet owed him and which Feet couldn't pay. He'd spoken in anger because this dinner, the money in his pocket, the so-called respect he'd been shown didn't mean a thing if Sal let Favore get away with this. This was a man who could pick up the phone and order Favore to forget the twenty percent monthly interest on the twenty-two dimes and make it stick. The question now was, would Sal do it?

Sal seemed more concerned with his gallbladder than with Feet's problems, the man sitting there holding his belly in both hands.

"You all right, Sal?"

Sal didn't answer him, held his belly tightly, then loosened, his face relaxing. He picked up his glass and turned to Catfeet casually, but he couldn't hide the fear in his eyes.

"Fuck it," Sal said. He smiled weakly.

"I ain't feeling good enough to play around with this shit. I'm gonna get the doc over here to check me out tonight, soon as you leave." He shook his head, and Catfeet could see sweat on his brow. Why wasn't he himself feeling sick? They'd eaten the same food and Feet sure wasn't used to things prepared that well, to food that heavy and spicy.

"Bobby, you used to be one of the best prowlers in this city. Respectful, too, always came to me, always paid your share, gave us a piece of everything you did. You know how many guys didn't play right? You got any idea? We took care of them, one way or the other, and we'd always give them one chance. I'd sit them down in that same chair you're sitting in and I'd tell them, 'Do the right thing, you got to do like Catfeet the Prowler does.' Some of them did, others didn't, but I'd put your name in their heads, let them know where you stood with me. You think that didn't stand you well with them? You ever think about how many times some idiot would have tried to take you off or down if they hadn't known I was behind you? Then you get into a gambling beef with one of the guys who'd like nothing better than to see me in my grave. You not only acted stupid, you insulted me, doing business with a guy everyone knows is my enemy."

Feet didn't beat around the bush or otherwise try to bullshit Sal. Decided to be straight with him because you didn't come to a man for help then lie to him.

He said: "I got called by a friend of yours, a guy I thought I could trust, in San Diego. He got this score lined up, twenty percent to me, one night's work, all I got to do is go in and open a safe, get out and hand over the contents to him.

"I go, they make me take some punk on the score with me, I open the safe and it's loaded with cocaine."

Sal didn't move, just watched him.

Catfeet said, "What was I supposed to do? Argue with them? They knew I'd balk, which was why they sent the punk. I make noise, he does me and brings back the yi-yo. Later the man hands me a hundred grand and I figure, sure as shit, I'm dead. They'll wait until I'm home and feeling secure, just in case I told you who I was working for, then they'll whack me for knowing about their drug business, seeing the way that shit almost brought the Chicago outfit down a few years back.

"So I come back home to take care of business, get my affairs in order.

"I pay off Charlie's last semester in college, buy him a new car so he won't try and steal one, he was still wild then. Drink, party, gamble the rest away, figuring for sure I'm gonna get aced. I got into Favore for that dough with every intention of not paying him back; how's he gonna get money from a corpse?

"But you know what happened? Nothing. The guy in San Diego, he must still like me and figure I'll keep my mouth shut, because nothing happens. He calls me a while later, talks in riddles, his point being he's sorry he got me into something he knew up front I didn't want to do. Shit, the guy beat me out of tens of thousands of dollars on the twenty percent I never got, then he apologizes.

"Still, I owed Favore. Was lining something up, to get his money 'cause the juice was running, and in the middle of it, I get subpoenaed. You figure he's right, Sal? Well, I don't, and with all due respect, he can kiss my ass if he thinks I'm gonna pay him millions of dollars for a twenty-two-grand marker. Besides, nobody pays juice when they're inside."

"Nobody with *us*, which you ain't."

Feet kept quiet. He'd already said more in this room than he had in the past twenty-eight months.

Sal shook his head. "That guy, Favore. My nephew. He's no good. A moneymaker, but his ideas are too big, he wants it all, the prick.

"Every time I talk to him he says to me at least once, 'Sal, I ever lie to you?' Watch yourself when someone says that, Bobby. It means they sure as hell have, and they're sending out feelers to see if they been found out."

Sal grabbed the bottle, got up and walked, seemingly without pain, over to Feet, poured him a double shot, then leaned over and put the bottle down at the foot of the chair. He didn't stand back up, grabbed the arms of the chair and leaned right into Feet's face.

Christ, the guy smelled sour. Something was wrong with him, and Feet wasn't at all sure it was the guy's gallbladder. Smelled like something had crawled into his belly and died. Sal made matters worse. He burped, not bothering to turn his face away, although he did squinch up his eyes, shut them tight and shook his head from side to side. He opened his eyes and stared straight into Feet's own, and now there was no fear in them or any other sign of weakness, just anger and determination. A man who'd killed a couple of dozen people himself and who'd ordered maybe a hundred more deaths didn't give in to heartburn very easily.

"I'm gonna tell you something, and you better hear me good. Darrin called me. He's got a lot more power than he did when you went away and he'd slash my throat in a second if he thought he could get away with it and not get killed for doing it, but still, he called me, told me about you, what happened this morning, what he thinks you owe him. I didn't say anything, wanted to see you for myself, see how you stood up inside.

"You come here, to my house, you eat dinner, you showed my wife respect and you didn't say shit about how tough it was, how hard you had it when you could have walked any time just by giving that man up. You did your time like a man and all you asked for was what you thought you had coming." He stood now, straight, nodding his head with his hands on his hips, Sal's belly almost in Feet's face. "That's good, Bobby." He spoke softly, then went hard again.

"But you were stupid, playing against us with those basketball games. Betting on a bunch of niggers running around a gymnasium, like some working stiff. Who did you think you were, some wiseguy? A thousand here, a thousand there, like a millionaire. When I heard about it, I thought you'd gone stupid. A first-rate prowler thinking he could beat the spread.

"I could have called you in, seen if you were burned out, if you had some troubles you needed help with, but I waited, I figured if you wanted something, you'd come to me like a man's supposed to."

"I scored big, Sal. I was just playing around before I died."

"Ah, but you got in over your head, then didn't die. Let the gambling into your bloodstream like heroin. All you had to do was to come to me, I would have straightened that San Diego guy out faster than you could make a bet on the Lakers. What'd you drop, fifty of your own? Then you got into Darrin for twenty-two, when you know goddamn well he and I hated each other, that he was trying to push me out. And you don't come to me because you don't want to be beholden. You want me to help you out now, though, don't you."

"I bet with Favore's people so you wouldn't find out."

"You think there's anything goes on in my business I don't know about? You think that, then you *are* stupid."

"Sal—"

Sal waved him off. "Just shut up and listen." He walked behind Feet, and Feet turned in his chair, watched the don of Chicago swagger around the room with his hands clasped behind his back. He looked pretty good now. Probably had an ulcer—you could get one having to watch your back all the time so some power-mad son of a bitch like Favore didn't stick a meat cleaver in it.

Sal stared into the fire for a minute, then turned around and walked back over to Feet's chair, stood in front of it regally, a king standing before a peasant.

"All right. I've seen what I wanted to see. And I don't forget how you took that kid Charlie in after his people died, raised him like your brother and took care of him after he had his troubles, helped him straighten out his life. That was more the act of an Italian than whatever you really are. That kid Charlie, you was good to him and that showed you were a man. You made him better than you and today's he's rich, working for a living instead of stealing like we do.

"Now, Bobbeet, I'm gonna ask you to leave and then I'm gonna make two phone calls. The first one's gonna be to my doctor, get him over here before this gallbladder explodes on me. The second one's gonna be to my nephew, to get you off the hook. You owe the twenty-two, and that's it. You got that in your pocket, plus six more to hold you until you get something going for yourself out there."

Sal leaned down and grasped the arms of the chair again, and for a second Feet felt his happiness fading, thought the man was about to change his mind or had only just been playing with him.

Sal stared at him hard, his ice-cold blue eyes boring into Feet's, and when he spoke his voice was a whisper, one Feet had heard before, just after someone had mistaken the don's kindness for weakness.

"You ever gamble on another game in this town, Bob-beet, and I'll take your hands off myself, mount 'em and stuff 'em and hang 'em on the wall of this den. This is gonna be hard enough, Favore thinking I owe him now, without you getting dumb and trying to play catchup from the Chicago Bulls."

"You knew all along, didn't you, Sal? Knew you were gonna help me. That's why the twenty-eight grand."

Sal allowed himself a small smile. "I had a idea, yeah." He leaned down to pick up the bottle, saying, "Now get outta here before I change my mind," leaned down and grasped the neck of the bottle but then kept leaning, a strangled sound coming out of his throat, leaning into Feet and then falling onto him, the bottle falling to the floor.

As Sal fell to his knees he twisted, his face turned upside down toward Feet, who stared at death on the hoof and felt terror. "Sal!" Feet jumped out of the chair and pushed Sal away from him, to the floor, the man's body hitting with a solid finality. Feet ran to the door, threw it open. His heart was sinking, his last hope for survival dying along with Sal.

"Help!" he screamed, "Goddamnit, *help*, the don's dying in here!"

Chapter 5

Darrin Favore was working late, keeping Femal there in the office, enjoying the fact that it was pissing her off, having to work late, because it meant that her kid, the half-breed she'd given birth to a year and a half back, would have to stay with Femal's mother a little longer than she liked.

As if Darrin gave two shits. He enjoyed her discomfort, the woman well aware of who he was and afraid to come right out and tell him off, Femal being aware too, of what she was and what she gave him; respectability and a legitimate front for his above-board dealings, of which there were now almost as many as there were of the other kind—his illegal businesses, the dope and the women and the gambling and the oh so many others.

She gave him legitimacy, this chick. With her MBA from Wharton and the fact that she was on the national board of directors of about a dozen major institutions. She'd sit on the dais at her NAACP meetings, or the UNCF—the United Negro College Fund—and he'd be right there next to her, her boss, the guy who made sure he donated more money than any other whitey because it would show everyone how liberal he was and how much class he had.

It was a two-edged sword, though. She could get a little mouthy with him sometimes and there wasn't much he could do about it, because if anything ever happened to her, the way it would to anyone else who cracked wise with him, he'd have Jesse Jackson—whose personally inscribed picture hung on the wall behind Femal's desk—and about every other *mullenjohn* in America pounding on his door, wanting to know what had happened to their precious little Femal.

He watched her working, taking the dictation, shooting little looks at her watch every time he paused to think.

It wasn't that he resented her or disliked her; she was the best secretary he'd ever had, honest to a fault, earned the large salary he gave her and the many bonuses he handed out for her having to work late or come in early, and she could keep her mouth shut. What bothered him was she wouldn't give him the time of day, when he was so goddamn crazy about her that looking at her sometimes broke his heart in two.

She'd sit there behind that desk, keeping the guys he didn't want to see away from him, Femal at five feet six and about a hundred and thirty just as tough as any of the slobs who came through his door. She'd yes, sir him and no, sir him when he was in the mood to play boss and give a little dictation, do her work as efficiently as ever when he was in a rage, as unafraid of him as she'd be on the days she'd come in and he'd have a couple dozen roses on her desk for her. The chick was fearless, never took a day off, didn't run up the corporate card in her purse, performed like a real trouper each and every day, as professional as any don he'd ever had to deal with, but when he'd hit on her, the many times he'd tried it, she'd told him no, flat and final. Acting like a virgin or a dyke, as if he wasn't her type, not in her league and never would be.

Which was okay, as far as that went. Darrin didn't

expect to really make time with a black chick who put Diana Ross to shame in the looks department. It was more the idea of the conquest, of her giving in to him the way so many other women did, ensnared by his power, drawn to it.

She was there for a purpose, and she served it. Worked harder than three white chicks would have, because she had to prove she wasn't the token shine. It wasn't part of the deal, spreading thigh for the boss, not in her job description. If she wanted to stay with her own kind after hours, that was her business.

But when that kid had been born half-white, it had really frosted his *cujones*.

All along, he'd been after her, doing things for her that made some of the boys think that maybe he was losing his mind. Taking her to lunch in his limo, making the boys call her Ms. Tyler, treating her better than he did his own wife, when it came down to it. And what does she do? Screws around with some other white guy, like Darrin wasn't good enough for her, didn't have enough class or wasn't man enough to please her. That hurt bad enough.

But when the guy who owed him and who worked for the county had slipped him a copy of the kid's birth certificate, when Darrin had learned who the father was, it had nearly killed him.

When he thought about it, it got his goat, so he let it go, never said anything about it to her. He hadn't gotten where he was by not recognizing talent. But the bastard who'd scored with her, Darrin would make *him* suffer.

But there was work to do tonight, and she'd have to stay until it was done, and the old lady who watched the kid would have to get a bonus for staying late, that's all.

That thought did give him a little pleasure. The longer she had to work, the less time she'd have to spend with her boyfriend.

She was looking up at him now, eyebrows raised, pencil poised, and he noticed that he'd stopped speaking. He hated that, when his mind went off on him. It made him afraid because if he ever did it when he was doing his other business, when there were people in the room he had no desire to have sex with, they might see him as slipping. Fifty-four and over the hill. And he knew what happened to guys who it turned out were slipping. Two in the back of the head and into the icy waters of Lake Michigan, that's what.

"Where was I?" he asked, knitting his brow at her, as if he'd been so deep in thought about really important matters that he'd lost all track of this mundane shit he was dictating.

"Where was I?" Darrin asked her, and Femal didn't miss a trick, said, " 'And furthermore, Mr. Parnell, due to the unconscionable . . .' " reading the last words he'd spoken back at him, hiding her smile at his macho show of movie-acting, the man looking all lost in thought. Big tough guy who thought nothing ever passed him by, unless he was thinking about making it with someone, which was probably exactly what he'd been doing. Man in his fifties saying "chick" and "babes" when he spoke about women, trying to act hip.

The two computer terminals behind her whirled, powerful things that she knew intimately, every aspect of their operation. They made her nearly indispensable to the man, who'd be hard-pressed to type on an old Underwood.

He was all right to work for, though, that was sure, the job certainly had its fringe benefits, even if he did all the time try to impress her with what an important man he was, how dangerous he could be when he wanted to.

She jotted down what he was saying, wishing he'd just talk into a recorder then bring her the cassette, so she didn't have to waste her time watching him think. It strained the man, thinking did. If he recorded his letters, as she'd asked him to, she could take the tape home and type it up, with little Elaine crawling around her feet, feeling the love pouring off of her mama.

As it was, she could do this dictation business with her mind in half-gear, free her brain matter up to think of other things, like how much she'd like to get out of here on time tonight, for one.

This job was fine, but it had a few drawbacks, the first and most important of which being that in Darrin Favore's general line of business, there wasn't much of a retirement plan.

He'd made it clear to her, in his silly way, how important a man he was in this city. When she'd first come to work for him seven years ago he'd even gone so far as to leave his office door open as he talked lower-level business, making sure she got the message. He'd act all secretive around her sometimes, talking in code over the telephone, speaking loud enough to make sure she heard. As if she couldn't read the papers, find out who this man was. From time to time he'd hand her something made of gold, telling her to go on and take it, it fell off a truck. That had become a game between them by now, Darrin offering her expensive items that fell off a truck and her refusing them. Her apparent honesty with him was probably one of the reasons he hadn't fired her by now and replaced her with one of his girlfriends, who'd run him skull under his desk and let his office go to hell, which he'd probably see as a fair trade. Her mother hadn't put Femal through college by washing white people's floors so her daughter could turn out to be a common small-time thief, even by implication. She could work for one, though, that was okay. By her mama's way of thinking, *all* white folks were thieves, had gotten whatever they had due to some conspiracy, being what she'd call tricknacious.

She thought of Mama, the woman illiterate, giving Femal her name by copying down the printing on her birth certificate, the word FEMALE printed next to the little box where the doctor had put an X, next to the word

SEX. Mama had known what *that* word meant; it was the act which had caused her all her problems. Mama had dropped the final *e*, thank God, her hand getting tired or maybe she just hadn't seen the final letter. Femal had forced her to get a passport, told Mama that someday she'd take her to the homeland, and there was an X above the signature line.

Mama was doing just fine these days, though, illiterate or not. Living in a condo on Lake Shore Drive that Femal had bought her after her first Christmas bonus from Mr. Darrin, the most tricknacious man Femal had ever come across. Mama would ride the bus over to Femal's fine house on the North Side and babysit little Elaine for free, so grateful was she to have a grandchild at last, even if the child didn't have a father around to look out for her.

Femal scribbled, biting her lower lip so Darrin would think she was concentrating, working hard.

It could be worse. She made a lot more money than she ever thought possible, even with a degree. She had Keogh plans for her retirement and for Elaine's education, and insurance policies against the unlikely fact that someone would gun Darrin down when she was in his presence and in the way. She had the stocks, the tips always coming in, someone wanting Darrin to owe him so giving him some insider bits that he used to his best and greatest good. There were other things she had, too, inside information, Femal who did the books for the business knowing where all the bodies were buried, where every penny of the accounts were . . .

Most importantly, though, she had Elaine. And hadn't heard a word from Darrin when she'd gotten pregnant, no wise remarks about race or why'd she wait until she was past thirteen, as she'd heard from some of his scummier associates. Remarks which were ignored by Femal, never mentioned to Darrin.

Anyone who had changed his name from DaMiccio Feveretti to Darrin Favore just so he could be socially accepted by the same WASPS he professed to hate was maybe vain enough to kill someone who insulted his executive secretary, just to impress her. That wasn't weight she was willing to carry.

"All right," Darrin said. "Type it up, have it on my desk by ten." He was looking at her oddly, probably wondering if she'd listened in on his telephone conversation with that hillbilly wildman nephew of his. Now *that* man frightened her.

"Good night, Mr. Favore," Femal said, thinking that all in all, the man was a good boss. A *very* good boss, compared to the ones she'd had while in college.

"You gonna type that up at home?"

"Yes, sir." Best to always keep it professional, no matter how many times he told her to call him Darrin. She would think of him by his first name and discuss him that way with others but would never call him that to his face. It was one of the ways that helped her keep him at his distance.

He had gone into his office and taken his camel's hair coat off his rack; his wide black hat was on his head. He stuck his arms in the coat, shrugged his shoulders so it would fall just right. Femal gathered her notes to her, shoved them into a folder, the folder into her briefcase.

"You take my advice about that new stock, the spaghetti sauce I was telling you about, Femal?" He shot her a furtive glance, playing his game, now seeing the two of them as conspirators.

She looked up, didn't smile. "Yes, sir, I did."

"How heavy you go?"

"Fifteen thousand." She halved it, didn't want him to know how heavily she had invested. There were times when half-honesty paid off, especially with a man like this one.

She was putting on her own coat, was about to set the answering machine when the phone rang, the private line that wasn't hooked up to any recorded message after hours. She lifted the phone, dreading it when she had to answer it because it was always one of the associates from his other business who called on this number.

"Darrin Favore's office, may I help you, sir?" It was the way she always answered that line, because no women ever called on that number.

A rough voice spoke to her, without inflection. "Gimme Dare."

She handed the phone to him, Darrin straightening his hat on his head, adjusting his tie before accepting the receiver, as if needing to visually impress someone who was on the other end of a telephone wire.

She took up her case and was walking for the door when she heard him say, "No shit!" Not hiding the glee in his voice. She was opening the half smoked glass door when she heard him say, "That's fucking great!" She was out the door and was closing it behind her, walking past the other secretaries' desks when he said, "Did the old fuck die alone in pain, if there's a God?" And was halfway to the bank of elevators in the center of the offices of the entire floor that he rented when she heard him laugh maniacally, between guffaws shouting into the phone, "Oh, Jesus, Oh, Jesus Christ, that's too fucking good to be true, the old man was with *that* bastard?!" She heard him pounding his hand on her desk, overjoyed at somebody's passing on.

Femal got into the elevator and was whisked silently down, to the subbasement where the garage was, wondering who had died.

It happened several times a year, that phone would ring and the next thing you knew Darrin was escorting her to someone's funeral, where the old white magpies in black dresses would stare at her with unmasked hostility. She doubted from the first that her presence was necessary, thinking that he probably only took her to avoid taking his wife, or maybe he was telling all his cronies that they were lovers and he was trying to prove it by taking her out socially, to funerals and such, agreeing to give money to the causes she was involved in, attending the dinners and fundraisers, sometimes even being the only white face in the room, which didn't seem to faze him one bit.

The elevator door opened and she stepped out into the heated garage, walked rapidly to her red Miata parked over there in its space, right next to Darrin's black Mercedes. One of the boys was standing next to Darrin's car, dressed in a black suit, his coat open so she could see the pistols hung on either side, under his armpits. The bodyguard-driver smiled when he saw her.

"Hey, Ms. Tyler, how's it going?"

"Fine, Lar, and you?" She smiled at him.

"How could it be better? That stock tip you gimme, that spaghetti gravy shit, went through the roof this week."

He held her car door open for her, ushered her in with a flourish.

"By February, Lar, it'll be worth fifty times what you paid for it."

"If you say so, ma'am." He shut the door and she started her car, giving him a little wave as she backed out of the space.

It never hurt to share little bits of information with the men who would never hear about things like stocks through their boss; it was amazing some of the things they told her in return, although she didn't care for that Lar much; he was smelly and mean looking and always seemed to rivet his eyes to her breasts.

She hit the button on the transmitter that raised the corrugated steel door, looked into the large curved mirrors that were hung up high on either side, bolted into the concrete. She waited for some pedestrian traffic to clear the sidewalk then pulled out onto South Michigan Avenue, heading north.

She had to attend a Mothers Against Gangs meeting over on the West Side then get home in time to spend some time with Elaine, bathe and feed her and get her ready for bed. She'd read the baby a story, teach her some words as the child lay in her crib. Give her a bottle to keep her comfortable through the night, tuck her in with her little bear. Then she had other plans.

Her man was coming over later tonight, and they hadn't been together in a while.

Chapter 6

Peter Silva was walking down a very cold far Northwest Side street when the cops stopped him, frisked him, calling him Pedro, even though he always insisted to them that his name was now Peter, he was an American and had even been naturalized, but they never believed him.

He hated it when they did that, pulled him over and gave him a toss, knowing they could get away with it because they were powerful and he was a single young male of Hispanic descent and he had no political clout. He hated it most when they put their hands upon him; nearly every time he had been in trouble in this country was because someone had decided that it was okay to push him around, a lot of them wanting to start trouble because he was tall and handsome but skinny. They didn't know that he could fight like the devil himself when riled, and once his temper was set off, it was difficult—sometimes impossible—to control.

People would push him, touch him, and he would teach them pretty quick that it wasn't the way to win his friendship.

Most of the time, though, he could be polite to people and show them respect, even if someone wanted to curse him or call his family names or insult his heritage. He did not pay a lot of attention to that. As long as they did not touch him.

But these men were the police, and he knew that it would be a major error in judgment to push the officer's hands away. It was the same in Mexico; the law ruled; fat men with guns and badges and mustaches abused the power given to them. He had not seen much change in that department since coming to this country as a young boy.

Sometimes they stopped him because they needed some mechanical or electrical work done on the fine houses they owned away from this neighborhood, and at those times Peter would do the work for free, seeing it as money in the bank, to be withdrawn at the time when he would need a favor. He hadn't done that in a while, though. As long as Merle Como wasn't coming around, Peter might not ever need to break his back for the police for free again. Merle had a strange way of being able to talk him into doing stupid things. He had not done anything stupid for a little while now, a month or so, and therefore had not needed to work for nothing.

Except for the gang leaders; for them he would work for nothing because as long as he did they would not recruit him, and therefore would not shoot him when he refused their offers to join their groups. He was a free agent, and had no gang affiliations, a rare thing for a young male of Hispanic descent in this neighborhood. On the leaders' houses, he would work for nothing. For other things that he could do for them, he was always paid in cash, and paid well.

Some cops were good guys, others were pure assholes. Peter had learned this lesson early, and not from television. Like this guy here, the fat one, Malone. He had a mustache like the man from the movies, Burt Reynolds, only he did not dress as well as the movie star, always dressed in the lumberjack coats and wearing the rolled up watch cap on his head. Malone, now he was an asshole. Running his hands around Peter's waist now, his fingers down inside his pants. Did the man not understand what an insult that was, how humiliating? Not to mention that it was very cold this night.

"Where you heading off to, bean?" Malone asked him.

"Can I zip my jacket up now, sir?"

"Naw. I got to keep mine open, in case I got to pull my shit and blow your bean head off for not answering my fucking questions. Why should you be warm if I can't be?"

Peter sighed. This one was an asshole of the finest cut.

"I am going to see my girlfriend, officer."

There were two of them, a couple of tac force guys who were known to him, both of them dressed in casual clothes, driving around in their unmarked car looking for people to whom they could give a hard time.

Peter wanted to ask them, Why aren't you out there arresting the Latin Kings or any of the other two hundred and sixteen different Hispanic gangs in this city, why are you harassing a man whose only recent crime was that he could not drive a car at this point in his life because of the prejudices of a judge who didn't care for Hispanics who had a few beers before driving home? He wanted to ask them this, but he did not. He knew better. Knew better than to even ask them to please not call him Pedro.

The second officer was named Dick Blandane. A lean man with dark hair who did not have a belly and who did not wear a mustache, a man who did his job and did not give people too much of a hard time. It was known that Blandane was not lazy like the others around this city, that he would not make something up to arrest you, that he did not like to tell lies. It was also known that he was not liked by his fellow officers on the tactical team. He had a feminine way of speaking, very soft and dainty, although he was a relatively big man, and it was thought on the street that he was homosexual, which was most likely why the other policemen did not seem to like him. At least publicly. Peter had a belief that most of these policemen, with their tough guy ways, were homosexual and did not even know it. Blandane was never known to approach anyone, though, never used the authority of his badge to coerce any gay people into performing for him, which made Peter doubt that he was gay. If he was, he would use that power, maybe even more than most police, just to prove he was still a man. Blandane did not give anyone a hard time unless they were giving him one first, and that made him a good guy in Peter's book.

Blandane was standing back and watching, stomping his feet on the ground and blowing into his hands while his partner Malone did give Peter a hard time.

"You want pussy tonight, Pedro?" Malone asked, then shot a look at Blandane. "And you go out on a night like this? What's the matter, you ain't got no sisters? Your mother work nights?"

Peter saw Blandane flinch, but kept his own face stony. "I do not understand what you are saying, officer."

Blandane tried to get him off the hook. He said, "Come on, Malone, it's cold."

But Malone wasn't through yet. He got right in Peter's face, his coat open, his hands at his sides now turned into fists.

"Get off my streets, Pedro. I see you again tonight, and I'm gonna kick your ass up and down the sidewalk, you understand?"

Peter had to fight his resentment, his outrage. Battle the urge to cry: They are *my* streets, too! at this Nazi, but he did not. He kept his mouth shut and his face a blank brown page, nodded his head up and down vigorously. Malone smirked at him, at what he saw as just another skinny little spic, never bothering to see the man behind the skin pigmentation. Malone backed away, then turned when he was out of Peter's reach, called out over his shoulder.

"Say goodbye to Blandane, Pedro. He's leaving us, going over to Gang Crimes tomorrow."

Peter said nothing, just watched the two men get back into their unmarked car and drive away, leaving him standing in the middle of the street, thinking about how easy it would be for him to rig a little package up for that pig, Malone, drop it off in the middle of the night and when the pig opened his door the next day to go off to work—BOOM—no more Malone.

He thought about it but he knew that he would not do it. He was an electrician, not a killer, and he didn't even steal much of anything these days as long as Merle Como wasn't around to talk him into doing crazy things.

He zipped up his leather jacket and stepped back onto the sidewalk, began walking down Broadway toward Terry's house, fighting his resentment at Malone's remarks.

He was a young man who had a gift; if it had wires and was broken he could fix it. As a child he'd built radios from scratch, had taken broken TVs he found in people's garbage or out of junkyards and within days had them working like new. He would look into a maze of wires and tubes and intuitively know what was wrong and how to make it right, as if a map of the proper way it should be was burned into his brain, and he would fiddle with the broken things until they were as his head and heart told them they should be.

He'd been making a living at it, lately, supporting his widowed mother and his seven younger brothers and sisters with his talents, saving neighbors and their friends and families thousands of dollars because when they called Peter he would charge them by the job, up front, and do the work fast, so they didn't have to worry about giving some white thief fifty dollars an hour to perform work that was only worth ten.

He could also walk into any drugstore and come out

five minutes later and have the makings of a bomb powerful enough to demolish a city block in a bag under his
arm, could put them together in five minutes with fingers
that didn't shake and could sell it for a thousand times
what it had cost him. He would do this sometimes for the
gangbangers, getting his money in front and making sure
that he built the bomb in the basements of *their* houses or
apartment buildings, giving them the subtle message that
if they beat him and took their money back that he could
build another bomb and pay them a visit, now that he
knew where they lived. It was a live-and-let-live existence. He expected nothing from life and that was usually
what he got.

Until he'd met Terry. An Anglo girl of seventeen who
liked him first as a friend, and then later as a lot more than
that.

Her father, though, he did not like Peter one bit. Had
sat him down on the living room couch and had ques-
tioned him intently the night of their first date. The man
drunk, drinking one beer after another. First trying to
convince Peter that he was not prejudiced, that he simply
thought his daughter was too young to be dating. Mr.
Pierce jumping back and forth between trying to be tough
and showing how afraid he truly was of Hispanics, ensnared by the trap of his middle-class beliefs—weren't
they all in street gangs, didn't they all carry knives?

"Too young? You kidding me?" Peter had said. "Why,
my mother had already given birth to me by the time she
was Terry's age." Which had been the wrong thing to say.
The man had asked him to leave and since then the two of
them had been forced to meet after Terry got out of class
at the all-girl Catholic high school she attended on the
West Side. They'd sometimes meet again later, at night,
Terry telling her drunken father she was going out with
her girlfriends.

Tonight, though, it looked as if he might be allowed
back into Terry's father's good graces. It seemed as if the
boiler in their radiant heat furnace had broken, and the

heating man had told Terry's father that it would cost three thousand dollars to repair the thing. Peter could fix it, he knew, put in a rebuilt one for less than five hundred. He would not charge the man for his labor, but would make it clear, if he was good enough to work in the man's house for free, he was good enough to date the man's daughter. See what the man said, how he took it.

Peter was beginning to love Terry very much. Now that she was a senior in her high school, the thought was in his mind that they might even get married next summer, after graduation. The father had nothing to worry about, Peter was not about to make his daughter pregnant. A woman with a good education was something to be proud of in the Silva family, and he wasn't about to waste the opportunity. He always carried some Trojans with him. Terry loved him, too, she had told him so.

He had to be a good guy, if a wonderful woman like Terry loved him, did he not?

He smiled, saw headlights turn the near corner, dropped the smile as the highly polished black Toyota came into view. He ducked into the hallway of an apartment building, glad that most of the vestibule doors in this neighborhood were broken. Those guys were with the Saints, probably looking for someone to shoot in a drive-by.

Not tonight, brothers. Peter did not have his shit with him, and besides, he had a boiler to fix.

He waited until they passed, watched until their taillights faded from sight, then got out of there, hurried down the street to Terry's block, turned and used the alley to approach from the back.

He didn't need to run into the tac guys again this close to Terry's house, get his ass kicked all over the sidewalk for being on Malone's streets.

Dick Blandane said to Malone, "Why you feel the need to threaten the kid, he wasn't doing anything," and Malone just grunted. It was like him, sitting there in the passenger seat feeling all superior, thinking that Blandane didn't have the street smarts to work this neighborhood because he'd gone to college instead of attending the School of Hard Knocks the way Malone and all of his cronies had.

The guy, he hadn't changed in the four months they'd been working together, always blurting out his words of wisdom as if he was the Dalai Lama, going on about how you couldn't trust your spics, how your niggers always lied to you. How your faggots were the worst, 'cause they'd spit on you and if they had AIDS it was all over. How you had to depersonalize them, call them by made-up stereotypical names so they'd know they were inferior to you. Malone had the social conscience of a flea, and about as much intelligence.

The problem, as far as Blandane could picture it, was that he seemed to see most of his partners in that light.

Was it him, or was it them? Blandane just wasn't sure. Seven years on the force and three of them in tac, rising fast and hard because he was smart and ambitious and worked his ass off, the brass seemed to think he was a pretty good cop, so why didn't any of his tac partners?

It had been fine on the street, working a squad car in uniform, back then they were fighting mostly a holding action and he got to work with members of all races and both sexes. He'd felt the unity, the oneness of the fraternity, even if he wasn't invited to a lot of the parties and didn't go drinking with the boys after work. It had been real police work, and although he felt somewhat of an outsider he had still enjoyed it, the action, constant and real. Things just seemed to change when he'd gone into plainclothes.

He'd watch the other guys, who sometimes seemed to be married to each other. They went drinking together, quit smoking together, went out on double dates, socialized together with their wives. They acted like family on the job and off and here Blandane was, sitting with the third man in his tac career that he saw to be a brutal racist Neanderthal. Was he right, or was he being too harsh?

"Pull over, Dicky," Malone said, "let's see what this jig's up to."

It was them, definitely.

He always backed his partners up, never waited in the car even when they were doing things he didn't agree with. Never argued with them when they spouted their gibberish, let his silence speak his piece for him, but they knew how he felt, could tell it by the way he would look at them. Knew, too, that they talked about him behind his back, called him an ass-kisser and brown-nose and faggot because he had no desire to sit on his backside for twenty years and then collect a city pension. Made fun of his criminology degree, too, as if education beyond high school was foolish. He'd see how much they laughed when he was a captain before he was thirty-five. If he didn't quit by then, he'd get there and they knew he'd get there, which was why they talked about him behind his back instead of right to his face. He'd be somebody someday and men like these didn't need powerful enemies.

He stood outside in the cold, behind the black man that Malone was frisking, wincing every time Malone called the man Wilbur or Willy, but not saying anything. He looked away when Malone made the man take his socks off, turning them inside out, looking for drugs while the man hopped from one foot to the other, the icy sidewalk tearing small patches of skin from his feet.

He would be glad when the shift was over. Tomorrow afternoon he'd report to Gang Crimes, and he would be surprised if it wasn't better than this. What did not surprise him, however, was the fact that there wasn't going to be a tac team party to send him off. To them, it would be good riddance. As far as Blandane was concerned, that was a two-way street.

•　•　•

Nobody said anything to him back at the station, close to the end of shift, but he felt their eyes on him, heard their snickers. It was something he was used to, had been used to since grade school when the ostracizing had begun. He was used to it, although it hurt. But he'd die inside, slowly, and never let them know they'd scored on him or it would only get worse. It came with practice.

He found the box as he was cleaning out his desk, his desk right in the middle of the squadroom, in the open without a partition for privacy. There were a couple dozen desks in this squadroom, and everyone could see everything, and he knew that they were watching. The box was small, square, wrapped in festive paper. As he lifted it out of his drawer he heard the guffaws, high-pitched and held back, laughter snorts shooting from the noses of men who were keeping their lips shut tight. Blandane tore the paper off. Inside the box were two figures from a wedding cake, only both of them were tiny tuxedoed males, hands entwined. One was white and the second doll's face was shoe-polished black, and it had a tiny Fila baseball cap on its head, turned at an angle. There was a card on the bottom of the box which read, *Good* lick *in finding a partner in Gang Crimes!*

Dick dropped the figures back into the box, put the cover back on top and left it in the middle of his desk, and continued cleaning his belongings out of his desk, ignoring the harsh laughter behind him.

Chapter 7

Charlie had known there was going to be a problem a couple of hours ago when Lina had breezed into the weight room wearing some multi-colored pastel nightmare Danskin thing that had probably cost a fortune. She'd come up to him, smelling of perfume and liquor, flirting with him, getting his attention the way she knew best. Which was a mistake. The way to Charlie's heart would not be found by a woman who ran around in front of a hundred men in two ounces of clothing which was cut so high on her thighs and the back of her legs that the bottom of her ass cheeks stuck out of them.

"So you and Doddy had your first fight." She said it sing-song, as if it wasn't important, something to laugh at. Charlie disagreed. He'd gotten her out of there before she tried to run on a treadmill and threw up on somebody, or died of a heart attack.

Now they were in their bedroom, Lance sleeping two rooms away, another bedroom between them—a "buffer" room, Lina called it—so they could go wild on each other in the bed and not have to worry about her son lying in his own bed listening, with only a thin wall separating him from his tortured imaginings.

Charlie was trying to get ready for bed but Lina's good-hearted kidding had now turned serious—sharp and harsh.

"He gave you your fucking *start*!" Lina shouted it, suddenly not so careful about what Lance might hear. Charlie pulled on his pajama top and buttoned it, his face blank, watching her, paying attention, but not responding.

"Goddamn you, don't pull that turtle shit with *me*, crawling into yourself every time someone says something you don't like!"

It was funny. People would say something to you and if you didn't respond they'd assume they were right. He'd noticed it before. Was there a pattern there, was it universal? Charlie wondered about it, indeed inside himself, she'd been right about that much. The fact was, also, she hadn't said anything important enough for him to respond to. Did he want to get laid? That would be the only reason he'd give in a little now, in bed, Lina was a tiger.

But she was a tiger who'd been drinking, and he didn't want to be smelling that liquor while they did it, tasting it when he kissed her . . .

"I take you into my house, I get you a job, I share my bed with you, I'll be a son of a bitch if I'm gonna sit here and let you give me the silent treatment, Mr. holier-than-thou, just because you don't want to hear what I'm say-ing." She paused, staring at him. Tiny chest heaving. He could see the pastel Danskin under the white shirt she was wearing. She hadn't worked out, so what was the use of showering and changing? Uh-oh, she was taking in a breath, about to give him more hell.

"You gonna fucking answer me, mister?!"

No, he wasn't. It seemed obvious that she and her father had had a little sit-down, and it was now Lina's job to get Charlie back in the fold, any way she had to do it. If sex didn't work, she'd try anger. The last resort would be crying, playing on his emotions and trying to make him feel guilty.

He turned his back on her, pulled down the covers and crawled into the bed, then almost smiled as he thought of a way to really get her going, a way to get her so mad that she'd forget about the last two scenes of the act.

He looked up at her, at tiny Lina standing there hopping mad, breathing heavily, hands on her hips, playing him for a wimp. Flashed her a half-smile and said, " 'Night, Lina," in a condescending, patronizing tone. She wanted her old man? He'd give her a taste of it.

He closed his eyes, said, "Turn out the light, will you please?" softly, then shook his head a little because she slammed the door hard on the way out, not even being polite enough to turn off the bedroom light.

The meeting was held in the living room of an apartment in the Rockwell Gardens projects, an area under siege. All of the outside walls were covered with gang graffiti, sprayed over and over again until the gang symbols were unidentifiable, surreal in the soft glow of the few working streetlights. Most of the windows at street level were shattered, and many higher up had bullet holes in them, the same holes that studded the concrete walls, everywhere. Femal locked and alarmed her car, walked confidently toward the building, ignoring the catcalls of a few stray punks, out in the night looking for trouble. She knocked on the door of the apartment and it opened a few inches then stopped, held in place by a chain, while one of the insiders checked her out, made sure it wasn't one of the enemy come to break up the play.

"Femal," the woman said, with relief. "You're late." The door closed and was reopened, thrown wide.

"Sorry." Femal entered the room and was grateful to see the black female faces, even those that weren't smiling. In here, it seemed, there was relative safety.

The woman who'd let her in was tall and heavy, with a large bosom that she wasn't trying to hide. The apartment was warm, and she was wearing a short-sleeved Winnie Wrap, a multi-colored African robe that cinched at the waist. She had a scarf tied around her hair that was made of the same material. Her name was Tashika, and she'd worked for months trying to get Femal to attend one of their weekly gatherings.

"I had to work until the last minute," Femal said, and smiled at the four other women in the room.

Two of them were smiling at her, one openly, one cautiously. Two of them were openly hostile. All the women in the room were black. Femal was the only one in a business suit.

"Knock on the door after six, we thinks it gots to be the bangsters, come to dis-rupt the meeting." The woman who spoke had processed hair, combed back. She was very slender, in her fifties, with a long, muscular throat. There were fingermarks on that throat, and her right eye and cheek were puffy. She had the suspicious, resentful glare of a woman who thought she was looking at an up-pity white woman, and that was a resentment that Femal would have to deal with right away if she was going to be able to help these women. Life was too short to waste weeks winning their trust before any real work could be done, and there were too many righteous causes out there, filled with people who wanted her and who wouldn't give her a hard time. She'd give them a chance, and if it didn't work out, she'd wasted an hour of her time and she could live with that.

Femal smiled at the woman, walked right over and held out her hand. "I'm Femal Tyler," she said, and the woman, startled, took Femal's hand and shook it.

"Chantay Tut."

Femal went around the room and shook the other women's hands, trying to put them at their ease by show-ing them her own, setting an example. Besides Chantay and Tashika, their names were Gloria, who appeared apprehensive, staring at Femal with a little hostility as she shook her hand; Johneara, a small, light-skinned woman who'd been smiling cautiously; and Lucille, who was friendly and open, and who had a firm grip and a ready smile.

"I *am* sorry to come late."

"It's just the bangsters, is all . . ." Chantay not putting much into it this time, just trying to save face.

"Boosheet," Lucille said. "We ain't no threat to them motherfuckers. I put a flyer under the door of every apartment in this hellhole my damn self. How many women in this room? Why the bangsters worry 'bout us for? We can't hurt them."

"That's where you're wrong," Femal said. She sat down on a cushion that was tossed on the floor, crossing her legs under her. It was a conscious move. She wanted to be lower than them, wanted to have to look up to them when she spoke. It would give them a sense of power, and perhaps their having that might ease their suspicions.

Tashika said, "We were hoping to have enough mothers here to organize a march, carry candles . . ." Her voice trailed off, the woman embarrassed that so few had shown on this cold November night.

"Got warned off, you bet," Gloria said. She looked straight into Femal's eyes. "Them boys out there ain't playin' around. By now, they got your license plate number, know where you live, and you'll be hearing from them. You ready for that action, Femal Tyler? We got to live under that eye twenny-four hour a day, seven day a week, with them watchin' and swearin' and threatenin' and sometimes actin', so you got to ask yourself right now, lady, with your downtown suit and your fancy haircut, can you handle it along with us?"

All right. Time to see if she could warm this crowd.

Femal said, "Gloria, I grew up about six blocks from here, in the Ogden Courts. Wasn't that damn long back, either." She put a little ghettoese into her voice, the urban twang. Let them know she wasn't all downtown.

"I saw fine young brothers fall under the gang's spell back then, drop out of school and run with them, wind up dead or in the prison house one, and nothing's gotten better."

Femal said, "I'm here tonight because nothing's changed, it's only gotten worse. Yesterday a young boy who was trying to learn something in school was brutally murdered, shot down because he wasn't a member of any gang. We've got sons who can't read but who can recite every word of 'Funky Cold Medina' and 'The Humpty Dance' in their sleep; daughters who can't write but who can Hippity-Hop dead along with Janet Jackson on any video she's ever done. We've got rappers who see all us women as bitches to be used for sex and mayors who make us all look bad, smoking crack and sleeping around and abusing their authority and power, and when they're caught, they feed the hatred of the white racist bastards because they lie to get out of it, try to put the blame on whitey. We've got thousands of us sitting around talking about genocide and how we're mistreated and ain't but a few of us standing up and taking what we want in a righteous, legal manner. We've got more black brothers in prison than we've got in college, and a full one fourth of our young men are in trouble with the criminal justice system." As she spoke Femal rolled onto her knees, put her hands on her thighs. She was getting worked up, was speaking to all the women in the room, although she never broke eye contact with Gloria.

Femal said, "This project, the Courts where I grew up, and thousands of other places like them across this nation are under attack right this second, Gloria. By gangs, by drugs, by AIDS, by girls who should still be playing with dolls having babies. We've got thousands of our own dying at the hands of blacks. We're at the point where gunshot is the leading cause of death of our young men, and AIDS the leading cause of death for our young women. Last summer there were eighty of us killed in the month of June, and more of us died violent deaths in this city last year than in any time in its history.

"I got out, and I've got a good job and I drive a nice car and I was one of eight people who had a private dinner in Detroit with Nelson Mandela, and I'll tell you why. Because thirty years ago, my Mama would sit me on her lap at night and tell me stories of the home country, hold me and hug me and talk to me about our pride and our traditions and our strengths, and there'd be awe in that woman's voice. She'd hold my diapered little body up in front of a mirror and she'd say 'Just *look* at that gorgeous black face!' She worked long, hard hours, slaving for the white man, and I got through college and now I can make a difference in this world, lady, instead of just sitting on my ass bitching about how the white man's holding me down."

Femal leaned back, flushed, and lowered her voice. "We've got six of us here. That's a start. You want to march in November? How many cameramen you think will show up? How many pretty little white reporters want the wind fussing with their hair this time of year, not to mention, how many of them would even come into this project at all the way things are?

"But let me tell you something, the six of us, if we go door to door in the daytime on the weekends, in three-women teams, we can cover this project and recruit before the warm weather comes. We can make up the flyers, get together and open a dialogue with the police, demand protection and if we work together, teaching and respecting and educating the women of this community, by summertime, when the march comes down, we'll be able to take back these streets, and you better believe that shit."

"But they ain't that weak, they ain't gonna let us." Gloria spoke softly, defeated.

"How they gonna stop us?" Femal said. "A thousand women, marching together, their black hands joined, singing to God. How they gonna stop us? You mention my license plate. That car is leased through the company, those cowards can't find me. And if they do, you think Mandela's the only black leader I've ever met? You think, if I have to, I couldn't get the Fruit of Islam into this place, marching with us?"

Tashika said, "Amen to *that*."

"So let's have no more of what we can't do, no more of what they'll *let* us do. Let's talk now about what we're *gonna* do."

Chantay said, "I want to meet Farrakhan, that what *I* wanna do. That man so fiiine!" And Femal sat back, relaxed, because now the ice was broken and maybe some progress could be made.

Two hours later Femal was wearing a maroon see-through teddy she'd picked up at Frederick's, which made her feel a little silly but which also turned her on a little bit. It wasn't a bad thing for a woman to do, if she knew who and what she was and didn't take it too seriously. It certainly showed off her body.

She stood looking at herself in the full-length mirror in her bedroom, admiring the way she'd bounced back from having Elaine, the tightness of her muscles, the taut thighs and flat belly she'd killed herself to regain. She had a garter belt holding up silk stockings, had spike-heeled black patent leather shoes on her feet. She smiled at herself and shook her head.

"Look at you," she said half-mockingly. "Fourth in your graduating class and you dress up like a hooker."

The little receiver that would alert her to any noises in the baby's room was on the headboard, turned low. She couldn't hear Elaine's soft breathing, as she usually could. She would lie in bed at night and let the sound of the baby sleeping lull her to sleep, her wonderful child in the room down the hall making baby sounds throughout the night.

But not this night. This night was reserved for somebody else.

She walked to the window that overlooked the street and sat in a chair a little away from it, so nobody looking up could see in and spot her dressed like this, maybe think she was a working girl and want to come up for a little high-priced action.

She wanted to catch him as soon as he walked up the street or pulled up in his car, did not want him to ring the doorbell and perhaps wake Elaine.

After some time she spotted him, recognizing his familiar swagger first as he strode down her street, stopping at the corner to look up at the street sign, making sure he was heading in the right direction.

She ran through the house, thrilled, stopped at the front door and caught her breath, put one hand on the doorknob and struck what she thought to be a sexy pose, thrusting her breasts out and putting a pout on her lips. Then she swung the door open.

And when she saw the look of despair on the face of Catfeet Millard she forgot all about being sexy; about her pose. All she could think of was that the man she hadn't seen in over two years was in trouble already.

"Bob? What's wrong?"

Catfeet smiled sadly. Came into her arms and pushed the door closed behind him.

"My God, Femal, my God, is it good to see you," he said, and held her tight.

Femal let him hug her, shushing him and rubbing the back of his head, holding him to her. It made her feel good, to give him comfort. As for his problems, whatever they were, he'd tell her about them when he got ready.

It was part of the deal they had; total honesty, but no prying. Neither had the right to demand explanations from the other, nor to demand that the other change; they accepted each other as they were.

It had worked out pretty well until he'd gone to jail.

She led him away from the door. She wasn't going to get ravished, that was obvious, so now she'd show him what she'd been planning to wait until later to display. If he acted the way she thought he would, great, they would discuss it and go on from there. If he turned into an idiot —and there was a chance of that, she really liked Catfeet but he had a penchant for foolishness and shortsightedness or he wouldn't be a thief—she would show him the door and burn the sexy little outfit in her fireplace.

She took him by the hand and led him toward the back bedroom, telling him, softly, "Come on, honey, there's somebody here that I want you to meet," pleased by the puzzled look that had come to his face. He looked as if he hadn't smiled for some time. They got to the door of the baby's room and Femal let go of his hand, put a finger to her lips and shushed him, then slowly pushed the door open.

Elaine was sleeping on her back, one tiny hand clutched around the empty plastic bottle, holding it against her cheek. She looked as innocent and as beautiful as Femal had ever seen her, like an angel without wings.

"Wha—" A whispered stammer from Catfeet.

"That's your daughter, Bobby," Femal whispered, and was pleased again because Catfeet raised his head quickly away from the crib and broke into a beatific smile, his eyes filled with tears and he stared at her, struck dumb.

She nodded vigorously, smiling widely. "That's right, Bobby Millard, you heard me; she's your daughter."

Elaine chose just that moment to make a satisfied baby sound and roll over onto her side. The bottle was caught under her cheek and she pushed it away with an awkward gesture, slapping at it to make sure it didn't come back, her little brow all furrowed. She settled back down, her chest rising and falling in her Dr. Denton's.

All Catfeet Millard could do was stare at the baby, his mouth hanging open, his eyes wide. Femal wondered what was going on in his mind, what he was thinking.

She didn't ask him, instead took his hand again and said, "Come on, Daddy, you'll have all of forever to get acquainted with her. Right now, I don't think I even want to know what's bothering you until you prove to me I didn't waste fifty dollars of my hard-earned money on this silly little nightgown."

It wasn't going as well as Peter Silva thought it would. He'd been let in by Terry's father and led back to the utility room, but the man, this Mr. Pierce, he acted as if he was doing Peter some kind of favor, allowing him to putter around in his filthy furnace and get his clothes all covered with soot.

Mr. Pierce would drink his beer, crushing it in his hand and disappearing for a minute into the kitchen to get himself another one, coming back and staring at Peter, maybe afraid that if he turned his back on him that Peter would steal his furnace or carry his washer and dryer out on his back. He was in a long-sleeved shirt because it was cold in here. Mr. Pierce was a tall man but with a shrunken chest and a large belly. Gray hair that had not been washed in some time. He had gray stubble on his cheeks. Peter gave him the benefit of the doubt. It had to be hard, your wife dying on you and leaving a child for you to raise and educate all alone.

Still, it was beginning to get to him, especially because Terry was nowhere to be seen.

"Think you can fix it?" Mr. Pierce asked him.

"I can fix it all right, that is not the problem." Peter was staring into the back of the boiler, at the small crack in it, wondering if this foolish man had somehow allowed it to freeze up last winter or if the break was fresh. It didn't look new to him.

"The question is, Mr. Pierce, if I can fix this boiler here or if you need a new one altogether."

Crush, went the can. Mr. Pierce seemed to think the act of crushing aluminum beer cans would impress Peter. Maybe he thought that Mexicans believed that the people over at Budweiser shipped their beverage in cans made of solid brass.

"The son of a bitch can't be fixed, goddamnit, the

heating man told me that." Mr. Pierce's voice came from the kitchen, filled with sarcasm, accompanied by the sound of the refrigerator opening and closing. Another beer, what, his seventh since Peter had arrived? Mr. Pierce had not offered him a beer. Nor a Pepsi or Coke, nor even a glass of water. Nor did he need to leave the beer in the refrigerator, as cold as it was in this house without heating. Why had the man waited so long to get this fixed?

Peter had pictured it in his mind, he and Mr. Pierce working on the boiler together and becoming great friends, Mr. Pierce learning what a swell human being Peter was once he got past his prejudice. He had pictured them drinking a few beers together, pictured himself telling Mr. Pierce about his mother's sickness, how almost all of his earnings now went to pay her doctor bills. Pictured them sitting on the couch, Peter having saved Mr. Pierce thousands of dollars, the house warm instead of the icehouse that it was now, the two of them close and tight.

But that was not to be.

Peter said, "That same man also told you it would cost three thousand dollars to fix this boiler," Peter was speaking loudly, so Mr. Pierce could hear him from the kitchen, but lowered his voice when he looked up and saw the man standing over him, glaring, finishing with, "Did he not?"

Mr. Pierce squinted his eyes at Peter, but did not say anything.

"I can fix this for you, Mr. Pierce," Peter said. He was wiping his hands on a dishtowel that had been hanging on a wire towel holder above the utility room sink, Peter's hands making the towel filthy with grease and rust.

"How much, three thousand pesos?" Mr. Pierce said it and laughed. An evil laugh, not one that invited you to join in. He was not being funny, which Peter could have lived with. Rather, he was making fun of Peter.

The same way the policemen always do.

"Much more than that, Mr. Pierce," Peter said. He

cleaned off the large pipe wrench he'd used to disconnect the water pipes, dropped the towel onto its wire holder and stood straight, stared Mr. Pierce right in the eye. He said, "For payment, you have to show me the same respect you would give to any other man who was doing you a favor, breaking his ass without pay so you can have heat in your home."

Mr. Pierce stopped short, squinted again. Maybe he thought that when he did that he looked like Clint Eastwood. Or meaner. All it really made him look like was a man trying to find his spectacles.

"You fucking my daughter, greaseball?" Mr. Pierce shouted, and Peter had enough.

"When you find your manhood, you ask your daughter to call me and I will fix your boiler."

Peter turned his back on the man and was about to put the pipe wrench back in Mr. Pierce's tool box when the man attacked him, crushing the Bud can on the back of Peter's head, beer flying all over everything and then the man dropped the can, put Peter into a tight headlock from behind.

What was happening, was this man insane? Peter began to see little black spots in front of his eyes, heard the sound of a waterfall rushing in his head and somewhere in the distance Terry's voice was screaming. Mr. Pierce was shouting something, calling him filthy names.

Peter began to feel the anger rise in him and knew that he was powerless to stop it. The pipe wrench was still in his hands. He said, "Stop it!" and Mr. Pierce shouted back, "*Fuck* you!"

Peter swung the wrench as hard as he could up and over his shoulder, both hands around the stem, felt it connect with something that yielded wetly, felt warm liquid run down the back of his shirt as the arms came away from his neck and fell to the floor along with the rest of Mr. Pierce.

He dropped the pipe wrench and clutched at his throat, gasping for breath, reached out with one hand and steadied himself on the furnace, turned slowly and saw Mr. Pierce lying on the tile floor with his eyes open and his skull crushed—dear mother of Christ, he could see the man's brain.

Terry was behind her father, looking down at him, her hands pulling at her hair, her face flushed red, screaming loudly enough to bring this house down around them. He staggered over the body and pushed her hard on the shoulder.

"Hey, shut up, will you?" Peter said.

She stared up at him, her mouth moving, trying to form words and failing.

Panic began to fill him as he wondered what the police would make of this; no one had been in the room with them, would they believe his story, the truth? They never had before.

"Terry!" he shouted. He reached out for her and tried to pull her into his arms, his thin strong arms which didn't tremble as they assembled deadly bombs but which were shaking terribly now. She pulled away from him, screeching, and ran through the house, Peter right behind her.

"Where are you going, what are you doing?" Did she think he had killed her father in cold blood? Hadn't she seen what had happened?

She was at the telephone now, hanging the thing up because her trembling fingers had misdialed the first time. He reached her, grabbed her, pushed her roughly away from the telephone and grabbed the thing, pulled its cord from the wall.

"No!" Terry shouted.

"What!" Peter hollered.

She came at him, fingers outstretched, those long nails that had dug lines into his back when she was in her passion now trying to tear his eyes out and what could he do except slap the phone against the side of her head?

Terry fell to the floor in a bundle, as her father had, lay there staring up at the ceiling as Peter tried to catch his breath, tried to make sense of what was going on in this madhouse.

There was a pounding on the door, someone had most likely heard Terry's screaming. Not the police, they'd kick the door down and come barging in with their guns drawn, and if that happened Peter would not have a chance, they'd take one look and shoot him deader than shit, and get away with it because Peter had been in trouble with the law many times in his life.

The pounding stopped and Peter thought that he had maybe five minutes tops to get out before the police arrived.

He ran into the utility room and grabbed the towel, rapidly wiped down the pipe wrench, the boiler, the furnace, the door frame, the light switch. Into the living room, where he cleaned the telephone, making an effort to keep his eyes off the motionless form of the girl he thought he'd loved. Back into the utility room, where he squatted down and with two fingers liberated Mr. Pierce's wallet from his pants pocket. He shook out the few bills inside and replaced the wallet.

When Peter ran out the back door, he took the towel with him, and stayed to the alleys all the way home because the night seemed to be alive with sirens and flashing blue and red lights and when you were in trouble in this neighborhood the alleys were your best friend.

Chapter 8

This was the part of it that Merle liked best, the action part.

They were in a grocery store Tuesday morning, he and Moonbeam, all made up now and lovey-dovey again, doing one of the things she thought was going to change the world.

She was the leader of the Florida Animals Rights Team, or, FART, whose battle cry was the same as all the rest of the animal activists'—in their world, it was a universal plea: Rat-pig-dog-boy. This hadn't made a lot of sense to Merle, but Moonbeam had explained that it was the natural evolution of things, that all living beings were one, and worthy of the same respect.

He never gave her any static about this, although he thought it was stupid and didn't have any problems sharing his thoughts and feelings with her. There was nothing he liked more than a rare steak smothered in mushrooms, he'd tell her, but the thought of eating a child, Jee-zus, it was enough to make you puke.

That was the whole idea, she'd told him.

Which was when he'd had his brainstorm.

They'd gone to the printer and had the clear labels printed up, the same kind you found in this grocery store, with the store's name and emblem on the top in capital letters: ISLAND FOODS, WHERE THE ELITES GET THEIR MEATS. Taken the labels home and it had been a simple thing to run them through her computer printer and to steal a price stamper from the Island Foods grocery store.

Now some of the labels read: BREAST OF MUR-DERED BABY FEMALE CHILD, with the weight and price stamped in the appropriate spots. Merle slid one of these out of his pocket and slapped it over the label on a breast of chicken. The LEGS OF MALE FETUS he stuck onto a package of drumsticks. The LIVER OF RAT he put across, naturally, a package of liver, and the ADULT FEMALE GENITAL GLANDS went onto the goose necks.

Moonbeam was fast at work on her own side of the meat freezer, not being as creative as Merle, slapping her labels on any damn thing just to get the job done. He'd hate to have her along on a score, a jittery woman like that. He wondered how she ever found the courage to plant bombs in college administration buildings and in Army draft registration centers as she'd claimed to have done. It was probably bullshit, like most everything else about Moonbeam.

All you had to do was act like you belonged, smile at the people next to you, slip your hand in and press the little label down, and nobody even noticed. The way Moonbeam was doing it, if it was later in the day and the store was more crowded, she'd have gotten her ass caught.

And then what? What could they charge her with, mislabeling chicken wings? Probably have to do some heavy time behind *that* charge.

Merle took the last label out of his pocket, slapped it

down on a large turkey leg. IMMATURE MALE PENIS. It never hurt to advertise.

They stood in the cereal section, right at the end of it so they could see the meat freezer, watch the women walk past it, most of them ordering their meats fresh cut from the butchers who'd come up front if you pressed a button. Rich people got spoiled on Palm Beach Island.

But right there came a couple of broads, a mother and daughter act it looked like, not Jews, goddamnit. Merle loved to scare the Hebes. They'd do in a pinch, though, these two.

The mother was about ninety, looked to have had about forty plastic surgeries, her skin so tight and tanned she looked like she'd died and been stuffed. The younger broad, maybe sixty, either a daughter or a paid companion, which was big on this side of the bridge, wasn't far behind in the skin department, all tanned and tight, too. They both wore the popular baggy shorts. The old woman had blue and red lines in her legs that direct exposure to the sun at a distance of fifteen yards wouldn't hide. If he were going to take a shot at one of them, though, he'd take the old lady. The daughter looked to be as tight-assed as a mouse stretched across a water barrel.

They walked through the meats, the younger woman picking up one of Merle's packages, oh, yes, PLACENTA OF GORILLA, one of his favorites. She looked at it funny, turning her head from side to side, not believing what she was reading, then holding it out at arm's length to her mama, pushing it at her a couple of times in a jittery fashion, trying to get her to read the label. The old woman pulled the daughter's hand toward her, impatient, looking as if she just wanted to humor the daughter and get on with her shopping, then she realized what she was seeing, gave a short cry and slapped at the hand, knocking the package to the floor, doing a little dance as it hit her shoe and broke open on the polished fake marble.

This set the younger one off and she started to scream, pointing at it, and the old broad joined in, ready to have a heart attack, dancing around the burst package of meat on the floor. Other shoppers were racing toward them, anxious to see what was going on, to be a part of it.

Merle and Moonbeam, their work done, walked slowly down the aisle, turned right and then out of the electric doors, to their car parked in the handicapped spot in front.

It was all in the way you saw things. Merle had gotten a nooner, was lying naked in the bed with his hands behind his neck, Moonbeam prowling the house somewhere, having a cigarette out there because Merle didn't allow smoking in bed.

He'd explained the plot to her and had then had to tell her the beauty of it, as she'd missed the point. It wasn't about scaring people once, it was about negative thought implantation. Subliminal shit like the advertising guys on Madison Avenue lay on you, shooting images at you in commercials faster than your eyes can spot them, giving you the urge to go out and buy their products.

Only this was the reverse procedure. Every time one of those people looked at a meat case again, they'd think about STILLBORN NEGRO HERMAPHRODITE or SIAMESE TWIN FECES, then pass the thing right by. How many of them, especially the retirees that filled South Florida, would ever eat hamburger again once they saw their ground beef stamped with BLOODY JEW BRAINS? A lot less of them than would have if the stuff had been left alone.

She'd gotten the drift, and had told Merle that he was a genius. Now he was a movie star *and* a genius. Shit, he'd been called worse.

He could always get her going, old Moonbeam. She'd tell him facts, trivia that she picked up somewhere, and he could twist it around to amuse her.

Like the time they'd had dinner in Miami and they strolled the sidewalk, in no hurry to get to their car, an early evening crowd all around them. They passed several couples standing in the middle of the sidewalk, walking around them, Merle satisfied with the meal and his life and not paying them any attention until Moonbeam told him about the study she'd read.

"When two people or a group of people meet on the street, they're more likely to stand in the center of the sidewalk than they are to step to the side."

Merle said, "Is that right?" and started paying attention, saw that she was right, and when they passed the next two men who were standing in the middle of the sidewalk talking he shoved one of them, hard, watched him fall to the ground then turned to the man's companion and told him he was an ignorant son of a bitch. Neither man had said anything in response.

Another time she told him that people were more likely to talk longer on a pay phone if they thought someone was waiting for it, so he'd taken to walking up to people and hanging up the phone on them, then standing there glaring, waiting to see what they'd say.

He smiled, there in the large bed in Moonbeam's mansion on Palm Beach. He was going to miss her, she was so easily amused.

The phone rang and he grabbed for it, Merle deriving great joy in giving Moonbeam's friends grief.

"Yo, 'ablamé," he said, but it wasn't one of her friends, or one of his, either.

It was his uncle Dare, telling him to get his ass on a plane, now, because old Sally Luchessa had finally cashed it in and he wanted Merle at the goddamn funeral.

Chapter 9

Feet was watching Femal feed the baby—his *daughter*—her cereal. Geez, how could she eat that stuff, mashed bananas and peas, for Christ's sake.

But she was his kid. His daughter.

The idea was hard to accept, although he knew that Femal would never lie. Still, a kid? Catfeet Millard the prowler with a kid? It changed things.

He wanted it to change things.

He wasn't getting any younger. By the time this kid was ready for college, he'd be sixty years old. And it wasn't like he had a pension plan, or any savings, for that matter.

Could he get a job, could he lay back and retire from this, give up the excitement, the rush of scoring? He didn't know, but he was going to find out, because there was one thing of which he was certain: This child would not be raised knowing her old man was in the joint. He would settle the problem with Favore, no matter what he had to do, get it behind him and get on with his life. With *their* lives. He wouldn't be living for himself anymore.

It gave him pleasure, thinking that.

He was standing by the sink, drinking coffee, wanting a cigarette but they were off-limits around the baby, trying to talk to Femal about his problem, which she was having none of.

"Children absorb everything they hear," she told him. "Even if they don't understand it right then, it stays in their subconscious. You can't ever fight around them, or curse or smoke or talk about bad things because it will impact upon them later, come back and haunt them. That's why so many adults run off to shrinks, because of the things that happened in the first two years of their lives."

Did she really believe this? He wondered if it were so. Wondered, too, if he were really here, in a nice new house with a woman who might love him and a kid there who was his daughter.

What had Femal just said, impact? He'd spent twenty-eight months around guys whose only desire was to impact your hemorrhoids. It was good to be around smart people again.

He hoped that some of it would rub off on him. Hoped, too, that Femal had thought about where this would lead. They'd have to get married, there was no doubt about that.

"We'll talk about it later, after I get home."

Femal gently pressed a little round silver spoonful of nanners and peasies, as she called them, into Elaine's mouth, wiped the overspill from her lips and ducked that in there, too.

"That's one of the things I been trying to tell you and can't say," he told her. "You're probably gonna wind up with the day off. For sure, tomorrow, to go to the funeral."

Femal stopped fussing with the spoon and looked at him, as if remembering something.

"Who—" She looked over at the child and caught herself. "Who d-i-e-d?"

"Kid's subconscious can't pick up spelling, is that what you're telling me, Femal?"

"I'm serious, Bob." He wiped the grin off his face and looked at her, saw that she was indeed serious.

He said, "S-a-l, L-u-" and Femal said, "That's enough," very softly. "I know who you're talking about," then didn't say anything else about it. But all of a sudden she wasn't cooing at the baby anymore, either.

When Femal's mother came Feet felt awkward, looking at this ancient skinny black woman who was standing right up to him, staring him down. Femal had to tell her the truth, too, right away, that he was Elaine's daddy. The first thing she said to him was, "You gonna marra mah baby?" and he didn't know what to say, managed to get into the living room and away from the woman when she spotted Elaine and the hardness fell off her face and she got all grandmotherly, full of love and warmth, smiling and forgetting about Feet to go over to the baby.

Femal was ready to leave, dressed in a suit that covered her but couldn't hide her. Carrying a little tiny black purse, her briefcase draped by a strap over her shoulder. He didn't let her catch him staring. There was a time for the little frilly teddys, and a time for the business suits, and the two didn't have any business being discussed in the same conversation.

"You'll be here tonight? When I get back?"

"Later, Femal. I got some things to take care of."

"Took care of some things last night, too, didn't you, you rascal." There she went, breaking her own rules. He never could figure her out.

Now she was serious, looking at him with—what— love?

"I know you got troubles, and I think there's a way out of them, I think I've got a way—"

"Forget about it, just don't go thinking up things that

haven't happened and won't happen. You work for the man but you don't know him."

"But I can handle him." She had her hands on her hips, and for a second, Feet believed her. Then remembered who they were talking about.

"No, you can't," he told her. She was getting mad, he could tell by the look on her face. Well, let her.

Feet said, "The guy's not what you think he is, Femal. I know he plays the game with you, puts on the bumbling fool act, I know he's pretty legit now too, but let me tell you something. When I was first starting out he was Sal's right hand, an enforcer, and he'd get sent out to do somebody, he'd get creative. Kill the guy then dress him up in women's clothes, let the cops or his family find him that way. Steal the last bit of dignity the man had left."

"Those are rumors."

"You don't believe them, Femal?"

"I know he's no saint, but like I said before, I can handle him."

Feet said, "Have a good day, Femal," and watched her walk out the door.

She could handle him.

Without Femal in the house the place seemed hostile. Feet could sense the animosity rolling off the old woman, who was no longer in the kitchen with the child, was now standing, holding the little girl in the doorway, glaring at him.

"Cold out today?" It was all he could think of to say.

"Hmmph." The woman was carrying the baby around the waist, had the baby's bottom propped up on her right hip, was rocking her up and down as she stared at Feet.

"Baby's name ain't Millard," Femal's mother said.

"Uh—I think I'd better go now."

"Uh-huh, that right, you get yo' ass right on out there." Little tiny woman she was, but Lord, could she look at you.

"Bye-bye, Elaine." Feet shoved his arms into his coat, waggled his fingers at his daughter. "Bye-bye . . ."

Before he could get out the door the old woman made sure he knew that Femal wouldn't be getting back until late; she had an Urban League meeting that night after work.

Feet told her that was fine with him, maybe he'd come back early and the two of them could sit around the fire-place, get acquainted with each other, sing some old civil rights songs. She didn't bother to respond to him, just stared at him silently, and as soon as the door closed behind him he heard her slapping home the deadbolt.

Catfeet headed for the bus stop, not feeling too good about acing out a woman who was more than likely in her seventies. He was on his way to see a man considerably younger than that, and he wondered if he'd be able to hold up half as well. Knew that if he didn't, he might well not get a chance to come back and sing any songs with the old woman. It was hard to warble "We Shall Overcome" when your throat had been slit.

The joy Darrin Favore had experienced over the death of his mortal enemy had been short-lived, lasting only until he'd gotten home.

The problem was, he hadn't married an old-world woman the way Sal had, that had been the beginning of his troubles.

Instead, he'd married Marlene the cat woman.

A woman from the homeland, all you had to do in order to silence her was give her an unfavorable look, and she'd lower her eyes. It was true, Darrin had seen Sal, in the old days when they were still friends, just *look* at his wife, and by God, she became silent, not wanting to further anger her master.

This one he was married to, Jesus, killing her wouldn't shut her mouth.

She'd been crying when he'd come home, then started

right in on him, about where the hell he'd been, who had he been drinking with.

Sure, he'd stopped off for a few at the home of a woman he kept, a black woman named LaVella who did things for him this uptight wife of his wouldn't dream of doing if he held a gun to her head, but he hadn't been long, hadn't even gotten laid, wanting to get home and into his office, onto the clean phone wires that were swept every day and learn all that he could about the final day of Don Salvatore.

He didn't tell Marlene about LaVella, although she probably had her suspicions. Nor did he slap her to shut her up. He'd laid his hands on his wife in anger only once, years ago, when he was still just a rising star instead of the kingpin he was now, and it hadn't worked out too well. She'd refused to make him a meal when he came home late and drunk, had gone off to bed after just waiting up long enough to check the time of his arrival. He'd eaten, wrecked the kitchen making something because he knew that if he didn't eat before he went to bed that he'd have a world-class hangover in the morning. Had gone off to the bedroom, folded his clothes over a chair, slipped between the sheets, and announced, "I ain't good enough to cook for, I ain't good enough to sleep with," and had shoved her out of the bed onto the hardwood floor.

Marlene had come up like Sugar Ray against Jake LaMotta, with a wooden club in her hands that she kept under the bed to fend off prowlers, and had whacked him in the head with it so hard that he lost his sight for a minute, by which time she'd been able to relax and improve her aim for the next couple of shots. When he'd come to consciousness, she'd been gone, and he was lying in about a gallon of his own blood, one eye swollen entirely shut, the other one only opening enough so he could see blurry images of everything he looked at. His nose was broken, and his entire chest looking like a sidewalk rainbow after a summer downpour.

As for Marlene, she'd taken off for the house of her uncle, who happened to be Salvatore Luchessa.

He found out where she'd been when Sal brought her home about ten minutes after Darrin had come to. Lord, how it had frightened him, seeing the man coming into his bedroom back then, the don short but powerful, holding Marlene by the elbow and shaking her as he spoke to Darrin.

"You ever touch my niece again and I'll kill you." Not said loudly, the don looking as if he were trying not to laugh at the sight of Darrin there on the bed. He'd turned and left, and from that day to this, he'd hated the don, and didn't have much use for Marlene, who didn't have the balls to fight her own battles.

"Uncle Sal's dead, you son of a bitch, and you go out and celebrate."

She'd said that to him last night and he'd thought about slapping her, one good stiff one across the mouth, just to see what she would do about it now that her protector was dead.

"He gave you your start and you spit on him." On and on, more of the same until he'd left the room. He'd heard the door slam a little while later and assumed she'd just gone out to comfort her aunt. Or maybe she had a boyfriend, who knew? He hoped to God she did. Why should he be the only man alive that Marlene could torment?

Even she, though, wasn't his biggest problem. His biggest problem had been how to convince the other leaders that he was the man to take Sal's place.

As he dressed for work this morning he still did not have an answer, knew that he might never have one; it would not be an easy task, convincing those people, even though he'd done more to legitimize the mob than anyone in the city.

He was their front man, their money launderer. They threw him pieces of the gambling action, the prostitution

—where he had found LaVella and retired her—small pieces of every pie, which he'd taken and had turned into a small dynasty, Darrin worth more than any other individual in the mob that he could think of. In return, one of Darrin's people sat down with them and accepted packages of small bills that were turned into tax-free municipals, insurance policies, IRAs and percentages of legitimate businesses that were little more than phony corporations, some of the money in blind trust funds whose beneficiaries were the children and grandchildren of the men who'd handed Darrin the packages. It was a sweetheart deal.

The best part of it was, the law could never touch him these days, because the other mobsters needed him; he was the single most important cog in their aging and slowing wheel. Even Sal himself went to bat for him when he'd needed the man, in order to keep Darrin's operation flowing smoothly.

Take a couple of years ago, after Mad Mike Tile had been killed and the cops thought it was going to be open game on the boys. Some stoolie had tricked Darrin out, telling a prosecutor a sad tale about the great businessman Darrin Favore's alleged ties to organized crime, about how he controlled the gambling south of 87th Street and east from the expressway to the lake. The punk, trying to walk Darrin into a trap so he himself could walk out of one of his own making. The prosecutor had gotten a special grand jury called quick, though, the bitch, trying to make her name on his downfall.

Well, he'd shown her, as he'd shown dozens of others over the years. "What good," he'd asked Sal and the other men, the dozen now who ran the city, "is our million a month doing us? Why are we paying the cops if these idiots keep calling grand juries against us?" It had been squashed, and the little fool, the snitch, he had done Darrin a solid in a way, because now Darrin owned Catfeet Millard, the best prowler in the nation, had him in the palm of his hand and was about to put the squeeze on him real slow. Teach him what happened to guys dumb enough to mess around with Darrin's secretary.

He was thinking such thoughts when he got into his Mercedes and had the driver take him to his South Michigan Avenue suite of offices, home of DFI—Darrin Favore Incorporated.

To find Femal hard at work, looking as sharp as usual.

"Morning, Femal," he said, and she told him that his letter to Mr. Parnell was on his desk, typed and ready for his signature.

He loved her, too.

He went into his office and signed the damn thing, the object of his greatest obsession out there discreetly answering calls, taking care of his business, the *real* brains behind this organization.

What would he do without her.

He heard the little buzzer go off that announced a visitor to his office, and looked up at his closed door because he wasn't expecting anybody this early, had no appointments. It must be one of the boys, coming to discuss the don's passing. Who else could get past the receptionist, down the hall and through the outer secretary's office without being announced?

He found out real quick when his door flew open, banged against the wall and he found himself staring eye to eye with Catfeet Millard, Femal right behind the arrogant bastard, outraged and grabbing at his arm. Darrin smiled.

"It's all right, Femal," Darrin said. "I'll see Mr. Millard a little earlier than I expected."

Chapter 10

"**C**ome on in, sit down, Catfeet. Good to see you out."
Darrin pushed the button on his intercom, said:
"Femal? Have Carol bring in a couple of coffees, would
you?" Let the circuit close before Femal could answer. He
sat back in his chair, took a look at Millard, searching for
traces of fear and seeing none, the man sitting forward in
his chair and staring at Darrin. Which was okay. Fear
could be instilled in the toughest of men if you knew the
way to implant it.

"How you take your coffee?" Darrin said, leaning forward, about to push the button again, "You want some
cream, some sugar?" He didn't wait for an answer, let go
of the switch and sat back again, grinning, and said, "You
bring my money, Catfeet?" Just like that, expecting to
throw the man off base, but the son of a bitch, he wasn't
going to be easy.

Millard reached into his jacket pocket and pulled out
a large envelope, tossed it onto Darrin's desk and said, "I
sure did," then sat back in his chair and smiled right back
at him.

• • •

Peter Silva did not sleep at all on Monday night. He hadn't spent the night at home, either. He knew that he hadn't been seen going into or out of the Pierce house, but someone, surely, would have told the police by now that he had been Terry's boyfriend.

He was in his cousin Arturo's house, the cousin taking him in without complaint or comment, simply giving his wife a look to shut her up when she had begun hollering at him about Peter having gotten them out of bed. He was on the couch, the sun rising quickly, the rays from its cold light entering the windows above him. The house was small, two of the children having to sleep with Arturo and his wife, three others sharing the only other bedroom, the children who would be up at any time now, wanting him to play with them as he always did when he visited.

Peter wasn't in any mood to be playing this Tuesday morning.

He got off the couch, found his coat and threw it over his shoulders. He searched the closet and found a wool navy blue and orange Bears watch cap, shoved it onto his head, dug around until he found some gloves. He walked over to the telephone and dialed Merle Como's number again, let it ring four times before the same recorded announcement he'd heard before came at him, telling him in Merle's slow drawl that he was gone for a while, but the dog was prowling and his roommate was a better shot than he himself was, so if this was a setup call, come ahead on, partner, but if it was someone who wanted a call back, to leave a message at the beep. When the sound came Peter left another message, begging Merle to call him right away, leaving Arturo's number and his mother's also, then hung up.

He left the house carefully, looking around the street for the police cruisers, and when he didn't see any he hurried down the street, heading east, away from the neighborhood as quickly as he could without running and bringing attention or suspicion to himself.

"Merle," Peter whispered, his head down, his eyes on the sidewalk, expecting a policeman to shoot him in the back with every step, "where in the hell are you *at!*"

In a shack in Palm Beach County, was where Merle was. Dressed in his traveling suit, looking safe and successful, Merle had left one of Moonbeam's cars out on the dirt road and was now entering his father's house.

Nothing ever changed out here. It was always the same, so damn depressing that Merle was sorry that he ever showed up.

There was dirt everywhere, the windows boarded up because his daddy never got around to fixing them after he broke them in a drunken rage. Mildew on everything and mold on the furniture. Decrepit-ass place, stinking of moonshine and B.O.

It was a two-room shack on state land that nobody ever bothered to throw his daddy off of, on a stretch of ground next to the dump. Out back was a pickup truck that hadn't run in Merle's lifetime, surrounded by used tires and hubcaps that the old man would try to sell when he got ambitious or ran out of people to beg or steal from.

Merle walked through the central room, aware that snakes could well be nesting in here, breathing through his mouth. Kee-rist, it stank something awful, how could the man live like this?

Found his daddy passed out on a mattress on the floor in the other room, a mostly empty jug next to his head.

The old man was dressed in urine-stained bib overalls, a filthy undershirt over his scrawny, sunken chest. His beard was yellow, hanging down to the middle of his chest, matted and foul. He was snoring, his mouth open, showing maybe three teeth still in there, and those looked green from where Merle was standing. Even the creases in the man's face had dirt in them.

"Daddy?" Merle spoke softly, hesitantly. Then, more boldly, "Daddy?" Still, the man did not move.

Merle kicked out at him lightly, but his father's breathing pattern didn't even change. Kicked harder and got a response, Daddy rolling over onto his side and slapping at his leg.

"Daddy!" Merle shouted, giving his father a good solid kick in the ass, and that finally motivated the man enough to where he opened his eyes, rolled over onto his back and stared hatred at the source of the noise.

"Go 'way," he muttered, not recognizing his son.

"Daddy, it's me."

"Said go 'way, motherfucker!" His eyes closed.

"Daddy!" Merle kicked sharply, on the outside of the upper leg, and the man rolled up into a crouch, one hand reaching into the overalls, as if for a weapon.

"Daddy, it's me, Merle!"

Slowly, the old man's hand came out of the front of his overalls. Merle's daddy squinting, shaking his head, a pained expression on his face.

"Who's there, goddamnit!"

"It's me, Merle." Last chance. If the old man didn't get it this time, Merle was on his way to the airport.

"Merle?!" Said in wonder. That was better. The old man said his name the way the Pope might say the name of the Lord if he had a sudden vision of Christ walking through the Vatican. "Son?" Daddy sat back against the wall, one hand reaching for the jug, still squinting, trying to make Merle come into his line of vision.

A quick shot of the juice and he seemed able to focus, blinked several times and looked at Merle, his eyes clearing, shaking his head in wonder. "Son." Merle's father guffawed painfully. "What you dressed up for, it Halloween already?"

Merle watched the man, his moves. It was pitiful, what had happened to him, and what scared Merle was the thought that this was where he would be thirty years from now, what he'd look like.

"I'm on my way to the airport, Daddy. Got to catch a plane to Chicago."

"See your mama?"

"She died, Daddy, you didn't know that?"

"Mama's dead?"

"Last year. Died in her sleep, year to the day after old Favore hisself. Her maid found her in bed one morning, stiff as a board."

"In her bed? They check, make sure she was dead? Way I recollect it, your mama never did do anything in bed but act like a dead woman." The old man chuckled, wheezing between laughs. Merle didn't join in; hillbilly humor had always eluded him.

"I wanted to come see you again, the plane don't leave for a couple hours."

"Glad to have you." He held up the jug. "Want a drink?"

Merle declined, although he could have used one. Watched the old man take his drink and couldn't think of anything else to say, was backing out of the room when his father told him to watch out for that gangster family his mama had married into, they were none of them no damned good, those goddamned wife-stealing guineas . . .

It wasn't the way he remembered his mother, and now his thoughts of her would always be tainted.

She'd been a high-assed woman, with large titties that jiggled when she walked. She had given birth to Merle when she'd been fifteen, the three of them living in a trailer park in Miami with his mama supporting them at her waitress job. Until the slick-talking gangster had come along and stolen her away.

He'd hear them, the pud who insisted that Merle call him Mr. Favore and his mother, going at it in the bedroom when he was a little boy, growing excited at the sound of his mama groaning, touching his little thing and feeling that delicious thrill of fear and guilt over what he was thinking.

Although it never stopped him. Now the old man says she was a cadaver between the sheets? Merle had had him a few of those, and could not believe it. They didn't moan when you banged them, didn't jiggle their tits when they walked, shake their asses or rouge their faces all up the way his mama did. The old man was just bitter. Drunken old fart thought the best living musician on the face of the earth was Zamfir, Master of the Pan Flute. Full of hate because the best woman he'd ever had had left him for a member of a race that Merle's family thought less of than niggers.

Merle got the drink he needed in the empty airport lounge, sat staring into it, thinking of his mother, the woman being the last thing on his mind ten minutes later when Peter Pudham himself walked in and Merle couldn't believe how lucky he suddenly was.

What the hell was going on here? Merle couldn't tell. Was this a blessing from God or what? The old man in the snazzy blue suit had walked in all full of himself, had acted as if Merle wasn't the only other person in the entire lounge, had come walking right up to him as if they had an appointment, plopped his fat ass on the stool at Merle's right.

The lounge was dark, decorated in different shades of red. The stools padded vinyl held together with cheap imitation brass studs, trying to give the impression that they were made of leather. Merle leaned back on his stool, swiveling to meet the man's gaze, his back to the bar now and his elbows on the wood. This little pud who was all excited and full of himself was sitting there bouncing around waiting for Merle to say something to him. It was obvious that he had something to say and couldn't wait to get it off his chest, show someone how damn smart he was. Obvious too was his glee over the fact that he wouldn't be just giving it to a lowly bartender.

"How's it going there, partner?" Merle said, and it was all the man needed to hear.

Favore looked at the envelope like it was a bug, didn't touch it. He turned his eyes away from it and smiled at Feet, the way a shark might at a ladleful of chum.

"That stuffed with million-dollar bills? Let me tell you something, Catman, so you know how slick you ain't. The old man hadn't died last night, there'd be about forty guys in this office right now, tearing you a new asshole. I sent them over to the house, to pay their respects to the family."

"There's still two in the garage, couple more in the outer office. Know what they said, Darrin? Nothing."

"Want me to get them in here, see what they have to say?"

"I want you to pick up your money and let me get out of here, I got things to do with my life."

"What life?" Darrin said. He picked up the envelope and tossed it back toward Feet, who let it hit his chest, made no move to catch it and didn't look at it as it fell to the floor. "You don't come up with my money, I'm gonna see to it that life as you knows it ceases to exist before this weekend."

"Your money's there, Favore, all of it. Sal gave me the word yesterday, what I owed you, and I'd bet that twenty-two to your nickel that the other bosses'll back my word on what he said. They know I ain't a liar . . ." He let it hang there between them for just a second, Catfeet telling Favore through implication that the other mobsters would see Favore as a liar. He let it sit a beat then continued. "They know me, know what happened, where I been and why. They'll back me."

"Over me?" Favore said, then grunted a laugh. "You really think so?"

Catfeet said, "I'm betting my life on it." And turned his back on the man, walked to the door and opened it, saw Femal right there with her arms crossed, staring at him. "Are you ready to?" he said over his shoulder, then had to hand it to the man, he had control of himself because as Feet was closing the door he shouted at him that he should wait, have his coffee, maybe a doughnut and a smoke, because every man deserves a last meal . . .

Femal hissed, "How *dare* you!" in a stage whisper, following him to the outer office door. When he didn't respond she grabbed his arm, turned him around and he glared at her, raised his hand in a violent gesture then stopped, put it down, turned his face away from the outraged, shocked Femal and slammed out of the office.

She'd be damned. He'd almost hit her. She turned and spotted Favore there leaning against his doorframe smiling at her, made sure she was composed as she walked back to her desk, sat down at the computer terminal and finished the money transfer she was working on.

"You get that two mill where it's supposed to be?" Favore spoke as if there had never been a problem, no confrontation with Catfeet at all.

She gave the same back to him. "Typing in the authorization codes now, sir. Shouldn't lose a day's interest, the way I've set it up."

"Good. Man needs to know his retirement fund's secure and growing." Something fell on the computer table, skidded into her, knocked into her wrist and she pulled her fingers from the keys instinctively, knowing that a mistake at this point could wipe out the transfer of two million dollars of what would soon be Favore's personal funds.

It was an envelope, folded over on itself and taped shut.

"You happen to see Millard, see that he gets this. Tell him he's short."

"What makes you think *I'd* see him? And what's in that?"

"Beats me," the man who'd risked two million dollars just to impress her with how tough he was said. "Either it's his, or else it fell off a truck. And Femal, I'm gonna need Sal's funds transferred here, today, liquid before the end of banking hours. I've gotta sit down with Mrs. Luchessa this evening, let her know how well her husband set her up. Can do?"

Can do? What the hell did he think she was working on? Did he think she didn't know he was robbing Sal blind before the man's soul had a chance to get out of his body? There'd be plenty left over for the family, more than enough, but nowhere near the amounts Sal had put into the offshore drilling franchise, the Bahamian banks . . .

She didn't mention any of this, though, wanted the man to think she was dumb enough not to remember whose money was whose. All she said was, "It's on its way, Mr. Favore," because there were times when he could be a frightening man, and the way he was standing there staring at her, the way he seemed to know that she and Feet were lovers, proved to her that this was one of them.

Chapter
11

Merle couldn't believe his luck, had to look around the bar all the time and walked into the bathroom twice when he didn't have to just to make sure this wasn't a setup, something the cops were pulling to screw him up.

He was half-convinced that this little shit was for real, and was having a hard time with it, having only an hour until his plane left and wanting to time what he wanted to do exactly right.

He ordered another round for them both, sipping his own beer from the bottle while the fat old gray-haired guy —"Just call me Jimbo"—sucked down the last of his manhattan, celebrating his good fortune and not being able to wait to impress his good new young friend with what a slick son of a bitch he was.

It was apparent in the clothes he wore. Jimbo wearing a snaggly electric blue suit, the old-fashioned kind that looked like someone had been picking at it with their fingertips. White shoes and belt, no socks. A hipster.

"So you told the old lady you'd follow her by the weekend, big deal. You're alone in Palm Beach for a couple of days, getting laid, what's so hot about that? Happens all the time out here, Jimbo." Make the guy work for it, that was the way to do it.

And it worked. The man's face fell, the little feather-duster mustache darted up and down there on his lip while the sucker bit his tongue, about to say something smart then thinking better of it. Jimbo took a sip of his fresh manhattan for courage, put it down smack in the middle of the cocktail napkin before he spoke.

"My friend, I can see you're young, you have a lot to learn." That was it, he was going to play teacher. Okay, Mr. Teach, give me something to work with. Impress me with your knowledge.

Which the old man had no trouble wanting to do.

"It's not a few *days*, my friend. It's forever, only she doesn't know it.

"I'm a retired salesman, you understand? It's what I did for forty years. The product didn't matter; what I was selling, every time I walked into a customer's office, was myself."

Good for you, asshole. The words thought but left unspoken, Merle putting his friendly face on, no more tough guy, the act dropped now that the man was in the process of selling himself to Merle. Not aware yet that if Merle got half a chance he would be buying a hell of a lot more than this pud had to sell.

"She knows that, knows how I do it, the way you finesse it, the subtle manipulation involved, the invocation of trust."

"So what'd you sell her?" Merle put his elbows on the bar, leaned in to be part of the conspiracy even though the bartender was a mile away at the other end of the bar, watching some game show on the portable TV. The man got into it now, leaning forward himself, speaking into Merle's face.

"I convinced her to put our money into a bank out here that had a higher interest rate than the ones in Chicago. Told her we'd buy some property for an investment

while we were at it. Shoved some papers under her nose
and she signed them without even looking at them. The
woman hasn't been able to stand the sight of me for
twenty years, but she knows I'm a first-rate businessman,
that I'm a moneymaker."

"So you're gonna ditch her? Not go back to Chicago
atoll?"

"Better than that." Jimbo snickered. It was getting
better and better. "One of the papers she signed was a
divorce decree, no fault, through Illinois, that my lawyer
will witness and swear was signed in his presence. She
not only loses me, she loses claim to any of my money!"

"This," Merle said, "calls for a drink."

Jimbo said, "My treat, though, this one's on me."

As the bartender mixed the manhattan, old Jimbo took
out his wallet, dropped a five on the bar, then held the
wallet out to Merle, Jesus Christ, offering it to him.

"First picture in the holder, son, take a look, go
ahead."

Merle obeyed him, his fingers telling him that the pigskin was filled with greenbacks, looked through the smoky
plastic and saw the ugliest woman he'd ever seen in his
life. Good God, what a prune-faced bitch.

"That's the woman of my dreams, the woman I've
been waiting for my entire life."

"This?!"

The old man looked, snatched the wallet back and
fussed around for a second and pulled the picture of the
prune-faced broad out, then turned the wallet in his
hands, flipped to the true front of the holder instead of the
back, handed the wallet back.

"*That* was my wife."

"Shit, no wonder you dumped her."

Jimbo had leaned over and grabbed a book of matches
out of a brandy snifter filled with them that was set into
the bar well, was lighting one, holding it to the picture of
prune-face. Dropped the smoldering snapshot into the
ashtray.

"That there, now, see what you think of that!"

It was a full-body long shot, taken on the beach, the woman in the picture being blond and maybe Merle's age, maybe a little younger. Full of breast and hip, posing for the camera in a World War Two cheesecake fashion, looking like she was enjoying herself. Looking like a two-dollar tramp, too.

"No shit!" Merle said.

The man was filled with joy at Merle's reaction. "No shit," he said.

Merle said, "You ready for a refill, there, Jimbo?" Shaking his head, letting the old fart know how amazed he was at Jimbo's intelligence.

"I'm around here somewhere, goddamnit, it's a white Cadillac."

That was a lot of help. Half the cars in this goddamned lot were white Cadillacs. Still, Merle was patient, accepting a ride "home" from the man, helping him find his car in the many-tiered short-term lot where all the levels of this concrete maze looked alike. He'd find Moonbeam's car before he found any particular white Cadillac. Still, it was good that they'd decided to leave, the bartender had been giving them funny looks.

The old man said, "There it is!" and pointed, swaying on his feet, walking toward the car with the odd dignity of the drunk trying to make a straight line.

Jimbo made it to the car and shut off the alarm, hit a button on the door and popped the locks for Merle then swung his ass onto the leather seat. The car's windows were tinted gray to keep out the hot Florida sun and to distract the rays that would reflect in off the car's polished white hood. Perfect.

Merle went around to his side, shooting a look at his watch, grateful that he'd checked his luggage early. Still, he'd have to hurry.

He slid into the passenger seat and closed the door

and didn't waste any time, lifted his arm and made a fist and delivered The Punch to the side of Jimbo's head, saw the man's eyes close and watched him slump down in his seat before he was ever aware of what hit him.

Merle was careful not to touch anything, wasn't about to leave any prints. He used two fingers to remove Jimbo's wallet from his pocket, slid the bills out of the pigskin, grabbed the credit cards and the old man's Rolex, dropped the wallet onto the floorboards and shoved the bills into his pocket. He'd count them on the plane, locked safely into the bathroom. He pushed Jimbo to the floor. Let him sleep it off there to wake up with a hangover and broke. It would be better than not waking up at all.

Merle looked around, through the tinted glass, saw nobody anywhere near the car, and slid out of it, walked rapidly to the elevators, hit the button and before he knew it was back in the terminal with plenty of time to spare.

Every neighborhood has one, everybody knows one. Even the sheltered children in the suburbs run into them from time to time, and everyone gives them a wide berth after that first encounter.

The person who looked innocuous, even innocent and weak, but had a punch like a mule and the disposition of a cat in a microwave.

There had been people in Merle's life who had learned it the hard way; the tough guys, the jocks in high school, the muscleheads who were dumb enough to think that lifting weights did anything to increase the size of the balls. He'd meet up with them, butt heads, hit them one time and it was all over.

He had The Punch, knew it, learned it early and now saw it as his due.

It rarely took more than one Punch, never more than two. Merle'd ball up that fist and swing away and it would be all over but the crying.

It was a true pleasure, seeing it in the eyes of his victims, the knowledge there that they'd fucked up. He'd enjoy it, their humiliation, would sometimes even lighten up on The Punch if he figured he could drag it out without any personal loss to himself.

Merle didn't know where it came from, nor did he care. All he was sure of was that the man hadn't been born who could withstand the onslaught. Too many had tried, too many had died.

He swaggered onto the plane, feeling no pain himself, smiling at the stewardess and telling her that prohibiting smoking on them damn planes was the smartest thing Congress had ever done, but they were still allowed to have a beer or two en route, weren't they? She assured him that he could, showed him to his seat, even took his arm and directed him and he kidded with her, laid on the farmboy charm until he spotted the passenger way in the back, in the last seat before the toilets, and the sight made his smile nothing short of beatific.

It was old prune-face. Jimbo's old lady. Should he say something to her, let her know the old man's plan?

She must have felt his staring because she looked up at him, caught his stare and gave him an ice cube glance that chilled him all the way up here in the center of the plane. Well, fuck her. She deserved whatever she got.

He said to the stewardess, "Could I maybe get one of them beers now, hon?" then had to assure her that he was just fine and not too drunk to fly when she asked him, smiling right back at him, if he was going to be a problem.

"Answer a question for me, honey? These pilots all go to hillbilly school or something, the way they drawl, or they just want me to feel at home?"

The stewardess giggled. "It goes back to Chuck Yeager. They all love him. It's something though, isn't it? I've met pilots from Boston who sound like they're from San Antonio and want to be called Lucky."

Merle smiled at her, wondering if he was going to join the Mile-High Club before the flight was through.

She winked at him and walked down the aisle and he sat in the seat, staring out the window awaiting takeoff and thinking that it would be fun, counting Jimbo's money with his little old prune-faced wife sitting there two feet away, broke, divorced and unaware of either fact.

The stewardess walked by, told him to fasten his seat belt then leaned down and whispered that she'd get him a beer just as soon as they reached cruising altitude, he wouldn't have to wait until the cart went by.

Merle said, "Why thank you, dear," and smiled innocently, letting her see how grateful he was.

Chapter
12

Even when Charlie was nervous inside, nobody could ever tell from looking at him. It was one of the things he prided himself on, showing them only what he wanted them to see, never letting them know when he was upset or even that he was. No one could ever be allowed to score on him, could ever know that they'd reached his center and caused him pain. Hide the buttons, with everyone, all the time, because even the people you think you like will turn around later and hurt you if you show them any form of weakness.

The prisons were filled with guys who'd talked too much. To family and friends as well as to stoolpigeons. Honor among thieves was dead. There was no such thing today, if there ever really had been. They'd turn on you, score you heavy time in order to keep themselves out of prison for just one lousy night. He knew these things as well as he knew his own name, knew instinctively that if he let anyone in, see the way he was really feeling, it could and probably would be used against him at a later time. Emotional blackmail was just as damaging as any other kind.

Which was why he came into work at the usual time, minding his own business and nodding good morning to the secretaries and the order-takers and Stell, his own secretary, who were all giving him guarded, curious looks as he passed. The word had probably got around. Charlie was out of here.

He sat behind his desk, thinking about what he should take with him, wondering if there was anything in the drawers that he wanted to have with him as mementos wherever he ended up. He could think of nothing.

It would be a good thing, striking out on his own. A divorce—which sounded better and better to him—would cause serious complications, no matter how good things were with the old man, what with Lina being the senior vice-president of the company. Let someone else have the office. Maybe he could get a buyout, get paid extra, some stock options or something to pay him back for all the time and effort he'd put into the company. If they gave him that, he'd even train his replacement, show him the ropes, instead of taking the hot files with him to start his own business with.

Charlie could picture his replacement, the man who would take his place in the business; could see him clearly in his mind. He'd gone to college with enough of the type to imagine what the man would be like.

He'd be a go-getter, serious and aggressive, slender, his hair combed straight back in the wet-look, maybe with a little ponytail down the back to show how daring he was. Dressed by Brooks Brothers and Hathaway and Gucci. With round frameless glasses like William Hurt wears in the movies. The man would talk about "kicking ass" without having any practical experience as to what the words meant, would say "destroy" with the same restrictions. Charlie could tell guys like that something about the art of ass-kicking, and he'd seen enough people

destroyed to know that the word didn't relate to beating
someone out in a business deal.

He'd been in college with people who'd come from
money and thought their book learning translated literally
to education, instead of being just a single part of the
process. He'd listen to them talk and would keep a
straight face and wonder if there was something wrong
with him because they all seemed so stupid, even the
smart ones. Until later, when he decided that what had
happened to him previous to his schooling had been the
best education any man could really have. Losing everything had gained him the world. At least it gave him the
insight he needed to know that in order to get ahead, to
truly survive, you had to be cold, cold as ice, and you
could never let them see that they'd gotten to you.

Like Lina, trying hard this morning to be the dutiful
little wife. Bustling around and making pancakes, humming, hell, even her kid had given her funny looks. She
was so transparent. Years ago, he would have been
brokenhearted at the thought of someone he thought he
might love using him for their own means. Now he knew
that it was part of the game, the way it was played. Everyone used everyone, if they thought they could get away
with it. The thing that surprised him the most about this
situation was that Lina could be so dumb, could be with
him for five years and live with him for over a year and
still believe she had any power over him.

Where had it gone wrong, when had it ended? He
knew just when; the day they'd gotten married.

Before that it had been sweetness and light, Lina accepting him as he was, never complaining, criticizing.

Right after the ceremony, though, the grooming had
begun, and now he couldn't take any more.

Charlie pushed his swivel chair back on its castors,
away from the desk and over to the little computer table
set up near the window, began to type away at the thing,
bringing up his passworded secret customer files, the
names, addresses and phone numbers of hot clients, the

ones he handled himself and wouldn't allow the order-takers, sales people, or even John himself anywhere near. He took their orders and billed them himself, cashed the checks in his own interest-bearing escrow account, then transferred the funds to the company once the checks cleared, keeping the interest as his due. As long as the cash flow was right in terms of product shipped from the warehouse John would never complain, and in his business affairs, Charlie was scrupulous.

Which might have been a mistake. He thought about this, as he transferred his files onto a floppy.

He could have made close to a million this past year, juggling the books and playing with the product order forms, the invoices. Embezzled all he'd wanted with no one the wiser.

Should he have? He wondered about it as the computer whirred, its little red HDD light flickering as the information was relocated.

Catfeet had taught him to be straightforward, to always let people know where you stood with them. Charlie'd believed him, as he'd believed every word Cat had ever said to him. Later, when Charlie'd screwed up, he thought that this one time, in that single instance, Cat had been wrong. It was best to always have your enemies think they were your best friend, and to keep your friends guessing. It made them respect you, gave you room to think and time to react to their behavior. The closeness he'd achieved with John, as a member of the family and as an integral part of the business, had put him in a position to be able to take him for all he was worth.

But what was the challenge there? How much satisfaction was there in robbing a drunk? On the other hand, if you were going to be a thief, did it matter who you robbed from? It would be better to steal from some fool who wouldn't even realize he'd been taken. But that would be a con, rather than a score. And the entire point of his going to school in the first place had been to keep from having to ever steal again, to never go back to where

stealing and the deadly aftermath of a broken robbery had
sent him . . .

Catfeet had known the odds would catch up with him,
had financed Charlie's education in order for them to get
into the legitimate world in a way that would not lessen
Cat's style of living, which might, in fact, raise it. After
Charlie's experiences as Cat's protégé, after what it had
cost him, the idea had seemed more than reasonable, go
to school and learn how to steal legally. They couldn't put
you in jail for that, or most of the real estate and insurance
salesmen in the country would be in the joint. The lawyers, forget about it, they'd get the death penalty. Charlie
had gone on to college, had used his native intelligence
and his true education and then his book learning and had
planned to parlay them into making him a powerhouse of
the business world.

Only Cat had gone to jail because he wasn't a rat and
Charlie had gotten married to Lina and had wound up
here, in a dead-end job where the profits went to everyone but him.

Well, he couldn't do anything about Cat, but he could
solve the other two problems right now.

The computer finished the transfer and Charlie removed the disc, put it in a sleeve, the sleeve into a plastic
disc mailer. He put it in his inner jacket pocket. Looked
at the information in the file and hit delete. The machine
seemed surprised. It read, DELETE CSTMER FILE?
(y) (n), the (n) flashing in red. Charlie hit y for yes, and the
machine still challenged him with: ARE YOU SURE?
This time the question mark blinked red. Charlie told the
machine he was, and he watched the screen go blank, the
only evidence of his secret files now in his possession.

He was wondering how long it would take to build his
own business, how much capital he'd need, when Stell
buzzed him and told him a Mr. Millard was there to
see him.

•   •   •

Catfeet had to get himself around someone who cared about him, and he knew that Charlie was one of the few people who did. Femal, well, the jury was out on her right now. There had been a time in his life when Feet would have bet his life on her love, but in the time he'd been gone, something had changed. There were differences in her that couldn't simply be put down to the passage of time, something that had once been an integral part of her makeup now gone. It wasn't something he could put his finger on just yet, but it would come to him if he thought about it enough, and would base his future decisions about her accordingly.

Maybe it was the kid. Going into labor and delivery all alone would change the way a woman looked at the father who wasn't there, would sour her toward him. He hadn't known about the child, and that wasn't right. Even though he'd made the rules himself, told everyone he knew not to write to him because he didn't want some small-time County hack reading the letters and invading the privacy of his loved ones, that was still one letter that should have been sent.

Did she love him? God, she'd better. Because Feet knew he could never again think of prowling; he had a kid to raise and a woman whose love, it seemed, had to be earned all over again.

So he'd talk to Charlie, see if the kid was still standup, if he respected their deal. Feet had made it only to get the kid to go to school but now it appeared more attractive. Take his half of the money and maybe open a legit business, a tavern or something, where he could set people up to meet others who needed something they had, take a percentage of whatever they worked out. He'd be like a real estate broker, stealing legally. But first, he had to find out if Femal would go for the deal.

Maybe it was *his* feelings toward her that changed, maybe his resentment at getting hit over the head with a daughter who was already a toddler screwed up his perspective. That had to be it, it couldn't be that Femal didn't care for him any longer, or she wouldn't have torn him up between the sheets as she had, with a vengeance, the night before, wouldn't have gotten all dolled up in the hooker's outfit for him. It wasn't her style, it was more of a message to him. She cared enough about him to do something against her grain because she thought that he'd enjoy it.

She wouldn't be doing it tonight, Feet knew. One of her rules was that their relationship would never get in the way of her career, was not supposed to even come to Favore's attention, as if the man wasn't powerful enough to find out whatever he wanted to know about her, her mother, the kid, and her ancestors going all the way back to the slave boat just by picking up the phone and making one call. Feet's going there this morning would be something it would take time for her to forgive, but she would forgive it. She'd have to. Wasn't he the father of her child? Wasn't he her future husband? Maybe he could win her love back. But what about the mother? Shit, that wasn't going to be easy.

He'd left Favore's office shaking, his hands in his coat pockets so the guards outside would not be able to see that they were trembling, would not know how afraid he was, and headed for Jerry's Tap on the West Side, around the corner from the main post office, a huge, ugly, bustling building that had an expressway running underneath. Had a few drinks with some of the rollers there, standup guys who welcomed him with hearty handshakes and tough talk, who bought him drinks as his welcome home present, their tribute to him for keeping his mouth shut and doing over two years in jail without having even done a crime to deserve it. As if a couple of J&Bs would pay him back. It was warm in there, almost cozy next to where he'd been all that time, but still, the fear wouldn't leave him.

Favore had the ability to do that to people. Could terrify them beyond the fear of God then sit down and eat a nice meal, discuss stock portfolios and long-term option deals as if nothing had ever happened, as if lives hadn't been altered, sometimes even altogether ended. Favore was a businessman, legitimate and, it seemed these days, beyond suspicion and reproach, but beneath it all, he was still just another two-bit mob punk, a guy who used fear and intimidation to get what he wanted. Only now he used it in the marketplace instead of on the street. The sad fact was that Feet knew there were thousands of kids in the city who had fancy educations and had gotten all the right breaks who admired the guy, were jealous of him, saw his whispered-about mob connections as the juice they wished they had. They would never think about what it does to you to order someone dead, what Favore had to be lacking in character to be able to do so arbitrarily.

And Feet had just insulted the man, took a slap at his honor, and didn't guys like Favore get high off that word?

Jesus Christ, one day out of jail and looking to get killed.

Feet had learned in Jerry's about Charlie, where he was, to whom he was married. The wife's name not meaning much to him, but the guys in the bar had told him that there was money behind it, that Charlie was doing all right and making a good buck. Hadn't Sal said last night that the kid was rich these days? Feet hadn't said anything, because he didn't want Sal to know that they hadn't stayed in touch. Nobody saw Charlie much, he learned, he didn't come around, hung around the country club these days, but everyone knew he was connected to Feet, that Feet had taken him in years ago when the mob had killed his folks, then paid his way through college after Charlie had his trouble.

So he'd left there, heading for the building in South Chicago using Petey One-ball's car, going to see the one person left in this screwy world whose presence alone would make him feel better. He could look at Charlie and know

that even if Favore had him killed that night, that right
before him was evidence that Feet had done at least one
thing right in his forty-some years. Like Sal had said, he'd
made Charlie better than himself.

That had to be worth something.

The building was bigger than Feet would have figured,
the lower floor having a loading dock with three truck
bays, all of them now full, the trucks big with white trail-
ers that had the company name stenciled across the sides
in large black letters. Loading vitamins. An Asian thief
had once told Feet that the Americans' passion for vitamins gave them something no other country had: The
healthiest piss in the world, and that's the way he saw it.
They were fine if you thought they were doing you some
good and you had the money to burn, but he'd get the
nutrition he needed from eating steaks and baked pota-
toes, maybe some broccoli on the side.

Still, it looked like a good scam, the semi trucks being
loaded as Feet watched them, standing in the cold and
smoking a cigarette, looking at what Charlie did for a
living and feeling good. Whatever Charlie did, whatever
straight job he held, it was better than doing time.

He would be happy to see him, was glad that he'd
come.

Still, he wondered how the kid would act when he saw
him. Was Feet a part of his past now? Was Charlie happy,
married and maybe with a kid of his own? A lot of things
could happen in twenty-eight months. Would he honor
their deal?

Feet walked past the trucks, into the man-door and up
to a guy with a white coat on, a supervisor of some kind,
asked him where he could find Charlie Lane. Listened to
the guy and took the warehouse way through instead of
going around outside again, mounted the steel stairway,
through a door and into a suite of offices and followed
directions given by harried phone operators and finally

found Charlie's corner office with hardly any trouble, his mind already made up.

If the kid was happy, if he liked what he was doing, Feet would back off, wouldn't make a big thing out of the deal they'd made six years ago. He'd fade out of Charlie's life and let him get on with it, let him be better than Feet and infinitely better than Charlie's own father had ever dreamed of being. He'd really only made the deal to keep the kid's pride from stopping him from doing what needed to be done. Talked the kid into it and the pride fell by the wayside. And it was a good thing, too, or Charlie wouldn't be here today, working for his father-in-law, making the big bucks.

Without an education, how far would a guy like Charlie get, after having done time for burglary-murder?

The old battle-axe secretary took his name and made it clear by the way she spoke to him that she didn't hold out much chance of Charlie's letting him in, her face falling and the old woman trying to control it as Charlie got excited, you could hear it over the intercom, tinny, but happy.

"You may go in now, sir," throwing in the sir as if that would make up for her treating him like shit.

It never ceased to amaze him, how many people there were in this world who didn't know how to act.

Forgetting about her when he saw someone who *did* know how to act, Charlie coming out of the office to meet him in the hallway, smiling broadly and pumping his hand, Catfeet happy to see him but aware enough of his surroundings to notice that everyone in that damn outer office was staring at them. What the hell was that all about?

"Perfect timing," Charlie said, "believe me when I tell you."

Cat smiling, even looking like a cat now, Charlie half-expecting to see feathers in the corner of the man's mouth.

"Jesus, look at you." Cat waved his hand around the office. "Not too shabby, huh? You think this was possible, six years ago?"

"Six, hell, ask me what I thought *seven* years ago!" Charlie opening up, smiling and happy, and Christ, did it feel good! It had been too long, he'd spent too much time keeping everything inside. But Cat had proven himself to Charlie, who else was willing to do that? Was prepared to sacrifice for him? To honor anyone else the way he honored Cat would be to insult the man who'd paid for his education. And that Charlie couldn't do and still maintain his integrity. No, it was better to stick with the way he was, stay cool and let them think he was an ice cube. It saved him a lot of trouble, getting hurt while trying to find out who could be trusted, maybe even loved.

"Education paid off, did it?"

"So far, but I think I'm leaving. I made fifty the last year, with bonuses. He tosses in a car with a phone, a portable cellular that folds up so he can reach me in the toilet, a membership in his country club, I'm supposed to be grateful."

"Nothing's wrong with fifty, unless you're bringing in a lot more than that for them."

Just like Cat, to get right to the heart of it.

"Plus, Cat, my wife, who runs around eating lunch with the wives of the customers, gets profit-sharing, made a buck-and-a-half last year, three times what I got, and I'm doing all the work."

"Where you gonna go?"

"I was just thinking about that, where I'd get the capital to start up for myself, when you came in."

Cat said, "Well, I got six grand . . ." and was about to laugh, then something stopped him. "Had to give the rest to that prick, Favore," the words said and then Charlie noticed that Lina was standing in the doorway, listening in and staring at the back of Feet's head. She set her face

in a determined expression and marched right in without
an invitation as Charlie forced himself to slip out of his
personality and back into his protective shell.

Catfeet watched the expression change on Charlie's face
and it was like watching a demonic possession. The man
all happy and smiling, then within the span of a couple of
seconds having a serious, thoughtful look on his face, like
a raincloud passing over the sun, Jesus.

Was that what all the staring in the outer office had
been about? Were they used to seeing Charlie like this,
never smiling, cold and tough? He hoped not.

The woman came in, Lina, whom he'd met once or
twice before, while Charlie had been in college. Tiny and
pretty but no Femal. There were no sensual signals being
sent off by this one, not even a hint of erotic promise. She
looked and acted like some model/actresses Feet had
known, aloof and arrogant, pretending to be sexy but
working too hard to gain the illusion. The difference between this woman and, say, a woman like Femal, was the
difference between a walking, talking, wetting baby doll
and a real living and breathing child. This one was all
plastic and pretense, in the way she walked and held herself, further confirming his judgment by the way she
played him, ignoring Feet and going right over to Charlie,
throwing her arms around him—not hardly even having
to bend over his chair. Looking at Feet now as if he was
an uninvited guest.

" 'Scuse me," said without even the hint of wanting or
needing to be excused, the woman turning her attention
to Charlie, giving him what she probably thought was a
dazzling smile, Charlie sitting there looking like a cigar
store Indian, no expression at all on his face.

"I just left Doddy, and he said to tell you you're on,
whatever it was you two cooked up last night, he's for it!"
Good God. He'd only seen her twice before in his life, but
Feet could tell that she was lying, that she knew good and

damn well what had been cooked up last night. Did she think that Charlie wouldn't? She giggled now. Feet hated gigglers. "He said if you ever try and hold him up again, he'll turn you in to your parole officer!" She did it again, giggled, obviously seeing Doddy as the wittiest man alive.

Feet didn't think it was such a clever thing to say.

"Well, aren't you going to introduce me to your friend?"

Feet stood up. "I'm Robert Millard, we met . . . ," and she left it hanging there, sized him up and made no move to come forward to shake his hand or hug him, which was just fine with Feet.

How could a little woman like this look down at you? Feet wondered it at the same time that he admired her ability to pull it off, the tiny woman looking down her nose at him, her lips twisting in a half-sneer as she remembered who he was.

She looked him up and down, spoke to Charlie but for Feet's benefit. "If the entire world was a nudist camp, people wouldn't let themselves get so out of shape now, would they?" She said, "I remember you now. Charlie's 'friend,' when we were in college. He told me how close you used to be." The woman said it and flashed a viper smile, let it drop and continued.

"And now he's married and has a job, and he doesn't have time for his jailhouse friends." Her tone was icy, the frozen, phony smile gone. She turned back to Charlie, hugged him tight around the neck. "Do you, Chaz?"

Chaz? Feet felt his eyebrows raise, tried to hide a smile and knew it wasn't working out. He could see Charlie staring at him, probably feeling betrayed. There was nothing he could do, though. If Charlie wanted to let some woman call him Chaz, he had to expect a little ribbing.

"Well, *Chaz*, I better let you get back to work. I was planning on staying at Femal's—" Charlie coming out of himself long enough to ask how Femal was, acting as if he really wanted to know, and did that anger his wife or what? Look at her, staring knives at Charlie.

"But now I don't know. If I'm not there, I'll be in one of the rooms above the 909 Club. They sold my clothes to pay the back rent while I was gone, all my stuff. But I like the joint."

"You were in prison again?!" Shit, he should have kept his mouth shut. "They sold your clothes?" She let go of Charlie, who still hadn't said one word directly to her since she'd come into the office. Came marching right up to him, and he had to look down to look her in the eye.

"I run a legitimate business here, mister. I can't be having ex-cons running around, interrupting the flow of our work. Can't you see my husband's busy?" Turning on Charlie now, giving him hell.

"Chaz, you should know better than to bring people like this into my daddy's building. My God, this element starts hanging around . . ."

"Shut up." Said softly, Charlie's voice carrying weight. She turned away from Feet, which was a good thing. She was just about tall enough for him to stick something into her mouth, see if that would shut her up. Probably never had one in there before, either.

The woman was aghast. She said, "What?! You can't speak to me like that!"

"I can't? All right. Shut the *fuck* up. That better?" Charlie got to his feet, walked around the desk without taking his eyes off his wife. Glaring now, lava instead of ice. "Get the hell out of my office, Lina, right now."

"You've got some *bum* in here and you kick me out? Who the hell do you think you are? This is my office, not yours, I *rent* it to you, you son of a bitch—" Charlie had her arm, was hustling her out the door, gave her a shove through the doorway and slammed the door behind her. He turned to Feet, looking sheepish.

"My wife," Charlie said, and shrugged.

Feet was smiling. He said, "Chaz? She calls you Chaz?"

Charlie said, "Jesus Christ, Cat, it sure isn't what I thought it would be," and Feet felt good inside because for the first time since he'd left Favore's office the fear had left him and he was able to laugh.

"You chump," he said to Charlie, "don't you know it's only as good as you fucking make it?"

Chapter 13

Merle dragged his suitcases out of the cab and let them fall to the sidewalk in front of his apartment house. He checked Jimbo's shiny gold Rolex before he even closed the cab door, the sun's glare causing his hangover to intensify, making his pulse pound in his temples. Goddamnit to hell, after two and would Uncle Dare believe it? No way. "'Ey," the cabby said, and Merle turned to him, saw the stinking little pud leaning with his elbow over the backseat, sneering at Merle. The greasy puke, probably saw Elvis do it in a movie once and thought it looked evil. All he needed was a jewel stuck into the middle of his forehead and a turban, and the image would be complete.

"You leave me no money for a tip and then you leave my cab door open? What were you, mister, born in some sort of a barn?"

Could you believe it? The plane had been on the ground for two hours in Palm Beach, then had to fly stacked up over the airport back home waiting for a runway, the entire trip taking over three hours longer than scheduled, then Merle had been forced to smell goat and garlic all the fucking way over from Midway as this god-damn Iranian breathed all over everything, and now the guy was giving him some lip.

Merle said, "Sure was, Abdul, raised by that bitch mama of yours, who's waiting for me right upstairs this very minute, gonna do the dance of the seven veils before she sucks my dick. So why don't you just go and fuck yourself?" then watched with some satisfaction as the fool gunned it, the open door smacking into a parked car be-fore the idiot remembered that it was open, Merle stand-ing there and laughing as the little brown turd got out of the cab and beat himself on his head, pounding his fists into the sides of his skull the way all those little gooks did at the Ayatollah's funeral, cursing Merle in Iranian, look-ing up the street at Merle, then back to his wrecked back door, like it was Merle's fault or something. Merle laughed but didn't move, wanted the little bastard to start something. It would be fun, pounding on this guy, and would pay back the hostages for all the time they'd had to spend with goat-eaters like this back when Merle was in high school. Maybe this guy was even one of them, one of the Black Sunday group or one of those other terrorist bands, here working undercover, spreading panic on the streets with their crazy-ass driving.

The guy was smarter than he looked though, he didn't move on Merle, just quit smacking himself in the head and threw a few gestures at Merle before he got back in his cab and raced away from the scene, not being too smart after all because he still hadn't had the common sense to close the fucking rear door. Merle watched it swing half-closed then open wide as the Iranian braked at the corner, cutting it too close to a BMW, the door smack-ing the Beamer's rear end and putting out a taillight.

Merle picked up his bags and began climbing the steps to his apartment, hearing the outraged high-pitched screams of the cabby behind him, Merle suddenly not having much of a hangover anymore, smiling . . .

Until the door to his apartment flew open before he reached it.

Merle dropped the bags and had his fist up, was about to deliver The Punch when he saw it was only his little mex buddy Peter, looking all sad-eyed and guilty. Merle picked up his bags and walked past him, into the apartment, dropping the bags right there on the hallway floor, his first instinct being to grab the guy and slam him through the wall, but he knew how Peter felt about being manhandled, and the boy had his uses. Instead Merle turned to eye him suspiciously.

"You weren't in here robbing your old buddy-boy Merle, now, was you, Peter?" Merle looked around the apartment, squinted at the VCR and the television, past them, his eyes roving around.

Peter said, "I knew that you did not truly have a roommate or a dog, so that meant to me that your machine message was not true. I am in trouble," and Merle slowly smiled. He was enjoying himself, first the Iranian, and now this, this little sad mex looking at him all solemn, wanting Merle to show him the way.

"Goddamn, Peter, I can't head down home for a few weeks without you getting yourself into some jackpot?" He grabbed a suitcase. "Get that other one, put it in the bedroom, then grab me a beer while I check my messages. We'll shoot down a few, find a way to get you out of your mess."

"I do not think it will be that easy this time, Merle."

Merle was walking through the apartment, heading for the bedroom. Over his shoulder he said, "What'd you do now, Peter, kill somebody?" And old Peter, he had to be a kidder, gave him a slow, wise No, dragging it out, then waiting a second before telling Merle that the fact was, he had actually killed *two* people.

Dick Blandane did not want to go in to work that afternoon, not after he'd read the morning papers.

The Supreme Court, in its wisdom, had decided that it was okay for the police to search someone's house without a warrant as long as the cops thought there was a reasonable possibility that danger might be lurking somewhere inside, and Dick had been a cop long enough to know what that would mean.

Whenever those wrinkly old bastards gave the police any new freedoms, the cops immediately put them to the test.

He sat in his kitchen, thinking about the decision because there wasn't much else there to think about.

The apartment was nearly empty of furniture, Dick having a used and battered sofa bed, a beat-up 19-inch portable color TV sitting on a microwave stand in front of the couch, a chest of drawers over against one corner. The kitchen nook was separated from the rest of the studio apartment by a waist-high counter. The bathroom was inside the closet. Dick was saving his money for his future. He believed in his future, even on days like this when he wasn't at all certain that it would be a bright one.

The little tuxedoed dolls were still on his mind, bothering him.

When he'd been a child his father could make him cry by just looking at him, and his mother would gather Dick up in her arms and hug him tight, kiss him, tell him that he was her sensitive little boy. It didn't mean much to him then, he didn't understand the word, but he figured that it had to be a pretty good thing to be, or his mother wouldn't be smiling and hugging him when she said it.

Daddy, now, he was another breed of cat. Big and strong, and he liked to stay out after work and have a few with the boys, which made Dick's mother sad. He'd go to her, try to comfort her when he knew she was down, and she'd pretend to be all cheery but he knew that it was just an act. He knew even then that he'd never drink or smoke cigarettes, that when he got married he'd come straight home from work and never give his wife a reason to cry.

All he had to do was to find the right woman, and it would be a pleasure to come home to her.

The only problem being, that he'd never found the right woman. Not yet. He'd keep looking, but he hadn't found her yet.

He knew about the rumors. What did he have to prove? His voice was the way it was, as were his mannerisms, and he wasn't going to waste money on a speech coach to try and change his voice now, to make it more masculine. At one point in his life he'd thought about it, though, after the problems in grade school, when they'd take his folders and write *HOMO* on them in big capital letters, or kid him because he was in the band. After high school when he'd get slapped around on his way to the chess or debate team meetings. Only in college, after his mother had died and his father would have nothing to do with him did he think about it, consider it, wanting to for once in his life impress that big retired steel worker, make him respect him. But he hadn't. If his father wanted to think he wasn't a man, then that was his problem.

Dick didn't visit his father much these days, only on Christmas, dropping a bottle of Scotch and a carton of Camels off and staying for no more than an hour, the two of them sitting there in awkward silence, the father staring at the son accusingly, the son staring back hostilely. The father wishing there had been ball games to attend, baseball dinners in his son's honor, the son bitter because the father had never once shown up at a debate or to watch him march in the band.

He'd stayed his mother's sensitive little boy, and his father had never been able to understand that, had never understood that Dick was gentle and kind. Dick would make the first move toward friendship with the other social outcasts, and sometimes they'd come over to the house and the old man would come home from work and just stand at the kitchen door and look in at them. Dick would remember the look on his father's face for as long as he lived. Disappointed and disgusted, that's how he'd looked.

He'd been tempted, every so often, to take a girlfriend over there when he had one, but he never did and he didn't know why. It just wouldn't have felt right. If the man wanted to live miserably in his paranoid notions of what his son was, then Dick would let him.

Now Dick sat at his counter sipping the coffee, dressed and ready to go, rested but still weary. A change in units didn't do much to excite him anymore.

He wondered how many cops would serve a warrant on someone today in this city, then tear the guy's house apart, just because he now had the authority to do so. A lot, he'd bet. If anyone beefed the cop could say he'd had a suspicion that there might be a dangerous individual hiding somewhere in the house, that he'd feared for his safety.

Lord, he was starting to sound like one of the bad guys.

Would it be a far jump? Dick knew more cops that fit the criminal profiles than he did criminals, so he had no true basis for comparison. What he did have, though, was his own ideas about law enforcement, and one of those ideas was that he didn't think that the laws handcuffed the police, Dick being maybe the only cop in Chicago who dared to think in such a manner. He believed he knew, however, what did indeed handcuff the police.

Laziness handcuffed the police, that's what handcuffed the police.

How many times had he seen it? The cops too lazy to do the work, the suspect being let go. They were trained in every phase of law enforcement, knew how to handle the paperwork and about the rights of suspects, but when they didn't do it by the rules, when the suspect walked, the cops would blame the courts.

Was it their fault, did the blame fall on the shoulders of the courts and the judges? Maybe years ago, when they were looking for excuses to shove the cops' noses in it to prove how liberal they were, but not anymore, not in the conservative 90s. Not when drugs were being kept illegal until all the rights of the average citizen were taken away, the same citizens who would allow it to happen because of their justifiable fear of the actions of the people who took and sold narcotics.

No, these days, it was cop laziness. He'd even heard the new line, the rationalization, the cops now telling one another, "Hey, if we didn't lie, we'd never put *anyone* in jail." Dick had never lied to put anyone away, and there were more than a few losers on the inside who blamed him for their sorrowful conditions.

He washed his cup and put it in the drainer, folded the newspaper in half and added it to the stack inside the recycling container that he would have to put out near the dumpster for its Wednesday pickup. Did these things and wondered if maybe he was in the wrong line of work.

It had to be him, it just had to be. He thought about it as he got his pride and joy—his one major expense, his black '68 Chevy Malibu—out of the garage, the garage that cost him almost as much per month as his overpriced studio apartment. Thought about it as he put the headphones on, as he popped a Buddy Holly tape into the cassette player and turned the volume up high.

Maybe he perceived things differently. Saw the world in a more optimistic light than his fellow officers. They never seemed to worry about things like this, didn't seem upset by bigotry or brutality.

Buddy took him a little way out of himself, out of the blues and onto a low level of cheerfulness, the driving guitar making him smile as his lips moved to the music, only half his mind on the big question:

Was it him?

He drove the car carefully down the mostly deserted narrow North Side streets, watching for darting pets or shallow yuppies racing away from the curb in foreign vehicles without a backward glance, thinking that because they were on the street it was everyone's job to look out for them.

He asked himself if it was him and even Buddy Holly couldn't jive away the fear that came when he wondered if it was.

He was no kid anymore, still single and living alone, didn't date much and when he did he never doubled with fellow cops—and didn't the guys like to throw *that* in his face in the locker room after he'd angered one of them. Was there something wrong with him? Instead of having too much of something—sensitivity or perception—was he maybe lacking something? Some simple gene or DNA thread that would make him be more like other men?

It was something to think about, but not when he was about to meet a new commander. The last thing he wanted the man to believe was that Dick Blandane was weak or afraid. Only Dick could ever be aware of these things about himself.

"The Death Stone Blood Ell Dees will be out in force tonight, at the funeral of one of their own, the kid who caught two in the head over at the school the other day. Keep a special lookout for them, don't let them congregate in front of the funeral parlor wearing colors or signifying." There was a general murmur in the room, the cops asking themselves: How the hell do we stop them?

So far, it was going all right.

Dick had met the commander and the guy had been pretty nice, at least he hadn't brought up any of Dick's prior problems with other cops. Five minutes with the boss then his new partner O'Brian had come in, introduced himself and led Dick into Roll Call with the rest of the Gang Crimes South afternoon shift, Dick so caught up in the general feeling of excitement in the air that he didn't even feel uncomfortable being the only cop in the room in a suit, with a topcoat. The rest of them were wearing jeans or other casual clothes. There were a lot of leather jackets tossed over the backs of wooden chairs.

"All right people, settle down." The duty sergeant was a large black guy, laid back but with an air of authority—Dick could feel it in the man's posture, heard evidence in his voice. This was not a man to anger. The sergeant was looking down at his clipboard, speaking in his low, forceful way, his face about to break into a smile as he read a line . . .

"The Alfredio brothers got pinched this afternoon—" the sergeant saying the words and the room breaking into applause and a few whistles, the cops settling down before the smile faded from the sergeant's face. "Got nailed trying to offload four keys to Martin and White. Arraignment's in the morning if any of you want the pleasure of seeing them in cuffs . . ." A few snorted laughs, a couple of men mumbling that they'd get up early to be there before the sergeant slapped the clipboard against his leg.

"Last item on the agenda, we got a new man today, Dick Blandane, just come over from Tac, so we can forgive the Dragnet getup." Dick rose and nodded, suddenly not feeling so comfortable anymore because most of the men and women in the room were staring hard at him, only a few smiling and nodding their welcome. His reputation had preceded him.

"He'll be with Obie," the sergeant said, "seeing's how Tank's retired." He looked up, nodded his head as Dick was sitting down. "That's it. Let's roll."

The thirty people in the room rose and began milling to the door as O'Brian grabbed Dick's arm and said, "C'mon, cherry, I'll show you around," and Dick felt strong hearing that, knowing now with certainty that it wasn't him at all, there was nothing lacking in his character, the fact of the matter was that these sons of bitches, they were all alike. None of them knew how to show respect.

Knowing this, he pulled his arm away, straightened his tie, looked the startled Obie right in the eye and said,

"The name's *Dick*, or Blandane. Not Richie, not Dicko, not Blandie and not Cherry, we got that straight?" And Obie rolled his eyes.

"I heard about you," Obie said. Then said, "Goddamn, why'd Tank have to fucking retire on me?" with feeling.

Chapter 14

It had been a while since Feet had gotten a bag on, and booze always tasted especially good when other guys were buying it.

Which they were, Jerry's joint hopping now in the late afternoon, guys he hadn't seen in years slapping him on the back, a few of them hugging him, all of them buying him a round, figuring him to be a little short of cash at the moment.

They didn't know about the six grand still in his pocket, and he wasn't volunteering the information.

Dean Martin was on the jukebox, singing soulfully, the mandolin-accompanied song sung half in English, the other half in Italian, Dino putting tears in his voice during the dago parts. Feet liked that, the ability the man had to touch you. It almost made him feel sad. If this wasn't his first entire day of freedom, he might have let go and been depressed, but how could he be, with all these guys lining up to buy him drinks, to welcome him home?

Thieves had no honor these days, Feet knew that, had taught it to Charlie. That *did* make him sad because he could remember a time when it was an honorable profession, when guys like himself and Charlie's father would take beatings from the law, vicious assaults which they'd endure silently, willing to go away for the rest of their lives before giving up another thief or telling the cops more than their names. He'd seen too many men sell their rap partners out to believe otherwise. He knew, too, that most of these guys were buttering him up, wanting to use him down the road to prowl a score for them, others wanting him to remember them the next time he set something up, wanting a part of some real action. He didn't say anything, didn't hold it against them, either. It was just the way it was.

He'd take their drinks, though, that's for sure.

There were four Scotches backed up on the bar in front of him, Feet now with a glass in his hand and his back to the bar, leaning into it with his elbows, his right foot up on the rail that ran along the base of the bar. When he couldn't hold his balance that way, he knew it would be time to go. But for now it was warm and hazy, inside the bar and inside his head, both places all right for the moment, people standing in line to hear what he was saying and not getting upset over the fact that he was slurring his words.

As they spoke to him he let his mind wander, caught himself smiling when he realized he was thinking of his daughter.

A daughter. Was she a pretty little thing or what, just like her mother. The resemblance was there, too, in the strong nose, the high forehead and cheekbones. She'd be pretty, all right. Educated and smart, go to the right schools and have the right friends and he wouldn't make the mistakes with her that he'd made with Charlie, wouldn't be gone all night stealing, leaving her to her own devices.

No, for his daughter there'd be Disney World and Great America, summers at the beaches and museums and winters learning to ski.

He could do that for her, yes he could. A man had to have something to remember him in this world after he was gone, and his daughter would do that just fine. First, though, he'd have to be the kind of man she could remember fondly, and it didn't look as if he'd get that way with Charlie.

What was the kid married to? Did she deball him? He'd seen it before, solid, standup guys being slowly castrated by women, the women telling them that it was for their own good, holding back the sex if the guy balked. Well, that might be all right for Charlie, but it wasn't for Feet.

He excused himself and went over to the phone booth next to the toilets, closed himself in, dropped in a quarter and punched out Femal's home number.

"She ain't here, she ain't gonna be here, and when she do get here she ain't gonna want to talk to no drunk." Femal's mother slammed the phone down in his ear while Feet was still trying to think up a snazzy comeback. He laughed, bitterly. Know-nothing woman talking down to him because he was white, only seeing him as a honkie wanting to bang her daughter.

What *did* he want to do to her daughter? He thought about that as he headed back to the bar, to the drinks stacked up and waiting for him, to the amber liquor he hadn't had a chance to pour down his throat for a while. In the County you could only get fermented potato skins or raisin jack, either of which could likely drive you blind or crazy and would definitely wreck your liver. Unless you had the cash to pay off one of the County hacks, have them bring you a bottle of Grant's or Jack Daniel's, the way a lot of guys did, score you some grass or some crank . . .

Which wasn't Foot's way; he saw The Man as the enemy, someone to neither bargain nor negotiate with. The bad news being that he was one of the few cons who saw things that way these days.

"Hey, Catman," the voice called to him and he turned,

saw Tony Juice waving at him, smiling like a long lost brother, this same son of a bitch Feet had gotten into for the gambling money that had caused all this trouble. "I heard you was back here!" Juice was smiling, the bastard. Feet smiled back. "C'mon over here, lemme buy you one, shit." Now the man was talking.

Darrin Favore sat at the living room table next to Mrs. Luchessa, looking at the old woman who was dressed in black and sobbing into her lace handkerchief. From time to time one of her old crone girlfriends would stick her head through the kitchen door and look in, solicitously, but Favore would purse his lips and shake his head, gently driving them away until the business was done. He knew that at the wake all these biddies would carry candles down the aisle, having turned off the lights in the funeral parlor, chanting in Italian and wailing behind Mrs. Luchessa, parroting her every word in unison. There would be children there who would have nightmares for weeks. He sure had, having seen his first Italian wake when he was five years old. He patted Mrs. Luchessa's back, rubbed her shoulder and muttered something sympathetic in a low, soft voice, paying token respect to her grief.

It was going even better than he expected. In her sorrow she was signing everything he put in front of her, Mrs. Luchessa still thinking that her husband was around, that he could maybe wield power or assert authority, frighten Darrin from the grave. That he could somehow still hurt Darrin. She was going through the motions, treating him the way the old man had, like a lackey, blaming him for the intrusion.

Yet he'd seen the gleam in her eye when he'd told her that her dearly departed had left her over a million dollars, liquid cash. "All you have to do, ma'am, is sign here, and I'll invest it, yes ma'am, right—there!" The proceeds being enough to pay all the bills around here, put a few grand in the bank for operating expenses, for pin money, yes, sign this one right here, thanks, Mrs. Luchessa.

You dumb, stupid bitch.

Darrin thought it but didn't say it, smiling sadly at the old woman, watching her facial hair and wondering why she didn't have it waxed. Nodding his head. Telling her it was going to be all right.

At last he had all the papers signed and was able to get out of there, going in through the kitchen and letting the women in there know that it was okay to go out to their friend, the women treating him with the distrust they kept in reserve for lawyers and child molesters. What was their problem? The priest down at the local church, they'd bow, kneel in front of him, kiss his hand as they handed over their money, thanking him for the privilege. Him, all he was doing was bringing her gifts, handing money over to a woman who had never done a thing to earn it, and they treated him as if he had the plague.

He checked his watch as he walked out the back door, squinting in the darkness. Darrin loved the fall, especially right after Halloween when it started to get dark early. He always had an affinity for the darkness, viewed it as his ally. It was only 5:15. He could get over to the club and have dinner, get a few drinks in him before the poker game began. He'd put two million, one, total, into his pocket in the past twenty-four hours, robbed it from the corpse of that old bastard, Luchessa. It was an act that brought him more pleasure than he'd had lately, and after pulling it off, after getting away with that one, fleecing the suckers over at the country club would be a piece of cake.

He got into his car, feeling so good that he didn't even hold anything against Catfeet Millard at the moment, and ordered his driver to deliver him to the club, telling the man to take his time, he was in no hurry, the driver turning to look at him, wondering why the boss was smiling so broadly after having just left the don's grieving widow. Well, screw him. What was he gonna do, report it to Don Luchessa? He thought that and then stopped smiling, began laughing. To the driver he said, "What are you waiting for, let's go!" then rolled the window halfway down so he could smell the crisp fall night air.

Charlie was sitting at the table, tearing open the decks and shuffling the cards, waiting for the five other Tuesday night regulars to come in out of the bar so the game could begin.

He could hear his wife in there, Lina loud and laughing, being attractive. Flirting with the men and elbowing the wives so they would know that she was only kidding. He kept his face impassive, though he wanted to wince at the high-pitched shrieks. Wanted, too, to yell in there, tell her to shut up, ask her if she couldn't see what a fool she was making out of herself. Shit, everyone else could.

It was over, and now it was just a matter of letting her know.

He'd break it to Lance first, because he knew Lina would make a scene, start a brawl that would only end when he left the house, her dramatics not over even then, at least not for the kid. She'd go on for days. He could picture it in his mind, Lina playing the part of the long-suffering, faithful little wife who had worked three jobs to put the hubby through medical school before getting dumped. She was tailor-made for the role, her entire life had prepared her to play the victim.

He riffled the deck, doing a few maneuvers, being slick because no one was watching and they wouldn't think that he was trying to impress them.

A couple of months ago he'd let Lina drag him to a book publishing party because he'd never been to one before and he'd wanted to see if the people in the Chicago writing community were any smarter than those in the vitamin business. The party had been a crashing bore, the room being full of slinky short-haired women slithering around, downing the men at every opportunity, the men all drinking too much and pretending to ignore the insults. A homosexual literary agent had sniffed at Lina when she tried to make conversation and then had put her down at every opportunity. The agent had spoken in French at every occasion, speaking to his young writer boyfriend but looking at Lina, obviously discussing her in a manner that wasn't flattering. On the way home Lina had asked him, "Do you think he hated me because I'm a woman, or because I'm a Jew?" asking it as if she really wanted to know, and Charlie had asked her if she'd ever considered the fact that the guy just might have thought that she was an asshole.

It had been the last time he had ever tried to share his opinion with her.

Shit, Favore was the first one in tonight, swaggering over from the bar and heading toward Charlie now, his bodyguard always in sight, in the background but around if Favore needed him. Favore had a sneaky smile on his face, as if he were planning to tear the table up tonight, had some insider's knowledge. Charlie knew that he himself was the one with the insider's knowledge. Which was the reason he had bothered to come tonight. He'd learned inside how to deal the cards the right way, had a plan to get back whatever amount Cat had turned over to this bastard. It was the only reason he was here tonight, to get Cat's money back, give this fool a taste of what it was like to lose something that was important to him, see how he liked it.

The problem being that he didn't know exactly how much that was. Lina had come into the room before Cat could tell him, and although Charlie had tried, he couldn't reach Cat at either the 909 or at Femal's. The clerk at the 909 had told him that there was nobody checked in under Cat's name. The old woman who answered the phone at Femal's hadn't been as kind, made it clear to him in her high whining voice that she wasn't running "no goddamnittyall answering service for ya'll's kind." The 909 he might try again in an hour or so. He wasn't about to try

Femal's number again until it was late enough to assume that Femal would be home.

Favore pulled out the chair directly across from Charlie and sat down, putting his drink in the little round leather-fringed hole cut into the edges of the card table for just that purpose, slapping his hands together and rubbing them quickly.

"Feel lucky tonight, Charlie?" His voice hearty and bluff, slightly slurred. Charlie could smell the whiskey on the man's breath. He would never be able to tell that Charlie was double-dealing. Maybe the bodyguard could tell, but he was bored, looking around, fidgeting and probably wishing that he was off duty this Tuesday night. As for the others, Charlie would drive them out in the first hour or so. He would get his hands on the cards every sixth deal, would set them up then, deal this fool Favore a hand good enough so he'd bet high and raise higher, forcing the others to drop out, then he'd deal himself a hand just a little bit better. He couldn't do it every time he dealt, but maybe every second time. If the cards were good enough, if Favore played into them, chasing his past losses, even once every third deal would be enough.

Now that Favore was there, the others began to wander in. By the time Charlie had the cards broken in the right way, the table was full and it was time to get down to business.

Favore won the deal and dealt Charlie a pair of queens. The guy to Charlie's immediate right opened for two bucks, and Charlie hesitated, making it clear that he wasn't quite sure, then raised the opener the same amount. Everyone commented, kidding around about the kid having beginner's luck, and after the discard Charlie drew the third queen.

As he bet a cautious twenty dollars Lina came meandering into the room, glassy-eyed and staring at him with laser-intensity, her lips loose. He knew that look. She was drunk and thinking that she was smart enough to tear him apart with her wit. All half of it. Charlie matched Favore's second raise, raised it himself for the last allowable time, then won the hand, his three queens beating Favore's two pair, someone else's pair of aces. He raked the pot in, saw Lina about to open her mouth and he raised his head to look at her and shot her a fast wink, a half-smile. It was so out of character for him that it threw her off base. Good. Maybe it would keep her off his ass for the two hours or so that he would need to clean Favore out.

Chapter
15

The gang crimes unit worked out of the Wentworth District, a predominantly black area which contained the Robert Taylor Homes, a sprawling project of high- and low-rise housing which contributed to the district's having one of the highest crime rates in the city. The district had been under scrutiny for a few years, since the time that a gambler had been arrested, then come into the station the next day, after making bond, inquiring as to whom he should speak in order to get this cleared up, seeing as he was paying the coppers three hundred a week to stay away from his game. This had been the beginning of an investigation which ended with the conviction of over a dozen people—cops, gamblers and drug dealers—and a black mark on the reputations of all the cops in the district, who took it personally, as anyone in any profession would when one percent of the members of that profession got in trouble and the general public painted the other ninety-nine percent with the same tarred brush. The black cops understood, as did the Italians; they'd been dealing with that kind of prejudice since arriving in America.

O'Brian had been working in the district when the indictments had been handed down. As he drove into the night on Dick's first shift in the unit he had told Dick about the anger, the frustration the other officers had dealt with during that time, although not using those words. What he'd said was: "They'd all been pissed off at the fuckers who'd sucked pusher cock for a few extra bucks," and Dick had laughed, in spite of himself.

Still in all, Obie told him, it was a great place to work, Wentworth was. Two of the city's best cops worked out of there, were attached to their unit, to Gang Crimes South, officers Fleming and Darling, who had the touch, the way to make the tough gangbangers open up and be ever so kind and oh so talkative . . .

If he hadn't called Dick cherry earlier, Dick might have begun to like the man, in spite of the fact that he talked way too much and didn't pay a lot of attention to what was happening on the street.

Would have maybe grown to like him if Obie's bladder hadn't been weak, if Obie hadn't pulled into the fast-food parking lot; would maybe have begun to identify with him just a little if Dick hadn't listened to the radio while his partner used the bathroom at McDonald's and when Obie came out Dick told him that there had been a rape on the north end and the son of a bitch, he had to blow it, had to tell Dick that within the Wentworth District perimeter, there *was* no such thing as rape, just bitches who got mad when the john decided not to pay . . .

He watched Obie at work, not bothering to hide his disgust, his mind already made up. He would ask the sergeant for another partner, maybe a woman, maybe a black, maybe, if he got lucky, either Fleming or Darling or the guy who'd introduced himself after Roll Call, Mike McNamara. He wouldn't work another day with this burned-out moron, this shift would be all he could take. He wasn't really even sure at this point if he could finish out the entire eight hours of this first night without maybe shooting this slob.

There he was, Obie, as insensitive as any male could ever be, sweet-talking the victim, making Dick ashamed that he was a member of the same sex. Obie was not being kind in order to try and get an identification, nor to be gentle on her emotions. What he was trying to do was talk her out of wanting a report filed. Right there in the office with cops milling around everywhere, this guy was trying to talk her out of any modicum of fairness and dignity she might rightly expect from an agent of the law.

The other cops never gave them a second glance, crying women being a common sight in the Wentworth District, far more common than happy women, unless the women were wearing uniforms.

She was a young girl, maybe seventeen or eighteen, black, her clothes old but clean, second-hand or handed-down Guess? jeans that she filled out pretty well, considering her young age and her generally thin build. The jeans looked older than she did. She was wearing a TROOP jacket with a pair of large leather dice stitched onto the back of the brown leather, a natural seven shown coming out. The jacket wasn't prophetic; this hadn't been her lucky night. And it was only getting worse.

There was no shirt under the jacket, no bra, either, Dick could tell, had to keep his eyes off her chest when she waved a hand at O'Brian in anger and the coat fell open, exposing the tops of her breasts, the creamy, smooth dark skin of her chest. Her hair was in cornrows, old-fashioned and time-consuming in this fast-paced decade, but the sight of them endeared her to him, reminded him of his high school days when that style was all the rage and blacks of both sexes bore the look proudly and didn't care how long it took to set the do and who didn't worry about the expense.

This girl wasn't very proud at the moment.

"What you mean I shouldn't bitch about this." Her voice was high-pitched and it carried. "I been raped, Jackson!" She was angry now and Dick thought that was a good thing for her to be. The way O'Brian was treating her, a weaker woman might have had a nervous breakdown by now. "So you get the forms or whatever it is you needin', and take my damned statement. And why the hell ain't a woman here with me? Why I got two mens, and two *white* mens at that!" She was looking around, trying to make eye contact with one of the black female uniformed officers, who were not even glancing their way.

"Come on, Claricia, it ain't like the thing got broke, like it ain't never been used rough before." O'Brian wasn't giving up, was talking sweetly, trying to coax her into changing her mind, standing over her and craning his neck, trying to see into the opening of the TROOP jacket.

"I wants a rape counselor, I wants a am-bu-lance, I wants a 'mergency room wheres I can get scraped and checked to make sure the sperm ain't got the Rock Hudsons in it, and last of alls I wants a shirt, that sumbitch done broke my zipper tearing my coat off and he stole off with my goddamn shirt."

"He didn't hurt the pants, though, eh?" Said suspiciously, O'Brian maybe trying to give her the impression that she hadn't been raped at all, planting the seed that perhaps she had made it all up, or, failing that, had somehow managed to rape herself.

Dick leaned against the wall, as far away as he could get from them without being out of earshot, his arms folded, a look of disgust on his face. He'd give it one more full minute. Sixty seconds, and if O'Brian didn't get off this line of questioning Dick would call the counselor himself, drive her to the hospital and wait with her, fill out the report and maybe even get someone up there with an Identikit. Even if it didn't do any good, it would at least give this woman the impression that the police gave a damn about her.

The sergeant came into the room, in a hurry, passing

through on his way to another office when he spotted the woman sitting there sniffling in the chair against the stone wall, one of the prisoner chairs that had handcuffs hung behind them, half of them attached to thick iron rings embedded in the stone. He looked at her, then at Blandane, then slowed his pace, stopped, crossed his arms and watched. O'Brian was so wrapped up in what he was doing that he did not even notice that the sergeant was there.

"You know the drill, Claricia, do you? Been through this routine before?" The sergeant flinched, and Dick nodded his head a centimeter, watching the man.

A good sized man, the sergeant was, looked like Mike Singletary after two weeks off the weights. Good arms, narrow waist, sloping shoulders and a high forehead, indicating intelligence, shadowing eyes that were now burning brightly.

Claricia said, "That ain't none of your *god*damn business, motherfucker, and you call me Miss Evans, you hear me?" and Dick turned back to watch her. Her voice was shrill now, she was beginning to lose it. Dick pushed himself away from his position and began to move in, quickly, when the sergeant's voice stopped him.

"Blandane, get this woman to Mercy, on the double." Dick moved toward her, smiling calmly, to reassure her, his back to O'Brian, then he was between the woman and the cop so that Claricia wouldn't have to look at O'Brian anymore. At the sound of the sergeant's voice O'Brian had jumped, turned, then tried to cover it up, turning back toward the woman quickly. Now he was attempting to move around Dick, to get in on the action as Blandane helped the woman to her feet.

"Not you, O'Brian," the sergeant said. "You, I want to see in my office. Right away."

"Uh-huh, you tell him, brother. Motherfucker don't deserve to be wearing no badge, way he treats people."

"Come along, Ms. Evans," Dick said, silently agreeing with her.

• • •

Merle maintained a somber appearance while all the time
he was smiling inside. It got better and better with every
word that Peter Silva spoke, and the little devil, he was
speaking a lot all of a sudden. This little mex who never
said shit if he had a mouthful now wouldn't shut up, was
going on and on in his softly accented voice, his command
of the language precise, speaking English even better
than Merle himself.

Was he bragging, was that it?

It sure sounded like it, old Peter looking up slyly as he
described the way his girlfriend's father had died, how
she had then died herself . . .

He'd lower his voice when he discussed how the story
had been on the Channel Five news—Peter had even
taped it on Merle's VCR—Peter discussing the manhunt
for him in an offhand way, trying to be modest and acting
a little scared, but it was obvious to Merle that the man
was proud of himself.

"You and me, we been pinched together a few times.
The cops will be coming around, you know." Merle said it
offhand, when he could get a word in edgewise, and Peter
looked up in shock, surprised that he hadn't thought of it.
It was then that Merle had his brainstorm.

Keep 'em humble, keep 'em guessing, and always, always make them think that they owed you, that their very
lives were dependent upon your generosity, your whim.
In this case, it wouldn't be far from the truth.

"I'll cover you. Even though hiding a fugitive could
put me away for ten years." Right. The cops most likely
wouldn't even be bothering to come around because on
Merle's rap sheet, where it said SUSPECTED CRIMI-
NAL ASSOCIATES, above the spot where Peter Silva's
name was typed in, was the name of Darrin Favore, and
there was no way a Chicago cop would want to anger that
suspected criminal associate. The feds, maybe, who didn't
care *who* they fucked with, but not the local precinct

boys. Uncle Darrin paid too well. Even if the cops did come around, Uncle Dare would get him off in a second, have some high-class lawyer claiming that Merle was out of town, how was he to know that his friend was a murderer? Dare would do it, too. As useful as Peter was to Merle, there was no contest if you compared it to how important Merle was to Darrin Favore.

"I got to do time," Merle shrugged, "fuck it, I'll do the time." He leaned forward, put his forearms on his knees, spoke earnestly and with all the charm he could muster, which was a considerable amount.

"I keep going in the bedroom, trying to reach my uncle. I'll get over there and see him as soon as he gets home, get this squared away."

"Do you believe that even a great man like him could get me out of this trouble, Merle?" There was a hint of skepticism in Peter's tone, almost disrespect. As if Peter was saying that he was such a hotshot criminal that nobody could help him now. A desperado. Merle blamed himself. This man was a D.P. and they weren't known for the strength of their intellect, and maybe he just wasn't getting his point across in the proper way.

"You don't want to ask for the help of the biggest outfit boss in the city, partner, you can just walk your ass out the door right now. You and me's close, but Darrin and me, we's family." Say it and pout, stare hard at the man and see what happened.

What happened was that Peter began to show a little true fear for the first time in a while, hastened to calm Merle down.

"No, no, *hombre*." That was better, the bean invoking his pet name for Merle, what he called him when he wanted to incur his favor. "It's just that this is so big, so important, such a serious crime that I wonder if even Don Salvatore himself could arrange for me to be delivered from it."

"Check the tape you made of yourself from the news, Peter," Merle told him. "The don is dead, keeled over with a heart attack, and who you think is the only guy in this city smart enough to take his place?"

That got him. Peter's eyes got all wide, not disbelieving for even a second now.

"All right, that is good. That is wonderful. So, your uncle can get me out of this?"

Listen to this monkey, one minute thinking he's the Frito Bandito, then after a little mind control, he was all of a sudden slobbering all over himself trying to get Merle to get him out of his messy diapers.

"No problem. But there's probably some things he'll want in return, for keeping you out of Stateville." Merle waited, having mentioned the state penitentiary on purpose, knowing that Peter was now seeing himself in prison stripes, maybe with the pants around his ankles, covering the ball and chain, slender little Peter bending over and pretending to like it while some big buck nigger shoved something in him.

"Anything he wants to put in the fix, to cover the *mordida*. You tell him that."

"Well now, Peter, I might not have to. I was thinking, if we brought him some presents, the sort of thing he might really *need* someday, he might be so pleased . . ." He let it hang and spread his hands, sat back and crossed his legs.

"What is it that I could bring him, what does a powerful man like your uncle need that he does not already have?"

Merle put a thoughtful expression on his face. "Let me think on that one, Peter. There's got to be *some*thing, shit. And while I'm thinking, do me a favor, run on into the kitchen and grab me another beer, will you? I always think better with a tall cool one in my hand."

Chapter 16

The wink seemed to have done the trick.

Lina was standing behind Charlie now, her elbows draped on his shoulders, the two of them conspirators, Lina seeing this as her way back into Charlie's heart. He could feel the back of his head resting between her breasts, in the valley there, the breasts on either side of his head. If they'd been larger, he might have had trouble hearing.

She'd been pretty good for a while, just standing there watching him, in the Men's Grille as if she was just one of the boys, Lina enjoying what she thought was her non-conformist attitude, her rebelliousness. Charlie saw her more as the spoiled child she was, the little kid who loved shocking adults, especially while in the presence of the type who were too polite to point out her shortcomings. But her presence helped his cause, was a distraction as the other men at the table were eyeing her discreetly as they played, buying her drinks, wondering how drunk she'd have to get before she'd take one of them on. If she hadn't already.

Charlie would have been doing pretty well even without cheating, he had a stack of bills in front of him that was ten times larger than the one he'd begun with an hour ago.

He'd play, rake in the money, and Lina would rub herself against the back of the chair, maybe trying to distract him, to see if he wanted her more than he wanted the money in the pot. Not much chance of that anymore. When he had ignored her, she'd moved in a little bit, into her present position. From time to time she would run a hand distractedly through his hair, then return it to its station slightly in front of him, her wrists hanging down limply, almost touching his chest. A proprietary gesture.

He wasn't paying her that much attention. She was about as important to him at this moment as the chair in which he was sitting, and just about as diverting. He was concentrating on the cards. He no longer wanted any part of the woman he once could not get enough of, and that fact neither upset nor saddened him, it was just the way it was.

"Flush," Charlie said, fanning his cards out on the green felt for all to see, and he felt Lina give a small jump of excitement when the man to his left said, "Shit," then threw his cards in the pot. The man beside that man said, calmly, "Beats me," and did likewise; the other player who'd stayed in shook his head and dropped his cards onto the pile.

While Darrin Favore sat staring at him, coldly. Charlie felt the exhilaration, the thrill of danger implicit in the man's stare. Around them other games flourished, louder games with more fun but nowhere near as much action. Players whooped it up and cursed each other good-naturedly and ordered rounds from the bartender but at this moment Charlie could hear none of it, he was tunneled-in on Favore, his eyes smiling into a pair that looked as alive as those painted on a department store dummy.

Only these eyes blinked. Once, then Favore dropped

his cards face up on the table, announced that he'd had a straight and Charlie smiled his pleasure, outwardly composed, pleased that his fingers weren't trembling as he raked in what had to be close to a thousand dollars in winnings.

"Take it *all*, Charlie." Lina, whispering in his ear. Sounding like a hooker begging for more of something she really had no use for, knowing it was the only way she could receive any pleasure from the act, knowing that inside she was really only making fun of the player, of the john. The mark. Charlie disregarded her, stacked the bills in accordance with their denominations atop their respective piles.

There had to be three or four grand there, a lot but not enough. Feet had made it clear by implication that he had turned over a considerable sum, far more than Charlie had won tonight. What had he said? "Well, I've got four grand . . ." then added bitterly, "Had to give the rest to that prick, Favore." As if there'd been far more in his kick before giving it up.

One of the players pushed the deck over to Charlie and said, "You win the deal, too, Mr. fucking lucky," kidding around, but with an edge in his tone because the game was getting out of hand, the stakes too high, and Charlie was pulling in every third pot.

Charlie said "Thanks," and began to shuffle, barely looking up as two of the players announced that they'd had enough and pushed their chairs away and another mentioned softly that maybe they should turn the stakes back down to a reasonable amount.

Charlie didn't say anything, continued to shuffle, with nowhere near the precision he'd shown when he'd been alone and practicing. Favore, though, he had something to say.

"No." Said softly, and Charlie looked up, saw that Favore was looking at him with the same faintly amused cold-eyed expression he'd had on his face when he'd announced that he'd raised into a straight. "Let's increase them," Favore said.

The man who'd asked that they be lowered excused himself, while the other player went to the front desk to cash a check and the word buzzed through the lounge, the scuttle as to what was going on. In a couple of minutes the player was back, and there were two more sitting there at the table, high-rollers who would be watching the deal well enough to make Charlie worry a little.

Two hours later, as Tuesday became Wednesday, Charlie had cleaned the original survivor out along with one of the high-rollers, and it was only he and Favore and the other high-roller, but that man didn't count one bit.

And it was at the stroke of midnight that Lina had to open her goddamn mouth, thinking she was hurting Charlie while in reality setting everything that he could hope for into motion.

Chapter
17

Femal had gone into the Urban League meeting with the hope that it would calm her down, bring her back into herself and out of the resentful funk she'd been in since that morning when Bobby had stormed into the office, deciding to play Rambo. No such luck.

It was good to be away from Darrin for a change, though, that was for sure. He usually lived for this kind of thing, reveled in the opportunity to show all the folks of color what a liberal he was, how successful . . . She often saw this as his way of showing them how superior he was to them, how far above them he was, then she would feel guilty, wondering if she was being unfair. But tonight, with Mr. Luchessa dead, he obviously had other things to do. At least he hadn't shown up, which she saw as a blessing.

She'd left the envelope on the computer table, not touching it, not opening it, not showing any outward curiosity about it throughout the day. It had still been sitting there when she'd left for the meeting, and Darrin had known that it was. He'd come to the door of his office, his suitcoat off, the sleeves of his shirt rolled up two turns so that he could impress her with the hair on his wrists and forearms. Had stood there leaning against the doorjamb and watched her put on her coat, smirking at her, the man acting as if she were dying of curiosity inside and hadn't touched the envelope simply to make him think that she wasn't concerned as to its contents.

What angered her about it was that he was right, she had indeed spent the entire day wondering about it, how much there was inside. It was obvious to her that there was money in the envelope, she could tell that from the shape of it, its outline against the tightly wrapped paper.

But how much was there? Bobby had made it clear that he owed Darrin millions. There wasn't *that* much in the envelope. So how damn much was there? Did Darrin know? Bobby sure would, but she wasn't sure if she would be asking him. He wasn't on her list of favorite people at the moment. And Darrin wouldn't tell her, would make her give in and sneak a look if she really wanted to know. She'd be damned if she'd do that.

She sat at a table for seven and fought to keep up her end of the conversation, but it was hard, she was distracted, her mind on Robert Millard, on the father of her child, wondering if the man wanted to get himself killed, barging in on a man who loved to brag about his underworld connections, Bobby treating him like some jailhouse adversary.

The company at the table wasn't doing much for her mood, either. Two of the dinner companions were all right, good people, but the other four were the sort of black males who made her ashamed of her race. The type who'd call in to the radio shows and talk about the white conspiracy to commit genocide to their race, fire off one-sided polemics to the editors of any newspaper that would print them, getting as big a thrill out of seeing their names in print as they did from spreading what they believed to be their message. These were the blacks who offended her—the enemy was real enough, his tactics terrifying enough, without these people conjuring up monsters which didn't exist. Couldn't they see how The Man laughed at them, at their foolish distractions? It only gave the enemy more ammunition, more reason to shake their heads and pat Africans atop theirs, as they continued their own destructive agenda, smiles gone, frowns in place, devil horns stuck in the middle of their skulls.

First the genocidists had blamed Reagan, spreading the rumor through the community that he had a full head of hair at his age because the mark of the beast was tattooed on his skull. The man was a demon, there was no way around that, but a biblical beast? Not hardly. Instead of waxing paranoiac, they should have banded together and voted his ass out of office, but what had they done instead? Stayed away from the voting booths in droves, using the same mentality they professed to hate; the slave bitching about the plantation master but not revolting against him.

Now it was Gorbachev who was the beast, the mark on the top of his head being the biblical warning of the beast, maybe in Russian so we couldn't understand it. This time, the devil was advertising. Femal believed that her people had to get away from superstition, as far away from that sort of thing as they could before they could ever achieve real power.

Of course, there were plenty of black politicians and preachers who didn't want that to happen. If the poor and uneducated lost their ignorance, they might see clearly, and for the first time, who two of their real enemies were: The politicians and the preachers who preyed on their distrust of whites to win votes, fatten bank accounts, and spread their hateful missive of paranoia.

Who was the speaker tonight? What would drag these sort of folks away from their radios and typewriters and out into the chilly November air? She tried to remember, tried to place the main after-dinner speaker, but she couldn't and didn't want to feel ignorant so she didn't ask.

There was nowhere near the sort of unity within the

middle-class black community that most African-Americans would have whites believe. Femal knew this and had learned to live with it, although sometimes it hurt, having your own kind mad at you simply because your skin was lighter or darker, your hair processed or natural. If it was up to her, she'd just shave it all off, the way Michael Jordan had, which would be a twofold blessing. She wouldn't have to bother with the silly controversy at all, and she would have a lot more time to sleep in the morning. As for the darkness of her skin, for that there was no defense, nor any which she would care to make. She was Femal, that's all, and wasn't about to change being who she was and definitely not about to feel inferior or inadequate around someone who could pass for white. Hell, wasn't that what the struggle was all about?

It seemed to be the hot topic of discussion at her table, that's for sure.

That smelly fat man from the suburbs—what was his name?—Carson, that's it, sitting there in his polyester suit smoking a cigar that smelled worse than he did, talking about the Jewish conspiracy to control the media and keep the black folk down. Arguing with Powers, who was a little more in line with Femal's political ideology. The other four people at the table, two other men and two women whose names escaped Femal, were watching them, taking little bites of their catered burnt chicken, their mostaciolli.

"What we got to do," Powers was saying, "is empower our*selves*, brother. Get our own newspapers, make our own editorial policy. Put our own board in charge and let them decide policy then never deviate from it. We can't sit back and blame the Jew for everything—"

Carson said, "I'm not blaming the Jew for everything, and I know more about journalism than you do."

Femal had heard enough of this. "You edit the suburban NAACP newsletter, Percival, that doesn't make you Ted Koppel." Said it and got a glare, kept her cool in the sudden silence that fell over the table, angry and upset only by the fact that the other two women at the table were staring at her as if she'd stepped out of character, had not known her place.

Carson said, "He a Jew, isn't he?" suspiciously, angrily.

Powers spoke as if Femal hadn't ever opened her mouth. "If you're not blaming the Jew for everything, then who *are* you blaming? You sure aren't taking any responsibility for your own actions."

"I blame all the white people, brother Powers, every last damn one of them. Femal there had to make fun of me, steal my respect by making fun of my newsletter, but you ever wonder where I'd be if I had this brain in a white body, this talent I possess? How many black faces you see in the newspaper every day around here?"

Femal jumped in again, an equal and making sure they knew it. "There's Clarence at the *Tribune*, and Jarrett at the *Sun-Times*. Jarrett's also on the editorial board of his paper, by the way. And while we're at it, there's Carl Rowan and more than a couple others gone national, syndicated all over the country, out of Washington and New York. Herbert at the *New York Daily News* is one of the most respected journalists in the country—"

"Girl, was I talking to you?" Carson was glaring.

"I thought your conversation was directed at the entire table." It was one of the other women, Femal didn't know her name, but at the moment, she wanted to kiss her. Although she wouldn't make the others aware of her feelings, Femal keeping her face straight, not about to give the woman even a glance of gratitude. This couldn't be turned into a sisterhood issue here. If they all weren't together here, it could get worse than it already was, turn into a man against woman against light skin against straight hair type of thing that she wasn't sure she'd be able to take.

"I was talking to William, Keneisha, not to Femal *or* to you."

Powers said, "Let them talk, brother, that's the way Harold would have wanted it."

"And speaking of Harold Washington," Femal said, "did you ever hear him talk any trash about blaming the white man for keeping *him* down? Did anyone give him any help putting him through Roosevelt University? He was the proudest man I ever met in my life, a *man*, now, Percival, not even getting into what he was as a black."

"As an African-American, Femal, that's what the man was, and don't you forget it. And while we're speaking of him, you ever see him outside of the public eye? Ever be alone with him? He had plenty to say about the white devil, you can believe it."

Keneisha said, "And you were privy to that, were you?" Smiling sweetly. Around them waiters were clearing the dinner dishes, others pouring coffee. There was clatter and the sound of loud conversation everywhere, more arguments heard around the room than there were laughs. Femal listened to it, took it in for a minute as she watched Keneisha go on the offensive.

"Clarence McClain said he was in on all Harold's secrets, too."

"You comparing me to that goddamn jailbird?"

Powers said, "Calm down, Percival."

"Calm down shit, this bitch just put me in the same class with a felon, brother, I don't have to sit here and take that."

"Who you calling a bitch?"

It was getting loud and ugly, and Femal felt the eyes of nearby guests watching them. There were maybe two hundred people in the room and she felt as if they were all focused on her, all of them seeing through her, inside her.

Well, that was just fine. She had nothing to hide. She jumped back into the discussion with vigor, even a little glee.

"Is that the way you respond to criticism, Carson, insult someone, hit them as low as you can? You just took

that route with Keneisha, yet if a white man does it to you,
if you frighten him or make him feel threatened the way
you just felt, and he calls you a nigger, which is not far
from what you just did to Keneisha, you'd want to shoot
him, wouldn't you? Or demand reparations, your own
goddamn state."

"That's a bad idea? You think separatism won't work
either?" Carson was shouting now, half out of his chair,
the cigar waving the air as he attacked, enjoying every
second of the attention he was getting.

"And who do *you* work for, Miss high and mighty,
huh? Not only the token nigger at a white business, but a
token nigger at a *gangster's* white business!"

"I'm nobody's token nothing, you bastard!"

Femal got to her feet, pointing her finger at the man's
chest as the room fell silent. Chairs scraped as people
turned in them to catch the show. She knew this wasn't
the way to act, knew this was improper. The thing was,
she simply didn't care.

"That's close to slander, Carson, and if I thought you
weren't at least half drunk and three-quarters brain dead
I'd tell my boss what you just said, see if you could prove
your allegations in court!" She could feel the sweat running down her ribs, tickling the sides of her breasts. The
elastic in her skirt felt damp. She was afraid but continued
in her anger before Carson could open his mouth to respond.

"You want to blame the white man for all your troubles? You go ahead, Carson, you be my guest. But *I'm* by
God not going to waste my energy. I'm going to make my
mark in *spite* of the white man, and when I get where I
want to be there won't be anyone to thank and bow down
to but myself and the mama who raised me and washed
floors for the white folks so I could get the education she
never had! I re*fuse* to use my race as a reason to stay
down, to be filled with hate and resentment. The prisons
are full of brilliant young brothers right now who were
never taught that they could be anything, whose *African-*

American parents never gave them any more of a chance than the system did! Is the system racist? You're goddamn right it is, Carson, owned and run by rich old white men who see us as the enemy. Well, the first rule of combat, brother, and don't you ever forget it, is *know your enemy!* I know him, and he isn't you, he isn't me, it's *them*, in their damn ivory towers throwing us bones and thinking we're ingrates for not chewing on them and being happy."

Carson had fallen back in his chair, was sitting there with the cigar hanging out of the corner of his mouth, a long ash about to spill on the jacket of his suit. She felt safe enough to take a deep breath, look at the room about her, pull herself up as tall as she could stand and then turn the full stare back at Carson, enjoying it when the man winced.

"*Our* job is to climb up there and topple them, climbing up one by one, reaching down and pulling others up along with us, Carson. I'm gonna get there, with or without your help. And I won't be dragged back down by some hateful separatist who thinks the proper way to respond to healthy debate is to call a fine young black woman a *bitch.*"

Femal turned on her heel, her head held high, ignoring the stares and the muttered comments that followed her out of the room, heading for the phones to get support from the one woman who was truly and surely on her side, never even noticing that the resentful funk she'd been in since that morning was now a thing of the past.

Realizing it only when it descended back down upon her, because the first thing her mother told her was that that tricknacious bastard who'd planted her with child had been calling all damn night, drunker than Uncle Samuel on Easter Sunday.

Chapter 18

Charlie had been ignoring her. Lina ordered a Tia Maria with one ice cube every time she caught a waiter's eye, getting drunker by the minute. She would run her fingers through his hair and he wouldn't move an inch, would not bother to acknowledge her.

He felt as if she were seeing this as the two of them against the world, Lina believing in her heart that after all she'd said and done, all the gaming and bitterness and bitchiness, that he still was on her side, the two of them one.

Bullshit.

He was no more on her side than he was on her father's. From Charlie's point of view, this was now more of a business arrangement than a marriage, something to work out in a court of law and get behind him.

He looked at Favore while the third man dealt, the two of them knowing that it was between them alone, only Charlie knowing why. All his fear inside himself, none of it showing to Favore or anyone else. Even Lina couldn't sense it, although she might be feeling the tension in his shoulders, the way she was leaning on him. Was she trying to be supportive or was she only using him to keep herself from flopping drunkenly to the floor?

Favore grinned, a serious loser not caring about his losses, having too much class to be angry, too much money to see this as anything but a temporary setback.

"You've got to have ten, twelve grand there, Charlie." Favore speaking as if it was pocket change. "Better than selling vitamins, isn't it?" Favore grunted a laugh. Making fun of Charlie. "Maybe you ought to go to Vegas, you want that? I could fix it up, give you a job, I've got friends at the Riviera."

The high-roller was through shuffling, began his deal. Charlie left the cards turned down before him, would not look at them or attempt to pick them up until Favore looked away. He stared right back at Favore, his face giving the man nothing. He let his mouth twitch in the beginning of a smile, just to see what Favore would make of it.

"Never seen a run of luck like that before in all the years I've been playing at this club, Charlie."

The third card fell, face down, and Charlie figured it was time to speak.

"Isn't this about where Gregory Peck puts his six-shooter down on the table, Darrin? Says something like, 'You calling me a cheater, Pard?' "

"Cheat? I don't think you're dumb enough to try and cheat me."

The other men in the Grille were listening carefully, intently. Gathered around to watch the big game, spectators now to a true and real dangerous occurrence.

Charlie ignored them, these overfed slobs whose closest brushes with violence were watching *Miami Vice* reruns. They wanted to see blood? Maybe he'd show them some. Not Favore's, though. Maybe, after he won, if he could clean this man out, he'd stand, stretch, and punch the smirk off the face of the first lawyer who stepped in his way.

To Favore, he said, "Thank you." In a way that offered no thanks.

The fifth card fell and Charlie heard Lina take in a breath, was gathering his cards to him with his right hand, still looking Favore dead in the eye, when she spoke.

"He wants it all, Darrin." Lina being cute, slurring her words, hissing them. "All that you took from his friend Millard."

That caught Darrin by surprise.

He shot his glance to Lina, his shock apparent, the words now spoken so Charlie could see no reason to react —he was almost grateful that she'd spoken them; in her ignorance she'd given Favore information he hadn't had before, which was a dangerous thing to give away for free, the upside being that she had at least cracked the man's cool facade.

But not for long. Favore got himself under control quickly, his shocked expression giving way to a broad smile as he calculated how the information could be used to his best advantage.

The other player at the table and the men around them were now silent, waiting for Favore. Charlie held the cards in his hand, hadn't yet looked at them; Favore's were still face down on the green felt.

Favore said, "Catfeet a friend of yours? Been so long since I been away from the street, I don't get the word from the grapevine."

"You been on the street, Darrin?" Charlie said it knowing the risk, wanting to get under the man's skin and push him into a menacing act, knowing that if he could get the man angry, make him do something dumb, that Charlie couldn't lose. Another man's anger was the best friend of the sensible person. "Not on *my* street." The words spoken and scoring, Favore's eyes narrowing into slits.

"I remember something about that, about some punk Millard took in. Word was Millard liked young boys. He like you, Charlie?" Favore playing the game now, too, wanting to get a reaction.

Instead only getting a smile as Charlie shook his head, bent it down to look at his cards, his poker face back in place. He said, "I'll open for a hundred," placed his cards face down on the table and tossed a hundred dollar bill into the pot. Folded his hands over his cards and turned a cold stare upon Favore, challenging him.

Favore picked up the gauntlet. "I'll go you one better than that. No sense in making this poor bastard here pay for your misplaced resentment." The other player said, "Hey . . ." without much emotion, knuckling under real fast when Favore's bodyguard put a hand on his shoulder to quiet him.

The guard had come over quietly, not making a thing about it, had somehow turned up just outside Charlie's field of vision, popping into it when he perceived a threat to his boss. Charlie sized him up. Beefy guy, big, with scar tissue over both eyes and a crooked nose. An ex-prize-fighter. A punch in the face wouldn't faze him, he would be used to that. Charlie wondered if he thought that the skin protecting his balls was any thicker than the next man's, wondered if he'd have the opportunity to show him that it wasn't.

But that was for later. There would be no frontal assaults inside the club. If it was to come, it would be later, outside, or better yet, a couple days from now, the stud coming at him from the shadows outside the office building. It wouldn't be here and now, and here and now was all that counted.

Favore continued, speaking in a friendly tone, with a trace of condescension, talking down at Charlie, trying to rile him.

"You want the money your boyfriend owed me? What he paid me?" He reached into his inside jacket pocket and took out a folded envelope, dropped it into the pot. "Put it up. There's twelve grand in front of you, I just put twenty-two on the table." Favore was smiling as he looked down, counted out the cash in front of him then reached into his pocket and riffled through his bills, told his bodyguard to give him all his money and counted it, added it to his pile, pushed it all into the middle of the table.

"Another seven grand, total of twenty-nine. Add seventeen to what you got there, sweetmeat, and we'll play showdown, five cards straight up, winner take all." Favore hesitated, looking all confused for a second, playing for the crowd, then looking wise and insightful, nodding his head.

"*I* get it. You don't have the cash, do you? Seventeen grand got to be half a year's pay for a player like you." He chuckled softly. "Let me see. From what I've heard your car's leased, your home belongs to your old lady, but maybe you got it in the bank? Put up the marker, Charlie, you're good for it. If not, I'll take the marker anyway, and you owe me six for five weekly until you pay it all back."

"Been off the *street* too long, have you, Darrin?" Charlie spoke coolly, in control of his fear. "Yet you remember the going rate, don't you?"

"Some things a man just never forgets."

"I lose and don't pay, what happens, you send this palooka over to break my knees, is that how it works?"

"Oh, you'll pay, Charlie. You're a man of *honor.*"

Charlie said, "It's good to know that one of us is," then said, "You're on, Darrin—twenty-nine grand, five cards up, winner takes all."

There was a buzz around the table. The evening club manager came over, took one look at what was going on, who was involved, and went quickly back to his office. Charlie was shuffling, expertly now, not even trying to give the impression that he did not know exactly what he was doing. Favore was no longer smiling, was leaning back in his chair, looking at the stacks of money in the center of the table, at the piece of white paper that Charlie had filled out that was useless in a court of law but which was legal tender in their world, better than a stock certificate. Favore waited until Charlie spread the cards into two halves, pushed them toward him and offered a cut before speaking up.

"I'll cut, but you don't deal."

"You don't either, Darrin, or your goon." Charlie felt the guard's presence behind him, threatening, but the man was smart enough to know that there was nothing he could do in this place. Even if he was psychotic enough to make his move in the club, he wouldn't be crazy enough to hit Charlie before his boss had his shot at Charlie's money.

"Hey, you!" Favore hollered over to the bartender, who ducked his head, got suddenly busy behind the bar, washing glasses. Favore shook his head in disgust, was about to holler again when the high-roller who'd been cut out of the play stepped up and said, "Gimme the cards."

Charlie's first card was an Ace and Favore's a three, the thrill Charlie felt upon seeing his first card gone right away, as his second card was a four and Favore's another three.

The dealer wasn't playing around, was shoving them out there fast and furious, earning back his self-esteem, his hands flying, dealing the first four cards in a frenzy then pausing dramatically at the moment of truth. Before Charlie was an Ace, four, seven and Queen. Favore had a pair of threes, a deuce and a King. "Hit me," Favore said, staring at Charlie, and the dealer dropped a nine onto Favore's pile, turned to Charlie and slowly dealt him his last card.

The Ace of Spades.

The gathered crowd that now included plenty of women made astonished noises, Lina cheering wildly as the last Ace fell, while Charlie ignored them all, leaned over and reached into the money pile with two fingers and pulled back his marker, carefully ripped it into small pieces which he dropped onto the table before allowing himself to smile, reaching in with both hands and dragging his winnings toward him.

The crowd quieted and Favore said, "Good hand, Charlie Lucky. You did well for yourself tonight." The gracious loser showing that there were no hard feelings.

Charlie said, "You want to do it again, Darrin? The cash that's here on the table against your marker? Naturally, if I win and don't get cash tonight, it's six for five, weekly."

The crowd got quiet, stared at the insolent young man who'd refused the great Darrin Favore's peace offering, had thrown it back into his face with an insult.

"Not tonight," Darrin said, apparently unfazed. "What I *will* do is buy you a drink to congratulate you." He paused for effect, then said, "Unless of course you're buying one for the house." Getting a rousing reaction from the crowd.

Charlie looked around him, sizing them up, wondering if any of them knew what they had just witnessed, what the repercussions might be. Although he didn't show it to them, he felt nothing but contempt.

He said, "Two things I'm careful about, Darrin. Who I eat with, and who I drink with. I'm gonna pass." Said it and got up to leave, stuffing the winnings into various pockets, not paying attention to Darrin who was now walking toward the bar with his admirers—the men and women who thought he was such a generous human being—following behind him like the children of Hamlin behind the pied piper.

Darrin let Charlie get to the door of the Grille before saying, "I can see you aren't real careful about who you fuck." There was a big burst of embarrassed laughter from the club members. Then Darrin walked into the bar, Charlie forgotten, Charlie, who walked through the door and out into the foyer of the club without responding, neither to Favore nor to Lina, who was stalking Charlie, drunkenly shouting at him.

"You gonna let that son of a bitch get *away* with that, you gonna let him talk about me like that? Where's your balls, Charlie!"

Did she really think he wasn't in possession of them, after what had just occurred, what she'd witnessed? She probably thought he didn't. Totally disregarded the danger he'd stepped into for a man he cared about, Lina thinking only of herself, about how her image had been damaged around the club by one of its most influential members. She would have enjoyed it if Charlie had thrown himself at the man, had been shot by the bodyguard in the process of defending her honor. Charlie could picture her telling her next husband about it, how Charlie had died for her, Lina playing the martyr and never letting the next fool stack up to him, never let him feel he was truly adequate. It was the way she was.

The money in his pocket now felt like an anchor around his neck as he walked ahead of her, ignoring her shrieks, knowing that he couldn't spend even one more night under the same roof with the woman.

In the bar, Favore bought a round, making a big thing out of having to charge them to his credit card as he was a little short on cash at the moment. He got his laughs, paid for the drinks and took his bodyguard into the bathroom with him, made sure nobody was in either of the stalls and that the door was locked before speaking to the man.

"I got a job for you. Call my nephew to go along with you. Lane's dangerous, but I want his ass *kicked*, not played with. Don't cripple him, just make sure he knows he's been in a fight."

"You want me to bust that punk up, it'll be a pleasure." The guard was breathing heavily through a nose that had the bone consistency of tissue paper. His manhood had been assaulted, Charlie had called him a palooka and a goon when he'd in fact been ranked number forty-seven in the world back in '69. Darrin didn't say anything about that, but he wanted to laugh.

What he did say was, "Not the kid, Mickey, his boy-friend. You and that wild-assed Merle find Catfeet Millard and split his head open for him, all right? I got a real good idea where you can find him, but make sure you get him on the street, alone. The woman he's with is a friend of mine . . ."

Mickey nodded, thinking being a big thing for him, and left, and Darrin followed him, but not back into the bar. Instead he went to the pay phones hanging between the men's and women's bathrooms, which nobody ever used because they always used the Princess behind the bar, rich people wanting to save the fucking quarter, and dialed a number. He identified himself to the man at the other end, then said, "Get me all you got on a Charlie Lane, if he got a record, anything at all," thanked the man and hung up, then went back to the bar, setting his face in a smile.

Chapter 19

Blandane waited for the woman at the hospital until almost nine, not because he had to—his job was to get her there and into the hands of the doctors and the rape counselor and he'd done that, she was now in the emergency room being cleaned up and counseled—but because he wanted to. Felt the urge to stay with her as if they shared some sort of bond, as if having met her first gave him a proprietary interest above all the others. The least he could do now was to wait for her, give her a ride home, show her through that simple act that he cared.

She came through the electric doors and seemed surprised to see him still there, stopped in her tracks then turned from him, walked back through the doors before they had even closed behind her.

What was going on? He got to his feet and found out in a second, as the rape counselor came through and told him that Ms. Evans had had enough harassment for one night, that if the police still insisted on giving her a hard time then she herself would have to report him to his superiors. "You're goddamn lucky I haven't gotten some-one out of bed already, the way you've treated her."

Dick looked at her, puzzled. The curled hair above her freckled face was red, too harsh and bright to be from a bottle. She had her hands on her hips and her mind was already made up so there wasn't a lot of point in arguing with her. He turned without a word.

He got into the car, thinking that maybe that was the way things worked in this town. That perhaps a citizen could have fifty cops help them out when they needed them, protect them and treat them with dignity, and would then stack that up against one who was a brutal idiot and think that the scales were even. How could they be so stupid, so shortsighted?

He was at a stoplight when it dawned on him that the sort of behavior he'd just been attributing to Claricia Evans was the same sort that he himself was guilty of exhibiting.

Things didn't get a lot better for him back at the Went-worth District. O'Brian was surly, churlish, exhibiting some pretty bizarre behavior himself. When Blandane came in Obie was leaning against the clerk's desk, sipping coffee from a Styrofoam cup, staring hatred at the door as Dick passed through. He didn't wait for Dick to approach him, just threw his cup in the general direction of the wastebasket and stomped toward him, reached for Dick's arm then thought better of it, just stormed past him and said, "C'mon."

He was silent in the car for a time, sitting against his door pouting, the anger a real and living thing between them. The black males on the street gave them the stare reserved for The Man, suspicious, filled with anger. In the squad car, when Dick had been in uniform, he would draw strength from his partner against those hate-filled looks. Fat chance of that happening now.

Dick drove as if nothing had happened, still a little

stung by the behavior of Claricia Evans and not wanting to hear anything just yet from the man who by tradition was supposed to be his closest friend on the department, but who now wasn't demonstrating anything near a confidant's attitude. When O'Brian at last spoke, his tone was harsh, a little hurt.

"You should'a backed me up back there, with the sarge." He steamed for a second, thinking about it. "Fuckin' jig, I was working the street when he was a teenaged basketball star in the ghetto, shooting melons through the goddamn bottoms of garbage cans hung on a telephone pole. He wasn't a jig, he'd still be in uniform. Fuckin' affirmative action bullshit."

Dick didn't say anything, didn't even shake his head. He kept his eyes on the road, his hands steady on the wheel.

"A partner's supposed to stand behind you, Blandane. Don't you know that by now?"

"I'll never not stand behind you on the street."

"Yeah, right."

Dick made the turn onto 47th Street, heading toward the Homes, to deliver a warrant to a man who probably hadn't given the arresting officers his proper address in the first place.

"I heard about you, Blandane." Then, sarcastically, "*Dicko.*" Silently daring Blandane to correct him. Dick did shake his head this time, disgustedly. "Heard you were a real asshole. Found out what I heard was true, too."

"Listen, why didn't you ask the sergeant for a different partner, you think I'm such an asshole? Or why don't you just work alone, go and eat all the free pizza and drink all the beer you want. Hell, you could go home and sleep the shift away, for all the work you seem to want to do. Bigtime gang crimer, all I've seen and heard so far is brutality and bitching, pal."

"I ain't your pal."

"You got that much right."

O'Brian muttered something under his breath and Dick was about to tell him to be man enough to speak up when the radio crackled and informed them that there was a riot in progress at the funeral home.

What had happened was not unusual, except in its complexity, such deeds usually being performed by simpleminded people who didn't have the sense to perform one task properly, let alone two.

The wake at the funeral parlor had been disrupted by rival gang members who'd done a drive-by, shot at the groups of teenagers who'd been congregating out in front of the place, some of them trying to get away from the grieving mother who'd been throwing herself on top of her son's lifeless body all night, others who'd just stepped out to have a smoke, bored. Some were gang members there to protect the integrity of their fallen brother's image in death, others out in front were just innocent bystanders, grieving young relatives and classmates who'd known the dead boy and respected him enough to dress up in their finest clothes and come there to say goodbye. The gang members were easily recognizable—they stood together and stared hard at the young men who weren't standing with them, flashing their sign at them, signifying with their hats turned sideways and down, bills low over their right eyes. Above bitter black faces who saw the gang as family and everyone outside it as their enemy.

The young people who weren't gang members stood uncomfortably, gangs a way of life with them, but one they'd somehow managed to avoid up until this night. Not one of them did not know several kids their own ages who'd been shot down in cold blood, blasted out of their lives because someone thought they might be in another gang. Not one of them had given into the pressure to join, had buckled under to the recruiters who sweet-talked them in class, who then got tough when these kids exerted the force of their character and stayed strong, still refusing the overtures. Not one of them hadn't lost their pocket money or taken an ass-kicking somewhere down the road. They walked to and from school in a hurry, as if in a war zone, under fire from all sides.

They stood together, their heads down, not wanting to make eye contact with the gangbangers, some of whom began taunting them, so wrapped up in the momentary demonstration of what they thought to be their manhood that they didn't notice the van, the war wagon, rolling slowly toward them, nor the black-masked head that was sticking out of the custom side window, pointing the short-barreled Uzi . . .

While three blocks away other soldiers in their army performed the second act of the play, snapping the lock on the door of the home that belonged to the family of the boy being waked.

It was a common enough occurrence; look in the paper for the names of the recently departed, copy them out of the obituary column, then look them up in the phone book. Who in the ghetto could afford an unlisted number? A phone itself was a luxury. Wait until the wake was in full force and then go on over and force the door, take everything that wasn't nailed down . . .

It happened so often that people got hip to it, had someone else house-sit while they mourned their dead, which was what had been happening at the home of the dead gang member, only it wasn't some gang member guarding the house with his automatic weapon, it was the dead boy's auntie, fifteen-year-old Jerrina with her six-teen-year-old boyfriend Marcus to keep her company through the night. The house was decrepit, like the ones around it, the neighborhood surviving on welfare checks and food stamps and resentment, the odd drug deal . . . You could get anything you wanted, meat, clothing, vege-tables, at a discount in the alley on Saturday morning, bought from the hustlers who were above peddling drugs or frightened by the drugger's pension plan, or from the junkies who'd shoplift the goods, sell them for peanuts in order to fill their needs. The windows in these homes were for the most part covered with sheets, except for the house on the corner, where Reggie the Pusher lived. Reggie only popped for old newspapers, taped to the glass. Every now and then you'd see an edge of the yellow paper pulled to one side, and a dark, wary eye would peek out scanning for the law.

Jerrina and Marcus were watching *Creature Features* on television, Jerrina involved in the program, Marcus more involved in her, his hands moving around her torso, his lips kissing her neck. Jerrina ignored him, absently pushed his hands away, sat forward and stared at the television set . . .

The door came off its hinges and Jerrina screamed, high-pitched and terrified, jumping to her feet and holding her trembling hands to her cheeks. Her boyfriend Marcus moved in front of her, saw that there were three of them, got to see that much before one of them hit him hard on the side of his head with something that made him see red for a second, then black.

Marcus coming to to the sound of his girlfriend's muffled screams, mingled with the sexual grunts of a male. Was she being raped? He opened his eyes, saw that he was on his back. Two of them were hurting his girlfriend Jerrina, one holding her hands down while the other tore at her clothes, the third now carrying a portable TV out of the kitchen door, probably to a waiting war wagon. Marcus knew that to attack the rapists would be futile. They would kill him, laugh, then return to their invasions of home and soul. So he waited until he figured the thief with the TV would be far enough away from the kitchen door, then he got to his feet, dizzily ran from the house and waited until he was two doors down before he raced up a stairway and began pounding on the rotted wood of the front door of the house, screaming and crying for someone to help him, please help him now.

As the door opened and an elderly man grabbed him by the arm and began to drag him into the house he looked back, saw that the thief by the van had a gun out and was pointing it at him. Marcus saw chips fly off the brick next to his head then heard the report of the pistol, then the door was slamming shut behind him and the old man was waving a baseball bat in his face and yelling at Marcus to tell him what in the fuck was going on with that shooting out there before he brained him.

When the smoke cleared at the funeral parlor there were three dead and seven wounded, four of them gravely. More mourning to be done over senseless death, far too soon visiting itself upon the very young. Gang Crimes was all over it, swarming the scene, angry because they'd been warned in advance and hadn't been able to stop the slaughter. All three of the dead had been kids who'd been standing on the non-gang section of the sidewalk, good kids come to pay respect to a fallen classmate.

Were the gangbangers cooperating, helping the cops, maybe giving them a license plate number to run down? They were staring somberly at the policemen who were questioning them, not saying a word, wanting only to get away from them and into their own wagons, stoking their own Uzi's and Aks as their van tore toward hostile turf.

Would it ever end? Blandane wondered. Too much drug money out there for things to ever change now. Too many weapons, too many hungry hearts ruling brains that should know better.

He stood staring at the puddles of blood at his feet, the blood reflecting the flashing red and blue and white lights from the squad car Mars lights, hearing the crackle of radios and the loud, mostly white male voices demanding obedience from young black men who saw them as their adversaries rather than their protectors. Hearing too the wailing of the women and men, the older ones, the sounds not just of grief but of desperation and hopelessness. Hearing in their tone the sounds of people who'd lost their dreams, their ability to expect anything but more misery from the shattered ruins that was, these days, their lives.

The sergeant was standing over to Blandane's right, speaking calmly to an obese grieving woman who was dressed all in black, holding her in his weightlifter's arms. "She'll be all right, your baby's all right," the sergeant said. Blandane wondered how he knew that was so, if he did or if he was just talking nonsense in order to calm her down.

The sergeant looked around him at the carnage, at the blood and bodies only now being carted away, and when he and Blandane made eye contact Blandane had to look away, uncomfortable at the pain he saw reflected in the eyes of a man who knew more about this than Blandane ever would, the eyes of a man who lived with this every day, maybe took some of the blame for it.

O'Brian wasn't feeling too uncomfortable. It was obvious in the way he was charging around the scene, exercising his authority.

"You better come up with something better than that, Wilbur," O'Brian said. Speaking to a young male with a tilted Fila baseball cap, a boy with a man's attitude, staring right through O'Brian. "Else your ass will be down at the station all goddamn night, believe me." O'Brian posturing, the young man staring at him insolently, as if he was wondering if O'Brian really thought a night in the slammer would truly inconvenience him.

"I ain't seen shit," the kid said.

O'Brian grabbed the boy's arm. "All right let's go." He pulled and the boy decided to resist, and two of his friends decided to help him just as the radios crackled that shots had been fired three blocks away and the responding units were to proceed with caution.

• • •

Marcus had convinced the old gray-haired man that he meant him no harm and had begged to use his phone, had been made to stand in the hallway as the old guy walked unsteadily over to the phone and dialed 911, his eyes never leaving Marcus, the baseball bat held threateningly in his left hand. "You move," the old man said, "and I'll brain you, I swear before Jesus."

Marcus didn't move, could only stand there and sob. Sixteen years old and until now able to avoid the violence of the streets through his quick wit, his way with words and women. Jerrina being his woman now, the one who had calmed him down, made him think about settling down. He could quit school any time he wanted, now that he was a man, was thinking of doing so, to get away from the gangs, maybe get his GED or go into the Navy and take Jerrina with him.

What would they have done to her? Was she alive? There was no way he would be able to walk into that house and find out, not alone. He would wait for the police and go in with them, describe the man who'd hit him, he'd had a good enough look at him.

Man. Marcus couldn't get the word out of his mind. He had fancied himself to be one, until this moment. Now he knew that he was nowhere near that level, that he was only a boy, and a cowardly boy at that. Who'd left his woman to fight off her attackers by herself.

He heard the old man talking rapidly into the telephone, understood that the guy was giving the police the street address. He could hear him through the ocean that was roaring in his ears, through the sounds of strange noises that he was surprised to figure out to be the sounds of his own sobs. Knowing that he was crying made his degradation profound; understanding that he'd peed himself made it eternal. He could never face Jerrina again, never in his life.

The old man walked past him, ignoring Marcus's mounting wails, and carefully pulled back the picture window bedsheet curtain, peered out into the night.

"They's gone. Their car and them with it. Po-lice on the way. Now you get your ass out there and tell them what they need to know, and if you gives them my name, if they come here looking for me, I'll beat the shit out of you with this here bat, you understand me? Shit. Boy y'all's age pissing on hisself. Get out my house 'fore you stink it up, motherfucker."

Still weeping, Marcus obeyed, staggered out to the street and sat down hard on the curb, his hands on his knees, his face aimed toward the dark, moonless sky, as if offering his degradation to God. Petitioning Christ to remove it from him. He looked toward the house where Jerrina was, wondering if she lay dying as he cried. He couldn't go and find out, he just couldn't. The thought made him fill with self-pity, the self-pity made him cry even harder.

He was still sitting there at the curb when the unmarked car screeched to a halt in front of him, missing his legs by a few short feet.

Chapter 20

Blandane took the wheel, followed the two squads out of the funeral parlor parking lot, grateful to be getting out of there, ungrateful for the fact that O'Brian had heard the call and had jumped into the shotgun seat. He'd been hoping that the gangbangers would do something constructive for a change, such as beating O'Brian to a pulp, maybe bad enough to force him into retirement.

No such luck. O'Brian was beside him, checking the load in his ancient revolver. A shots fired call was never taken lightly.

O'Brian seemed to have forgotten about the words they'd been exchanging when the call had come about the drive-by shooting, was now acting as if they were partners, speaking rapidly, breathing just as quickly.

"We're sitting at a stoplight one night, me and Tank minding our own business, and this carload of shines pulls up next to us. I look over, see them, give them the eye back, and this one fucker, he lifts a Saturday night special up and lets a cap go. I duck, Tank ducks, the round goes through the windshield and the chase begins." Dick drove fast, not paying a lot of attention, following the squads through turf unfamiliar to him. The sound of O'Brian's voice was soothing, though, even as nervous as the man was. It made Dick feel safe, made him believe that the man would cover his ass, no matter how he felt about Dick personally, even though he knew that O'Brian was only talking to hear the sound of his own voice, only telling the story to bolster his own courage.

"We catch up to them and ram them off the street, into a storefront, the driver dying on impact, two others trapped in there and burning up when the thing explodes.

"The prick with the piece, though, he's out the door and running before the car goes up, shooting at us behind his back, like he's Roy fucking Rogers, gonna hit us through the gun hand on the run." Another block, that was all, then they'd know if it was war or a false alarm. Dick felt the adrenalin rush, the surge of blood through his veins. It was welcome, made him feel good. It was what he'd joined the force to experience.

"I hear the guy's gun clicking, know it's empty, but my piece is out and I catch up to him on the steps of a fucking church!" O'Brian chuckling at the thought. "He turns, dry-fires at me a few times, his jig eyes all up in his head like he was Buckwheat got caught raiding the cookie jar, and I let him have it, empty my piece, hitting the church door three times but I caught him in the arm twice, and somehow, scared as I was, I still put the third round right through his chest. I go over to him and kick the gun out of his reach and you know what he says, his last words on earth? He says, 'Man, you done killed me good.' Famous jig last words."

The squads were slowing down, stopping diagonally in the middle of the street, blocking egress of any fleeing felons still on the block.

O'Brian said, "That was the last time I fired a shot on duty, killed me a jig who was stupid enough to congratulate me on my marksmanship."

Blandane halted the car and threw the gear shift into

Park, left it running and while opening his door decided that he just better let it pass. If there were gangs warring in one of these houses, he'd need this man on his side.

In front of him sitting on the curb was a young man in some kind of serious agony, his hands folded in front of his chest as if in prayer, eyes squeezed tightly shut and his face raised to heaven. Tears streaked that face, the boy silently crying, praying. His lips were compressed, turned down into a scowl, the child looking young and helpless, alone and terrified on a curb of a street that held no hope for people like him, sitting there crying as if he'd just suddenly understood that, figured it out for the first time.

Blandane saw the squad cops surrounding the house, guns drawn, the cops entering it, heard no shots, no calls for help. Whoever had fired the shots was long gone, Blandane was sure of it.

He crouched down next to the boy, afraid to touch him, to intrude on his grief. There was a low helpless sound issuing from deep down inside this child, the kid fighting to keep it in, not to let the world see or share his suffering. He wanted to help him, but how?

He heard O'Brian slamming the car door behind him, heard him shouting, O'Brian saying, "Whattaya got, boy, what's in them hands?" Dick wondered for a second if there was a chance O'Brian might shoot the youngster, then forced the thought from his mind. His problem right now wasn't O'Brian. His problem was finding a way to help this young man without intruding on his grief, without making it worse.

O'Brian had no such problem. He walked up to the kid and stood before him, kicked him hard on the leg.

"Hey, Wilbur, what the fuck you doing out here?" The boy opened his eyes and looked at them, then turned his head away, unclasping his hands, digging them into his pockets.

"Look out!" O'Brian shouted, leaning down and shoving his pistol into the boy's cheek. "Take your hands out of your pockets, nigger, now!" The child obeyed, eyes wide, tears still streaming, staring at O'Brian with terror and bewilderment. His mouth was open now and he was drooling, his lips working with no sound coming forth. O'Brian dragged the boy to his feet.

"You the nigger with the trigger? Huh?" Patting him down. "You the fuckin' nigger with the trigger, Wilbur?" O'Brian shouted it in the kid's face, enjoying himself, working out his anger and frustration at the world and taking it out on someone whom they both knew had no defense against the acts. Blandane saw the dark stain on the front of the boy's pants. Knew right then what it was that he had to do.

He stepped between them, forced O'Brian away from the boy and, disregarding the gun in O'Brian's hand as well as the curses O'Brian was shouting at him, hit him hard, one time, square on the button, knocking the vicious son of a bitch right into the gutter where he belonged.

Chapter 21

"The old lady, she's all of a sudden Florence Nightingale, taking care of this quadriplegic lives down the block, young good-looking kid got fucked up in a car wreck." Johnny Red was telling his story to Catfeet, who was half-listening, looking at his stack of drinks there on the bar and wondering if there were three rock glasses filled with Scotch in front of him or six. Someone had put Sinatra back on the jukebox, and Feet had to fight the urge to go over and kick the thing in, break it before he heard another song. He would hear Frank singing and think about Sal, good old Sal dying in Feet's lap, his heart bursting while Sinatra sang Christmas songs in the background through hidden quadraphonic speakers.

Quadraphonic, quadriplegic, was it the same thing? What the hell was this guy Red talking about, anyway? Jesus.

"Me," Red said, "I'm a thief," pronouncing it "teef" in a way that showed he was proud of it. "Bring home the bacon, take care of the woman, don't go in for no perverted shit, like a lot of guys done time get into once they get home." Little Johnny Red took a sip of his drink, put the glass back right in the middle of the Budweiser coaster and twisted it, so that it stuck there. Short stocky guy maybe fifty, fifty-five, with a hangdog look Feet didn't remember him having the last time he'd seen him. Around them there was pandemonium as men who made their livings illegally partied, telling war stories, getting rid of Mr. Stress. Everyone had been giving Johnny Red a wide berth, but he'd buttonholed Feet, who hadn't seen him in a while and was now learning why no one else had seemed happy to see the little guy.

How many cops were in here? Feet wondered. Undercover guys who'd have to do no more investigating than buy you a drink and sit back and listen to you brag on yourself. Feet hadn't been drunk in years, mostly because he didn't want to be out of control, didn't want to do something stupid. But what was the risk now? What was he going to do, tell these guys about the scene he'd made in Favore's office that morning? Or, worse, brag about Favore wanting Femal so bad he could taste it when all the time it was Feet himself who had her between the sheets? Had her, and might now have lost her. She wouldn't put up with some guy hitting her, and today he'd come close.

"I drive down the block, there's the missus, pushing this crip around. I see it all the time and it makes me feel good inside, you know? Knowing my old lady is doing something for someone else, like maybe we're like everyone else for once.

"One night I come home early, don't stop for no drinks, and there it is for me to figure out, the crip out of his wheelchair, lying flat on his back on my living room rug, the old lady crouched over his face. I can hear him licking from the front door."

"That's rough, Johnny," Feet said. Why was the man telling him this?

"Yeah." Red paused for effect, then said, "I'm the only guy you ever met who got eaten out of house and home."

The punchline spoken but there was no laughter in Red's voice, no crinkling around his eyes, which were wet, red and sorrowful.

"What are you gonna do, eh?" Red said, and Feet told him that he'd see him later, he had to make a phone call, taking his drink with him as he walked to the back of the bar. He wasn't about to come back and listen to more of this.

Sinatra went off and Feet steeled himself for another round of the guy, the phone stuck between his ear and his shoulder, the drink in his left hand and a smoldering cigarette between the fingers of his right, his index finger stuck into his right ear so he could hear whoever answered the phone. Have to go another round with Femal's mama, too, probably. So he was pleased on both counts when first Dean Martin came over the speaker, singing "Return To Me," at the same time that Femal answered the phone herself.

It hadn't, all in all, been a good day for Femal. She was a woman who prided herself on having it all together, in fact on having it all, and suddenly she was feeling inadequate, almost as if she had nothing.

Except for Elaine, she had her baby, that was for sure. But what else was there? Since Robert had gotten home, just in the past twenty-four hours, so many things had changed!

She thought about this as she sat moodily in her rocking chair, looking down on the North Side street below her. It was Tuesday night, Wednesday morning now, late, after midnight. She'd left the meeting after seeing a poster of Gus Savage in all his glory in the vestibule near the phones, a sign beneath the poster telling her that Savage would be the main after-dinner speaker at the meeting, and she knew that she just couldn't stay.

Knew, too, that the others in the room would see her as having caved in, backed down and been afraid to reenter the room and face that bastard, Carson. Well, let them think what they wanted. They would anyway. She had enough on her mind without sitting there listening to a state representative who, while on a congressional junket to Africa, apparently told a black woman that if she didn't sleep with him she was a traitor to the movement. A man who'd defended his racist attacks on Israel by saying that "There ain't no such thing as black racism, there's only one kind of racism, and that's *white* racism." She was in no mood to listen to a man whose response to reporters he didn't agree with was to call them faggots. He would play right into the hands of the Carsons of the world, talking about the white-run media and the Jewish conspiracy to rule the world, to keep the black folk down. Like some of them needed any help with that.

She could tell that little shit a few things about black racism. Sexism, too. But why bother, he wouldn't listen. Would probably hit on her then see her as a lesbian when she rejected him.

Femal had the urge to go in and wake up the baby, bring her into the bedroom with her and just hold her tight, rock her in her arms and look down at her softly sleeping face. Her precious face. She could not remember ever feeling so alone, so out of place. So damned *inadequate.*

Where did she fit in? What the hell was her place? Was she going to the top, the way she'd told Carson she would? Or was she as high as she'd ever go, resigned to working for a white man who never missed an opportunity to brag about his criminal affiliations?

Was that a smart move? Good Lord, no. How could it be? The FBI had to be looking into Favore, maybe even the Justice Department was in on the act, doing an undercover audit or whatever it was they did. Even with Femal's safeguards on the computer, her passwords and codes, someone with the proper computer knowledge could get inside their hardware, find out where all the money was.

She'd caught a couple of hackers at it and had been afraid that it was the government, her fear eased when she'd done a silent trace and learned that it was only college students, feeling their way around Favore's electronic fiefdom. At least that's what she suspected had happened. All she could do was learn what computer was tracking her and where it was, and both times it had turned out to be computer time rented from one of the universities. Femal had informed Darrin of the intruders, and the problems had gone away.

Now she wondered how he'd handled it, what he'd done. Was there blood on her hands that she was unaware of? Maybe it was time to begin searching for a new job.

Her confidence level was lower than she could ever remember it being, her self-esteem in jeopardy. It was, she hoped, because she was alone. Tomorrow, in front of the boss and the lesser secretaries, it would come right back, and she'd wear her attitude proudly, appear confident and strong, a role model for the younger women wanting to work their way up the corporate ladder at DFI. For some of the men, too.

But would it be real, would she truly be feeling strong or would it be just an act? Would that matter, as long as it was the way the white world saw her? Did it make a difference?

Heavy post-midnight thoughts on a cold November's morning.

She told herself things would look better in the morning. That she could come to grips with it all at that time, with Feet, with her argument with Carson, with the guilt over the things she was doing, her fear of getting caught. With her feelings toward her boss and even with her mother's hatred of Robert Millard. That might even have been the catalyst for Femal's depression, having to come home and face her mother's no longer silent scorn over the fact that she'd slept with and had the child of a white man. Maybe her mother saw her as a traitor to the movement, she didn't know.

What she did know, what she was sure of, was that there was no positive action to be taken this night. She needed some sleep, a good night's rest before she wrestled with the demons surrounding her, overwhelming her . . .

She brushed her teeth and looked in on the baby, tiptoeing into Elaine's room and smiling down at her, feeling almost renewed at the sight of her daughter. As long as that baby was with her, nothing could really get her down, surely nothing could defeat her.

She was slipping between the blankets, listening to the baby breathing over the speaker on her headboard when the phone rang and she jumped, grabbed the Princess on the nightstand before it could ring again and awaken Elaine.

She heard the string music in the background, some angelic female voices raised in choir along with it, ascending and descending in syncopated rhythms, then a moment's silence before Robert's voice came over the phone wires, accompanied by Dean Martin in the background.

"Re-turn to meee, oh my dear, I'm so sorry," Robert singing in a voice that should make him glad he was a reasonably good thief, as he'd never make it in Motown. "Hurry back, hurry home, won't you please hurry home I am yours," dragging it out, his voice warbling. Femal had heard enough.

She said, "Knock off the bullshit, Millard, and state your piece."

"I'm drunk."

"That's a surprise. What is it with you? You get a few under your belt and you're Italian all of a sudden?"

"I'm sorry." He didn't sound it. "Tell you what. I'll head over to the South Side, go into one of your people's joints and call you back, sing some Smokey Robinson to you, all right?"

"Is that supposed to be a joke?"

"My darling," the half-wit was singing again, putting olive oil into his voice, "if I hurt you I'm sorry. Forgive me, and please say you are mine, all mine, all mine. Re—" Femal hung up on him, waited, grabbed the phone on the half-ring when he called back.

She didn't even wait for him to say hello. "Let me tell you something, Millard, you think I got time for this, you're crazy." She said it and regretted last night's homecoming, the teddy, the sex. Suddenly her reaction to his release made her feel cheap. Had he even once hugged Elaine? She didn't think so, at least she couldn't remember it happening.

"I got no place to go," he said.

She could hear the song winding down in the background, Dino whining, pleading, sounding better than Millard ever could but still not even being a corn on Smokey's feet, when it came to singing.

"I'm running a hotel for drunks now, is that what you think? For suicidal fools?" It was time to wrap this up, as it was useless to argue with drunks. They never remembered what you said to them the next day, anyway. Or claimed that they didn't. "Get this straight, get it right the first time. Don't you ever call me again when you been drinking."

"I tried to call before I started—"

"You got no place, you got the spare bedroom, that's it. And if you upset Elaine or give Mama a hard time tomorrow, she'll have my permission to shoot you, you understand me?"

"Why you being so tough?"

"You got fifteen minutes to get over here, Millard, or the deal's off." Instead of a reply all she heard from him was the last words of the song, Dean and Robert Millard singing together, "So lo tu, so lo tu, so lo tu, so lo tu, mi a-more." Then she hung up.

Chapter 22

Twice now, she'd hung up on him. Feet said hello a couple of times just to be sure that she had, then hung up, shaking his head. He turned, unsteady on his feet, banged into the wall as he lost his balance, put his hand out to steady himself, spilling half his drink on the floor. He said Shit, then stood there until he got his sea legs. Staggered over to the end of the bar and asked the bartender to bring his drinks over. Watched the man go and get them, saw the quick hurt look that passed across Johnny Red's face as the bartender said something to him. Feet turned his gaze to the smoked mirror behind the back bar. He didn't want to carry the weight for hurting Johnny Red. There were enough things in his life to feel guilty about.

Wasn't freedom beautiful? It sure beat the alternative.

The beginning of his lack of which had been a bus with forty-four other guys on it that drove through the gates of the County Jail complex at 26th and California, where they'd been processed, forced to look through an IBM computer they called an Eye-dentification System that locked you into the system forever, quicker than fingerprints, and from that point on all the County ever had to do was get you to look into the viewer again and you were theirs, from the date you were born until your last pinch, its resolution. The bored official working the machine had said that one eye match had a million to one chance of being wrong, both eyes, five billion to one. From there they'd been forced into a bullpen, a hundred and thirty guys considered to be on the new, crowded in a cage built to seat forty-five for the ten hours it took to process them in, the weakest forced to the floor, to eat their lunch with the roaches and rats while the head gangbangers sat proudly with their feet up on the concrete seats, taking up two spaces to prove their importance. Feet remembered looking around and wondering if white guys committed any crimes these days. From what he could see, there weren't too many of them. There were black faces everywhere, angry and mean.

Feet stayed at the front of the cage, busy countering the jostling, the players wanting to get him in the middle of the cage where the guards on the other side of the chain link fence couldn't see what they would do to him. That bullpen was the best of it for some of those guys.

They'd taken them out one by one and processed them through the system, psych workers and paramedics right there with the hacks in their dark blue County uniforms. Asking you questions: Are you gay? Do you cross-dress? Feet heard the rumors, what happened to you if you answered yes. You'd do relatively easy time, closely watched, but in the morning on the Gump Unit—otherwise known as D-1 and 2—they had to pry guys off each other in the bunks and the shower room. Some gangbangers knowing they were going to be in there for a long time as pre-trial detainees would ask for relocation to the unit, to receive what they thought would be free sexual services, but soon found out that the girls in the unit had their own set of rules: If you pitched one night, you caught the next, were forced to take part in it whether you liked it or not. When Feet's turn came, he told them that he wasn't gay.

Another good scam a lot of the guys used was to tell the workers that they had a history of mental problems, so they could go right down the hall from the gumps to the psych section, where they'd let you stay for twenty-four to forty-eight hours under observation. Under the influence of drugs, too, which were administered in the morning and then again at night. Good jailing, if you could hack it, exhibit strange enough behavior so the medics would keep you there. If you screwed up or hurt another detainee you could be sent to an iso unit for up to twenty-nine days, locked into a bare cell all alone with no outside contact.

Either way you went, gump or psycho, it stayed with you, on your jacket if you got convicted and they transferred you to a state joint during the Friday movements. It wasn't a risk Feet wanted to take. The prison system had a grapevine that was better than intercell fax machines, and he couldn't picture it, his someday going to a state joint and the word being around that he was a gump or a psycho.

He'd wound up doing his county time in Division One, the oldest part of the county jail complex, the design of the place the exact diametric opposite of the newer, more recently built wings. Everything was supposedly electronic in the new wings, all modern and clean. Division One was clean, mostly, because a convict could earn ten bucks a week toward commissary if he had a job and did it right and any convict could make a store for forty-five bucks a week worth of goods if they had the money on the books. Cigarettes, candy, pop, potato chips, almost anything except gum, because if you chewed it up you could stick it in the locks and it would play hell with the door once it dried up.

The county officials would admit to the place having

over five thousand prisoners in there at any given time, counting the Department of Corrections prisoners, who had lower bails and lived in a slightly safer environment, but that was bullshit. On any given day, there were eight thousand people in a place built to hold less than half that number. There were fifteen hundred guards. "You figure it out," a hack had told him when he was on the new. "Who's gonna cover your ass for you?" Subtly telling Feet that he had to join one of the white gangs. Which he hadn't had to do, mainly because of Sergeant Ellis.

His first day there, a burly black sergeant had told him that the "Bitch who'd built the place had her a cold, cold heart," and it didn't take Feet long to learn that the man had spoken the truth. The speaker had been Sergeant Ellis, a man almost as wide around the shoulders as he was tall, who walked the tier without a trace of fear and commanded respect from the convicts.

He wasn't a man who was afraid to mix it up, would show any con the respect a human being had coming, no matter what crime he was awaiting trial for. Ellis showed that respect and demanded it in return, and if a prisoner decided not to give it up Ellis would be forced to, as he called it, "Get in the cat's ass," whup up on him to let him know who was in charge.

Ellis didn't cotton to the "just us" theory of justice, either. Would tell the black political activists—who caught that activism inside the same way a lot of white prisoners caught religion—"who doin' all the crime, youngblood?" He didn't go in much for sociological theories, didn't want or care to know about such things; he was a good hack and he did his job to the best of his ability.

He took a liking to Feet because he was standup, hadn't ratted out to get free when he had his chance; and Ellis told him he respected that, seeing that on any given day he had to deal with more rats and stoolpigeons than he did any other type of human being, the rat telling him things in order to curry his favor. They'd snitch and get

their favors, but in doing so would lose Ellis's respect.
That wasn't a risk Feet was willing to take.

Not when he was living in a place that was fifty feet
long by twenty feet wide, which housed sixty-five convicts. There was no privacy there, except for the sheet the
hacks let them hang over the shower because there were
women guards now, and some of them were sensitive to
such sights. No, on Division One, the only way to survive
was through the earning of respect, by minding your own
business and never touching anything that wasn't yours,
never bitching about what was playing on the television
or telling some other con to turn his rap music down.

Feet later learned that a woman had indeed designed
the jail, its architecture dating back to the twenties, the
cells tiny with two men living in each one, without privacy. He would lie there after eleven o'clock lights out
and wonder if some man had broken her heart, if that was
the reason for her cruelty.

Division One was maximum security, no dorms in
there as in other areas, no private two-man cells with steel
doors such as the ones in the school dorms. In here, you
didn't work, you just did your time, sat in the dayroom
from after breakfast until the change of shift at three,
when they'd slam you down again and count you, make
sure nobody had osmosed through the walls. Then you'd
come out again, vegetate some more until supper and
lights out. Fights? Constantly, and Feet had his share of
them. He was one of three white men on the tier and
nobody ever let him forget it, now that the shoe was on
the other foot and he was a minority.

Doing that, that sort of thing for twenty-eight months,
after having never even been accused of a crime. It just
didn't seem fair.

And what had he come out to, what was out here for
him? Femal and a new daughter he hadn't known he'd
had. He wouldn't let Femal visit him because on the ABO
—Abnormal Behavior Observation unit—the visitors had
to walk through the cons to get to the visiting rooms, and

then you had to communicate through glass, speaking through a tiny speaker set in steel. It just wasn't worth it. The guards treated the visitors as if they were all bringing in contraband, and they weren't far off the mark. They found everything in there after a visitor left, jailhouse joints rolled so tightly that you could slip them between the tiniest of cracks between the glass and the steel door of the visiting room, drugs stuck with gum on the underside of the bars where someone with your gang affiliation would come along and pick them up as they were cleaning the place. Cash money was at a premium, as more than one hack had been known to take a bribe. Feet wouldn't allow Femal or Charlie to suffer such indignities, couldn't let them be put through that.

And Charlie, how about that kid? Seeming happy to see him this morning, but how about the way he'd changed when his wife had entered the room? He hoped Charlie hadn't called Femal's, hadn't had to take a load of shit from her mother.

He checked his drinks, there were either two or four left. Could he catch a ride over to her house? There was a question he wanted to ask her, something she had said that morning . . .

He'd make one more call, speak to her one more time. Ask her over the phone and then forget about her. She had a good job, a child to raise, what did she need with him? That was it, he'd say goodbye over the phone, have another reason to feel sorry for himself. Speaking to her, to anyone right now, had to be better than sitting here thinking about that damned County Jail Complex, or the mess he'd made out of his life, about the death of the don, about the millions he owed Darrin Favore. Who had he thought he was, thinking about raising the kid and giving up the life? He couldn't be good enough for Femal, no matter how much he tried to change. As for the kid, forget about it. It wouldn't even be close. She deserved better. The noble thing to do was to blow them off, let them start over without him. He just couldn't wreck their lives, the way he'd wrecked his own. Feet staggered to the phone, wondering how much booze it would take to wipe out the ugly memories he knew would haunt him forever.

And all along he thought he'd been drinking to forget.

Femal wasn't sleeping. She was lying awake in the dark staring at the ceiling, wondering where she'd gone wrong.

It wasn't the way she thought it would be, in her mind's eye she'd seen Robert taking one look at the baby then falling to his knees, asking her to marry him. She would have taken him up on it, too.

But something had changed inside the man, something had turned sour. He'd come to her door looking haggard, and from what he'd said the next morning it was obvious that he knew something about the death of old Sal, that sweet old man, who always took the time to come out and speak with her after his business with Darrin.

Warning her about Darrin, too, as if she couldn't handle him herself. Did jail do that to a man, make him paranoid? Maybe it just broke a man down, took away his heart and zest for life.

There had been a time when Feet had been one of the happiest men she had ever known, always smiling and laughing, making love with abandon. That man was gone. Forever? She didn't know. He'd only been home one day, but from what she was seeing, he was no longer the sort of man she wanted to spend a lot of time with. Coming to Darrin's office and arguing with him, raising his hand in anger toward her. She wasn't a therapist, going to sit around and play nanny to him until he came back to life, got his heart back.

The sad fact, one she had to face, though, was that maybe it was over. It wasn't the way she thought it would be, and that was fine with her.

She thought about it, about her twenty-eight-month fantasy gone wrong, and felt strong. She'd been through worse. One thing was for sure, she wasn't about to sit up nights waiting for some drunk to call her up, thinking he was making her night by singing stupid thirty-year-old dago songs to her over the phone. She wouldn't put herself through that, and she damn sure wouldn't put her child through that.

She was beginning to feel better. She'd just get the man out of her life and do whatever she had to in order to prosper. It was for the best. She told herself this and began to relax, to feel a little sleepy. She pulled the covers to her neck and curled up, a slight, sad smile on her lips, and was just drowsing off when the damn phone went off again.

Feet heard it ring once, twice, then Femal's voice, cold as he'd ever heard it, said, *"Yes."* Shortly. It was too late to back out now, she would know it was him. Her first hint being the same background noises from his previous calls.

He got cold feet, didn't want it to end like this. Feet said, "Femal? I'm waiting for a cab, you still want me to come over."

"I never wanted you to come over. I said that you could, half an hour ago. You don't have anyplace to go, you can stay in the extra bedroom, one night only. You come here wanting to talk, or make a scene, I swear to God, I'll have you arrested."

His first instinct was to argue with her, his anger right there on the surface, his pride hurt. Who the hell was she to speak to him like this? But something stopped him, maybe the tone of her voice. She didn't sound mad, or hurt. Just cold. Cold as the woman architect who'd built the County Jail.

He said, "Femal? There's something I want to ask you." He took her silence as a positive response, hurried into the breach. "You said, this morning, when we were talking, you said you had a way out for me, something you were working on . . . ?" He let it hang there, it's what she'd said, wasn't it?

He couldn't tell from what she was saying, which was nothing. Femal taking her time, so long that Feet thought that she'd hung up on him. He was about to hang up himself when she spoke again, her voice no longer cold, now sounding hurt, as if she'd had a daydream interrupted, rudely.

"Forget about it, Robert. It was nothing, just me talking. Now you coming over or not? I have to work in the morning."

"I'll be there in twenty minutes," Feet said, not calling her honey or anything as he signed off, speaking to her now as he would to a man who was offering him a bed for the night. His heart was heavy as he thought that it seemed to all of a sudden be a business deal now between them, and not a whole lot more.

Chapter
23

Merle grabbed the phone on the third ring and said through his beer hangover, "Who is this and what do you want?" then right away terrified that it might be his Uncle Dare. Shit, how could he answer the phone that way, with the people he was related to. Sometimes he scared himself. He'd gotten that line from someone else, from some dip who owed someone some money, someone who offered Merle twenty percent if he could collect. The ower speaking the words, being cute, as Merle, in his best stupid-hillbilly act, had entered the pud's office. "Who are you and what do you want?" the man had asked him, and Merle had said, "I'm the devil and I want your soul, asshole." A pretty good comeback, but he'd liked the original line better. If he hadn't been having a bad dream he would never have answered his phone that way, though. It was a line he usually only used when he could see the person right there in front of him.

He'd been dreaming that he was in bed with Moonbeam, doing things to her, with his Daddy lying on the other side of the bed, a jug of shine in his hands, watching them with laughing eyes, silently scorning them, making fun of them. When he heard Mickey's voice on the line he was grateful. That it wasn't his Daddy or his Uncle Dare. Losing his gratitude as soon as he heard what it was that Mickey was telling him he had to do.

He said, "Shit, it's *cold* out there, Jackson." And "Since when am I a goddamned watchdog?" Trying to talk his way out of it, but Mickey wouldn't quit, told him that his uncle had told him to call, had ordered him to call. Showing respect, not giving Merle orders, which he appreciated, but still, the man was letting Merle know that he had no choice.

Shit. He hung up the phone and got out of bed, shivering in his Fruit of the Looms, tightening his muscles to warm them. Where was that little devil mex? Not in bed with him, that's for sure. He dressed quietly, snuck out of the house and out to the garage where he paid three bills a month for the privilege of housing his vehicle, got into the old white Chevy and it started right up, even after sitting here for weeks on end in the cold.

Merle wasn't a man to take to the high life. He liked to dress up sometimes and get out there amongst them, to mingle with the other half, seeing how they lived and usually wondering how they could live that way at all, spending all their time at restaurants and shit. He didn't carry hordes of cash with him, wore no jewelry, drove an older sedan that would draw no attention on the street. He was of the philosophy that if he wanted to impress someone, he would give them a taste of The Punch, and that would work better whipping out a Gold Card any day.

He let the car warm up, then backed out of the garage, hit the button attached to his visor that would lower the door. There was a fifty-dollar fine if they could prove that you left the door open. He drove out of the alley and headed north, thinking that he might have given old

Mickey an argument if he hadn't told Merle that they had to beat a guy up who was more than likely at Femal's.

He didn't know why his uncle liked that spade chick, what he saw in her. It would be a pleasure to do what had to be done in front of her. Maybe, even, if the guy didn't show up, Merle could climb up her fire escape or onto her balcony, catch a look at her in her nighty and find out what the fuss was all about.

Fifteen minutes later he was parked down the street from her fancy two-story house, Mickey in the passenger's seat passing Merle a flask. He was angry now, listening to this pud.

"We can't kill him, your uncle was strict about that." Strict? Schoolteachers were strict, his uncle wasn't strict. His uncle just told people what to do, then killed them if they fucked it up.

How much was Darrin paying this jig broad? Merle wondered. Had to be a lot for her to be living in this neighborhood. Area had *trees* for God's sake. Cobblestone sidewalks with little grates around the trees, which was cute. Probably made the people who lived here feel all safe and sound, secure against the marauding hordes. If you pretend something isn't there, then it isn't. Her building had two stained-glass windows, one on the bottom floor and another on the second, and a high black iron gate that didn't seem to be locked, although the tips of the fence bars appeared to be sharp. The bricks of the home were faded and old. Real toney and high-classed. Shit, Merle lived in a hole compared to this. Maybe he should hit his uncle up for a raise.

Mickey said, "Catfeet, too, of all people. I really like that guy."

"I can't remember anyone named Catfeet." Merle took a sip of the flask and winced because it was bourbon. He hated bourbon. Still, it was better than a cup of White Hen Pantry coffee.

"You remember Millard, for Christ's sake, Merle. Not too big, kind of slender, the prowler."

"Didn't rat out Uncle Dare?"

"*That's* the guy. Just got out of jail for that, now we got to kick his ass. Seems wrong, don't it?"

"Wrong, right, what's the difference, we're getting paid, ain't we?"

"Still . . ." Mickey reached for the flask and Merle let him take it, although he'd flirted with the idea of holding it back from him, to see how Mickey reacted. He liked to test people, particularly those who couldn't do him any harm.

"I don't believe this shit, we got to sit in a freezing car and wait for some bum might not come here all night, might even already be in there, getting laid."

"He's not there, at least not yet. I talked to Tony the Juice earlier, Catfeet was in Jerry's, looked like he was gonna be there awhile."

"Why don't we go over there and drag him out of the joint, bust him up in the alley, shit, get Darrin's money for him."

"This ain't about Darrin's money, one, and two, your uncle owns Jerry's since Barboza got himself whacked. Don't want no trouble in there." Mickey paused, capped the flask and put it in his inside coat pocket, the greedy puke.

"Besides," Mickey said, "I think this got something to do with Femal, with Darrin for some reason wanting her to know that he had the guy's ass kicked; I think it's personal." He paused, as if waiting for Merle to give him the inside scoop on this Millard's personal relationship with Femal, how it affected Darrin's business. Merle wasn't about to tell him that he didn't know.

Instead he said, "Hell, *every* prowler's ass belongs to us, only sometimes they just don't understand that until we tell them."

Mickey shifted in the seat. "Well, it looks like this is

one prowling cat we get to tell about it, and right now, because here his ass comes."

The sign on the desk said, EDWARD SIMMONS, SGT. The words cut into brass, mounted on the plaque. Simmons was in charge now, the duty sergeant for the night shift and the one who, Blandane was sure, was going to have the honor of firing him, right now on the spot.

The man sure looked about to pull his badge, sitting behind that desk with his big beefy arms crossed, scowling.

The door to the office was closed, it was just the two of them now, Blandane and Simmons staring each other down. Blandane would be damned if he'd look away first.

At last Simmons rocked twice in the chair and said, "Got quite a file on you, killer. You brought some serious baggage with you into this unit."

Blandane said nothing. If the sergeant intended to pull his badge, there'd be more people in the room than just the two of them. There'd at least be a representative from the union, seeing as how this would be no insubordination or other spur of the moment suspension. Blandane was surprised that there wasn't someone in the room from Internal Affairs. He knew damn well that he'd be speaking to someone from OPS, the Office of Professional Standards, the civilian group which investigated cases of brutality. If the kid—Marcus, his name was—didn't file charges against O'Brian, then Blandane would file them himself.

"We got a call from the same man called in the original nine-eleven, the same voice. He was hollering on top of his lungs about some white-ass cop beating the shit out of some young boy on the sidewalk in front of his house. Wouldn't leave a name, but it was easy to find out who he was and where he lived, as soon as the street cops tore you off O'Brian."

"That's why I've been sitting outside for three hours,

Sarge? So you could speak to some civilian to see if I was telling the truth?"

"You're damn right that's what you were waiting for. We got your story, the kid's story, the old man's story and we got O'Brian's story. Guess which three were similar?" The sarge wasn't smiling, merely stating a fact, perhaps embarrassed that one of his men had done what O'Brian had.

So where did they go from here? It would be up to Simmons. The sergeant who was sitting there looking colder than a December morning in Minnesota, biceps straining the material of his shirt.

"You think every goddamn ranking officer's out to get you, don't you? You been watching too many television shows, Blandane."

What was this? What was the man trying to tell him?

Simmons said, "I let you sit there for ten minutes, not saying a word to you, and do you look to me for help, try and explain your side? Did you see me as a man, Blandane? A black man? Or just as another one of *them*. That was one of my people out there nearly got his head blown off for no reason, son." Simmons using the paternal term in a way that conveyed no biological warmth. He glared at Dick, hotly.

"Same as they were my people got shot all to hell at the funeral parlor for standing on the wrong side of the doors outside the place. Innocent black folk, who we're supposed to protect the same as innocent whites. Don't work that way much, though, does it?"

Blandane opened his mouth to speak and Simmons uncrossed his arms, held up a hand for silence, got it. He said, "See, your problem is, you got too much damn pride. Only way you see me as your friend is if I had raced across the room and grabbed your hand when you came in here, slapped you on the back and told you what a splendid job you'd done, beating O'Brian's ass."

"That's not so."

"Hell it isn't. You been sitting there all along waiting for me to demand your gun and badge, haven't you?" Blandane didn't answer, and Simmons snorted, both of them knowing he'd spoken the truth.

"I was young on the job once, Blandane. Saw more of that shit than you have in my first years, some partners getting more brutal than usual with my people because they wanted to show me something, teach me a lesson about who was really in charge."

"What would you have done tonight, Sarge, tell me that. The kid was crying like a baby, he wasn't a threat. He was sticking his hands in his pockets because he didn't know what else to do with them."

"Maybe I'd'a pulled my piece and sent O'Brian to cop heaven with some friendly fire, way I was feeling after that funeral parlor shooting. But that's not what did happen, is it? What happened is, you beat the shit out of a senior officer who claims he was performing his duty."

"You know better than that, though, don't you, Sarge."

"Don't tell me what I know or don't know, son." Simmons being his daddy again and Blandane sat back, chastised. He'd gotten too familiar with the man, it was his own fault and he had it coming. He kept his mouth shut, deciding to let the man say what he wanted to without any further interference or comment.

"Way I see it," Simmons said, "is one thing. The review board might see it another way altogether. But I doubt it.

"I suspended O'Brian while you were still downstairs giving your statement. He's off duty pending investigation by OPS. They'll want to talk to you in the morning, too. So you'd better get some sleep. I figure the kid's lawyer'll want to have a few words with you too, preparing his suit against the city. You stay on the job, for now, we'll let the review board make their decision before taking any action. Way it looks, the worst you'll come out of this with is a recommendation, maybe a medal. The last thing the department needs right now is another goddamn racial incident with its white officers."

"I'll have a good time getting partnered tomorrow," Dick said. There was irony in his voice.

"No, you won't. You stay in Gang Crimes, but in Gang Crimes North. The commander there's a friend of mine, he'll find something for you to do solo."

"I can't work solo out of this unit?"

"You could, but there's a good chance you'll get a call, head out on it and find a bullet waiting for you. O'Brian is pretty well liked around here."

Blandane kept quiet, watching the man, Simmons returning the stare, sizing him up. Simmons shook his head.

"Too much pride, Blandane. You got too much pride. You did a good thing tonight, or I'd still be chewing your ass out, you come in here and stare at me like I'm the enemy. See what you're doing, acting like that? The same thing O'Brian does every time he looks at a black face and sees an opponent instead of a man."

"I thought you were going to can me."

"See what I said? You been watching too much TV, seeing too many movies. Ranking officers have more to do in this department than to stand around shouting at street cops, taking their guns and badges. What you think this is, *Baretta*? This is real life, Blandane, and you better figure on showing us respect if you're running around demanding it for yourself." He paused, looked hard at Dick to see that he'd made his point, then said, "Now get the hell out of my office, go take care of your cockatoo or whatever the hell that bird was."

"Bird?"

"The white fucking bird, whatever it was, didn't you ever watch *Baretta*, for Christ's sake?"

There had been frustrations in Blandane's career. Once, with tac, he'd been on a drug bust and they'd beaten the steel door down and been confronted with concertina wire, sharp as razor blades, loops of the stuff there in the doorframe making entry impossible. The pusher had walked by casually, waggled his fingers at them and said, "How's it going, there, officers?" and proceeded into the toilet with a paper bag, managing to flush all his dope away before anyone could figure out how the hell to break down the barrier.

And there'd been some high points along the way. He'd been on another drug bust where the dealer had stashed balloons up his backside, had volunteered that information to the officers, so they'd had the right to make him drop his drawers and strip search him at the station, wondering how to get him to pass the balloons. The dealer had decided to cooperate no further, after his initial terror at the thought of arrest he was now telling them that he had lied, that there was nothing up there, that he was constipated and if they wanted to shove their fingers up there they could go ahead, if that was the way they got their kicks. Dick had had a brainstorm and had left the room, had come back unraveling a wire coat hanger, whistling, had told the dealer to bend over. Five minutes later, the dealer passed the cocaine naturally, no problem.

Frustration and elevation, the two strongest emotions in his career.

Dick feeling the latter now as he left the sergeant's office, thinking about what the man had said. The sergeant had been right, he couldn't see all officers as the enemy, had to give them all a chance, one at a time, not lumping them into stereotypes or labeling them. There were guys like O'Brian around, sure, the force was full of them. But there were also guys like Simmons.

And like himself. He couldn't forget that. There were men like himself and that was a pretty good thing to think about. Maybe he could find one tomorrow, over at Gang Crimes North, if someone didn't lay him out with some friendly fire, first.

He walked through the squadroom, the men and

women in there staring at him, whispering amongst themselves, Dick feeling a thread of fear worm through him because he knew what they were saying. They'd classified him as one of the enemy now, he was as much the enemy as the criminals out there on the street. Which was all right with him. Screw them. He wasn't about to back up the lies of some brutal son of a bitch like O'Brian, would resign from the force, first. And if they were the type of officers who would do a thing like that, he didn't want anything to do with them. He felt sure, passing them by without a glance, that Simmons would feel the same way.

As he stepped out of the squadroom and into the hallway a dark figure approached him from behind and he half-turned, frightened, his hand reaching for his weapon.

It was Marcus, small and embarrassed. Dick relaxed, asked him how he was doing. Marcus was self-conscious, nervous. He shrugged.

"Jerrina's gonna be okay, they say over to the hospital. She didn't get rapeded. She fought them and they ran away as soon as they heard the sirens coming. She beated up pretty good, but she heal."

"So you did right, by taking off. I knew you were worried about that." The boy stood there, there wasn't much more to say.

"You look through the photos?" he asked, and the boy nodded.

"Didn't see nobody I could recognize."

Dick knew right away that he was lying. He'd probably seen the thieves, recognized their mug shots, and knew the gang they were with, what they'd do to him if he signed a complaint against them or tried to testify against them in a court of law. He couldn't blame the boy, he had to live here.

"Well, good luck to you, Marcus."

"Officer?" Blandane had been turning to leave and now he spun back on his heel, his eyebrows raised in question.

"Why he do that to me? How come he stuck that pistol up in my face?"

Dick didn't hesitate. He said, "Because he is an asshole," and Marcus seemed to understand that, nodded his head and turned and walked away.

Chapter 24

Femal had hung up and sighed, not looking forward to this, wondering if there was some way she could avoid a confrontation with him, at least until morning. One thing was for sure, she wouldn't be taking any backtalk from the man. If he wanted to use the spare bedroom that was fine with her. He'd be safe for the night, and she'd at least know where he'd be . . .

Where he'd be? What the hell did it matter where this damn man was? She sat in her rocking chair, looking down at the sidewalk, at the concrete that now looked black under the soft incandescence of the cadmium light, wondering about that.

Was it important to her where he was, who he was with? She fought with the idea of jealousy, it wasn't her way. Sure, she'd been mad at him, he'd been calling all night from some bar instead of coming over and waiting for her here at the house, here to support her after her rough day. Here so the two of them could sit down and put their heads together, figure out how in the hell Darrin had learned about their relationship. He hadn't been there, though, because he'd been out boozing it up.

But could she blame him for that? Mama had made it clear that morning that he wasn't one of her favorite people. And he *had* been gone a long time. Was there anything wrong with his having a few drinks with his friends? She chortled, remembering him singing to her over the phone, acting like some Italian crooner. An hour ago it had infuriated her, now she could see it as cute.

God, if only she could make up her mind about him!

Femal looked out at the street, up one way then down the other, wondering if he was really taking a cab or if someone would be dropping him off or if he'd be taking a bus, as he had last night. Maybe he was walking. She hoped not, it was a cold night and he'd been drinking. A middle-aged man who'd gone without exercise for over two years would be courting some serious health problems out walking around drunk on a night like this. She gave a short laugh. Robert's lack of exercise hadn't done him any harm last night, over there on the bed. Of course, Femal had done without any exercise to that particular muscle group for as long as he had, and she'd somehow gotten by.

What was different out there? That car at the curb down the street, that's what. Was someone waiting for someone else to come out of one of the houses? Femal was curious; it was late and this was a good neighborhood, well-to-do working people who didn't sit out in their cars and neck late on Tuesday nights, inside beat-up old cars. She walked to the closet and rummaged around, found some old 20x50 binoculars and walked back to the window, held them to her eyes, then drew in her breath quickly.

What the hell were *they* doing here? She recognized them right away, Darrin's night driver, Mickey, and that hillbilly wildman nephew of his, Merle Como. Sitting in the car talking, casually. Did Darrin think she needed bodyguards for some reason? Did he think that the don's enemies were out to get Femal? She shivered, then got herself under control. That wasn't logical. She had no enemies, nobody was aware of the extent of her knowledge of the operation, not even Darrin. Especially not Darrin. And old Sal had always liked her. So what were these gorillas doing out there in the middle of the night?

She found out in a second as she saw Mickey stiffen, say something to Merle then look back out his window. Femal turned her glasses to the street, saw Robert there at the corner swaying slightly as he stared up at the street sign, confused. She watched as he nodded his head, started walking down the street—heading the wrong way! She cheered him on silently—keep going, keep heading down the wrong street!—as she dropped the glasses to the bed and grabbed for the phone, dialed 911 as fast as her fingers would fly, frantically telling the man who answered that there were two men attacking another man down the street from her building, gave him the cross streets instead of her address and told him to hurry it up, they were killing him.

It was a lie, they hadn't touched Robert as far as she knew, but she somehow knew that they were planning to, that he was the reason they were out there. Knew, too, that the cops would head out there faster if they thought they'd catch a murder in progress, maybe get their faces in the paper or on the news.

She dropped the phone and grabbed the glasses, went to the window and looked at the car, but it was empty. She turned the glasses to the street, but couldn't see any of the men there.

"Come on," Femal said, suddenly and desperately back in love with Robert again. "Come *on*, goddamnit," she whispered to the cops, then dropped the glasses to the floor and began to tear at the window lock, trying to get it to open.

• • •

Merle had been in a Miami Beach pet store with Moonbeam once and had stopped to admire a sleeping African parrot, surprised at two things. First, that the parrot was able to sleep at all, at its ability to shut out all the dickheads standing around its cage trying to get it to repeat the cuss words they were whispering at it, and second that it had the ability to turn its head on its little parrot shoulders, all the way around, its bird chin down there on its back, tiny eyes closed. He'd asked Moonbeam how in the fuck the parrot was able to do that, and she didn't know, Moonbeam all gaga over the cuteness of all the animals, finding something lovable even in the snakes, incensed because they were caged when she believed they should all be let out, to run wild in their natural environment. She didn't pay much attention to his question, but a woman standing next to him did.

"Their necks are on a kind of swivel," the woman told him. "Sort of like being double-jointed." Merle had looked at her, wondering if she was setting him up, making fun of him. The woman said, "Don't you wish you could do that?" and he told her that he did, because then he could give himself a blow job.

He thought of that parrot now, because Millard reminded him of it, although old Catfeet wasn't even thinking about sleeping, the man walking fast down the street, half-running now that he'd spotted them.

"Come on, Catfeet," Mickey hollered, whining, the two of them a half-block behind Millard and closing fast, "don't make us run after you, it'll only be harder on you." Mickey was puffing and Merle told him to shut the hell up, he liked the chase.

Millard would go a few paces then swivel his head around, looking over his shoulder, the way the parrot might have in Africa, with a monkey chasing it through the trees. Merle smiled at him, waved at him to encourage him.

"Goddamnit," Mickey said, "I ain't got time to be running around like this," Mickey huffing and puffing. Out of shape.

Millard broke into what he must have figured to be a full-out run, but what was more of a fast stagger. They caught up to him when he stumbled over a hydrant and Merle pushed Mickey aside, the guy resenting it because he'd gotten to Millard first but fuck him, what was he going to do?

Merle grinned at Millard, through the sour smell of Scotch on the man's breath, and something else there to be smelled, the stench of fear. Coward. Merle balled his hand into a fist and was about to deliver the first of many Punches when the ear-piercing scream broke the neighborhood quiet, so loud and shrill that lights began coming on in the houses and apartments before he could even turn his head to see where it was coming from. Merle said Shit and pushed Millard up against the wall, gave him a short one in the gut to keep him from running away, then turned and looked up the street.

The jig bitch was leaning out her window, had to be a full block away, screaming louder than a police siren. Merle turned back to Millard, angry. He'd been looking forward to this and now it was going to have to be shortened because of some spade broad who didn't know the rules.

Millard was breathing in gasps, bent over, his hands around his middle. Mickey grabbed Merle's arm and was pulling at it, saying something, Merle could barely hear him through his laser-like concentration, his sudden hatred of the man in front of him, seeing only Millard.

"Go get the car, Mickey," Merle said and Mickey asked him which one. Merle turned to him. "You got keys for *my* car, dickweed?" Then turned back to Millard, who had straightened up, was fighting to put his face next to Merle's. He heard Mickey running down the street away from them. Good. This guy had something to say? Merle would hear his confession, then deliver a couple of good ones before Mickey turned up in the getaway car.

"What's that, buddy?" he said, leaning in to Millard, his hand already a fist, wanting the guy to just say one word, think they were friends before Merle laid him out.

Millard was breathing in short gasps, was clutching Merle, his mouth wide open, almost as if he was carefully aiming his next words toward Merle's ear. Merle, curious, leaned in further, and it was then that Millard let the vomit go, all over Merle's face.

Catfeet had felt it coming as soon as he'd started running, all the drinking he'd done on an empty stomach, then the sudden unexpected exercise as he ran away from the two goons he knew were up to no good. What did they want from him? He didn't know, and wasn't about to stick around and find out. He tried to run, dizzy now, feeling his stomach rolling over and then he was falling over a fire hydrant, then getting shoved up against the wall before the young one—what was his name—Como, hit him in the belly.

It took all of his concentration to wait, to aim it at this bastard. If he couldn't fight him he could at least insult him.

He let it go and Merle screamed as the stuff hit his face, shrieked louder than the voice down the street, Femal he thought it was, wailing and attracting attention, God bless her. Feet staggered back, sickened by the sight of what he'd done, weaving back without conscious thought but wanting to get away from Como before he got himself together and decided to retaliate.

Which wasn't long in coming. Como stopped screaming and bent over the sidewalk, bent far over, at a ninety-degree angle, wiped the stuff out of his eyes with his forearms, his fingers splayed wide, then stood, a mix of terror and loathing and disgust on his face, disbelieving eyes frantically searching for Feet. Focused on him and moved in, bellowing in rage.

Feet let him come, glad that the man was enraged; it

would give him a slight chance. He stood there swaying, waiting as Como advanced, stepped back as the man was nearly to him then kicked out, hard, the leather heel of his shoe connecting with Como's shin, the kick driving Feet off balance, off his feet into the gutter.

Where Como already was, covered with puke, holding his leg just below the knee, screaming again.

Feet sat up, pushed himself back with his hands, sliding on his backside, away from the man.

It didn't do him a lot of good.

Como spotted him, let go of his leg and roared, tried to stand but his leg wouldn't support him so he began to crawl toward Feet, looking in need of an exorcism, his face as ugly and angry as any Feet had encountered.

Feet felt terror mixed with elation—he'd stopped the man in his tracks once and might be able to do it again. He got his back against the curb and waited, feeling the urge to throw up again, fighting it because this guy wasn't going to give him another chance to get that close. He drew his knees back into his chest and struck out with his feet and kicked as headlights blinded him, felt the heels of his shoes connect with Como's face as the headlights got closer, remembering that this bastard had a partner. Feet closed his eyes and waited for the bumper to crush his face, happy because he had at least gone out fighting.

Chapter
25

But it hadn't been Mickey, it had been the cops. Rolling in with their sirens off, the neighborhood too classy for such action. On the South Side the cops wouldn't think twice about waking up the entire block, but out here the rules were different, the game played by an entirely different edict.

They got out of the car and took one look then stepped back, not wanting to touch either man—with the chance that the AIDS virus might be floating around in all that vomit and blood—one cop talking to them from a distance, once they were sure that there was no longer a fight in progress or any weapons being flaunted. One officer spoke to them while the other stood back with his hand on his holster, just in case.

"This guy was getting mugged," Merle said, jutting his chin over at Catfeet, who stared at him for a moment then nodded in assent. "I come to help him and Je-zus, they turned on me." The cop told them that the dispatcher had reported about the same thing, two men beating the shit

out of one, except that it hadn't mentioned a savior, the
woman who'd called in had said nothing about the good
Samaritan over there doing all the talking. Told them it
sure looked as if they'd been going at it pretty good when
they'd rolled up in the black and white.

"Well, hell," Merle said, exasperated, "I musta come
on the scene *after* the call came in." He disregarded the
cop's last statement, asked if he could go home now, he
had puke all over him that he wanted to wash off and was
this the way the cops acted up North, giving a kindly
passerby a hard time while the fucking muggers escaped
on foot? "You hurry, you might still catch them running
around the streets, there ain't too many niggers in Fila
caps strolling around this neighborhood this time of night
is there?" Then caught himself, the cop over on the side
with his hand on his pistol was black. A black cop who
squinted as Merle spoke, then spoke himself for the first
time.

"Phone call didn't say anything about race, did it?"
Then looked at Merle, said, "You look awful familiar,
boy."

"Don't know why, just come in on a airplane this afternoon from Palm Beach, eff-ell-ay."

"Got many niggers down that way?" the black cop
asked.

"Just the ones, work for us," Merle said, and the white
cop smirked.

Feet sat back and watched the interplay, Como acting the
outraged citizen who'd gotten involved and now regretted
it, maybe even believing the story he was laying out.
Standing there touching his face gently now and again,
looking in wonder at the blood on his hands.

Feet was sitting on the curb, his elbows on his knees,
breathing heavily while Como stood and talked to the
coppers, and it scared him. Even worse than he'd been
when he'd been fighting this psycho.

Como would look over at him as he spoke and there
would be a benevolent expression on his face, none of the
smoldering anger that should be there when one man
looked at another man who, a few minutes ago, had puked
on him and then kicked him in the knee, then in the face
both times hard. The first cop spoke to him, and he
stopped staring at Como, looked over at the officer.

"You hurt at all?" the cop asked. "Need to get checked
at the hospital? You look all right."

"I'm fine," Catfeet said, nodding his head. "This guy
took all the grief when he came up to help me."

"So it happened the way he ran it down?" The black
cop's tone made it clear that he did not believe either one
of them.

"Exactly that way," Feet said, struggling to his feet,
then he said, "Can I leave? I don't want to file any report,
the muggers are gone, there's no way you're gonna
catch them, and all I want to do is get home, take a
shower and get into bed."

"You don't want to file a report? You're the victim
here, mister, are you sure?"

Catfeet began to slowly move down the sidewalk, toward where Femal lived. If she really did live down that
side of the street. He'd been sure he'd been going in the
right direction, but he'd been drunk and he must have
been screwed up, because the screaming had been coming from behind him, not in front of him, and it had to
have been Femal screaming. At least he hoped so. He
didn't want the cops to leave him alone on the street with
this crazy man, that was for sure. He was no longer drunk
nor feeling especially brave at the moment.

"I just live down the street here," Feet said.

"What's your address?"

Como said, "Fourteen-eleven, isn't that what you told
me, buddy?" and Feet said, "Yeah."

The cops were looking at each other, puzzled. "I gotta
go," Feet said, and Como walked right up to him, took his

hand, began to pump it, then, with his back to the officers, winked at Catfeet and said, "Good thing I come along when I did, eh, buddy? You mighta got hurt otherwise." Then stood back and waited, Jesus, enjoying this, setting Feet up.

Catfeet said, "Thanks a lot, pal," not about to call him mister or sir. He'd go to jail, first.

The first cop said, "Well, we got a choice here, way I see it. Either run them in all bloody and full of puke, put them in the car, and be at the station all fucking night, writing paper, or let it end here and now, what do you think?"

Feet was walking backwards, ready to try to escape, watching Como with his full attention and the cops out of the corner of his eye, the man standing there grinning at him, blood dripping down his face from where Feet had kicked him, puke on his shirt, sticking his tongue out, waggling it at him as if this was all some kind of joke, somehow funny.

The black cop said, "Ah, fuck it, they ain't worth it. Probably a couple of queers had a fight," and Como heard it, caught it and tossed it at Feet through a blown, silent kiss, nodding his head at him as Feet turned and hurried down the block.

Behind him he heard Como thank the officers for their trouble, telling them that it sure was good to know that the Chicago po-lice were on their toes, especially after all the stories he'd heard about them down home, shit. Heard them talking back to him, asking him questions, and Feet moved as fast as he could, wanting to be safe with Femal before the cops got back into their squad and rolled away from the madman. The killer clown.

He sat in her living room, considering the fact that it had only been a couple of minutes ago that he'd been thinking that in here, he would be safe. He sure wasn't feeling very safe at the moment.

Femal was ignoring him now, holding Elaine in her arms, shushing the child as she rocked her back to sleep. Humming. When he'd first come in she'd been singing a song to the still-sobbing child in a hoarse voice, "Rock-a-bye Baby" with Femal's own poison lyrics, directed at Feet.

> "You rotten-bastard,
> How dare-you-do,
> This goddamn-thing,
> To-your-child-and-me."

He'd listened to her singing, her voice never rising, Femal appearing calm, her tone steady and soft as the kid rocked and slowly closed its eyes. His hands were shaking, there was vomit on his pantleg and shirt, covering his topcoat. His bloody shoes were by the door. He had the urge to sing back, something about how you weren't supposed to curse in front of the kid or she'd pick it up, be calling everyone assholes before she was two years old.

The baby reached up and patted Femal's face, gently, absently, then her little hand dropped like a stone onto her chest and he suddenly understood Femal's anger.

They knew where she lived, knew about the kid.

He'd been sitting gingerly on the edge of the couch, not wanting to soil the dark, silk-like material. He rose, walked to the first floor picture window and peered out. Nothing, there was no one out there waiting. He buttoned his coat and walked to the door, Femal rising, bouncing the kid in her arms, glaring at him.

> "Don't you da-are,
> Leave us a-lone."

Femal began to walk toward the stairs, to put the baby back in her crib, then she probably planned to come back down here and give him hell. He carefully took off his topcoat, turned it inside out so as not to get any of the mess from it on the carpet, and walked on stockinged feet toward the kitchen, looking for the door that would lead him to the basement.

Chapter 26

Femal put her precious child down on her stomach in the crib and hummed to her, patting her back, until she was sure Elaine would not awaken, then backed toward the door, still humming, watching the crib. She walked out, closed the door and tore down the hall then stormed down the steps, searching for him, heard a noise downstairs and was glad. In the basement, she could say whatever she wanted, as loud as she wanted, and she would not have to worry about her voice waking Elaine again.

He was over by the washing machine, in his underwear, staring at the label inside his suit, trying to figure out if he'd wreck it by washing it. Femal came down the stairs and spotted him, crossed her arms and composed herself. She would not let him win. She'd been undignified enough for one night.

"My child woke up in fear for the first time in her entire life, tonight."

Feet looked at her, a little surprised. "Can I just wash this on cold? Will it wreck the fabric?"

"Did you hear what I said to you, Millard?"

"Yeah, I heard you, and what do you want me to say? You want me to take the weight for a couple of guys work for your boss? For what they did? Bullshit. I got enough problems here without worrying about your sensitivities." He tossed the clothes into the washer, topcoat and all, poured in some liquid detergent and shut the lid, pulled the knob to start the machine. "Probably wreck the fucking suit."

"That's all you're worried about, your goddamn *suit*? Your *daughter* was terrorized here a few minutes ago!"

"Because her mother was screaming her ass off out the window." He seemed calm now, at ease. Had probably been through more violent encounters than this when he'd been doing time at the County. Well, she had news for him. Her home was no jailhouse.

He said, "I didn't ask for you to do it, you know," and took the wind out of her sails, because he was right. She'd done it of her own volition, no one had prompted her. See if she'd do it again, though. Then knew that she would. The two of them, they were entirely different breeds. If he'd seen it he would have done one of two things; would have run out in the street to protect whomever it was, or would have ignored it, depending on how he was feeling at the moment, or maybe on who it was taking the beating.

She felt the tension drain out of her because standing before her was a man who lived by his own set of conditions, under circumstances he put himself into without even knowing it.

Would he ever understand? She doubted it. Femal stood looking at him with her arms crossed, relaxing with her mind made up. She'd been right the first time. She'd be better off without this man in her life.

He was standing there shivering in a dago tee-shirt and jockey pants, black silk socks on his feet, standing on the concrete, not smiling but not frowning, either, running his hands over the gooseflesh on his arms. It was just part of the game to him, something that happened in his line of work.

If she pointed the fact out to him that he'd turned her home into a war zone he would tell her that he had called, that she had invited him over, would turn it around so she'd have to take some of the blame. She knew this and the knowledge stopped her from speaking her mind. It was no longer a matter of the heart, it was a matter of survival now.

How could she have been so wrong?

"Do you think Darrin sent them?"

"Who, the boss that you can handle, no problem? Would he do a thing like this?" He looked around the room. "You got a robe might fit me?" He stared at her, dropped his arms. "Let me tell you one last time. If there was a profit in it, Favore'd come into this house, shoot you, and eat that baby upstairs without a second thought. Believe me, don't believe me, it's up to you."

She had a vision of that, of Darrin killing her and Elaine. She remembered him standing in his office doorway that afternoon, smiling at her, his shirtsleeves rolled up twice. Grinning at her in a way that had seemed buffoonish then as he kidded her about the envelope but which seemed frightening now. He'd worn the look of the predator about to strike, wearing the smile she'd seen on lions on PBS as they were about to pounce on hyenas. The smile of the great white shark as it attacked the fishing boat. She thought about that and couldn't help herself, she had to tell this man what she thought because before he came home, everything had been in order, everything had been going fine. Now she was jumping on her own people at meetings, was seeing her boss as a killer.

She said, "You rotten bastard, how could you bring this on me?"

And he told her, "You brought it on yourself, the day you decided to go out with me. Three, four years ago. You knew up front how Favore felt about me. You made your decisions. Now you got to live with them."

Did he really believe that? Did he think that she had given it thought, weighed it and considered it and had chosen him knowing something like this could eventually happen? Good Lord, how could she have ever thought that she'd been in love with a man like this?

"I thought at first that they were here to protect me."

"They were sent here to hurt me. Favore wanted to send me a message. The money I gave him wasn't enough, Femal, he wants millions and he's making that clear."

"And he knows about us, right?"

He just looked at her.

"If he knows about us, then he must know that Elaine's your daughter, isn't that so?"

"I wouldn't doubt it."

"So, if he wants money from you, and beating you up doesn't do the trick, what do you think his next move will be?"

Robert Millard looked at her a minute, until he got it, then he said, "Jesus Christ, Femal."

"What'd you just say he'd do if he saw a profit for himself, Robert?" Her voice was calm, her tone even, her demeanor relaxed, but when she was certain that Robert believed her boss capable of harming Elaine, she went all cold and dead inside.

"We've got to stop him, Robert." Her throat hurt when she spoke, it was sore, tender inside. She wondered if she'd ripped something in there, if she'd done any permanent damage when she'd been screaming, trying to save the life of this man before her who hadn't even thanked her, who'd turned it all around and made it look as if this was all her fault. She kept the anger out of her voice, managed to speak calmly and coolly, not giving him any sense as to the extent of her resentment, her anger. She said, "We have to find a way to get him off you. Before he hurts my baby."

"Yeah," Robert said, looking straight at her. "You got any bright ideas?"

Merle entered his apartment and slammed the door, forgetting all about the little mex who suddenly started whimpering and whining, thinking the cops had come to get him. Merle flipped on a light, let the mex see that it was him and then shut the light off so Silva could go back to sleep on the couch. He hurried into his bedroom and grabbed the phone book off the nightstand. He found Mickey's number, angrily punched the lighted digits on the phone, sat there fuming as the phone buzzed in his ear.

"Merle, that you?" Mickey whispering, probably not wanting to wake his wife—or more likely, his boyfriend—lying beside him in the bed in their nice safe house.

"You're fucking right it's me," Merle said. "Where the hell did you run off to?"

"Shit, the cops was there, what was I s'posed to do? What could I do, Merle?"

"No sense in all of us maybe getting in trouble, is that what you were thinking?"

"One of us had to stand by with the bond money, right, Merle?" That Mickey, always thinking. Mickey said, "Wait a minute," and Merle heard the clatter of the phone as he laid it down on something, probably the nightstand, then there was silence for a minute until Mickey said, "Yeah, Merle," no longer whispering. Maybe he'd gone into the kitchen or somewhere, where he could act like a man without worrying about pissing off his old lady.

"You tell my uncle about this?"

"Not a word, I wanted to see how you wanted to play it." Mickey paused, searching for words. "I mean, we was sent out there to kick some ass and the guy, he was working you over pretty good when the cops came."

Was he laughing at him, making fun of him? Kee-rist,

this guy would have to go before he told anyone else about this.

"Didn't say a word to Darrin, that what you're saying?"

"Ain't talked to him, Merle. You know how it is, he tells you to do something then he forgets about it; who's stupid enough to not do what he tells them to?"

"You better keep your mouth shut about this, Mickey. Any of the boys find out about this and you know it'll get back to Darrin, and you know what he does to guys who fuck things up he tells them to do?"

"Shit, I take care of that business for him, you kidding me? My lips are sealed." Was there another laugh in his voice? Oh, Mickey, you bastard, pounding the nails in your own casket and not even smart enough to figure out why was it getting dark all around you.

"He should ask, tell him we took care of it."

"Merle, wait! What happened with the cops?" Mickey spoke quickly, wanting to get the question in before Merle hung up.

Merle said, "You wanted to know, you shoulda hung around. All you got to know is that *I* took care of the job we was sent out to do, by myself," then slammed the phone down hard. Give the man something to think about before he shot off his big trap.

He took a shower, put all the clothes he was wearing right down to the shoes into a large plastic garbage bag, closed it tight with the little plastic-coated wire the bag people gave away, twenty to the box. He put the bag inside his garbage can in the kitchen, listening to the little mex Silva pretending to be asleep and knowing that the man was wide awake, wanting desperately to know what the phone conversation had been all about, why Merle was covered with puke, with blood . . .

He'd have to give that some thought before he went to bed, the best way to use the boy's anxiety. Find a way to work it so that it looked as if whatever Merle had been talking about concerned him, his problem, a way to get him out of it. He needed the boy grateful for a while, at least until he killed that son of a bitch Millard and that big-mouth run-away no balls Mickey. Maybe even his uncle, too, if he found out about Merle's shame.

The cops weren't a problem, he felt no animosity toward them, they were doing what cops got paid to do; fucking with people, and besides, he'd gone mouthy on them. He'd given them a hard time and hurt the nigger's racial pride. Up here, that was a pretty big deal these days. What had he expected of them? Millard had snuck away and they'd gotten a little tough with him, demanded to see some ID, the usual shit that cops did when they were pissed off but knew that eyes may well be watching from behind windowshades. If not for that, Merle knew, things would have been a lot different. He'd have taken a serious ass-kicking.

The cops had checked his Rolex—thank God there was nothing on there but a bunch of numbers they couldn't trace to anybody—went through his wallet piece by piece, then cut him loose, no big deal. You give the cops a hard time and that's what happened. No problem, it was a part of doing business.

But Millard, he'd done that puking shit on purpose, and would have to die for it. Mickey too, for making fun of him.

Merle thought about it, lying in bed with his hands cupped behind his head, staring thoughtfully up at the cracked plaster ceiling.

Those two, at least, the prowler and Mickey, they'd have to die. And maybe the jig bitch, for calling the cops, making a scene about it and waking up the whole neighborhood. Hell, that made what happened afterward all her goddamn fault.

Why was he blaming her? Femal wondered. She was lying awake, Robert passed out next to her, showered, his teeth brushed, but his breath still giving off a faint smell of sourness, of stale whiskey and vomit. Femal was sitting up against the hand-carved wooden headboard that went all the way up to the ceiling. Last night she'd gripped the sides of this same damn headboard and moaned her pleasure to high heaven; tonight it was her wailing wall, sharing her grief.

Millard sure wasn't, lying there snoring.

He was in his underwear, she had made him take it off and had washed it out in the basement sink while he took a hot shower, the underwear dry and ironed before he came out of the bathroom. She'd taken care of his suit, too. Good thing it had been a cheap one, it took the wash without a whole lot of damage and when she ironed it it came out pretty much like new, or as new as it had looked when he'd worn it out of the gates of the County Jail. It was a little tight on him, these days, she'd noticed. The suit and his shirt were hanging in her closet, the shoes wiped down and polished quickly with the liquid stuff, under the bed with his still-damp socks rolled up inside.

She'd performed the tasks because she wanted him on her side, at least for a little while. No longer seeing him as a man she loved or one she even cared a whole lot about. It wasn't about insecurity anymore; no more boy-girl bullshit as it had been earlier. Now, it was a matter of survival. When he'd been talking downstairs, showing her sides of him she hadn't ever known existed, she'd gone all cold inside, looked at him and saw nothing, feeling only revulsion. He'd walked her into this trap, jeopardized not only her job, which she could live without, but maybe even her life and worse, Elaine's. Did it without guilt, with no real understanding of the word. Standing down there playing with his clothes and talking about "weight" as if he had an intimate connection with the word. As far as she was now concerned, he was nothing. Someone to use to get what she wanted, which she was loathe to do.

She sighed, hunkered down and pulled the comforter up around her neck, exhausted but too frightened to sleep. How could he roll over and just pass out like that?

What was wrong with this person? Didn't he feel fear, was he so deranged that he could blame her for his troubles, so out of touch with reality that he wasn't even aware that they were all in danger?

Or was that what he enjoyed, the danger part of the whole thing? Some men lived for it, she knew. Weren't happy unless they were on the edge, living in danger and loving it, never knowing that their self-destructive urges were insane or even wrong. Thinking they would live forever, somehow charmed.

How could she have been so wrong about him?

She thought this and shivered, because if she could be that wrong about him, what made her think that she was right about Darrin Favore? Was he on to her every move, watching her all the time and giving her just enough rope before he stepped into things, wrapped the damn rope around her neck and tossed her out his South Michigan Avenue window?

Femal shivered again, the down comforter scant shelter from the numbing coldness that came from her soul. "Lord," she whispered, her eyes squeezed shut the way she used to do it when she was a little girl, "deliver me from these tricknacious white devils . . ." Then decided to hedge her bets with a being she hadn't turned to in a while. "For the baby's sake if not my own . . . ?"

She drifted off, relaxed, sleepy darkness coming, engulfing her. Awoke with a start when she heard her front door slam and she sat up in bed, terrified.

There was sunlight streaming in from her window, approaching the edge of the bed with stealth. She was alone. The clock on the nightstand said that it was 7 A.M.

"Femal? Where you at, girl?" Her mama's voice called up to her from the bottom of the stairs and she realized that she'd overslept, then thought about Elaine.

Ran into her room and her baby was lying there giggling, staring up at the mobile dangling from the ceiling, slapping a hand at it and kicking her feet with glee as the thing spun on its wire. Femal brightened.

"How's my girl this morning?" she said, tickling the baby's belly and ripping the fasteners off her diaper.

"Mah," Elaine said.

From the doorway, Mama said, "You oversleep? Good job like you got and you oversleep in the middle of the week? Get a move on girl, you ain't even showered yet." Mama moved in to take care of the baby and Femal let her, thinking of something.

She didn't smell coffee, hadn't heard any banging around, it would have got her up, she was a light sleeper.

So where the hell was Robert?

She put him out of her mind, knowing he wasn't in the house or Mama would have said something, insulted him in some way when she'd entered the room.

What could she do? No matter what happened, she had a job to do, and not much sleep going for her. She couldn't waste time worrying about him, she had to get ready because after what had happened last night, what she'd figured out about her boss's character, she'd need all her wits about her when she went into work that morning.

Chapter 27

As soon as she entered her office Femal learned that she'd need only most of her wits after all, because the boss had left a message for her on the machine; he'd be going straight to the wake from his house and had some business to conduct later, he'd call in and tell her what time he'd pick her up for the funeral tomorrow.

Just like that. Was he afraid to face her, ashamed after what he'd done last night? That couldn't be it, not if he was the type of man she now believed him to be. The man Robert said he was.

All right, so she had a reprieve. There was plenty she could do here today with the man gone, not around to throw any dictation at her. There was a lot of work she had to catch up on.

Was halfway through it when the delivery man brought her the roses at eleven, Femal thanking him, looking at them quizzically. She opened the card and saw Darrin's chickenscratch printing, all capitals, the note telling her that the flowers were for the best executive secretary in the city of Chicago.

Was he scary or what? She found a vase, put water in it then stuffed the flowers in there because she knew him, the way he acted. He'd be in later today and would know something was wrong if the flowers weren't on her desk, prominently displayed. She didn't want him to know she knew about him, the sort of person he truly was. She'd let him take the first shot, make him show his hand and hope that it would be something weak, not a vital blow. Something, as Millard would say, lightweight.

Femal turned her attention from the flowers and went back to her computer terminal, had to reenter the thing and call forth the document she'd been working on because she'd exited the program the second she'd heard the knock on the door. Got back to where she'd been and, with the smell of fresh roses filling the air around her, began to type on the keyboard with strong, determined strokes.

Charlie decided that he would come back to the house at lunchtime, would pack his things and get the hell out, let her tell the kid anything she damn well pleased. He'd spent the last half hour trying to get through to the kid and it looked as if he was making it, then Lina had to come in, started in on him all over again. She was starting to get on his nerves with this constant carping, the nagging and bitching, and he had to figure that there was something wrong with him if a woman of Lina's emotional depth could make him angry. Or maybe it was just that she was a pro at it, had so much damn experience.

It had begun the night before, after they'd gotten home, Lina incensed because he hadn't thrown himself at Favore, kicked his ass for insulting her. She didn't understand two simple things: It was really only the man's way of saving face, and it had been she who had started the final hand, shooting off her big mouth and insulting Favore's pride, his ego. Could she expect a man like Favore to let that pass, to forget about it? Especially when you took into account the fact that technically, she had no business being there in the first place, a woman in the Men's Grille. She wanted to act like one of them and Favore had accommodated her, given her her wish, treated her the way he would any man who'd stepped into his path and made a stupid remark.

Could she understand any of this? Not one word of it, which was why he didn't bother saying any of it aloud. She wasn't showing him the same respect, though, that was for sure.

Carrying it over from last night when she'd called him a coward, a wimp, a pussy who didn't have the backbone to defend her. Told him that her father damn sure would have, calling him "Doddy," or "Dod," as if she'd gone to Vassar instead of the University of Chicago. He'd told her that he had thirty-some grand in his pockets, the money spilling out of his suit jacket, his pants, the pockets of his coat. Taken from Favore and the guy had to give something back, some parting shot.

He'd told Lina this but he'd known better, Charlie knowing what had really happened and didn't want to even try and tell her the truth, which was that Charlie, too, had insulted Favore in front of everybody, refusing the man's offer of a drink, telling him that Charlie didn't consider him good enough to drink with. Favore had responded with the jailhouse manners of a man who'd never been behind stone walls, saying what he'd thought a man inside would say, not knowing that such words, behind state steel, would get his ass cut in two, no matter *how* many bodyguards he had. But Charlie knew it, knew that it was just profiling, the man blowing wind. It hadn't offended him, so why had it offended her? If she hadn't been in there, Favore wouldn't have even bothered to mention her name, it was just his way of trying to get Charlie to jump, so his gorilla could do some damage. Not a game that Charlie was willing to play.

She hadn't understood his explanation last night, had

kept at him until he figured that it was his turn to hit the third bedroom, had gone and locked himself in there and found some peace, a quiet place to count his money and wonder at the sight of it; he'd never seen that much cash at one time before in his entire life, had gone to prison for five long years over far less. Still, he'd heard her voice through the walls, heard, too, Lance, crying on the other side of the bedroom.

Things didn't seem to have gotten any better this morning, either.

Lance was sitting at the kitchen table, his head stuck down in a bowl of cereal, shoveling it in his mouth mechanically, trying to ignore his mother's sudden whining, the two of them only noticing that she'd entered the room when she started bitching. The second she did, though, Lance dove into that bowl. Intimidated, more than likely. Charlie could understand it.

She came into the kitchen and said, "Mr. big shot," directed it at Charlie, spitefully, spitting it out as she poured herself some of the coffee he'd put on earlier. He'd been talking to the boy, throwing hints his way, letting him know that he might not be around much longer without coming right out and saying it, and Lance had seemed hurt, confused but also appreciative, Charlie wasn't talking down to him the way his mother did, the way his father most likely did on the weekends that Lance spent with him.

"Mr. asshole, is more like it," Lina said.

"Lina . . ." He was speaking to her but looking at Lance, at the top of the boy's head.

"Yeah, what. He's not your kid, what interest you have in him? Huh?" She smiled. "Maybe that's where the problem is, huh, Charlie? Think your parole officer would like to hear about that, your fondness for young boys?" She knew the ways to hurt him, paid attention to his schedule, too. Knew that this was the third Wednesday of the month and he always reported on that day. She'd do it, too, tell The Man that he was a pedophile, if she knew how to contact his PO—and that wouldn't be a hard thing for her to find out—he wouldn't put it past her. If she called him the PO would raise the price of Charlie's freedom accordingly. It was the type of man he was, always looking for a reason to raise the ante.

Lance was looking at him now, eyes wide. He didn't know about Charlie's past, about his trouble.

The boy was smart, though, smart enough to keep his mouth shut, Lance not about to ask any questions. When his mother was like this she'd answer them in a way that he didn't want to hear and he knew this, had that much insight into her personality.

He'd asked Charlie once, "What happened to Mom, why has she changed?" Said it slowly, guiltily. Lance asking a stranger to explain the ways of blood, and Charlie had told him that he did not know, wondered about it a lot himself, lately.

Although he knew. Found the empty whiskey bottles and others that weren't so empty, the Didrex and green and clears, hidden under the medicine cabinet in their bathroom right next to the Darvon and Nembutal, which would bring her down. There were water pills in there, some diuretics. He wondered if she took something that made her hungry, another pill to make her horny. One to make her talk, one to make her friendly. Once you got into mixing booze and pills, he'd learned in the stone village, they owned you and there was no way out that was easy. Just Say No didn't cut it except as a battle cry for middle-class suburban white kids who had never touched the shit.

He looked into Lance's eyes, shook his head quickly— a mistake—and the boy looked back into his bowl as Lina started in on him again.

"Don't you dare patronize me, don't you *dare* give signals to my son!"

Charlie stood up. Was about to say something but

Lance was making sniffling noises, trying to keep it together but not quite making it, and he figured that anything he said would only hurt the kid worse. He looked at
her, at his wife. Then turned and left the room without a
word.

Chapter 28

Darrin was impatient, had had a tough night himself and now the Dragon Lady was giving him some shit. "Family visitation's at ten, goddamnit," Marlene said to him at a quarter till. "I'm leaving," and he'd told her to go, to get the fuck out, were his exact words. She'd given him a dirty, hurt look, had spun on her heels and slammed the door behind her. A few minutes later he'd heard her car giving up some of its rubber to the street as she'd pulled out of the driveway.

What had she expected, consoling words and reassuring hugs? She'd been holding the old man over his head for years, had driven the wedge between the two of them and now here she was, middle-aged and expecting him to bow his head and weep when her favorite weapon broke.

In the beginning, like all of them, Darrin had been a hitter, had had to do it to prove himself to men who trusted no one who hadn't been born with the same last name as them. He'd been good at it and had enjoyed his work, had begun his criminal career with a gun and a large set of balls, only later finding out that he had the smarts to make it big using his other abilities, that his education hadn't been wasted, that there was more to stealing than sticking a gun in someone's ribs. If you played your cards right, you could make more with one phone call than fifty thieves with cannons could make in a decade.

Try telling that to his brother's stepkid, though. Dumb hillbilly idiot. "College?" Merle would say to him when the topic came up, squinching his face up as if Darrin had asked him to identify planets in another galaxy, by name. "The fuck you want me to go to college for?" Darrin would tell him that it would make his father proud of him, from wherever his dad was, and Merle would say, "Shit, my daddy's proud of me, you don't believe me, give a holler down to Florida. He'll tell you so." Trying to get Darrin's goat. The kid had known which father Darrin had been referring to, and it hadn't been that drunken hick living in his tarpaper shack down South.

He'd tell Merle, "You're smart, Merle, look at the scams you come up with. Learn how to use that brain, goddamnit, I won't always be here to look after you." Pleading with the kid and Merle would look at him blankly, tell him that he'd been getting along all right without any damn diploma.

Merle, the fool he couldn't reach this morning, the man who was going to make him late for his wife's uncle's wake.

All he could get was some frightened idiot with an Hispanic accent, telling him that Señor Como was not in just then, and could he please take a message, sir? Finally calling Mickey, finding out that the job had been taken care of. Sort of.

"Is the guy crippled up good?" Darrin didn't need the prowler waltzing into the wake or showing up at the funeral; he had important business to discuss at both places.

Mickey hesitated, said, "Uh," and Darrin had to ask him what in the fuck was wrong with him.

"You got to ask Merle about that part, chief. I waited in the car because he wanted to take care of him himself."

"Well, were you watching?"

"Well, you see, I was watching the street, boss. Looking for the heat."

"Mickey?" Darrin's patience was gone, there was too much damn stress in his life. He waited until the dumb bastard said Yeah before he told him, "You're full of shit, Mickey," not knowing if he was or not, but wanting to make him think. Then he hung up, dialed Merle's number again.

The sad, respectful spic came back on, "Allo, please?" sounding scared. Darrin slammed the phone down in his ear. Grabbed his coat and went out to get his own car out of the garage. He had given Larry the morning off, would drive himself to the wake. The old bastards who would be there paying homage to Sal's corpse would see it as a sign of respect.

Merle stood outside the door of the hardware and lumber store, wondering how thieves were supposed to get ahead these days, the way everything was protected. No wonder the jigs had gone back to smashing old ladies' skulls in to get dope money, what with every place from the local 7-Eleven to the bigger chains now having their own security guards, cameras and everything.

Take this place here. Right there in the window, next to the poster of the smiling bearded guy with the tool belt holding up a finished door—the poster an advertisement for the paint that was on sale inside—was a yellow diamond-shaped sign that warned in bold black letters that this store had its own camera and private security crew working inside.

Ain't that the way they do you? Puds. Spending a fortune on security and who has to pay? Three guesses. The customer, that's who. He hated the way these hypocrites acted, talking about how shoplifting cost them billions a year. Bull*shit*. It cost the people who shopped in the stores billions of dollars, because these jive-time fools would jack up the price of the shoplifting maybe fifty times up past what it was, then raise their prices accordingly.

He watched the folks walking in and out, everyone self-important, wrapped up in their own little projects, Merle aware that the only people smiling would be the store owners and you'd have to break into the manager's office to see them, raking their fingers through the greenbacks and greedily looking out at the crowds through one-way mirrors, at the suckers. Why were they suckers? Guess who paid for the security guards, the cameras and the alarms? The cost passed on to the painters and electricians and tile layers and the rest of the army of homemakers who weren't about to pay top price to the professionals to fix something they themselves thought that they could do. These goofs paid for the security, then the store got itself a full tax writeoff, too.

Sometimes, it was almost worth thinking about, giving up crime and going into business for himself. He'd be a millionaire in a year. Have to get up before first light, too, though. That wouldn't be worth any amount of money.

Merle was standing in front of the store, looking down at the carefully written list of things he'd be needing, knowing he could not buy everything at one place. Some rent-a-cop who subscribed to *Soldier of Fortune* magazine might realize what he was purchasing, figure him for a terrorist, and shoot him dead with the gun the State had made him take eight hours of instruction with before turning him loose to protect society. If it hadn't been for Millard, he might have given it a shot, tried picking up everything at one store, but his forehead had an ugly gash in it where Millard's heels had connected, and his shin hurt like hell, there was no way he could walk straight today, probably not even for a couple of days. He could still smell the puke on him. He'd be easily recognizable.

He was thinking that he didn't want to blow his cash

reserves—he never felt secure unless there was a couple of grand in his pocket—and this wasn't exactly a business expense he could ask his uncle to pay him back for. It wasn't a good place to be standing around thinking, either, in the heart of the West Side, a block or so away from a Buddy Bear store that had posted a huge sign in the window when it was being remodeled— THIS STORE UNDER CONSTRUCTION AND NEW MANAGEMENT—THERE WILL BE NO ARABS INVOLVED IN THIS STORE! The owner trying to calm down the jigs, who hated the A-rabs for coming into their neighborhood and making money off them. There were times when Merle's social conscience got the best of him and he wanted to call someone at the Nigger Guild or someplace and ask them, Why don't you open up your own stores, burrheads? Solve the problem right there.

Still in all, it was a bad neighborhood and he was a slender white guy standing out front of a store. If he didn't get a move on, the cash in his wallet would disappear without his ever having made a purchase.

He walked into the store, thinking that his problem was that he liked to party too much. Spent the money on the booze and the broads, taking care of them the way Moonbeam had taken care of him. He had to take good care of them so that they would be willing to submit to his desires, which sometimes got a little out of hand. He could get carried away, he knew it and it was a problem he was working on, even now as he pushed a cart down the aisle, grabbing the first of the things he'd be needing, he was thinking on it.

He'd be okay, maybe even feeling the desire to be gentle, but then his dick would get hard and he'd have to do things. Some of the women enjoyed what he did, others balked. All of them got well taken care of before and after the act—even the ones who wouldn't go out with him anymore—because he didn't need a rape charge laid on him later.

Merle acquired what he needed, got in line behind

some fat slob with a cart full of the paint that was on sale, the stuff that was advertised on the store windows. More than he'd need to paint St. Pat's, inside and out. Wanted to save money. After his purchases were rung up, he reached into his back pocket and took out his wallet, lifted the hidden-compartment flap and took out good old Jimbo's MasterCard, handed it to the clerk and signed the slip when it was presented to him, made up a phone number and wrote that down too, where the clerk had marked the X. He'd use the VISA at the next stop, to get the rest of the things he needed, because he didn't know how high Jimbo's limit was on the cards, whether the man had them maxed out or what, then would talk to a guy he knew over on the South Side who'd give him three hundred apiece for them, no questions asked.

As he pushed his cart down the parking aisle toward his car—walking with a slight limp, his shin hurt like hell —he realized that it was a pretty good thing to be a frugal shopper, because now, even if he never found an immediate use for the bombs that Peter would make for him, there would be no financial loss to him personally, Jimbo would get his bills next month and there would be a few hundred dollars on them charged to a couple of different hardware stores in Chicago. If he'd called the company right away as soon as he'd woke up, he wouldn't have to pay anything at all. It was the way Merle liked to do business; keep everybody happy and there would be no complaints.

He watched Peter make the bombs, standing behind him as the boy worked on Merle's little two-person glass and steel kitchen table, Merle listening to his rap while he worked, the mex putting on a terrorist's clinic for Merle's benefit. Showing off his single talent.

"With just what equipment you have given me, Merle, I can make you three or four far separate types of devices." Devices. Merle liked that, but not as much as bombs. Bombs sounded better, tougher. The mex was carefully spreading steady fingers over a compound he'd mixed up, rubbing it, patting it, gently kneading it. The gunk looked more like plastic explosives that had been left out in the rain than it did like gunpowder, which was what Merle expected from the stuff he'd bought.

But it sure wasn't gunpowder. It was pliant, almost putty-like, wet, and it stunk to high heaven. It sweated, and Peter would run a finger across its shape and gather the liquid into his palm, drop it onto the middle of the bundle that he was skillfully molding into the shape of an un-baked loaf of bread, then would fold it over on itself again, begin kneading it some more. Looked like he was jerking it off and shoving the jisum back into the pecker.

"I can make a pressure device, such as you might want if you desired to place it under the seat of someone's car. He sits down," Silva raised his hands off the explosives, opened them and spread them around, forming a mushroom shape. "Boom." Said softly.

"Or, I can make a simple pipe device, with a fuse. You light it and run and it will explode." Merle had once held a ladyfinger firecracker too long in his hand, watching it burn down. It had gone off and he had closed his eyes and looked away, not sure if he'd have fingers left when he looked back. The fuse type, fuck that, it was out of the question.

"I can make a good one that you simply apply to the hot wire onto a car's starter, a very simple device, really, Merle, you just run a wire onto it and as soon as the person starts the car . . ." Peter shrugged.

"Let me ask you about the pressure device deal, partner . . ."

"Yes?" Silva never took his eyes away from his task, rarely moved his hands off the gunk except when to make a point. Cut off a spic's hands, and he'll lose the power of speech.

"Can you turn that around? Say, a guy sits down,

drives his car around, but it doesn't blow up until he steps out of the car?"

"That is even less trouble, Merle, and I can make it even less troublesome than that, where you don't even have to go near the man's car." Silva nodded his head at the stack of little slim metal tubes he had lying next to his explosives. They looked like steel pencils cut in half, with wires coming out of them. "I can apply a small hook onto one of my triggers. You simply hook a wire around the hook, tie the other end of the wire around the doorknob of the front door of the person you wish to harm. Then you go home and go to sleep. He opens his door . . ." The shoulder shrug again.

Merle studied the triggers. "That what they call blasting caps?"

"Caps, triggers, fuses, is all the same thing to me."

"How many can you make altogether with what I got you there?" He hoped a lot. He had already sold the hot cards to his South Side connection.

Silva considered this, said, "Four good devices, Merle."

"How good? Maybe we only need two, if we're stealing firepower from them." There didn't look to be enough there to make even one good bomb.

"Any of the four, Merle, it would be powerful enough to destroy this room and everything in it. Everyone, too, even someone who saw it and hid behind the sofa."

"Strong as, say, a grenade?" Merle didn't think so. The stuff was too compact, not big enough to do that kind of harm.

"Much more than a grenade," Silva said, then added, "Or, in a way you would better understand, you know the silver salute firework?"

"They's a fourth of a grenade, right?"

"One quarter, they say. Each device I build you will be seven times the strength of that silver salute, and less than half the size of a single one, believe me."

"How you know that?"

"Because when I was young I used to make silver salutes for people who wanted them at the Fourth of July time, that is how I know." Then, a little irritated, disgust sneaking into Silva's voice, "How do you think I know, Mother of Christ, Merle."

Goddamn. Merle had him a sensitive La-tin-o on his hands. A couple of quick responses came to mind, but he didn't think it would be wise to hurt the boy's feelings while he was playing around with that deadly bread dough. He said, "I was just asking, Jeez. Didn't you ever watch a pro at work and wonder how he does what he does, how he knows about it?"

Even from behind him, Merle could see Peter stiffen with pride, the little peacock. Maybe after he made the bombs Merle would turn his ass in, if there was a reward. In a week the bikers would have him wearing mascara, Maybelline pancake makeup on his face. If they didn't sell him to the niggers first.

Merle said, "You spend all damn morning making that stuff?" He'd left him alone here for three hours while he'd taken care of the credit card business, and Peter had been bent over the dining room table when Merle had come home.

"Just began this, this is the easy part. The hard part is the triggers."

"Just like with a woman, is that right, Peter?" Merle almost slapped him on the back, pulled his hand away. He didn't know how dangerous the stuff there on the table was. "Once you got their triggers pulled, you own them."

"That is correct, I guess," Peter said, sadly, and Merle decided that he was thinking about his little dead white girlfriend. He should have kept his mouth shut.

He said, "I got to go take a bath, Peter, I got a wake to go to."

"Will you be speaking to your uncle at this wake, Merle? About my problem?"

Well, look here. Wiseass little shit getting cocky because he had some dynamite or whatever he had in his hands. Let him be that way, see how far it got him.

To Peter, Merle said, "Wouldn't be a bit surprised if you were the major topic of conversation, Peter," then strolled off toward the bathroom.

Chapter 29

At noon, Charlie left the office and got into his car, stopped off at a liquor store and bought a bottle of bourbon, then headed off for 26th and California, to the Adult Probation Department, which was in the same ancient complex of buildings as the Criminal Court of Cook County. Also in the complex, in the back behind a high stone wall topped with several rows of razor-sharp wire, was the Cook County Jail.

The manila envelope with his money stuck inside was pushed down his pants, in front. He'd have to find a safe place for it. He hadn't had time yet, not since winning it.

Once a month he'd have to check in, see his man, take the guy a bottle of booze, a case of Scotch at Christmastime. Five more years of this, and maybe if he upped the ante the man would let him mail his form in, like some other guys Charlie had heard about were granted the privilege of doing. The system was corrupt, his parole officer a stone thief. Still, it beat doing time, hands down.

Cat had been behind that wall for twenty-eight of the sixty-one months that Charlie had been coming here, but he'd never gone in to see him, although he'd wanted to. As a convicted felon, he no longer had the right to visit people housed in such places. Which was dumb. He was good enough to spend time in there with them, but not good enough to come back and visit, go figure it.

Not that he had a great desire to hear the sound of metal slamming shut behind him. Sometimes even on him, because some of the hacks were cruel, would pump the hydraulic arm that closed the cell door without warning and if you weren't paying attention, whammo, the rolling steel would hit you with enough force to knock you out.

He finally found a spot to park across the street on the one-way Boulevard, waiting, holding up traffic while an entire family of black people walked across the grass, took their time getting into their car, strapping on their seat belts and everything while behind him, horns blared. When the car finally pulled out, Charlie pulled in, got out of the car and locked it, began walking across the grass toward the steps of the place, looking up at the wall, the wire, seeing the guard towers up there, remembering.

Dragging himself back to the here and now with a start, angry at himself for delving into a past that was painful when he didn't have to, when it would serve no useful purpose. He hadn't been inside this place as a prisoner since the early '80s, when he'd been awaiting trial. Everything had probably changed inside there by now.

Jesus, early '80s? Five years in, a little over five years out, leaving an entire decade in between since the moment he'd been arrested, since he'd broken into that damn house trying to impress Cat with how good he was, going in alone and the old man had been home and son of a bitch what had happened then shouldn't have happened to a dog . . .

Charlie walked into the Adult Probation Office, the name stenciled on the thick sheet of glass in large black letters. Sat in an uncomfortable molded plastic chair and waited, being ignored and listening closely and pretending not to while his PO, Brimley, stood deep in conversation with a County hack who was probably screwing off.

"What more do those criminoids *want*," the hack was saying, whining and bitching, a white guy, probably one of Brimley's protégés. He was like that, would bring a man into the county department and sponsor him, set him up somewhere in the County of Cook, planted around the area to be there when Brimley needed him. "I mean, they got radios, fans, even. Some of them even got fucking color TVs! You know how it makes me feel, seeing those bastards living like that?"

Charlie wanted to ask this guy how he thought the *prisoners* felt, locked in there, accused of a crime but not convicted of anything yet. And their keepers, their low-pay no-account son of a bitching keepers thought they had too *much*? When you take away a man's freedom, he has nothing. That was the way Charlie looked at it, and that was the way it was.

"And the captain tells me, I hit one more of those fuckers, I'm fired. What kind of shit is that, Matt? It's bullshit, is what it is." The guard was next to tears and he turned his head, shot Charlie a withering glance, knowing why Charlie was there, that he was an ex-con. A twelve grand a year punk in a blue uniform looking down on him. It mattered, but Charlie didn't let the fact that it did show on his face.

He shut his ears off, a habit you had to pick up in prison or the noise would drive you insane. Charlie tuning these fools out and going into himself, to the place that the sight of the wire, the stone wall, had started to take him when he'd still been outside . . .

Did he want to go there, to that place in his head, the place of memories? He wondered that on some level, if he really wanted to go into that particular area, if the memories would be too painful. Brimley had a hand on the screw's shoulder, was leading him into his inner office,

Brimley a prick, always speaking in a low, down home voice, you'd think he was a Bible salesman from the tone of his voice, from the farmer's go-to-meeting suits the man wore. He closed the door to the office behind him, and Charlie knew that he'd be in there awhile, calming the man down. Brimley probably needed him to mule in marijuana or cocaine to the prisoners, not being the type of man who would counsel someone just to be friendly.

So be it. Charlie could handle it. And it was probably a good thing, doing it in this place. Everything that went on in here was forgotten the second he walked out the door, anyway. He leaned back and closed his eyes, the fat envelope stuffed down the front of his pants, his coat over his belly so no one coming in or out would be able to see it down there, the bottle held loosely atop the coat, in his lap. Charlie closed his eyes and allowed the memories to come to him.

A father who didn't love him, but took care of him because it was the manly thing to do, the right thing. A mother who tried but who was too busy taking care of her old man, the hit-man thief. The old man being a full-time project.

Charlie vaguely remembered them, not unpleasantly. They were distant, cold but never cruel, the old man grunting when Charlie brought home straight-A report cards, the mother baking a cake on his birthday and the two of them singing him Happy Birthday, Charlie blowing out the candles and then the old man was out of there, back to whatever he'd been doing before getting called into the kitchen.

School? What about that. He'd never had a problem during grade school, excelled in his studies. Looking back, it might have been because of the home situation. Approval from adults was important, and when he got good grades he got the approval of the teachers. Became one of their pets, young Charlie a studier who did his homework on time and neatly. He never took a sick day, never played hooky. He'd sit at home and study his parents, taking his quietness from them, his father's strength envied but too great to be simulated until he was older. So he only imitated him, walking as his father walked, speaking in the same patterns, winning the man's approval by putting a mirror up before him. It was never lost on Charlie, the way the old man would light up when someone remarked on the resemblance. It was about the only time he ever saw his father smile.

Took that from him, too, eventually. Charlie becoming a studier, a watcher. Quiet and reticent, somber, always thinking and never acting without first having weighed the consequences.

Not that he never acted at all; just that he waited for his shot, learned early to lay in the weeds and await his chance.

A school bully named Tomkiss had razzed him when Charlie was a freshman in high school, at Washington on the East Side, not far from where Charlie the adult would earn his honest living. Tomkiss a tall athletic black who played three sports, giving Charlie grief in the cafeteria where you had to go at lunch time, as there were no stores close enough to walk to. You either went home to eat if you lived close enough, or you went to the lunchroom, where you would be at the mercy of the Tomkisses of the world.

Tomkiss would trip him, stick his foot out as Charlie walked by, call him names because Tomkiss was a dummy and Charlie was pulling A's out of his ass, without a whole lot of effort. Charlie would look at him, glare sometimes, and Tomkiss would make sucking noises or stand up, either making fun of Charlie or trying to egg him into a fight, waving his hands toward himself, saying C'mon, motherfuck, depending on his mood, how he felt that afternoon. The only positive thing about it was that the lunchroom was the only place where Charlie would have to put up with him. Tomkiss would have to stay after school every day to practice whatever sport was in season, and, being two years older than Charlie and a junior, they shared no classes.

He could have put up with it, taken it for forty minutes a day and let it go, if other students hadn't seen it and tried the same thing, giving him trouble, knowing that Tomkiss had gotten away with it so why shouldn't they?

Charlie thought about it, how to handle the situation. He couldn't fight him and win, call him out before class and have it out with him once and for all, as he had nowhere near Tomkiss's strength and power, the kid's speed. It would only make things worse, Tomkiss then would beat him up at every opportunity, maybe other kids would, too. It took him a week, during which Charlie went back and forth, vacillating because the only solution he came up with would be one that could get him expelled, but when on a Thursday afternoon Tomkiss hollered to him that he was going to make Charlie his bitch, Charlie knew he would have to act, and soon. He had no idea what the kid really meant by that, but he knew that it couldn't be in his own best interest.

Charlie's last class before lunch was shop, and he slipped a short length of heavy pipe up his sleeve just before the bell rang, leaned over the table and wrote a quick note to Tomkiss on a piece of paper torn from his spiral notebook: YOU ASSHOLE—IF YOU HAVE THE BALLS, COME INTO THE WASHROOM ALONE! He did not sign the note.

Passed it to Tomkiss as he took his tray to the garbage can, scraped it and dropped it in the dirty rack, turned and entered the bathroom, heard the scrape of the chair, heard Tomkiss tell his jock friends to "keep yo asses right where they is," heard a grunt of anger, as Tomkiss charged after him.

Charlie was standing inside the bathroom, facing the door and ready. As soon as the door banged open he swung, the pipe in his sleeve hitting Tomkiss above the eye, opening a wide gash that spurted blood all over

Charlie's shirt. Tomkiss threw his hands to his head, let out a frightened shriek, and Charlie let him have one in the belly, low, but not in the balls; he wanted this guy to be able to move on his own, he was too heavy to carry. Charlie dropped his pipe-loaded arm, leaned over and grabbed Tomkiss with both hands, pulled him over to the toilets, threw him into the stall and Tomkiss fell over the commode, landed on his knees facing it, and Charlie did what he'd been planning to do. He stuck Tomkiss's face in there, in the water, held it down as the powerful muscles in the boy's neck bunched, fought for freedom. Tomkiss couldn't get a grip on the rim with his hands, if he had Charlie would have had to hit him again, to get him back down in there, but every time his fingers closed around the bowl they'd slip off, Tomkiss panicking, thrashing around with Charlie now sitting on his back, holding him down, pressing hard.

Let him up only when the fight went out of the boy and Charlie knew he'd be safe.

He pulled Tomkiss's head out of the commode, bashed it once against the porcelain side of the toilet, leaned down close so Tomkiss could see his face.

"That was a kiss, punk," Charlie said. Speaking in his normal voice, surprised that he was able to pull it off. His hands weren't shaking. "You ever bother me again, in any way, and I'll turn it into a fucking, you understand?"

Tomkiss, eyes wide, tears flowing down his cheeks mixed in with the toilet water, nodded his head and Charlie punched him, once, in the mouth.

"Talk to me when I speak to you, motherfucker."

"I hear you, I hear you, I understand!" The badass was gone, there wasn't even a hint of the ghetto drawl in his speech. Tomkiss was waving his hands around his face, his eyes squeezed shut now, his face twisted and ugly. Charlie let him go, walked out of the bathroom with his hands in his pockets, seeing the smirks drop off the faces of the other kids who'd been staring at the door in gleeful anticipation. He looked around, none of the toughs want-

ing to meet his eye, and casually strolled out of the lunchroom, to the shop, to return the pipe before its absence
was noticed.

He figured it would be more effective if he had already left the room when Tomkiss came out of the can
whining and crying, his upper body soaked with toilet
water and blood.

Chapter
30

That had been the beginning for him, the first time he'd seen what unexpected violence could do to completely change a person's attitude around. He learned from the lesson, used it to his best advantage, although his grades began to slip and he found himself hanging with a wilder crowd, a group of boys who admired his coolness, his attitude, the fact that he could drop whatever he was doing and fight at the wrong tone of voice, over a perceived insult. Vanquish his foe and then pick up his can of beer or jump back into his conversation, as if nothing had ever happened.

He even got suspended once for fighting on the school grounds, and that was the first time he had ever really known fear, wondering what the old man would do to him when he found out.

Which was nothing. His father had listened impatiently until his mother got to the part about the fistfight, then he'd turned on Charlie, angrily.

"You win?" he'd demanded.

Charlie nodded.

"Win good?"

"Busted him up, and he was older than me, bigger."

"That's good. That's good. You ever lose, you're locked out of this house until you go back and win, you got it?" His father said this and turned, walked out of the room, his wife behind him, wondering aloud if this was the proper thing to be teaching their kid.

He never heard a word about his fistfights, nor about the grades which had, by the time he was a junior, gone all to seed.

Never saw his father violent, either, or heard him raise his voice. Even when the man was drunk, he was in control. He would bring his new younger friend over, his father calling the man Cat but making Charlie call him Mr. Millard, and the two of them would sit on the sofa and watch baseball games, drinking beer, sometimes coming in rapidly and heading into the bedroom, where Charlie would hear excited voices and the sound of laughter, of money being counted, coming at him through the thin wooden door. His mother was fiercely loyal to her husband, backed him before all others, and did the cooking, the cleaning, and stayed out of Charlie's way, never gave him a hard time.

Three weeks after Charlie turned seventeen his father was arrested for murder, and things began to change quickly.

In the first place, he got out on bond, and that was strange. It made Charlie happy because his father was home, but it gave him pause for thought. How did you get bond for a murder rap?

The murder itself didn't surprise Charlie. He'd known about his father for some time, what he did. Knew he was a thief because he was always bringing dresses home for Charlie's mother that still had the price tags on them, watches that were still in the box with their tags attached, too. The man didn't work except at night and sometimes during the day when he and Mr. Millard would disappear, usually on Sundays, and it didn't take Charlie long to figure out that they were hitting stores that were closed on Sunday, that hadn't had a chance to deposit their Saturday receipts and wouldn't until Monday. He would picture them in his mind, busting into a safe, and be forced out of his normal reticence, would get excited at the thought of his being a thief, of working with his father and Mr. Millard.

He would feel that and wonder about it, why it was that he felt that way. Was it a way to please his father, to win his approval, or just a desire to be like him, strong and tough, taking orders from no man?

His father got out on bond and right after that Charlie would hear him yelling a lot over the telephone, amazed at the sound of his father's voice raised in anger. Sometimes it would be his mother doing the yelling, telling whoever it was on the other end that they better damn well leave her husband alone, she knew where the bodies were buried . . .

Brimley's door opened and the hack came out, red-faced, stormed past Charlie and out the door, into the corridor of the courts building, not even glancing Charlie's way. Brimley was standing at the door to his office, looking at Charlie the way a principal might at a troublesome student, stern and angry because he'd believed the student to be bright enough to stay out of trouble. He crooked his finger at Charlie, turned and walked out of sight and Charlie rose, not bothered by the look or the curtness of Brimley's greeting, rather, feeling relieved because the time for reminiscence was over.

Brimley said, "Well, there, Charlie—" looking down to read Charlie's name off his folder, as if he couldn't remember his name without help. A busy man who didn't have time to dawdle. "I got a call today, from your wife, yeah?" Leaving it up in the air, wanting Charlie to explain.

Lina, you bitch.

Charlie said nothing, put a look of surprise on his face —What could *Lina* want with his PO?—and sat back, the envelope making him feel conspicuous, the coat over it scant camouflage.

"It 'pears she thinks there's some sort of hanky-panky going on 'tween you and her young'n, Charlie." Brimley was a tall man who took advantage of it, sitting behind his desk, looking with disapproval down his broken-veined nose at Charlie, the two of them knowing what happened to child molesters in the joint.

It broke Charlie's reserve. This man could pick up the phone on his desk and make one call, and Charlie would not see daylight again for at least five years, until the term left of his special parole was served in full. He squeezed his coat, hard, so Brimley couldn't see that his hands were shaking.

Charlie, speaking too fast, said, "Mr. Brimley, there's trouble in the marriage. I'm gonna divorce her, and she's gonna say anything she can, do anything she can to hurt me."

"Hateful bitch, yeah?"

"Oh, yeah, Mr. Brimley."

"The same hateful bitch you told me was the best thing ever happened to you, there, Charlie? Remember that? And why haven't I heard about this before, about the trouble in paradise?"

"I've been trying to keep this together, Mr. Brimley, wanting to make it work. She's drinking, she's taking drugs, poisoning the kid's mind against me."

"Says that you been spewing some poison yourself, there, what she says."

"Mr. Brimley, she's a liar. All she has to do is call the DCFS, and they'd come out, check it and see that it's a lie from talking to the kid. She didn't do that, or go to the cops, 'cause she knows it's bullshit. She wants me to go back to prison as punishment for leaving her, that's all."

"What about the job, Charlie? You work for her daddy, don't you? What about that?"

Charlie felt a trickle of sweat on the back of his neck, felt drops of it working their way down the side of his throat, into his shirt collar. Saw Brimley smiling in approval, happy because he had another con pleading for his freedom. He felt ashamed, humiliated, but was willing to lose the face, the self-esteem, in order to stay out of the joint. He couldn't go back, not over something like this.

He said, "Mr. Brimley, John, her father, would let me work there until retirement if I wanted to. I've doubled his business, easy. I'm gonna quit, though, I want you to know that. If she's this hateful, hates me this bad, I'm out of there. It'd only cause me trouble, staying, but I won't have a problem getting another job, hell, I'm constantly turning down job offers from the competition; I'll just call one of them up, I'll have a job in a week . . ."

Brimley was loving this, Charlie could see it in his eyes. He knew he'd been rambling, near begging, but he couldn't make himself stop, the thought of losing his freedom after making something of himself, after going to college and busting his ass to get ahead, terrified him. Was he this weak, this much of a punk? He didn't have time to think about that now. Now, his problem was staying out of prison.

"Mr. Brimley, I never hurt anyone in my life, and I'd never hurt a kid—"

Brimley put his right hand in the air to stop Charlie, deepening his humiliation but not having time to listen to him beg. Charlie forced himself to shut up, to not overstep his bounds. He'd have to eat this, take it and live with it. It was part of the payment due for what he'd done ten years before.

Brimley lowered his hand, straightened the knot in his tie, in charge, knowing it, and enjoying it.

"Never hurt anyone, there, Charlie? How about the man, died when you were burglarizing his house, yeah?"

"Mr. Brimley, he was a recent bypass patient, home convalescing instead of at work like my information said he'd be. He had an attack when he saw me, I didn't even know he was there or I wouldn't have gone in, I swear to Christ."

"Got nailed for Burglary-Murder, though, didn't you."

"Bargained down to Home Invasion, sir," Charlie spoke and saw the anger in Brimley's eyes, again forced himself silent.

"I don't much care what the conviction's for, son, don't mean shit to me what you did *time* for, all I cares about is what you actually *did*, and from my reading of your record, son, from the fact that you pled guilty to anything, tells me you killed that man same as if you'd'a shot him, there." Brimley sat back and let Charlie squirm, staring at him, the PO self-satisfied and righteous. Charlie bit his tongue, knowing that the man had no idea what he was talking about, but was in a position to let his ignorance win the argument simply because he was in the power seat. Charlie could picture him, carrying anti-abortion posters outside a doctor's office, telling women what to do with their bodies and wearing that same smirk, as if he had a direct pipeline to God's lips.

For a second he reminded Charlie of a male Lina, knowing everything, perfect and wondering why everybody didn't just do what he said, secure in the knowledge that if everyone did, it would be a flawless world.

Brimley was sitting back in his chair, Charlie's life and future in his hands, then jutted his chin at an old typewriter on a stand in the corner.

"Know what that is, there, Charlie boy?" Charlie said he didn't.

"That's the Kiss of Death, over there, son. Never type anything on it but a beef sheet, what they call a parole revocation." There was a sheet of paper in there already, rolled in with some spaces already filled in, Charlie could see that much. The paper was about half-typed.

"That's your ticket back to the penitentiary in that machine, Charlie. Give me a reason to cancel it."

Charlie's mind raced, looking for that reason and knowing it could only be one thing. Brimley wouldn't care about his degree, about the year he'd spent working his tail off. Nor would he give a damn about Charlie's character, what type of man he was. All this guy would care about was money, and if Charlie had to, he was willing, right now, to hand the entire contents of the envelope in his pants over to the man, just to walk out that door to freedom.

He calmed himself, took deep breaths. Brimley was expecting an answer.

Or was he? This was a man who got off on power, who seized control and never let go. He might even be offended if Charlie made an offer that was too low, or even too high. He would not want Charlie to be in the position of strength; if the idea didn't come from Brimley himself, it would be rejected and the ante would rise.

Charlie congratulated himself because he was thinking again in spite of his panic. He would get out of this, even though it would cost him. He told himself that Brimley wasn't going to beef him and send him back, convinced himself that this was true. Otherwise, he might lose it, leap over the desk and choke this bastard, and if that happened, Lina would win.

He said, "Mr. Brimley, I just don't know how we can make this right."

It had been the right thing to say, Brimley had been waiting for it. That was obvious in the way he pushed himself forward in his chair, and smiled.

"Well, now, Charlie, there's a way all right." Spoke and stopped, smiling.

"What's that, sir?"

"See, what we can do here, Charlie, is forget about the

damn bottle of booze every month. What you can do, what can make us all happy here, is to get you out of the house, right off, away from the child. Then, starting the next time you come see me, you come in a little early, before I'm in here, while I'm at lunch, and you bring an envelope with a thousand dollars in it, put it inside one of the books that'll be sitting on top of this desk." Brimley paused, waiting for Charlie to complain. When he didn't, didn't even open his mouth to bargain, Brimley continued.

"Then all you got to do is turn around and walk out. No conversation, not even a face-to-face anymore. You think that's a little steep, do you, Charlie?"

"Mr. Brimley, I got no complaints."

"That's a good thing, because I do. See, for five years now, you come in here once a month, we have a little chat, find out how it's going at school, how things are with the girlfriend, who's now your wife. This last year we talked about the job, the way you were succeeding in the business world, hell, you had me all proud of you, son." Brimley sat back again, looking a little sheepish, smiling ruefully.

"I spend about ninety-nine percent of my time chasing down niggers don't want to be found, Charlie, and it was almost re*freshing* to meet a boy like you, doing what no other con I ever met was able to do. Which is, get out of the joint and lead a productive, happy life. I got to feeling a little paternal, so I cut you some slack. Gave you a break and settled for a bottle of booze every month just as a token of your respect, and how do you think I feel, there, when I find out that all along you been conning me same as the niggers? That you're a bullshitter too?"

"Mr. Brimley—"

"Don't even try it, son. I won't even see you again until the day I sign you off parole, what, fifty-eight or -nine months from now. Only way you can screw things up after this is to lie to me, which I expect from most of the assholes don't know how the business is done, but which I won't take from them that do.

"I had me a nice talk with your missus, today, Charlie. Found out all about your little pal, Robert Millard. About your friendship with Darrin Favore, too. All this time you been raking it in and here was Mr. Brimley, being played for a fool.

"You think I don't know what you make? I say to you you got to pay me twelve grand a year out of a gross of fifty before taxes, and you don't even blink an eye. That tells me you're making a hell of a lot more than that fifty. Hear tell you won you a heap last night in a card game over to your damn country club." Brimley shook his head. "I *explained* to you that you couldn't gamble, couldn't ass-o-ciate with no known criminals, and all this time, you been pulling old Mr. Brimley's leg. Which is why you got to pay so much, son. To make up for all the lies you been telling me all this time.

"But that's ancient history, Charlie. Now, we're in business, yeah? So what you do, is, you go about your prowler business with your friend Catfeet, and you do your business with Favore, and if you get caught you call me and we'll negotiate you a settlement fee. A man with over twenny year in the business can do you a lot of good, you get in trouble, you unnerstand what I'm telling you?"

"Yes, sir."

"All right then, get on out of here, and you can take the bottle with you. But don't you ever be late with my stipend, Charlie, not even once. I can take an insult once, son, can even admire it. But *no*body screws me twice and gets away with it, you hear?"

Charlie rose, said, "Yes, sir," began walking hurriedly to the door and was reaching for the knob when Brimley called his name. He turned, said again, "Yes, sir?"

And Matt Brimley smiled his down-home smile, told him, "At Christmastime, every year, I get five extra as my gift, Charlie, and I do mean thousand." Then looked back down at the papers on his desk, marking Charlie's file.

Charlie didn't answer him, just accepted it, turned and was opening the door when Brimley said, "That's only four weeks away, Charlie, that Christmastime visit, right?"

And, yet again, Charlie said, "Yes, sir."

Chapter 31

Feet had a hangover, which wasn't making him feel any better about things. All told, those things would have been more than bad enough without it.

Good God, had he actually kicked the shit out of that psycho nephew of Favore's? All he'd had to do was take the ass-kicking, and it would have been forgotten. It had probably been Favore's way of telling him that they were even. What with Sal's death, and with Favore maybe jockeying for position, the last thing the man needed was Feet popping up at the wake, telling the other Men of Respect about the way Favore was doing him, screwing him around after Feet had done hard time rather than rat him out.

Why couldn't he just accept it, let it happen and then get on with his life? He had six grand to his name, a few dollars less after last night's partying, enough to hold him over until he could set up a score. Which he could have done, no problem, as he healed from whatever beating Favore had ordered upon him.

Now, it would be worse than a beating. Now, if he couldn't square the beef, he'd have to die.

Catfeet knew it and the thought frightened him, almost as badly as the fashion his death would probably take. He could see it, that crazy man torturing him, all the while giving him the impression that he was going to let Feet live. It was the kind of man he was, one who knew the politics of fear just as well as he knew the violent application, the manifestation of that emotion, how to draw on it for strength and use it to win his battles.

He'd been in a tavern one night at 10:30, drinking peacefully and discussing business, and he'd heard the news go off and *Nightline* come on, heard sudden singing and lifted his head from his conversation, seen Como at the end of the bar, the idiot actually creating lyrics to the *Nightline* theme song. "Da-da-da, this is Night-line, starring Te-ed Ko-pple; ta-da, this is Nightline, whe-ere we'll show you some fools!" Como smiling and creating, drawing stares and grins. Some dunce had said something, made some joke about Como, and the next thing you knew, Como was strolling down the bar toward him, grinning peaceably, still singing his song, stopping when he got to the man who'd made the joke, his face going all of a sudden ugly as he spun, swung, and hit the man hard in the throat, then swaggered back to his position at the bar without even looking back to see if he'd killed the guy.

This was the man he'd vomited on, then kicked the shit out of.

Feet was sitting on his bed in a room above the 909 Club, in his underpants but with his shirt still on. He'd come here just before dawn from Femal's, had checked in, the 909 night clerk a new guy, not familiar to him, had paid for the month and hit the sack and had fallen asleep right away, passed out for seven hours, which was a shock. At Femal's, he hadn't lasted more than two, three hours. Then the nerves in his ankles had begun twitching, waking him, Feet suddenly antsy and high-strung, lying there afraid.

Now Feet said, "*Damn*it," shaking his head. What had he done, how the hell could he have been so stupid?

The thought passed through his mind, in there a second then out, as if testing his courage. Get out. Get out, right now. It felt good to think about it, but it was something he couldn't do. Sal had known about Charlie, and if Sal knew, others did, too. Maybe not Favore, not someone at his level, a businessman who didn't think it was important to know everything about your enemies, about their personal lives, but some others sure would know, some of the oldtimers. And they would tell him if Favore was looking hard enough for Catfeet, tell him all about Charlie. That wasn't something he could let the kid carry, not after all the years of trying to help Charlie become a success as a man. He had paid for the kid's education and taken care of him for a part of his upbringing, but still, he owed Charlie more than that, couldn't throw him to the wolves.

And what about Femal, and the kid? She said it was his and he believed her. Admired her, too, because she'd never said a word about his helping out, helping to support the kid, and that took pride, because she knew the sort of money Feet was capable of generating.

He'd been trying to throw a scare into her, saying what he had about Favore, but now he wondered if it were true, if the guy was truly a menace to her, to her child.

Favore was a big shot now, no longer a cruel beast of the night. He liked Femal, too, wanted her, Feet knew that much. Knew, too, that Femal took the man too lightly, didn't perceive him as a true threat, or hadn't before last night. Either way, it was a good thing that he'd said what he had, she'd at least be on her toes now, be looking for Favore to make his move.

He wondered why she didn't just quit. What was the point of sticking there? She had a good education, connections throughout the entire nationwide black network, she'd been recognized as an up and coming power in the black structure well before he'd gone away, and she hadn't lost any ground that he'd known of in his absence. So why was she working for Favore? Was the money that damn good?

Feet felt lightheaded, his breath rasped in his lungs. He lit a cigarette and took a deep drag, another, and felt a little better. Maybe a drink, to take away the pain. No, he'd always believed that drinking in the morning would start him down the path, and he'd seen too many guys fall by the wayside from the booze, reliable men who couldn't keep a grip on the bottle, on the monsters it produced. The guys suddenly not so reliable anymore, reaching the point where people didn't call them for things, left them alone to their buddy, booze. No, if he started now, began to drink in the morning, then next month he'd be sitting next to Johnny Red, laughing as the guy told him again about being eaten out of house and home, seeing the line as funny because if he laughed maybe Red would pop for a drink.

Feet rose slowly, held a hand out and grasped the wall for support. He needed a shave, bad. Needed a shower, a toothbrush, a new shirt, at least that, maybe even a new suit. The shower he could take care of right now. He headed into the bathroom, the cigarette stuck between his teeth, smoke dragging in and out with each breath he took, Feet hacking around the filter. He decided that if he lived through the day, he'd give the damn things up, quit cold turkey. If he could figure a way out of this mess he was in, he could do anything.

Darrin looked around him, in the lounge of the funeral parlor, surrounded by the other bosses, thinking that it had been a big mistake not to bring at least one driver, maybe two or three other boys. Not that he would need them here, he was safe from all harm with all the women around, just upstairs. One of them his wife Marlene, out there wailing her grief, the rest of the whining old black-dressed bitches carrying on, following Mrs. Luchessa's lead, groaning and moaning about their beloved Sal. His problem was that he was the only ranking boss who didn't have a couple of guys hanging around and lighting his cigars, getting him water or coffee. He wondered how the other dons saw this, if they took it as an insult, saw it as a sign of his independence from the rest of them, or, worse, a sign of his arrogance. He was about to begin laying the groundwork for a takeover of Sal's position, and everyone in this parlor wanted the same thing. He couldn't afford to lose face in front of them, to have them see him as anything but a boss, a power to be reckoned with . . .

And even as he was thinking it, there was Merle, coming through the door of the funeral parlor lounge, looking around at all the heavyweights, dismissing the guards with a sneer. Darrin smiled. It was genuinely good to see the boy for once, the kid showing good timing for a change.

What was that on his forehead, though, and was he limping?

Merle had a rule of thumb that he lived by and which served him well: Live by your instincts. Sometimes his instincts would tell him to relax, to calm down and not make a scene because there had to be a cop in the area. Other times they told him to attack, kick ass and kill if he wanted to, there was no way he could get caught. Right now, his instincts were telling him not to let any of these lames see that he was afraid of them, so he came strutting into the room as if he owned it. Spotted Uncle Dare over there on a couch talking to a couple of old fat guys, looking at him and smiling, aw, the old pud was glad to see him. The sight of Merle probably made him less afraid, himself.

Merle walked over to him, stood with his hands clasped before him, waiting for a break in the conversation, until Darrin could acknowledge him, and as soon as he did Merle slid onto the sofa next to him, letting these guys know that he wasn't some bodyguard, was above that, wasn't about to stand against the wall all day and look tough.

Which didn't mean that he didn't know how to show respect.

"Uncle Darrin," Merle said, "I'm sorry about your loss."

Darrin was staring knives at him, as if he had just lifted the toupee off his head or some damn thing. Now all of a sudden not looking so happy to see him.

"You pay your respects to Mrs. Luchessa, Merle?"

"Yes, I surely did. Along with the other ladies, Aunt Marlene, too. She told me you were down here."

Uncle Darrin smiled tightly, nodded a couple of times, his anger apparent. Merle knew when he wasn't wanted, and besides, he'd made his point.

"I'll just go ahead back on in there and make sure everything stays cool."

"Yes, you do that, Merle."

Merle got up, nodded his goodbyes to the fat old guys who looked as if he'd slapped them, and swaggered from the room. His instincts told him it was time to get the fuck out of there.

Catfeet looked better, the cold outside air rejuvenated him, although he still wasn't feeling so good. His head was pounding, and he was wondering when he'd had his last meal. Had it been the dinner with Sal, a day and a half ago? No, it couldn't be. He must have had a sandwich somewhere, a bowl of soup or at least a hamburger.

He walked from the store to his hotel, quickly. His stomach felt raw, as if it consisted of two soft steel plates that were rubbing together. On fire and sour. Throat sore from smoking one after another at the bar last night. His toes hurt, from where he'd kicked Como in the shin. He wondered how Como's shin felt.

He was wearing a new suit, off the rack but it fit all

right, maybe a little snug in the shoulders. New topcoat, too, the other one was all wrinkled and hadn't come out of the wash too well; he'd told the guy in the men's clothing store to dump it along with the suit. He had a couple of boxes under his arm, new shirts and ties, matching accessories. He had shiny new shoes on his feet, Florsheim's. Even his socks were new. He'd change into the new underwear back at the hotel, after he took another shower and shaved, brushed his teeth and gargled.

He entered his room and locked the door behind him, dropped his packages on the bed and took off his coat, checked himself out in the mirror. Looked good, except for the stubble, the red eyes, the slight paunch. After he got this problem fixed, he'd start swimming again, get back into shape. Hell, the way he was going, he'd be down to a hundred and a half in no time, just from not eating.

Feet undressed and threw the jail-bought underwear into the trash can, went into the bathroom and shaved, brushed, gargled, then showered again, passing up the hotel soap, using the three dollar a cake stuff he'd bought at the men's store. Smelled good and musky, somehow dark, even a little sinister. He scrubbed his head with the shampoo that was the same brand as the soap. He'd even bought some cologne of the same scent. He got dressed again, slapped on some of the cologne, checked the paper to make sure he had the address he was heading for down in his mind, then picked up his topcoat and began to walk out of the room. He stopped with the door half-open and looked back, regretfully.

It was a smaller suite than the one he'd rented before, the 909 being his base of operations for many years before his trouble. His regular place was rented out, this was all that was left for him. Eight, nine years he'd lived here, tipping the maid weekly, giving the night clerks racing tips, the doormen presents four times a year on top of the buck he'd hand them coming in and going out, and every time they hailed him a cab. Been back around ten hours and had anyone come up to see him, ask him how he was? And now he was heading out to maybe get himself killed, and there was really no one to say goodbye to.

Well, two people really, three if you counted the kid, who didn't even know him and probably never would, even if he lived to be a hundred.

Feet closed the door behind him and dropped his top-coat on the bed, picked up the phone and dialed information, got two numbers from the woman and hung up.

The first call was routed through two other people before he heard Femal's professional voice, all cool and businesslike. "Darrin Favore's office, may I help you." Her inflection making it clear that she didn't think that she could.

"It's me," Feet said.

"Yes." Flat and emotionless. He was bothering her.

"Femal . . ." She didn't say anything, let him squirm.

"I'm sorry."

"Not as sorry as I am, Robert." He heard her breathing, wondered if she was through. At last, she said, "Listen to me. I've got a good life, a good job. I'm in control. There's no room in my life for someone like you, not anymore. Don't bother me again, or drag me into your little soap opera life, all right?"

"What about the kid, isn't the kid mine?!"

Softly, Femal said, "Tell me her name, Robert. Go ahead, speak your daughter's name."

He racked his brain, frantically trying to come up with the kid's name, he knew she'd told it to him. He remembered thinking it, knowing it last night. But last night, when he was drinking, he wasn't under any pressure. He just couldn't do it, the name escaped him.

He said, "That's not fair, I—"

"You make my case for me, Robert. Now don't bother me here, and don't bother me at home. Is that clear?" Then she hung up, obviously not too concerned as to whether it was or was not clear in Feet's mind.

He looked at the phone, puzzled, then placed it in its cradle.

The second call went a little smoother, at least he got through right away, even though he could tell from the way the secretary answered the phone that something wasn't right. The secretary said, "Mr. Lane's office?" as if she wasn't quite sure, the woman sounding scared, breathing fast.

"Let me speak to Charlie Lane," Feet said. "Tell him it's Bob Millard," and the woman told him that she wasn't sure if Mr. Lane could come to the phone right now . . . Hell, was she about to start crying?

"Mr. Lane?" The woman called tentatively. "Sir? It's a Mr. Millard?"

There was a pause, during which Catfeet could hear Charlie speaking loudly in the background. Then he heard, "Yeah, what?"

"Charlie, is that you?"

"Feet, where the hell you at, tell me, I got to see you right away."

"I'm at the 909."

"I'll be there in ten minutes, if I don't kill somebody first."

Feet said, "Wait a minute, calm down, now goddamnit, don't throw it all away, she ain't worth it."

"How you know who I'm mad at, huh?" Charlie challenging him, angry at himself because he was angry. Feet didn't take it personally. He'd rather Charlie was mad at him than at that flyweight broad he was married to. Maybe he could use it, get the kid out of the office and on his way over to the 909, steaming, before he did something he'd be revoked for.

"It's always over a woman, Charlie, you remember that, a woman or dough. Everybody in the joint's there for one of those two reasons. I'm at the 909, and you get your ass over here before you say another word in that place."

There was a pause, he heard the phone bang on some-

thing, then he heard Charlie's voice, disembodied, floating to him.

"*Fuck* you, John, and that hateful bitch you raised." In
the background he could hear a woman, Charlie's old lady
probably, shrieking something, telling Charlie he was a
child molester and she'd see him behind bars. Feet heard
a door slam and then someone grabbed the phone, a male
voice fighting for control spoke in Feet's ear.

"Yes, who's there?"

"You don't know me," Feet said, "but I got a friend of
yours in the room with me. Your wife."

"I beg your pardon?" Feet loved it when they got outraged, acted superior.

He said, "She wanted to tell you something, but she's
busy right now."

"Who is this?" the voice said. "My wife's with you?
What's wrong with her?"

"Nothing, she's just fine. Listen, she's got something
in her mouth right now, I'll have her call you as soon as
she's done, all right?" Feet, smiling, hung up the phone
on whoever it was who had helped put Charlie in such a
bad mood.

Then right away felt badly about what he'd done. The
guy, John, and Lina, God bless them, they'd brought
Charlie back from the dead, had somehow got him mad
enough where the jailhouse attitude stopped being important to him.

Feet took off his suit jacket and sat down on the chair
next to the bed, picked up the paper and scanned the
front page, fighting hard to keep Femal and the daughter
he'd never know out of his mind, waiting for the Charlie
he'd raised to come and see him.

Chapter
32

Blandane had taken his violin lesson and listened patiently while the teacher chewed him out, told him what a fool he was, wasting his money on the instrument and the lessons. Why invest that kind of time, energy and money if you did not love the music enough to practice? The man had told him that his playing sounded like cats screaming. Dick had listened, apologized, paid and left, vowing to find the time to practice before next Wednesday's lesson. When you were dealing with artists, you had to make some concessions.

One good thing about it, the lesson and ass-chewing had taken his mind off his problems, off his work.

He hadn't heard from Internal Affairs, yet, although he knew he would. OPS had grilled him for most of the morning, making their case against O'Brian and getting it right in their minds that they didn't have to make one against him. He'd have to testify, something he wasn't looking forward to.

He'd tried to make it clear to them, what it was all about. He'd done what he had the night before because he had no choice, and he resented the fact that departmental politicians were using his actions to step up the ladder. He'd testify if he had to, do whatever else he had to do to make sure that O'Brian would never be allowed back onto the street, but he just wanted it on the record that he wasn't doing it for any other reason than to see justice served. He'd made this statement and had found himself with five pairs of eyes upon him, all looking puzzled. Then one of them had said, "Uh, right, we got you, amigo, now, you want to tell us again why you flattened your partner last night?"

Sometimes it wasn't easy.

He locked the violin in the trunk of his car, grateful that it was mid-November and unseasonably cold, nearing the freezing mark. He wouldn't have time to take the thing home, and if it had been hot it might have warped in the trunk. He couldn't see himself carrying it into a new precinct house, locking it in his locker. There'd be enough gossip floating around about him as it was.

He drove quickly through the near-deserted afternoon streets, down to Police Headquarters at 11th and State, parked, locked and set the alarm on the car and headed into the station, anxious.

Dick found the shift commander of Gang Crimes North sitting behind his desk in an office that was large for a lieutenant, stood there until the man noticed him then introduced himself, saw the curiosity fall off the man's face, replaced by aversion. The lieutenant was not happy to see him.

"Sit down, Blandane."

Dick sat. The chair was wooden, with the curved seat with the little carved wooden valley that always stuck to his pants, made his butt sweat. He sat straight, staring right into the man's eyes, with nothing to hide. He'd made his decision when he'd been with the OPS people that morning; this job just wasn't worth it. If this guy gave him one ounce of trouble, he'd quit, take his degree and his idealistic attitude and put them to work in the private sector, where he might even make a decent buck without worrying about getting his ass shot off every night, by friend or foe, one.

The lieutenant picked up a phone and told someone to have Sergeant Hurtah come into his office, then he hung up, appraised Dick with an open glare.

"Simmons says you're solid." Dick said nothing. The lieutenant grunted. "Said you had an attitude problem, too."

"Only with people who don't deserve a liberal attitude, sir."

"Well, there's more of them out there than there are in here," the boss nodding his head toward the window then back, telling Dick who the enemy was, that it wasn't his fellow cops.

The lieutenant said, "Sergeant Hurtah's going to explain some of the facts of life around here to you, Blandane. Then he's going to give you your assignment. Before he gets here, I want you to know something." The lieutenant sat forward and crossed his hands on the desk, hunched his shoulders, sharing a secret.

He was a tall, lean man, sandy hair receding rapidly, young for an officer, the baldness giving him an air of authority, of age. He looked more like an accountant than a cop.

The lieutenant said, "If you ever see one of my people acting brutally toward the citizens of this city, I not only expect you to react the way you did last night, but I expect you to take it a little further, put the son of a bitch in the hospital so we can get him fired before he's able to hit the street, waiting for some departmental hearing. But, if you ever, and I stress the word *ever*, take it upon yourself to go to OPS or IA without bringing it first through proper channels, then I'm going to make a project out of you, Blandane, make you my own personal assignment. You won't use my unit to further your personal agenda, is that understood?"

"I have no agenda, sir."

"Your record shows you've beefed something like eight people in seven years. You're getting attention, Blandane, but you're making some serious enemies along the way."

"Only people who aren't worth being friends with, sir."

The lieutenant opened his mouth to speak but his attention was drawn behind Dick, and he shut his mouth, saving it for another time when there were no witnesses. Dick turned in his chair, saw a short stocky man standing in the doorway, watching and listening.

"Sergeant Hurtah, come in." Dick stood, at parade rest, then held his own hand out when he saw that Hurtah was doing so as he approached, shook the man's hand and they introduced themselves.

"You through with him, boss?" Hurtah didn't wait for an answer, said, "Come with me, Blandane."

The sergeant's desk was cluttered. Half a sandwich was on a sheet of waxed paper, a cardboard cup of coffee on the paper next to it, emitting steam. Hurtah sat behind the desk, shoulder holster riding high, another, larger pistol sticking out of the left side of his pants, butt out.

"Here's the deal," Hurtah said. "The lieutenant's a lot like you, college boy with ambitions. Going far. But not too far with me, that ain't the way I operate. You tell him I said that and I'll catch your ass in the toilet, cut your tongue out for you with my razor."

Dick wondered if he was kidding. He looked as if he could pull it off without a lot of trouble. He had wide shoulders and a big waist, going to fat, but not soft. Hurtah lit a cigarette and Dick tried not to make a face at the smoke filling up the tiny room.

"Me, now, I'm another story. Hell, me and Simmons go back a way, and if he tells me you're all right, then that's the way it is, and I don't care what the street cops think." Hurtah paused, took a sip of his coffee, a deep drag off the cigarette. "Coffee serves no purpose without a cigarette.

"The problem we got here, is our unit's kind of elite, we got a grapevine never stops yacking, so everyone knows about you and O'Brian, and even the people who agree with what you did ain't about to say it in public. They'll treat you OK in roll call, but nobody wants to work with you."

"I can work alone, Sergeant."

"I'm Emory, you're Dick. Save that sergeant crap for the politicians who need the thrill." Hurtah took a bite out of the sandwich, made a face, dropped it back on the paper, spoke around it.

"I've got the only teenage son alive can fuck up making a sandwich." He didn't wait for a response from Blandane, said, "We got something last night might be of interest, I want you to look into it." He fished around on his desk, found a report and shook it free, tossed it across the desk at Dick.

"Got a nine-eleven about a couple of guys beating another guy to death. Victim refused to sign a complaint, said his attackers left before the squad rolled up. Thing was, the officers saw two men rolling all over the gutter, and when they pulled up they got another story, one claimed to be a good Samaritan. Who then got mouthy, and the officers tossed him. Turned out he's known to us, got quite a rep for himself. Name's Merle Como, know him?" Dick shook his head. "He's Darrin Favore's nephew, runs errands for him."

"I know of Favore."

"You and everyone else on the force. Blockhead sits there in his office laundering money, pretending he's legitimate and thinking we're not onto him."

"*Are* we onto him?"

"Only from an intelligence point of view." Hurtah stopped, looked pointedly at Dick, letting him know that someone else, more than likely Uncle Sam, was onto Favore, and the Chicago Police Department could only pass on any information obtained on him to them. "You get my drift?"

"I'm not dumb," Blandane told him, and Hurtah said that Dick couldn't prove that by him.

"Your job, starting now until further notice, Dick, is to look into him, see what Como's up to, and what, if anything, it has to do with his uncle's gang."

"We can't go after the head, we'll take an arm, is that what you're saying?"

"That's what *you're* saying, Dick, not me. Don't put words in my mouth, I got too many of them in there already. What I'm saying—" The black phone on his desk rang and Hurtah held up a finger, said, "is that there ain't no other fucking thing for you to do, pal." He picked up the phone and spoke softly for a minute, swiveling around in his chair to face a filthy window. He turned back and hung up, looked in Dick's direction, reflectively, through him rather than at him. "Hm," the sergeant said.

Then, to Dick, "You've got the report, the information on last night's occurrence. Look into it."

Dick wondered if he was being dismissed, then had another thought, thinking about what the man had said before answering his phone. He looked at his new boss, wondering how far he would be able to go, the man now distracted, thinking about something else, the phone call, probably. Blandane said, "Sergeant? Emory?" Waited for the man to look up then said, "Is this bullshit, to get me out of the way because nobody wants to work with me?" and the sergeant told him to get the hell out of his office.

Chapter 33

What else could he possibly have expected? Hurtah was a damn sergeant in gang crimes, not assigned to the shrink's office, and he damned sure wasn't a priest. It could have gone far worse, if Dick had pushed it or if the guy really didn't like him. If he wanted the man's respect, he'd have to earn it.

So, if it wasn't bullshit, he wouldn't treat it as such. And if it was, he'd damn sure change it around, make it important. Nail Como to the cross and look innocently at Hurtah, at the lieutenant, tell them, along with the feds, that he was only following orders.

Maybe it was for real, anyway, just maybe they were giving him some responsibility, testing him to see if he could handle it, working without strict supervision.

Blandane sat at the computer terminal, punching in numbers, first drawing out Como's driver's license information, then his two-sheet according to Sound-Dent, where you put in the target's name and got a couple of pages of criminal histories of people with the same name, or one that sounded like that name, good for finding out aliases. They'd pop out two sheets at a time, and if your man's name wasn't on those two, you hit a key and two more would print out. The point being that most crooks used aliases that sounded close to their true name, being creative geniuses, and weighed the same no matter what name they were using, had the same hair color and placement of scars.

Finally, he tapped into the FBI sheet, accessed all of Como's arrests, the disposition of those cases.

Was this interesting reading, or what? Blandane thought so, was fascinated by the report in front of him, looking it over as he absently stripped the perforated edges of the computer paper away from the report, eight pages altogether, including the license report and the Sound-Dent sheet.

Twenty-four arrests as an adult, with no felony convictions. Everything this guy did was plea bargained down to a misdemeanor or thrown out of court. How the hell old was he? Thirties. Old enough to have been plying his trade in the wild days, when justice was done in the hallways of the court buildings. Before the feds started slamming down the crooked judges. Still, Greylord had begun when this man was still in his mid-twenties, most of the judges pinched for taking bribes had by now been released from prison, having served two or three years of their fifteen-year sentences before being paroled. So, either Como or one of his cronies had got next to the victim, or the witnesses, or they'd reached the cops. There was no judge in the county stupid enough to take bribes from small-time hoodlums like Como anymore.

Interesting.

The Federal Organized Crime Strike Force had been ravaged in this city a few years ago, officially a victim of cut funding, while law enforcement officials throughout the state knew better, were aware that the real reason for its decimation had been that the US attorney at the time had thought that the Force was getting too powerful. It had been a political decision. But even so, someone, somewhere, should have noticed this, seen this known associate of gangsters getting away with everything short of murder . . .

Right at the top of the printout were the words: *****CAUTION/SUSP DEVIATE SEX ASLT***** the proclamation being made that this person was a dangerous sexual felon, at least had been arrested as one. There were three arrests for deviate sexual assault—which could have been anything from wagging his penis at schoolkids to attempted rape—pleaded down, disposed of, Blandane assumed, after promises of counseling or psychiatric care.

Intimidation—there were four arrests for that. Not a single conviction. Seventeen Battery arrests, fifteen thrown out, one pleaded down to misdemeanor assault, one somehow disposed of before Como had even left the police station.

Blandane read the police report from the previous night, holding it on top of the computer printout. Como had been wearing a Rolex, with several numbers stamped on the back, the responding officer had jotted them down but Dick wasn't sure if one of them was a 7 or a 1; another could have been a 3 or a 0. The other five numbers were clear. He dropped the sheets on the desk and punched his ID number into the machine, accessing FBI and local police departments around the nation, squinting at the officer's cramped printing and typing in the numbers and the suspected numbers, doing them both ways, requesting information on a stolen Rolex watch with those specific numbers. A waste of time, more than likely, but some Rolexes had a price tag in six figures, and if he could put one of those on Como's wrist, he'd have some leverage with the man, at the very least something to hold over his head, legally bring him in for questioning on any other matters that might arise in the course of his investigation.

Christ, it felt good to be acting like a cop again, to use what he'd learned from his long years of study of the criminal mind, his ways . . .

"Need the computer, bloods."

Blandane turned, saw one of the largest black men he'd ever laid eyes on, the man standing there patiently, nonthreatening. "Follow-up on an ongoing investigation. You mind?"

Dick told him not at all, lifted his sheets and gave up the chair.

The man stood there, looking at Dick calmly. He had a dapper little pencil-mustache, short-cropped hair razor-parted on the left. He was dressed in blue jeans, wore a plaid lumberjack shirt with a sleeveless down vest over. The curving handle of his pistol stuck out of the left armpit of the vest. It looked like a cap gun, next to that massive chest.

"You seeking info, it'll come over the line, wait on hold for the computer to free up." The man stood there, wanting something.

"Thanks," Dick said. Around them other officers were filing out of the roll call that Dick hadn't attended. He'd already checked in and was assigned his duty. The big man looked around him, curiously, not furtively. Then spoke softly for Dick's benefit.

"You got friends, bloods, here and in South, too. 'Bout time somebody kicked that Irish fool in the ass." He said this then sat down in the chair, not bothering to introduce himself.

He might have friends, Blandane decided, but they were definitely working undercover.

His next move was to speak with the responding officers from last night's 911 call, interviewing them quickly over coffee at a 7-Eleven, the three of them leaning against the squad car, informally.

"Man called me a nigger, and my partner laughed," the black cop said, not mad about it. Dick couldn't tell if the man was making a statement or voicing a complaint. For all he knew, the guy was putting his partner on.

The white cop told him, "Soon as he shot off his

mouth, I decided to toss him. Never heard of him before, but I figured, what was a slob like this, like this hillbilly, doing over there in *that* neighborhood? He wasn't even close to Uptown, where most of his type lives. Why I wrote down the Rolex numbers, too. Guy's rolling in the gutter, wearing about twenty bucks worth of clothes, fighting some other idiot, and he's got a *Rolex* on his wrist? It didn't make sense."

"Victim wouldn't file a report?"

"Didn't want to. He was drunk, both of them had puke all over them. He was either scared of the loud-mouth, or didn't want to snitch on him."

"You think this Como might have attacked the other man?"

"Looked the other way around, when we got there. The other guy was kicking at him, but crawling away, scooching along the gutter on his ass."

"You pat this Como down?"

"Sure did, didn't have rubber gloves with me, either, and the guy had puke all over him."

"I heard you the first time. But you didn't search the other guy?"

"Nah, he looked harmless. Middle-aged, overweight, had a suit on. Wouldn't have even bothered to file a report at all, if Como hadn't called Crier here a nigger. I figured it would be a good idea, have it on file in case any houses got robbed that night, or someone turned up shot."

"You follow the victim home, find out *any*thing about him?"

"Now wait a minute, we ain't running a cab service." The black cop, Crier, was showing his anger. Did he think gang crimes worked for Internal Affairs, or what?

"This isn't an investigation into your practices, Crier. It's on Como, I want a case on him, not you."

"Well, just so you know . . ."

The white cop said, "Crier's sensitive, all the time crying; it's in the blood, genetic. It's how they got the name in the slave days."

Crier said, "Fuck you man, that shit ain't funny."

The white cop said, "The guy, Como, he knew the other guy's address, that, or made one up."

"Knew his address?"

"Told us where the guy lived, anyway, maybe even trying to keep the victim silent, letting him know that he knew where the guy lived."

It was difficult for Dick to remain calm. These guys were street cops? Responsible for keeping the public peace? He forced himself to speak with composure, said, "Either of you remember that address, by any chance?"

The black cop looked thoughtful, while his partner didn't even seem to be thinking about it, seemed more interested in Crier than in the question Blandane had asked. He smiled at Crier, as if silently encouraging him on.

Crier said, "Fourteen-eleven," then nodded his head, sure of himself.

The white cop said, "I got an idiot savant for a partner, Blandane. Can't remember his wife's name, but give him a phone number he heard in passing ten years ago, he got it on the tip of his tongue."

"I can remember *your* wife's name, man, amongst other things 'bout her, that's all I need to remember."

Impressed, Blandane said, "What street was that on, again, Officer Crier?"

Chapter
34

Charlie had tried to keep the anger inside, had given it his best shot and had been amazed when he'd failed. He'd had it in his mind when he'd left Brimley's office not to let his humiliation affect his judgment. All he had to do was stay alert, cool, for a couple more hours and everything would be all right.

Except for the fact that half the Adult Probation Department now thought he was a child molester. And the fact that he'd have to hand over a thousand dollars every month to some fat, sweet-talking, conniving piece of shit, all because Lina's pride had been hurt.

He packed his clothes, in a hurry, taking the suitcases from the closet, the good ones she'd had before they'd even met, maybe bought by her first husband or given to her by her parents. His anger mounted with each trip to the car, with every step, his surprise at it rising accordingly.

Hadn't he survived five years in Menard by staying cool? Here he was, going berserk now, over something he perceived to be unfair. What could be more unfair than prison life?

The difference between then and now struck him as he locked the door and threw his house keys into the bushes. Struck him with such force that he stopped on the sidewalk leading to the street.

Inside, in prison, people were aware of the damage their actions could cause them, the pain; sometimes, even, the loss of life itself.

Charlie walked to the car, got inside, and drove to the office, thinking about it.

Inside, you walked hard and looked straight ahead, never away from anyone. They tested you constantly, stood in your way until you proved yourself to them. Inside, people died for ignoring someone's greeting, for making another man lose face, real or perceived. You knew that, learned it quickly if you were to make it through.

Out here, people thought they could say and do whatever they wanted, whenever they wanted, with no repercussions.

It had blown him away, when he'd seen it the first time, some kid at the college trying to be his friend when Charlie was still feeling anxious about his freedom, sitting next to him, talking bad about his own girlfriend, what a bitch she was, how he was cheating on her every chance he could. Charlie would see the guy later, with his arm around the girl's waist, whispering in her ear, lovers for all the world to see and envy, and he'd feel repulsed.

It wasn't just the males, either. More than once Lina's own closest friends had come on to him, let him know that they were available, that the two of them could carry on a short or long term affair and Lina would never have to find out.

He'd wondered back then if it would bring them some kind of twisted pleasure, cause them joy to hurt a friend.

To Charlie, friendship was forever, gained through behavior and lost the same way. His few friends in prison were men he was willing to stand and die for, and he was sure they would do the same for him. Was there any way he could hurt Cat? Not in this life, and he knew the same held true for Millard, his truest friend, more a brother than a mere buddy or pal.

He would have to speak to Cat, tell him about this, the hypocrisy he saw in this outside world, more dangerous and life-threatening than any lifestyle in any prison on earth.

Out here, people did, by design and intent, things that would automatically end their existence in the world in which Charlie had lived for so long.

What frustrated him, he realized, was the fact that they nearly always got away with it.

He entered his office and got his client disc out of the locked drawer, shook his head because it was payday and he might have to slap John a time or two to get him to cough up his check. Which was all right with Charlie, he was tired of playing by the wrong set of rules, for the benefit of people who didn't even come close to understanding him, why he was the way he was. Tired, too, of being the butt of their jokes, their sideways glances, of having them think things about him that were absolutely false. So damn tired of being in control . . .

He sat down behind his desk, taking a few minutes to calm down. It wouldn't do to get pinched in here for doing something stupid, it would cost too much to square. He had to relax, hold on for a few more minutes, just that long.

But boy, did it feel good, letting it out for a change.

He had the urge to go over to the country club and drop some weights on the toes of some of the traders, the brokers, the real estate assholes who equated muscle mass with strength. Wouldn't that be fun, tearing them up then going into the bar and letting the older corporate frauds know what he truly thought of them?

He felt the anger, let it roll over him, enjoyed its company after such a prolonged absence.

Frustration, man, it was there in bunches. On the inside, if someone's foolishness had cost him a monthly fee, the deal would be obvious to everyone involved, even the other man's closest friends; the liar would have to pay the monthly due or he would die, deservedly so. Out here, people could get away with shit like this.

Or could they?

Charlie grabbed his Rolodex, zipped through it, looking for the card he'd made up yesterday, the day before, when he thought that he might need the woman's name and number, if she ever turned up looking for trouble again . . .

There it was, Lorraine Williams, with a phone number and address. Charlie got up and went to his file cabinet, pulled out the drawer and grabbed her file, found the release form the woman had signed. Took it back to his desk and swept the While You Were Out messages onto the floor, dropped the file where the messages had been and dialed the woman's number.

"Mrs. Williams, Charlie Lane, remember me, the check-writer from the other day?" He put all his salesmanship into his voice, all his sincerity, not faking it at all.

"Yes?" Poor fat Mrs. Williams lost the cheeriness that had been in her hello, now wary, on guard.

"Mrs. Williams," Charlie said, "I've had a change of heart. It seems that I've made an error, and allowed you to make one, also."

"You can't have the money back, if that's what this is about." The anonymity of distance, of being safe in her own kitchen, gave the woman strength. Courage enough to stand up to him. He admired that in her. Charlie felt very secure around greedy people, it was easy to understand them, their motivations.

"Oh, no, the money's yours, that was from my own personal checking account, my gift to you."

"Then what do you want?"

Charlie held the phone to his ear with his shoulder, took her release form and held it close to the mouthpiece, ripped it in half, then again, then again, and let it fall to the floor with the messages.

"You hear that, Mrs. Williams? That was the release form you signed. My wife, ma'am, perpetrated a fraud upon you. Misstated our product and willfully misled you. All three of which are wrong, the first of which is illegal. You see, the picture she showed you, where she was so heavy? She was pregnant in that picture, Mrs. Williams, Lina has never been an ounce overweight in her entire life." He finished the sentence and looked up to see John Lofgren standing in his doorway, looking puzzled, a payroll envelope in his right hand.

"Hold on a second, Mrs. Williams."

Charlie put the phone on the desk and rose, his smile warm and welcoming, walked over to John and plucked the envelope out of the man's hand. "My check? Thanks, Doddy."

John, puzzled, said, "I prorated your raise, is why it took so long to get down here, and you won't complain about the size of the monthly bonus, either . . . Who you talking to?"

"Listen up, you'll get the drift." Whispered, as if he and John were in on a secret. Charlie walked back to his desk, swept all the papers off it except for Mrs. Williams's empty file folder, put his feet up on the desk and smiled at John, tossed him a wink.

"Mrs. Williams, I'm back, sorry for the delay." He reached into the middle drawer of his desk, found the picture of Lina, and put it in his breast pocket, right next to the disc with the special clients.

"Yes, you heard me right, she defrauded you, just like Jim Bakker did to all those TV people, that's right, and she could go to jail for it." He covered the mouthpiece while Mrs. Williams shot questions at him, stage-whispered to John, "Wait, you're gonna love this next part," then said into the phone, "Can you sue her?! You can sue the *shit* out of her, Mrs. Williams, and her daddy, too, who, I'm willing to testify, put her up to the entire thing.

Yes, that's right." He paused, listening, then said, "I wouldn't be a bit surprised, Mrs. Williams, you might just win the entire business, yes, ma'am, 'Mrs. Williams Vi-ta-mins, help you go from fats to thins.' Pretty catchy, huh?" He was having a hard time trying to keep himself from laughing, seeing the look on John's face.

"What you do, ma'am, is let the rest of your dieter's group in on it. No, the business has insurance to cover this, a set amount for each claim, it won't take a dime away from you. Now, listen carefully to the next phrase. *Willful Misrepresentation.* Mrs. Williams, make sure your lawyer hears that phrase, that's the one that can win you the family fortune. And in the meantime, ma'am, watch your mail and keep your receipts from the company, you're gonna need them." Charlie looked at John, Mrs. Williams blabbering into the phone. He held it away from his ear, grinned widely and shook his head. "She's excited," he whispered to John, then he put the phone back next to his ear.

"You'll get the incriminating photo in the mail in the next day or two, certified, from me. That's right, I'm quitting, Mrs. Williams, and best of luck to you in your lawsuit. Class action? That sounds good, right, yes, bye now, and remember, willful misrepresentation!" Charlie hung up, feeling better than he had in his adult life.

"Gonna cost your ass a bundle, Doddy."

John's face was on fire, his eyes wide, staring. He did not believe what he had just heard. "What was that all about?"

"Lina's lies just cost me sixty grand, more than I make in this joint in a year. I figure it should cost her something, too, maybe every fucking thing you've got. I can't afford to work for you anymore, John, raise or no raise. Being married to your daughter, it's just too damn expensive."

John's face was darkening further with each of Charlie's words. The sight made Charlie feel good. He rose, slapped the payroll envelope against his leg, began to walk past John just as Lina came through the door, and Charlie smiled. Little Miss in a hurry, stopping and giving him the large-eyed, little-girl-lost look that he'd once loved so much.

"The dieter's group scam, Lina?" Charlie kissed her forehead, shook his head and walked past her. "It was your best move yet." He waited until he was in the middle of the office, the order-takers and secretaries all sitting there watching John preparing for his stroke, then said, "If your lies hurt Lance even once, lady, I'll have him taken away from you."

"I'll see you back in jail, first, you bastard!" Lina was shouting, the woman-child gone, the office seeing her the way Charlie did most every night.

"Good. I got better sex in there than I ever got from you, believe me." Charlie smiled at his secretary, the woman watching him as she automatically picked up the ringing phone, answered it in a frightened tone.

"See? See, Doddy?! I told you he was a faggot!"

"Faggot, hell, you'd turn Hefner gay. A blow-up doll is more lively in the sack than you've ever been!" He was enjoying this, shouting over his shoulder, walking past the secretary, who was holding the phone out, telling Charlie it was for him . . .

Now, driving to Cat's hotel, he felt elated, alive and renewed. What was wrong with him? This wasn't him, he was quiet, thoughtful, kept everything inside. Here out of a clear blue sky he was blowing it all off, giving it up because of a few stupid words she'd spoken over the phone in anger to his PO.

But what was he supposed to have done, waited until things quieted down and then killed her? It's what he would have done in prison, no doubt about it.

Only he wasn't in prison anymore. There were new rules to be learned, and it was about time he began to learn them. Talking to Mrs. Williams was a good start, it showed him he was picking the rules up, fast.

He found a place to park and got out of the car, the envelope inside his pants crinkling as he stood. The bottle that he'd never given to Brimley was in his hand. He'd walked out of the office clutching it to him, his security blanket. Brimley's price had gone way, way up. Scotch would no longer cut it with the man.

Cat opened the door before Charlie got to it, had obviously seen him from the window of the hotel room.

"Charlie?" Cat concerned, half-smiling, half-puzzled.

"Cat, man, I got to talk to you."

Chapter 35

But it wasn't that easy.

Charlie sat in the flower-patterned chair next to Cat's bed, the bottle on the nightstand, a full glass in his hand. An ice bucket was next to the Scotch bottle, sweating water onto the wood.

How to begin? To open up? It wasn't something he was used to doing.

Cat was sitting on the bed, patient, waiting him out, his hands on his legs, his head cocked, studying Charlie. When Cat had first taken him in, Charlie had seen him as an old man. It wasn't that way anymore.

Charlie said, "Cat, fuck it, I got sick of it. They're frauds out here, pretenders, man . . ." He thought of a way to explain it, a way Cat might understand.

"I worked in the clinic at Menard, you know that? We'd sometimes have to go to Death Row because unless they had to be street hospitalized the walking dead weren't allowed out of the area. Gacy was there, John Gacy, the fag kid-killer?" Charlie took a sip of his drink, turned it into a long pull, thinking about the right way to say this, he didn't want to screw it up.

"There's an extra set of bars sets off the area from general population, it's guarded from outside and in, and it's off limits, but the cons on janitorial crew clean the area; wax and buff the floors, wash the steel walls.

"Gacy, see, now you got to understand this, he's a soft, fat, short-eyed, short-ass punk. Swaggers around there because he's cut off from everyone else, the guys who would turn him out his first night in population, I mean a sissy like Gacy, he wouldn't even get *tested*."

"Negligees and Max Factor," Cat said, encouragingly.

"That's right. But see, we'd be there working on some dead man's tooth, stitching his forehead where he banged it against the wall or the bars, trying to knock his brains out and save the State the trouble, and one of the janitors would say something to this punk, he'd get all tough. 'You feel froggy, jump,' he'd yell it out, like a badass.

"But what you got to understand, see, is that set of *bars* is there. We'd get let out and the dead men would have to get locked down and this sissy would be sticking his middle finger up through the bars, like he's bad. But *he was safe*, see? Could afford to play the game. He knew goddamn well if it hadn't been for that set of bars he'd be ordering out for knee pads, Cat. He wouldn't stand a chance with any of us, the guy got the muscle tone of a five-year-old. But *he was safe*. He knew he could get away with it and he did."

"What're you saying, Charlie?"

"I don't know, shit." Charlie rubbed the glass around between the palms of his hands, set it down on the nightstand and began to pace the room. "I guess I'm saying that's how I see the outside world, the people in it, Cat. They're all huff and puff, talk shit because they know they can get away with it, feel safe . . ."

"Yeah, Charlie, sure, but inside, what you got in there? Society's best and brightest? Come *on*. The rules got to change out here, and you got to live by them. Otherwise, you go back in, and they throw away the key."

"You know what she did to me today?"

Cat said he didn't and Charlie told him, and all Cat wanted to know was why she'd called Brimley. Charlie took the envelope out of his pants and tossed it onto the bed next to Cat.

"That's why, Cat. Your money's in there, I think, from what Favore said last night. I took it from him in a card game. Your dough, and nineteen more."

Cat said, "Jesus, Charlie," holding the envelope in his hands, lifting it up and looking at it, in wonder. Then, softly, again, "Jesus . . ."

"I've had it with this bullshit, Cat."

"Charlie," Cat put the envelope back down on the bed, slapped it with his hand, hard. "Charlie, you got to listen to me. I ain't seen you like this since you were in high school, for Christ's sake, when you were gonna kill everyone because of what happened."

"Nice way to put it, Cat. 'What happened.' What *happened* was they killed my folks, drove them off the road and shot them down like dogs in the street."

"It don't matter anymore, Charlie, it's history. What matters now is you got an education, you can get a good job. Pay this idiot off for the next five years 'cause that's the way he does his business, you got no choice." Cat talked and Charlie watched him, slowly eased back down in his chair, crossed his legs. He'd drop the bombshell as soon as Cat stopped talking.

"You use what I gave you, Charlie, and pay attention to me for once. You know what this reminds me of? It reminds me of the fight we had ten years ago, when you were gonna try and be me, be a thief, after you got out of high school. I had college money put *aside* for you, kid, and what'd you do with it? You threw it away, spent a couple of years out there being a tough guy and wound your ass up in the joint."

"Where you never were."

"Because I'm careful. I don't let emotions get in the way. And don't you say it, don't hand me that shit, 'cause I know you. That whole act, the way you were after prison, it didn't mean nothing to me, I saw through it. It was *all* emotion, Charlie, the way you acted."

"It was control, Cat."

"It was fear."

"Bull*shit*."

"You talk about them being hypocrites? Take a look at yourself, kid. A PO gets under the surface, makes you scared and you go nuts, quit your job, leave the old lady, come running in here with God knows what garbage about some skinner on Death Row won't see next year anyway, look at yourself."

"You'd'a done different?"

"Damn right I would have." Cat had been looking at the bottle throughout the conversation, his eyes going to it involuntarily, gazing longingly. Now he got up and went into the bathroom, got the other glass and opened the ice bucket, grabbed a handful of cubes and dropped them into the glass, filled it with liquor. He stood with his back turned to Charlie, downed the glass and gave himself a refill, left the glass on the table after he capped the bottle and lit a cigarette, turned and sat down, looking somewhat calmed down.

Charlie wasn't letting him off the hook.

"What would you have done, Cat?"

Cat blew smoke over Charlie's head. "Me?" He crossed his legs, reached out and picked up his glass, drank half of it down. Cat set the glass on the nightstand and took a deep drag on his cigarette, staring hard at Charlie, talked around the smoke drifting past his lips.

"I'd have waited, sweet-talked the wife, put the sauseege to her every night, made her think I loved her above life. A week, two weeks from then, I'd have her feeling so goddamn guilty about what she'd done that writing a letter to the PO would have been the least she would want to do, maybe even talk her into going to see him, run him some head to get me off the hook. If that failed, I'd go to the US attorney, tell him about the scam and let him know that for complete termination of parole, I'd wear a wire, hang the PO by his balls for him. Turning in a cop ain't snitching, it's getting even. But the bit with the wife would work, if you played it right."

"You'd be able to do that, be that phony with a woman?"

"Let me tell you how it was with you, Charlie." Cat was staring at him straight in the eye, giving Charlie what he thought was the gospel, finishing that second drink now, sucking on the smoke.

"She was all over you, sweet and kind and loving, doing things to you that you only used to dream about in the joint, right? But the second the ring got on her finger things changed, though, didn't they?"

"Cat, she went from day to night in a week, and it's gone downhill since then."

"What's more phony than that?" Cat said it and sat back, his case made.

"So you could be the same as her, just as phony?"

"In a minute, and that's the difference between us. Charlie, you think with your heart, and I use my head. That's why I'm a thief and you're a college-educated salesman. You went into the joint and after five years knew goddamn well that you could never go back, came out and became what you should have been all along, because you got the heart. Me, I get pinched, go inside, I'd spend the time figuring out what I did wrong, and the day I got out I'd be setting up another score."

Charlie didn't like the way it was going. He'd come over here with every intention of going into business with Cat, living up to what Lina and Brimley and everyone else seemed to think of him, put it to use and profit. Now he was hearing that he'd made a mistake, that he was wrong again.

"You know how sick they make me, Cat? They take

one look at you and figure they got you sized up, file you away and forget about you. You see it all the time, someone says, What do you do for a living, you tell them you're a salesman and they think you're gonna talk their ear off. Women see you in a bar without your wife and come up to you, immediately assume that they can seduce you, that you're as self-absorbed as they are. They never look any deeper than the surface . . ."

"How you think Bundy lasted so long, that DeSalvo guy, Gacy, even? Charlie, they *counted* on people taking one look at them and figuring out what they were, and that's the only way to get ahead. Get them to thinking one thing, then pounce on them with the truth when their backs are turned. The serial killers don't know the way to do it either, because if you play it right, the mark won't even know you've been there 'til you're gone."

"It's the way a thief works, is that what you're telling me?"

There he went again, to the bottle, sitting there pouring a drink, lighting another cigarette from the butt of the last and crushing the worn butt in the little white Club 909 ashtray.

"It's the way *I* work, the way your father worked. Not the way you work. You work with your brains, with your mind, I said you *think* with your heart, I didn't say you work with it. Me, I think with my brain, and work with my heart. Go where it tells me. Like to the safe in a K-Mart after closing."

"You got to be as phony as they are, isn't that what you said, work from inside and play their game?"

"That's right, Charlie."

"All right. Let me ask you this. Is Favore a thief?"

"Favore, Sal, God rest his soul, all of them, they're all thieves at heart. Like me."

"But not me, huh? Well, you're wrong there. Cat, if they're thieves, if we're thieves, then why don't we rob *them*?"

"Rob Darrin Favore?" Cat grunted, dismissively. "It's been tried, more than once. Guys get found with their hands cut off and stuck up their asses, down their throats." He sipped his drink.

"You see what I'm saying to you, Charlie? About your heart? You blame Favore and your old lady for your problems, so you screw her around, leave her, quit your job, now you want to rob him. Don't you have any idea of how it works? Christ, you'd be the second guy they'd look for. Me, I'd be the first. I got enough troubles right now, brother, just forget about robbing any of those guys." Cat shook his head. "See what I was saying? You're all emotion, Charlie."

"And you're not?"

"Charlie, I hardly ever do anything doesn't turn me a profit."

"Except time, like the last two years. And taking me in fourteen years ago, how about that? Getting me through a year and a half of high school, two years after that supporting me. Later on, putting me through college, buying me clothes and cars."

"I told your old man I'd look after you if anything ever happened to him. And besides, you and me, we had a deal, plain and simple. You're my retirement plan, Charlie. We split the proceeds of your work down the middle, fifty-fifty, remember?"

"That was just bullshit and you know it, you only said that so I'd take your money."

"You think so?" Cat picked up the envelope, said, "What's in here, forty-one?" and counted out nine thousand dollars, tossed it on one side of the bed.

"The twenty-five's mine. Half of what you made last year."

"You don't mean that."

"Hell I don't. Now go find a job, Charlie, before your bright ideas get the both of us killed."

"Go find a job, just like that. And what about you?"

"Me?" Cat said, rising. "I got a wake to attend, an old friend of mine had a heart attack. But stick around, Charlie, get some rest, relax. I don't come back, all of that," he gestured toward the bed, toward the two piles of money fanned out on the bedspread, "is yours."

Chapter 36

The first place Blandane went after he left the squad cops was the house where the victim was supposed to live, and right away got told through the storm door that there wasn't no white man ever lived there, wasn't no white man living there now, and wasn't no white man ever *gonna* be living there.

"Can I come in?" he'd asked, and was told, "Does you gots a warrant?"

So, it was either a bogus address or the maid or whoever it was didn't want to give her boss up to the cops. He'd come back later, after normal working hours. It was four or so now, whoever lived here would be home probably no later than six.

It was time to perhaps confront the perpetrator, this Merle Como person. At the very least get a glimpse of him, check him out and make him aware that they were onto him. With punks like this, that could scare them into doing something stupid. If Como truly was a member of organized crime, he'd either be sleeping now, hung over, or he'd be jockeying for position at the funeral of Salvatore Luchessa. Dick hadn't so much as looked at a newspaper in the past two or three days, as busy as he'd been, but even he was aware that the leader of the Chicago outfit had caught himself a heart attack.

He would find Como, run him down and then, from seeing how the man looked, feeling his attitude, would know how to play him, whether to have a face-to-face, or do the legwork first. If the guy looked like a hard rock case, or if Dick had doubts, he could always say he was following up on the squaddies' case report from last night. He'd play it by ear and see what happened, see how he felt, if he should approach the man or leave him alone.

It would be easier, closer for him, to check Como's apartment first, though, just take a ride past, maybe park for a while, see if the white Chevy was on the street. He had a fax of Como's driver's license, so he knew what he looked like, but still, it was always easier for him to do his work when he knew his enemy, had had some sort of personal contact with the man.

He put his Malibu in gear and waited for a break in the early rush hour traffic, people taking shortcuts down what they thought were untraveled North Side streets causing more of a tie-up than there was down Michigan Avenue. To pass the time Dick put his headphones on, letting the car idle, warming up. What did he feel like listening to today? How about a little bit of the King.

He popped the cassette into the machine and waited, listened, started to sing "Love Me" along with Elvis as a kindly woman driver with very short brown hair combed all over to one side waved him ahead of her Volvo, the cars behind her honking their anger at her civility. Dick waved his thanks and broke away from the curb, smiling, singing, alive and ready.

It had been some time since he'd felt so much like a real cop.

•   •   •

Had Merle's faux pas cost him? Darrin didn't know. These guys, they played their cards so damn close to the vest, you never could tell what was on their minds.

Something sure was, though, or the eleven leaders wouldn't be sitting alone, without even bodyguards, in the lounge.

The dons had eaten, the eleven of them in the room dining on spaghetti and meatballs cooked by their grieving wives, the women making enough for three hundred men. Neckbones held in fat fingers and sucked dry with disgusting noises by men for whom eating was one of life's great pleasures. Most of the food was growing cold, sitting on various tables around the lounge, to be eaten by the bodyguards and the mourners after this meeting was over. Darrin wondered if there was anything more disgusting than cold spaghetti, knowing as he thought it that most of the people upstairs would scarf the greasy noodles down happily, feeling themselves to be a part of the family if they shared food with them.

Now it was time for wine and cigars, the smoke circling the ceiling, getting caught in the rotating fans and dying instantly. The smell, though, that didn't disappear anywhere near as quickly as the cigars' visual proof. It lingered, got into Darrin's clothes and hair. He wouldn't be getting laid tonight, not stinking like this. A thought that depressed him. That meant that he would have to stay home with Marlene, rather than be out screwing LaVella, who didn't even allow cigarette smoke in her apartment.

He wondered how Femal felt about smoke, if it bothered her if her lovers had the habit.

The talking was petering out, just small talk about what a nice guy Sal had been, most of it. The leaders speaking together in pairs, in cliques, none of which seemed to include Darrin. Was this something to worry about, had somebody learned something? If they even suspected him or anyone else of serious wrongdoing, there would be hell to pay. These weren't men who waited for evidence before judging you, convicting you, sentencing you . . .

At last Don Moretti spoke up, directing his comments at Darrin without preamble. The room, as if on cue, fell silent as the fat old bastard raised his voice.

"I got a call today, Darrin," Moretti said, "that somewhat disturbed me." The don puffed on his cigar and let the words hang between them, Darrin feeling ten pairs of eyes glaring at him, hard.

"Is that right?" Darrin said.

"Yes, unfortunately, that's exactly right." Talking around wet sucks, white smoke billowing and turning blue, heading toward Darrin.

This fat bastard, he thought he was in a movie, had center stage and was loving it.

Moretti had been close to Sal, they called themselves "brothers," and the first time Darrin had heard about that he'd laughed, asked the people he was with if the two of them had pricked their fingers, mingled a drop of their blood. It didn't seem so funny to him now. If this guy somehow took Sal's spot, was voted into the top position, Darrin could be in a lot of trouble. It was no secret how Darrin felt about Sal, Marlene's uncle or not, and when it came to brutality, Sal was a pussycat next to this Moretti.

But he was damned if he'd buy into this, play guilty. The guy wanted to wait him out? Well, Darrin could wait, too.

Although it wasn't easy, the way the others were staring at him, accusing eyes glaring . . .

Don Moretti never spoke a sentence in his life in which the word fuck wasn't spoken at least once, usually several times. But now he was playing it cool, speaking slowly and menacingly, without cursing and using ten-dollar words he must have learned from watching television. Being Don Corleone for the others in the room, impressing them with his knowledge, the way he could handle the situation. Maybe jockeying for position, for their votes. The prick.

All eleven surviving men would have to vote on Sal's replacement, the same way all of them would have to vote on moving someone up to fill the vacant spot. It was outfit law now in Chicago, there had to be a ruling party of twelve. As Christ had his disciples, so did the devil.

"Mrs. Luchessa called me." That old bitch? What the hell did *she* want?

In spite of himself, Darrin felt the need to hurry the man up, at least to show that he wasn't concerned.

He said, "Yeah, so what, Lorenzo?"

"The so what, Darrin, is what bothers me." Moretti waved his cigar around the room. "Bothers *us.*"

"You guys gonna let me in on the goddamn secret?" That was the way to do it, act all morally outraged that they'd been speaking about him behind his back. For all Darrin knew, this might even be a lead-in to their telling him that he had Sal's spot, was now The Man. Lord knows, these people had weird senses of humor.

"She says," Moretti said, slowly, raising his eyes to pin Darrin with close scrutiny, checking his reaction, "that you set her up with two mill worth of stuff, that she'd be seeing interest from it forever, from Sal."

Is that what this was all about? Thank God. For a minute, Darrin had thought that maybe they'd found something on him.

"That's right. Two mill for the old girl, and it wasn't easy explaining it to her, either, believe me." Darrin tried a laugh and it came out a little dry. "With seven old hens dressed in their funeral black running around the kitchen, clucking and crying." Shit! Some of those hens might well have been the wives of some of the men in this room. Too late now. He'd been trying to be funny, that's all. He hoped he didn't laugh himself to death.

Darrin continued.

"She's got interests in the Bahamas, some even in Switzerland, even though most of our action is out of there, now that the IRS can get into the numbered accounts—"

"I don't need to know specifics, Darrin."

Specifics? Who'd taught this ignorant bastard these words?

"What I need to know is, what happened to the other three mill?"

Oh Jesus, oh dear God in Heaven. The other three mill. How had Lorenzo Moretti found out about that?

Darrin composed himself, tried to, while he felt his heart begin to pound, the sweat roll down his armpits and down his back, into his pants. He took a slow breath, not being obvious about it, put what he hoped was a quizzical expression on his face.

"What other three mill?"

"Sal and me, we was close. You don't think he'd tell someone close to him how much of his action was with you, what you were burying for him?"

That was bullshit and Darrin knew it. These guys, the oldtimers, they'd never tell *anyone* their business, what or how much they had. If they did, even their closest associates would begin thinking about ways to take it away from them.

Still, he had to think of something. He couldn't challenge the man on his knowledge, couldn't insult him or the late Sal Luchessa.

There were a couple of ways Darrin could play this. He forced his mind to race over them as the men stared at him, as the sweat dripped . . .

He could say, Oh, *that* three mill, and get himself killed. The ten men with him here at this moment were looking for a reason to kill him, of that he was certain. Acting stupid was out.

He could tell them that he and Sal had plans together, had invested in things that hadn't worked out, in an offshore drilling lease in Louisiana before the bottom fell out of the oil market. That would cover it. Yet he'd have to come up with proof of that, with signed papers in Sal's handwriting, postdated.

He played the only card in his hand.

Darrin rose slowly to his feet, staring at Moretti for all he was worth, and said, "The Don's estate was worth nearly two million, even, Don Moretti, a little more with the change. I've doubled his investment, the million he kept with me. You guys know how he distrusted me in these later years, he was always calling me, collecting cash, I thought he was putting it away somewhere else. But the million that I doubled, I have proof of that. If you think I'm gonna sit here and be called a liar, a thief, you're thinking about the wrong guy."

The two men's eyes locked, neither giving an inch. It was now Darrin's word against a dead man's, and his indignity might go a way with these guys. As for Sal, he couldn't defend himself to anyone anymore.

Almost as one, the ten other outfit bosses rose too, stood staring at him, silent and scornful.

"Sit down, Darrin," Moretti said, and Darrin looked at him, knew he was as close as he'd ever be to dying without his heart actually stopping, and wondered if he should force it, walk past them, or sit down and try to reason his way out of this.

He sat down.

The other men joined him. Sat, but did not relax.

Moretti, the uneducated ignoramus who was suddenly now the spokesman for the entire goddamn mob, said, "Mrs. Luchessa's happy, Darrin. Two million's more than her entire clan has ever had at one time, ancestors included back to Adam and Eve. She ain't complaining; hell, she called to thank me for looking out for her, even told me that she knew you would have stolen all of it from her if I wasn't around to keep you honest." Moretti hesitated, allowed that to sink in with the group.

"And Sal, he's gone. He ain't around to stand up for himself, tell us what he left with you and what he didn't." Moretti sat forward, stubbed his cigar out in the brass standing ashtray provided by the mortuary. The base of the thing had the funeral parlor's name engraved on it, in cursive. Like that would keep somebody from lifting it.

Moretti said, "Sal was a friend of mine, but now he's gone and we're here, eleven of us left to carry on." He sighed. "I'm taking Sal's place, Darrin."

"I don't get a vote?"

One of the three younger men, the new dons who were brought up through attrition, sitting in the back there, what was his name, Joey something, yeah, Joey the Blade Gambiosi, said, "You're lucky you got a throat left, asshole," and Don Moretti turned on him like a cat, hissing.

"Joseph, you shut the fuck up!"

That was more like it, this was the Moretti Darrin knew and hated. At this moment, though, seeing Moretti revert to type was cold comfort.

To Darrin, Moretti said, "I'm in and that's all there is to it." There was a general murmur of conversation around the room, the others agreeing with Moretti, grumbling about Darrin's disrespect, someone speaking soothingly to Joey, telling him to calm down and relax.

Moretti said, "Sal was worried about you, and he brought his worries to me. Said you was charging juice, keeping the meter running, on that prowler did time rather than give you up. That was wrong, Darrin."

"He's a *thief*, for Christ's sake! This is about some two-bit *thief*?"

"Wasn't no two-bit thief, uh-uh, you're wrong about that one, too, Darrin. Shit, when he was in his twenties and thirties, Millard was one of the best thiefs this city ever *seen*! And he was special to us, to Sal and me.

"Years ago, see, we made a deal with this guy, when we took down his partner, the guy's wife, too, who couldn't keep her fucking mouth shut, was threatening to go to the newspapers and the U.S. attorney if we hurt her old man.

"There was a kid involved, and we had a discussion about him, Sal and me, wondering if he was as goofy as the rest of the family, had a big mouth and maybe got told too much by his old man.

"So what we did, we called the thief in. He was always good with us, this Millard, always paid his ten percent off the top and never tried to bullshit us about how little he scored. He told us the kid knew nothing and wasn't after anybody, and if we wanted the kid, we'd have to take *him* out, too, and did we want to lose that source of income? So we struck us a deal.

"We left the kid alone, and Millard doubled the ante. Gave us twenty points for all his scores. Now, that is considerable money, Darrin, when you think about some of the things he set up, the armored cars, the supermarkets. So what happens? He gets into you for some gambling dough, does you a favor and keeps his mouth shut but he goes to jail when he could have sung and got a new ID, caused us all kinds of hell, and guess what? My twenty points are gone, Darrin."

"I didn't know about that deal."

"It weren't none of your business. It was between me, Sal, and the prowler."

"But I didn't call the grand jury, I didn't send him to the County. He could have talked, and then you'd have lost your money, anyway."

"Don't you count on it. The prowler might have done us a favor, the way it turned out, putting your ass away in prison for twenty years."

Moretti cleared his throat and leaned forward, his gut hanging way over his pants, between his wide-spread knees, and grabbed a glass of wine off a small coffee table in front of him. He sipped from it, loudly, put it back and wiped his lips with the back of his hand.

"You see, Darrin, Sal always loved Marlene, she was the daughter he never had. He nearly raised her, took her to the zoo, shit like that, can you see him doing that— Sal?" Moretti chuckled, as did everyone except Joey, in the back, still stinging from the rebuke. And Darrin himself. Darrin wasn't laughing. Darrin didn't see anything as being funny anymore.

"You married her, he took you in with us, helped you

out, but he found out about the other stuff, the talking, the badmouthing you'd do, the ba-deep ba-doop with the nigger broads." Moretti dry-spit at the floor. "Jesus Christ, how fucking disgusting. You even hired one of them to work for you, Darrin, flaunted her in front of Marlene, Sal, and everybody."

"I made a lot of money for this group, here, Don."

"Did you?" Moretti said. Again, murmuring from the others.

"We thought you did, so did Sal. But the thing with the thief, fucking him over like that, that bothered Sal, made him wonder about you, why you never came to him, wanting to do something for a man was doing time rather than put you in a trick bag."

What could he say, could he tell them about Femal, about the baby? Like hell he could. They'd see it as another error of judgment, letting his personal feelings cloud over his business sense.

"You could do something like that with this Millard guy, not see the honorable thing to do, what other fuckups you might be making, that's what I'm wondering, Darrin."

"I don't make fuckups, Don Moretti." That was the way to play it now, cool, formal and respectful, yet act a little dangerous, as if Moretti was walking on thin ice. No more first names with any of them. Be above them. God only knew how many in the room hated Moretti's guts as badly as he did, were on Darrin's side privately.

Darrin felt confident, in control, sure in the belief that he would live. He had their money, didn't he? There was no way they could get that back with Darrin dead. All he had to do was get out of this room and start making phone calls to the others, especially to the younger ones. Moretti would have made a mortal enemy of Joey the Blade with his insult, and there would be others, more men on his side. Maybe even a majority.

"You don't make fuckups? Ain't what I heard."

"Tell me what, Don Moretti, besides this missing three mill I never had." Good, call him a liar without saying it, plant the seeds in the others' minds that this was all bullshit, Moretti's way of getting back at him because old Sal wasn't man enough to bury Darrin when he was alive.

"Well, for one, there's rumblings that there's a federal investigation into your dealings." Moretti spoke and Darrin felt his face drain of blood. This guy, he had to be kidding.

"And, there's no way around it, the three mill, fairy tale or not, it got us thinking."

"I can account for every dime every one of you in this room has ever given me, with interest, minus cleaning fees. You knew going in that I would take three points off your profits, every year, I made that clear up front. Outside of that, every dime's accounted for."

"Well, you better hope it is, Darrin, on account of I want the three and a half mill you got of mine, by the end of the week, no check over nine and a half grand, no personal checks, neither."

Darrin felt a little dizzy.

"Fine. You'll take bearer bonds?"

"Darrin, I'll take it in fucking gold bullion if that's the only way you can get it to me. I want it all, and I want it in two days. No, I'll give you till next Tuesday, seeing's the funeral's tomorrow, and the next day's Friday, all the banking fucks run out of town at noon."

"As you wish." Acting as if that kind of money was chicken feed.

"And you ain't with us no more, you got to understand that. You ain't on the committee. No decisions, no input. As Sal's nephew, you keep what you got, the gambling, the broads, the dope on the far South Side, the Hegewisch area. That's all that's out there anymore, anyway, is dopes." Moretti chuckled, as did a few of the others.

"But that's it, Darrin, you're out of decision making, and you answer to Joey for our piece of your action, for everything."

Jesus, wasn't that just like this guy? Insult the man one minute and favor him the next, making it all fine.

"Thank you, Don Moretti," Joey the Blade said, standing and formally nodding at Moretti, his eyes never coming off Darrin's, throwing ice his way.

Darrin couldn't resist taking a shot at this punk. He said, "How about you, Joe? You want the fast seventeen grand you invested with me back, too?"

"Fucking right I do, Favore," Joey said, "and it better be twenty by now, with interest."

"Me, too, I want mine back," another slob said, then another and another and by the time the last don spoke, Darrin felt no hope, because there was no way on earth he could get that kind of money back into the country, out of his own accounts and back into theirs, in the amount of time they'd given him without sending up red flags to every government agency in five nations. Gave up, too, the possibility that any of these men might be on his side.

And he wasn't a fool. They could talk all they wanted about his being Sal's nephew, but the second all their money was accounted for, Darrin would catch one in the back of the head and get a chain-escorted ride right down to the bottom of Lake Michigan. Moretti hadn't given Joey collecting rights over Darrin, what he'd been doing was handing Joey Darrin's action.

With as much dignity as he could muster, Darrin stood, nodded his assent to Moretti's terms. It wasn't the time to tell them he thought they were making a mistake, nor was it a time to argue or even to try an appeal to their reason. It was time to do only one thing: To run, that's what time it was.

Darrin said, "Gentlemen, you'll be hearing from me before Tuesday, every one of you."

"We fucking well better," Moretti said, as Darrin was walking out of the room, "or else, Favore, there'll be no place on earth that you'll be able to hide." And Darrin had to bite his tongue to stop himself from saying, Wanna bet?

Chapter 37

He found Merle sitting on the floor in the upstairs chapel, his legs crossed, Indian-style. Looking all relaxed, not a bit embarrassed. Hick punk probably felt more at home this way, would be even more so if the floor had been made of dirt and there was a goat or two sniffing around, the smell of chicken shit in the air.

Every chair in the room was full, Sal being paid high respect in death, most of the mourners either old women or young men who were there looking to catch the attention of the men they feared yet wanted desperately to join forces with.

Darrin ignored the pleading glances of the young men, the resentful stares of the old women. He particularly ignored his wife, who was somehow managing to moan and glare at him at the same time. He nudged Como with his foot. "Merle, let's go."

Merle looked up at him quizzically, struggled to his feet. "You didn't have to kick me." Whining little idiot. Did he really think Darrin gave a shit about how that kick appeared to the punks in the chairs? And if Merle was so concerned about his image, why hadn't he kicked one of them out of their seats, taken it as his own?

The boy would never be a don, that was for sure.

But then again, he himself wasn't a don anymore, either. He said, "Let's go, Merle, right now," whispering, the old women eyeing them, whispering to each other about the kick he had given Merle. Well, to hell with them.

"Let me say goodbye to Mrs. Luchessa."

No longer whispering, Darrin said, "Fuck it," turned, and walked out of the room. If Merle wasn't right behind him when he hit the door, he'd shoot that little bastard.

But he was, hurrying to keep up, catching him right outside and half-jogging, painfully, next to Darrin.

Darrin turned to glance at him, saw the familiar puppy dog look the kid always got on his face when he wanted something, or thought he was in trouble.

"What's the matter, Uncle Dare?" Smarmy little shit. "Uncle Dare?"

But Darrin wasn't watching him, his eyes were on another man now, a shorter, stocky guy who was strolling purposely toward the funeral parlor, his face set in a determined way . . .

Catfeet Millard. That son of a bitch.

To Merle, he said, "You got a piece in the car?"

"Sure . . ." Merle must have looked in the direction Darrin was staring; from the corner of his eye, Darrin saw him jump. Merle said, "But I don't need no gun for this guy," and before Darrin could stop him, Merle headed off toward Millard at a full-tilt run.

Femal had left the job in mid-afternoon, with important things to do and little time to accomplish them. She'd thought about calling her mama and telling her a lie, but couldn't bring herself to do that; there had been too many lies in Femal's life just lately.

Her first stop was a leather shop inside Water Tower

Place, where she bought a clinging soft black leather mini-skirt, a low-cut top to match. She'd wear her own underwear. Next, she stopped at a wig shop.

She took her purchases into the bathroom on Level Six and locked herself in the stall, changed clothes quickly, her regular clothing shoved into the bag the leather goods had come in. She got out of the stall, walked to the mirror and applied her makeup, heavily. Pouted at herself in the mirror, wondering if she could pull it off. She left the bathroom and practiced her strut, swung it out there, saw that even the white men who were walking by with their fur-coated wives were giving her furtive glances, and she felt confident. She made two more stops, first at a kitchen utensil store that had a hand-painted sign in the window: YES, WE HAVE THE GINSU KNIVES! then at the Citibank Cash Station on Level Seven, drawing the limit on her Citicard, then on her Visa and Master-Card.

Femal, dressed to kill, with plenty of cash in the purse swinging from her shoulder, locked her bag in one of the lockers, went to the elevator and hit the Down button, leaned against the outside of the elevator waiting for it, winking at a couple of young black boys who walked by her.

One of them said, "How much, bitch?" boldly, and she told them she was off duty, turned her back and smiled secretly at her reflection in the glass of the elevator's door.

Catfeet saw him coming but there wasn't a thing he could do about it. He caught Merle's first punch high, Feet trying to duck, the fist hitting him in the top of the head and poleaxing him, driving him to his hands and knees.

Was the man wearing brass knuckles? Christ, it sure felt like it.

He tried to rise and found that he couldn't, he was paralyzed. If he moved at all it would be downward, face-first onto the pavement of the funeral parlor parking lot. With a heroic effort he managed to raise his head in Merle's direction, seeing first the man's shoes, then his legs, waist, and when he got to Merle's belly he noticed a fist coming at him, and was powerless to even try to duck it. He felt a heavy pressure on his cheek and then saw black.

Merle looked at his uncle, who was standing there gawking, nervously glancing around the parking lot, making sure there were no witnesses.

"What the hell'd you hit him with?"

"The Punch, Unc. Laid it on his ass."

"Christ, Merle, get the car will you, before someone comes out and sees him laying here."

Dick Blandane sat in his parked Malibu across the street from Como's building. If his apartment faced the street, he might have a problem, as the curtains in that apartment had been pulled back an inch or so two or three times in the half-hour he'd been sitting there, someone inside there anxious, looking for someone.

Or at someone. Namely, him.

Should he walk up, introduce himself? No, not yet. If the man was wise to him, he might be prepared for anything, and Dick did not wish to walk into a trap, not when the real possibility existed that no backup units would respond to a call for help from a man they saw as a snitch. He sat there, thinking about it, listening to his tape through the headphones, to Johnny Mathis now, smooth-voiced and cool, Blandane singing along with him a little bit as the song wound down to the end.

"Well chances are your chances are, awfully goood! Well chances are those chances are, aw-fully good," then da-da-daed while the music slowed, piano tinkling, his off-key voice fading out with the sound.

No sense hanging around here. Dick took the car key out of the Accessory position, twisted it and fired it up, put it in gear and drove slowly past the apartment, seeing the drapes pull back again as he did so, then quickly pulled shut when whoever it was inside spotted Dick looking at the window.

He'd shaken the guy up, there was no doubt now that this was Como, that he'd spotted Dick. Dick cruised past, nodding his head. Anyone acting this guilty had something to hide, and he'd find it in a hurry, even if he had to come back here and prowl the apartment himself, when he was sure that Como was gone.

Femal walked into the bar with her exaggerated swagger, heard some wolf whistles and smiled at them, sashayed right up to the bar and ordered a brandy for courage. What she was about to do would take more strength than she would be able to muster without additional fortitude, even if it had to be artificial. It was one thing to act the part, another to live it, to actually speak with one of these animals.

There was blues music blasting from a jukebox in the corner, an ancient female voice screaming her pain out to the world, trapped for eternity on scratchy vinyl. The floor was cracked and filthy tile, and she could see the sticky areas where last night, drinks had been spilled and never mopped up. The place smelled of vomit and fear and excitement, and she felt her blood race in her veins. It was even worse than she'd expected.

It was a pimp's bar. The days were long gone when they wore fur coats and the big wide-brim hats, drove the custom-made Cadillacs and beat their girls on the street in broad daylight. These days they were more likely to wear Brooks Brothers and drive BMWs, but their viciousness was still the same, that hadn't changed and never would. They spoke loudly, above the din of the music, above the chatter of the several working women in the place, most of them giving Femal vicious looks every time she caught their eyes.

"That's on me," a voice said, and Femal saw a large hand drop a bill on the bar, then rest there, looked up and saw a scar-faced thin man with a dozen razor-slashed punk cuts sheared into the sides of his head, fashioned in lightning bolts.

"You with someone, baby?" the man said. "Someone got your action? You don't look familiar to me."

Femal looked at him closely, at the cut of his suit, her eyes appraising.

"Like what you see?"

Femal lifted the brandy snifter off the bar, walked past him and said, "No."

She struck pay dirt with the third man she spoke to.

"Sit down, mama," the man in the booth said. There were obvious bulges at both sides of his waist. She did.

"You shot them two motherfuckers down, and that's good, they's shit, the two of them rolled together don't make one man."

Femal said, "And you do?"

"Get cute with me, bitch, and you'll be carried out this place, believe me." The man was short, fat, with lips that reminded her of fat red worms. He spoke and stared at her, looking ready to move on her if she tried to leave the booth. It might have been a tactical error, her sitting down. The others, she had just breezed by, after looking them over real good.

"I'm Montague Rayford, but you can call me Monte."

"Monte, I'm Toni, with an 'eye.' "

"First thing you gots to do is change that name, sweetie. You got any idea how many ho's names is Toni? With or without a fucking 'eye'? Shit, many as there are named Crystal. Man gets it in his mind that you a regular long-time ho, you don't get the real action. Lots of them wants to think you new, just doing it to stay off the welfare, feed your kids or somethin'." He gave her a look she'd seen before, on men whose very ignorance gave them reason to believe they were smart. "See why you needs a man like me in your life?"

Femal gave him the slow look, up and down, put her brandy down on the table.

"You got something else I need, Monte."

"I don't doubt that, sweetie. Mr. Monte, he gots what *alls* you ladies need, and he deliver, don't just talk on it." Monte grunted, satisfied, raised his glass to his lips and sucked some of it in. "You wants, we can get out of here and talk about it."

"I thought you'd never ask," Femal said.

The types of the cars never changed, although the style did. The Cadillac was rolling down the now dark South Side street, Monte driving quickly, trying to confuse her, she knew. He didn't want her able to find her way back to the bar, or for that matter out of whatever neighborhood he was taking her into.

She was cold, though the heater was on. For maximum effect, she'd carried her coat over her arm, showing herself off to best advantage, and hadn't put it on for the short walk to the car. From the iciness coming up off the red leather seats, Monte must have been in that bar for a while. The car smelled of strawberry spray, sweat, and liquor.

"Why you alone in there, Monte, how come you wasn't with none of those other girls?"

"I is a businessman, sweetie. Doesn't mess with my wares. Half them ho's in there right now drinking up what I give them, looking around for a better deal and knowing I kill the man try and move in on me. Stupid, ain't they? The bitches?" Monte smiled, looked over at her, let one hand drop onto her left thigh. He rubbed it, squeezed. "You gonna be smart, though, ain't you, Toni?"

"Thought you didn't mess with the wares."

"You buy a car without giving it a test drive?"

Femal said, "Monte, I got you out of that bar, well, let's say, under false pretenses."

"You a cop?!" Monte jerked his hand off her leg. He was outraged. "You a fucking cop? Well, you ain't got shit on me, bitch, I ain't said or did nothing illegal." Monte regained his composure, looked at her and smiled, leaned his head toward her breasts and spoke loudly toward them, as if at a hidden microphone. "Ya'll hear that? I ain't said *shit* illegal!"

Femal had to think about that for a second. Should she play the part of a cop, let him think that's what she was and get what she wanted that way? No, she'd only mess that up, he'd more than likely been arrested enough times over the years to spot an amateur the second one opened her mouth.

Femal said, "I ain't no cop, and you *still* got something I want."

This gave him pause, and he slowed down, caught a red light and put one hand on the seat between them, curled into a fist.

"What reason you give me to not kick your ass right now and throw you out my car, bitch?"

"Two reasons," Femal said. "First, I'm offering you nine hundred dollars for just one of those guns in your pants, and secondly, you lay a hand on me," she pulled the ginsu knife out of the folds of her coat, "and I'll slash your throat from one ear to the next."

"*How* much you say you gonna pay me for the gun, sweetie?" Monte said.

Chapter 38

Charlie wished that he had gone with Cat, hadn't been so hurt by the man's words that he'd allowed him to walk out of the hotel alone. At the very least, he should have given his car to Cat. It was too damn cold to take a bus or even walk around looking for a cab. Eventually, John would report it stolen, if he hadn't already. He'd bet that the car phone and the small fold-up cellular phone numbers had already been disconnected.

November wasn't supposed to be like this. He remembered times when he'd been in the joint, Novembers that were so damn beautiful that it broke his heart to be where he was, missing out on Indian Summer, Charlie locked down at an age and during a time of year when he should have been taking hikes with a girl through the forest preserves, booted feet kicking at leaves . . .

He thought about that the only time he left the hotel room, when he'd gone to the bank to cash his check before his father-in-law had a chance to call them and have them stop payment. Thought about that and almost anything else rather than having to think about Cat, what he'd said . . .

It had been a mistake, letting the armor down. Cat would never understand it but he'd bet that Lina would, was willing to bet, too, that she was right now in some bar, her diet pills in her purse, some of them flowing through her bloodstream, feeling as if she'd accomplished her life's goal.

But maybe not.

He thought about it as he sat in the hotel room, the money stacked now, something he'd done to pass the time, counting it and stacking it into two neat, separate piles.

Would Lina be happy that she'd gotten him to break out of his character, made him angry? Maybe that had been her goal all along.

But Charlie had given Lorraine Williams and her entire crew legal grounds for a lawsuit, had done it in front of John, had rubbed the old drunk's nose in it and what satisfaction was there in that? In hurting a harmless old man?

Cat had been right. If you wanted to live by prison rules, you belonged in a prison.

He tried Femal's house for maybe the tenth time and was getting a little sick of the snotty old woman who answered the phone, the way she talked to him, insultingly, seeing him as a honkie. Yet he was polite, Femal was Cat's woman and you had to respect that, had to show her mother or whoever that woman was the same respect you would afford the woman herself.

He hung up, looked at his watch again, wondering where in the hell Cat was.

Charlie felt his coldness slip over him, covering him like a blanket, a well-liked roommate who'd taken a short trip returning home, welcomed and warmly received. It had been a mistake, losing his temper. Coldness was all and you could never let them see that you hurt, never let them know your pain.

The phone rang and he grabbed it, said, "Hello, Femal!" urgently, hoping that Cat was with her, forgetting about being cold.

But it wasn't Femal. A voice he'd heard over a card table the night before, Darrin Favore's voice, spoke chillingly into his ear.

"So he *was* telling the truth." Favore chuckled. "Lane, you better get out into the alley behind your new digs, clean up your fucking garbage. And then start running, 'cause you're next." There was a click and a dial tone, and Charlie looked at the phone, trying to put what the man said into place in his mind.

How did he even know where Charlie was? Lina wouldn't know, and even if Favore was calling from the country club and was sitting next to Lina at the bar, she wouldn't tell him if she knew, no matter how drunk she was. And what was that about cleaning up his garbage?

He got it then. Only Cat knew where he was, and Favore had somehow gotten Cat to talk, wanting Charlie, a piece of him, wanting to tear him up for taking his money and dignity from him the night before.

But first, before killing him, Favore wanted Charlie to suffer.

Dear God, what had they done to Cat to make him give Charlie up?

He ran out of the club through the rear service entrance, forgetting about the weather, his suit jacket off, his shirt and thin pants the only protection from the biting wind but they were enough, that and his rage.

He found Cat in the hotel dumpster, crumpled there, bloody, nearly unrecognizable.

Cat's face was a round ball of ground beef, bloody and raw. One eye hung out of its socket, down on Cat's cheek, looking into the dumpster, the other open, unfocused, looking at the cold November sky. His arms were broken, both of them twisted around with the hands open, the fingers bent grotesquely. Charlie couldn't see his legs.

He flipped himself into the dumpster, landed on a pile

of garbage and fell onto Cat's chest and quickly flipped himself off, scrabbling around for position, Cat grunting, moaning, moving his head around and trying to see who was hurting him now, maybe wondering how much more there was for them to do to him.

Christ, they'd killed him, beaten him to death.

"Cat?" Charlie spoke softly, next to tears. "Cat, can you hear me?" There was a catch in his voice, a lump in his throat. "Cat, don't die!" A whispered petition as Charlie pressed his face into Cat's chest and began to sob.

"Charlie?" Cat spoke in a soft voice which sounded incredulous. "*Char*lie? I can't *see*! They blinded me!"

"Who?"

Cat spoke with terror, trembling as he whispered the name. "*Merle Como*," spoken with near reverence. "And Favore."

Cat couldn't move, couldn't even clutch at Charlie. Should Charlie leave, call an ambulance? No, he'd smelled death before, more than once, and Cat was dying, it was in the air.

Cat relaxed in Charlie's arms and a faraway look settled over his bloody face. He spoke one word calmly, and smiled. "Elaine." Charlie couldn't see any teeth left in Cat's mouth.

"What's that, Cat?"

"Elaine," Cat said, and nodded. His body relaxed further, permanently in Charlie's arms, went limp. His battered face was almost serene. He was dying, but he'd given Charlie all that he needed. The names of the men who'd killed him.

Cat nodded again. "Elaine," Cat said, with conviction, then died.

He didn't know how long he stayed there, holding the body. But it was dark and he was cold and stiff when he stuck his head out of the dumpster and looked around, saw that he was alone and jumped out, landed lightly on his feet on the old-fashioned cobblestone alley floor. Charlie squared his shoulders, tightened his muscles, and let his prison attitude adjust itself, waited, taking deep breaths, fighting the cold until it did, until he felt the coldness seep into his bones, into his soul, where it belonged.

He looked into the dumpster and saw a bunch of meat, which would soon rot, smell, and attract attention. Charlie closed the lid on the thing, without taking another look. That wasn't Cat in there, wasn't the man he'd loved, the guy who'd taken him in and treated him like a son. That thing in there was only a corpse. Cat was gone. Cat had been killed.

And the guys who'd killed him would have to be dealt with, and there was no way Charlie could deal with them unless he had nothing left inside him that they could take away from him; no fear. No courage. Nothing.

When he was ready, he left the alley and entered the club the same way he'd come out, went up to get his fingerprints out of the room, collect his clothing and his money. It was all his now, every dime of it.

Soon, he knew, there'd be a lot more, or he'd be dead, and he didn't care a whole lot about which way it went, as long as somebody paid for Cat.

"Mama," Femal said, dressed in her regular clothes but with the makeup still caked on her face—she hadn't had time to wash it off in the Water Tower Place bathroom— "I want you to go home right away, Mama, and don't ask me any questions about this. Get the hell out of here and back to your place, and take the baby. And don't ask me any questions. I'll be over there in two hours to pick you up."

"Now, Femal, don't play that secret shit with me. I ain't goin' *no*wheres in two hours. I watchin' Arsenio on the cable then I'm goin' to bed."

"Mama, trust me on this one, you *want* to come with me tonight."

The old woman was standing in the middle of the room, watching as Elaine pulled herself up on the couch, took a few steps away from it then flopped down on her butt. Undaunted, she crawled toward the couch, began the process all over again.

"Good," Elaine said, clear as a bell, and Mama's face lit up.

"You hear that? Girl be spouting off any day now, talking your ear off. You spend two years tryin' to get 'em to talk and the next twenty tellin' 'em to shut up." Mama clapped her hands. "Good," she said, encouraging the baby.

"Mama . . ."

"Femal, you come into this house lookin' like some kind of hoo-re, don't pay no attention to your child's steps, to her talkin', what's wrong with you, girl? Tell your mama."

"Mama, I can't right now." Femal walked over and scooped up the baby, began carrying her toward the stairs, Elaine protesting, angry, wanting to practice her walking. "I have to get Elaine ready for bed, she'll fall asleep on the bus and I want her bathed and in her pajamas, dry before you take her out into this cold."

"Is cold for November, ain't it?"

"Mama, are you gonna do what I tell you on this, or aren't you?"

"Ain't nobody told me what to do since the day you got out of college and I stopped working for the devils in their rich houses. You ain't never told me what to do in your entire life, and I reckon it ain't likely for you to begin tellin' me what to do now." She walked to Femal, took the struggling baby out her arms. "Too cold for any damn bus, too. You pack, do whatever you want to do, and I'll bathe the child. Then the two of you can drive me home. And on the way you can tell me what's got my daughter so damn scared all of a sudden." She shushed the child, walked her up the stairs, saying Good and waiting for Elaine to answer her before saying the word again. "Whatever you been up to, you can trust that I'm with you, girl." Said simply, firmly. It made Femal want to cry.

When Mama was out of sight Femal sighed, took the gun out of her purse and set it on the small desk next to the computer terminal.

Monte had taken the money and even seemed to appreciate Femal's courage, showing her how to load it, where the safety was. It was a small automatic, a .25, and he'd warned her that they sometimes jammed and didn't have a lot of stopping power but if you hit a man in the head or belly, the fight would be gone out of him. Femal had watched him work, her eyes on him, her hand clutching the knife. She'd wondered if she'd have the nerve to stick him with it if he made a move with the weapon, if he tried to steal her money.

But she never had to find out because he hadn't, Monte had become a gentleman once he'd figured out that she wasn't on the market. A businessman making a deal, more than likely tripling his investment in a weapon that had probably, as Darrin would have said, fallen off a truck.

She felt a distant security at the weapon's presence, a certain safety. She was no longer dependent on her wits alone to get her by. Even a subhuman such as Merle Como would think twice before getting tough with her now. She stopped, shocked at her thought, hearing the water running upstairs in the bathtub, Mama singing soothingly. She placed her Golden Disc, the key to the kingdom, into her computer, turned the machine on and began to type, tapping into her modem to check facts and figures every few seconds, double-checking, from time to time her eyes gazing over toward the gun, for reassurance.

Is this what it's like for a man? she wondered. Did the

gun make him feel strong? Is that why so many of them carried them around?

Her thoughts were interrupted by the doorbell, and she jumped, spun, reaching for the gun with one hand even as she was hurrying to her feet.

Chapter 39

Blandane was driving back to the house where Como's victim supposedly lived, feeling pretty sure of himself, certain that he would have Como in his grasp for something no later than the end of the shift. Either for possession of stolen property or maybe even assault or worse, if he could get this guy to talk, to open up to him.

He was practicing his lines, going over them in his mind when his radio squawked, the dispatcher telling him to report in by phone to Gang Crimes South, right now.

What the hell did they want?

He found out right away, because as soon as he found a working pay phone and dialed the number he was patched through to Simmons, who told him that Internal Affairs wanted to talk to him immediately, as O'Brian had just died on the job.

Femal went to the door without hesitation, thumbing the safety off the gun as she walked, jacking a round into the chamber as if she were an old hand at it, and it was only when she reached the door that she thought that the weapon seemed very small, almost puny in her hand.

Would it do the job, would it stop an enraged Merle Como? He might put on his innocent yokel act at first, playing all cute and childish, but the second he saw the gun, the other side of him would come out, the Mr. Hyde in him.

She didn't have time to waste on that.

Femal slid the curtain back with her free hand, then sighed her relief. It was Charlie, Robert's cousin, or nephew or something.

She opened the door, the weapon still in her hand, not too happy to see him but relieved that it wasn't someone else. Como, or worse, Darrin himself.

"Femal." Charlie said it flatly, staring at her, not even glancing at the gun. "So you know."

"Know?" She stepped back, put the gun behind her back, embarrassed now. She was distracted, hearing the water still running, Mama singing, the sound of Elaine up there splashing around in the half-filled tub, laughing through the open bathroom door because Grandma was letting her get her all wet. Charlie came in, closed the door behind him before she found the presence of mind to say, "Know what?"

Charlie looked at her, and she shivered, in spite of the fact that she had the pistol, held all the cards, and they were standing inside her own house. Something in those eyes frightened her, he was opening his mouth to tell her something that she knew she did not want to hear.

"Favore didn't call you?"

Femal was trying to put the safety back on the gun with her hand behind her back, and it wasn't working.

"Why would he call me?" Her fear was mounting, her anxiety level high. Here it comes, she thought.

"Femal, Cat's dead."

It hit her with stunning force, the words driving her back, on wobbly legs, Femal putting her hands out in front of her, as if to ward off any further words that Charlie might speak. She felt the back of her knees hit something and she sat down hard, found herself perched on the edge of the computer chair. She reached a shaking hand out and dropped the pistol onto the table, into the space between the printer and the machine itself. She looked at it, blankly, the gun insignificant, mostly hidden by the computer, covered it with a sheet of typing paper, trying to hide from anything that could cause sudden and brutal death, then looked at Charlie, and when she saw two of him she realized that she was crying.

"No." Spoken softly, with foreboding. She did not want to know how it had happened.

"You're in danger here, Femal, you and the kid."

Femal felt her anger rise, blocking out her grief. She raised her head to look at Charlie, angrily swiped at the tears on her cheek, her hands coming away smeared with makeup. "My child's name is Elaine, mister," and that stopped him, staggered him.

"*What's* her name?"

More softly, puzzled, Femal said, "Elaine."

Charlie said, "Oh my God, oh Jesus. Now I get it."

"Charlie, what is it?"

"That name was the last word Cat spoke on this earth."

"Oh my God," Femal said, and began crying again.

Darrin had a plan. Had it for a while, too, awaiting this day. Hoping it would never come but preparing himself for it all the same. He wasn't some punk kid who sat around smoking one cigarette after another, thinking cancer would never come his way. He'd learned early on that if you played with fire, you could get yourself burned, no matter how many times you lit the damn thing up.

So now he was putting his plan into effect.

Marlene wouldn't be home until after the funeral parlor closed at ten, maybe even later than that as she would probably be going over to her aunt's, the bunch of them sitting around talking about what a miserable bastard he was, cussing in front of everybody at the wake.

So what? What would anybody do to him?

Merle had started to give him some lip about cursing like that in front of the women, too, and he'd had to set him straight, told him the facts of life.

Darrin could walk up to the casket and piss all over Sal's corpse, and there wasn't a thing they would do about it. Not until after Tuesday. Once they had their money they would take him somewhere and cut little pieces off of his body and make him eat them, but until then, Darrin had them by the balls.

He had his nephew drop him off at the house with orders to take the car over to the car wash right now, run it through the automatic thing four or five times, vacuum out the trunk and shampoo it, too, if they had one of those machines in there. The kid, Merle, he'd gotten his sexual pleasure for the day, beating Millard, breaking his bones one by one.

It amazed Darrin, watching that. How Merle knew just how to do it, what would make the prowler pass out, how long he'd be out, how to bring him around. Seeing that harmless-looking young kid smiling, talking soothingly to Millard as he worked, raising his voice when the guy would scream in anguish. Darrin hadn't known that one man could take so much pain and survive, had expressed this view to Merle and been told that the son of a bitch wouldn't survive for long, that was for sure, but that he'd last long enough.

He was in his basement now, putting his contingency plan into operation as smoothly as paramedics around an airport went into their crash plans when a bird went down, both plans having the same training hope, that they would never have to put this into use, but if the worst case ever arose, they would damn sure be ready.

Darrin was carefully prying out pieces of bricks, pulling them out and setting them aside on the floor beside him. Then he'd reach in and remove packets of money, shrink-wrapped, tightly. He'd been at it an hour and already there were seventeen bundles of hundred dollar bills on the concrete floor, each holding twenty thousand dollars, cash. Eight more and he'd have his escape money, nine more and he'd be set.

He was sweating despite the chill in the basement, waiting for someone to come and catch him, either the dons or his wife, knowing that either case would bring him death. He hurried, replacing the bricks haphazardly. Marlene would not come down here until well after the funeral, and once she did, it would be too late. Hell, he wanted her to find the evidence, turn it over to the dons and let them tear their hair out, thinking about their money, about their life's work down the tubes. It would serve them right, the way they treated him. Maybe they'd all have heart attacks, like Sal.

Merle had not wanted it to end, had wanted to go after Charlie Lane right away, keep the hard-on he more than likely had gotten from doing Millard. Darrin had told him no, that he had to wait two days, let that smug little bastard suffer.

And hadn't it been a kick, finding out what they had about old Charlie? He'd lost his job, his parole had nearly been revoked, and he'd been over at Millard's hotel, cooling his heels.

Darrin knew the punk wouldn't go to the cops. It wasn't his style. There was no chance on earth of it happening, but even if it did, no cop would question him on the word of a convicted killer, at least until after the funeral, until Sal had been lain to rest. And by then it would be too late.

At last he had all the money out of the walls, and the extra package that held the documents, wrapped as safely and securely as the cash, of equal importance. Darrin put the last brick back, stacked the money in a suitcase, surprised at the bulk of it, the weight. He'd put the packets in there one by one, over a period of several years. He'd never seen it all at once like this before. Although he was worth many times this amount, counting what he'd skimmed from the dons, it still made him feel important, a man of substance. This many greenbacks would take him on a roundabout trip around the world, to a place where they'd never find him.

They'd be looking in Europe, maybe the Caribbean, thinking that all the money was in some easily accessible spot that they'd known of for years. Well, let them look. They'd never find him, never in a million years and it would only take maybe ten before they were all dead anyway, and the young turks would write off the old man's money, wanting to protect their own, why would they care? No, he could hide from them for ten years without half-trying.

In Peru. That's where he'd be, sitting in luxury and watching his investment take shape as the forest fell, the land was leveled off and the hotels were built, and he'd own more than one of them. Hell, ten years from now, he'd be the Donald Trump of Peru.

He liked that idea, liked it fine.

Darrin lugged the suitcase into a corner of the basement, shoved it under the workbench he'd never used. It would be safe there, who would dare rob from him? He'd need easy access to it, would leave the funeral as soon as the casket was lowered to the ground, feigning grief, would pass up the dinner at Sal's house where everyone would spend hours eating spaghetti and drinking wine, telling Sal stories. By the time most of them left, Darrin would be on the first leg of his journey.

He'd thought that out, too, thought about it again as he showered the sweat off him, soaped away his fear.

He had three separate passports in that suitcase, each one showing a different Darrin, having a different name. He had the stamps, too, bought at great expense, which he would use to validate the new passports, make them appear legal and above reproach, and if anyone gave him any trouble he could always dip into his suitcase and hand over a little cash to calm them down.

The first documents had his likeness, what he looked like now. On the first stop he'd stay awhile, grow the mustache and beard that was on the second passport, then move along. At the next stop he would rent a hotel room and shave his head, then be on his way immediately, bald, bearded, the facial hair and the fringes he'd leave on his head, above his ears, dyed gray. When he hit Peru he'd be a sixty-year-old businessman, and had set things up to prove residency there for many years, in a place where he would have a safe retreat for the rest of his life.

Darrin dried himself and called a cab before he dressed, wanting it there when he was ready, not wanting to wait for some Iranian fool to find his way over. Merle had his car, might have it for a while, and what Darrin had to do couldn't wait. He wound up waiting anyhow, and therefore didn't tip the driver when the incompetent fool dropped him off at his office.

Inside the dark office he went right to the computer, only needing five minutes here to do what had to be done, then it would be over to LaVella's, to say goodbye.

He wished it was Femal he'd be seeing, kissing her goodbye, maybe even taking her with him. She would enjoy that, life in a place like Peru, where nobody ever thought of going for fun. Darrin knew better, knew all about it, although he'd never dare gone there. The boys would be onto his records, would grill Marlene about them and would send people to any place Darrin had ever gone to in his life, to places he'd even discussed someday going to. They weren't dumb, just stupid.

So stupid that if it hadn't been for their terror of the IRS, they'd have their money in passbook accounts at the local banks, collecting five and a half and thinking they were getting over. So stupid that they believed him when he told them that he'd doubled their money, when in fact he at least tripled some of their investments, had quadrupled others. All you had to do was have the touch, know enough to get into what was about to become hot, know when to get out before it went cold.

Darrin had that touch.

The computer was warmed up, and Darrin waggled his fingers over the keyboard. It was all on hard disc, he knew. Femal had copied everything onto the hard disc so he wouldn't have to play around, looking through her files for the right floppies every time he wanted to survey his fortune. But there were two things he'd added, that even Femal didn't know about.

With one stroke of the keyboard, Darrin would transfer everything into other accounts, so quickly, through so many different banks that no one, not even the FBI, would be able to trace it.

Secondly, there was a virus, and with a second stroke he would set it off, the bug eating his trail, wiping out everything that had ever been on file anywhere in his computer system, leaving nothing but a blank screen for anyone to look at.

Marlene would have nothing. Femal would find a job. LaVella would have her happy memories and within a month would have to hit the street, a box of Trojans in her purse, and would have to worry about things far more dangerous than secondhand smoke.

And Darrin would have approximately forty million dollars spread out over eleven South American banks, at his immediate disposal, that amount approximate because he hadn't checked his earnings lately, the interest. It could well be more.

He thought that would be a good deal all the way around.

He tapped into the file, hit the modem and waited, got a little shock when the bottom of the screen flashed, telling him to punch in the password, feeling, as he always did, that this time his memory would fail him, that he wouldn't be able to access the machine. Darrin shook himself and tapped in: E-L-A-I-N-E, then waited.

WRONG PASSWORD, the machine told him, and he

punched it in again, thinking he had obviously typed in a wrong letter, the password letters not appearing on the screen, staying hidden and secret.

It was on the third try that he began to suspect that something was wrong, and it was after the fifth that he punched the keyboard hard, then spun away from it and reached for the phone, dialed his car phone number.

Merle's voice said, "Yeah?" not sounding happy.

Darrin said, "Merle, you get over to that bitch's house right now, that nigger bitch's house, and you take care of her, the kid, too, right now."

"What?"

"Goddamnit, are you deaf?" Darrin forced himself to calm down, took some deep breaths. When he was under control he said, "Merle, listen carefully. I'm going to tell you exactly how to do it. You get into that house, I don't care if you have to kick the door in. Then you get your hands on that half-breed kid. Put your pistol in its ear and tell Femal that if she doesn't give you the password, the kid is dead. Then you call me at the office before you do another thing, you got that?"

"You want the password, right, some password from her?" Merle's voice was almost obscured with static, crackling over the lines.

"Get that password then call me before you let that kid go."

"Uncle Dare?"

"What!"

"After she gives it to you, can I kill the kid? I never done a kid before."

Chapter 40

"**I** want you to have this," Charlie said, and extended a manila envelope toward her.

Femal looked at it. Was that the same damn thing that Darrin had thrown at her in the office the other day? It sure looked like it. A little dirtier, wrinkled, but obviously stuffed with money.

"For Elaine," Charlie said, "for her education."

Femal looked at it, then at Charlie's face. He seemed sincere. She said, "After I got to know him I asked him once, what made him do what he did, and you know what he told me? He said right after the war, he was sitting in the VA office, waiting for a counselor to come talk to him about a problem he was having, beating people up in bars. He said some kids came in, about his age, with long hair but dressed in business suits, stood there looking around, and when the secretary asked what they wanted, they told her they needed the sheet, the list of foreclosed veterans' homes, so they could bid on them at auction. You heard this story?" Charlie didn't say anything, he just shook his head. He seemed interested, though. "He said he walked out of the counselor's office and forgot all about trying to find a job, he didn't see any percentage in it after that." She was quiet for a minute, thinking, then thought of something far more important than fond reminiscence of a now dead thief she'd once loved.

"I don't want that." Femal rose, getting herself back together. "If Darrin had Robert killed, then I'm in more danger than I thought, me and Elaine. I want you to go now so I can—so I can think about what I have to do."

"He had Cat killed, he called me and told me about it. I'm next, too, I got that message."

"You'd better go, Charlie."

"First, you tell me something, or I'll never leave. You know a man named Merle Como?"

"That's Darrin's nephew, Merle Como."

"Tell me where he lives and I'll be out of your life."

Femal went to the computer and typed for a second, standing up, waited, then pressed another button and the printer buzzed, lasered out a white sheet of paper. She handed it to Charlie.

"This is his information, home address, phone number, driver's license number, anything you need. Darrin's, too, if you want it."

"Oh, I want it," Charlie said, then said, "Thanks," and left without waiting for Femal to walk him to the door.

Upstairs the noise had stopped, Femal couldn't hear anything, but she assumed that Mama would be dressing the baby, getting her ready to leave. She cleared the screen and went back to her work, hurriedly typing, and a few minutes later when the doorbell rang again she started and said angrily, "*Now* what does he want!" got out of her chair and marched over to the door, threw it open and her heart leaped in her chest as Merle Como smiled down at her.

•   •   •

"Hey, baby," Merle said, and pushed her hard, knocking her off her feet and to the floor, then came in and kicked the door shut hard behind himself. "Mind if I come in?"

Femal didn't know what to do, was only aware due to some elemental instinct that she had best not look toward the computer table, toward the gun. It was her only hope, to somehow reach it before he spotted it lying there, saw its shape under the paper. She crawled away from him, toward the door, so he'd turn his back on the table, Femal praying again, getting into the habit these past couple of days.

At all costs, she had to protect Elaine.

As if reading her mind, Como said, "Where's the kid, sleeping already?" He was grinning innocently, as if he really cared. "Bet you take good care of her, don't you? Don't smoke crack around her, don't let her see the white guys you fuck around with. What do you do, make them leave before she wakes up?"

Femal stayed silent, staring up at him. She was terrified, but that terror was balanced by the thought that she wasn't alone, that there was an innocent who counted on her for survival, two innocents really, because she had always taken care of Mama, always seen to her needs.

"Ain't you scared, honey?" Como swaggered over to her, kneeled down. She could see the butt of a large gun stuck in the waistband of his pants. He was smiling.

"Good thing the baby's sleeping. Give us some time to get acquainted, if we hurry."

He began to touch her, softly, then with urgency, squeezing, pinching. Femal did not cry out, did not whimper, did not pull away from his touch. "You like that?" He sounded surprised. "I'll be damned. I'll bet those big fat lips of yours can suck them a hell of a dick, can't they?"

From the stairs, Mama's voice called out, "What in the hell's all that noise down here about?" Mama seeing it then, her face falling and she was trying to climb the steps but Como was on his feet and to Mama as fast as Femal had ever seen anyone move. He grabbed her, tore the child from her arms and Elaine began to cry, wail, her arms reaching out to her grandmother, terrified of this beast who held her in one hand, pulled Mama down the stairs with the other. Mama was hitting at the back of his head, calling for the child, screaming but not in terror, rather in anger.

Femal got to her feet and was rushing him as Como pushed Mama hard, used the free hand to pull the weapon out of his waistband and point it right at Elaine's head.

Femal stopped dead in her tracks. She held up her hands in supplication, seeing Mama twisting around in agony, half-lying across the computer table, her hands holding her belly, her head down on the printer.

"No, don't do it, I'll do anything you want, *any*thing, but don't hurt that child."

Como smiled, looking his most handsome, as if he'd just stepped off a movie set and was meeting an admirer for the first time.

It was as if the scene with Mama had never happened, as if he wasn't holding a shrieking child in his arms, wasn't holding a deadly weapon to her head.

"I get a hard-on hearing you beg, you know it?" He walked toward her, eased back the hammer on the pistol. "There's three pounds of pull between life and death for this caterwauler. Give me the password, honey, and we'll see how good a receiver you are." He pulled Elaine back quickly, as if he was a quarterback about to throw a living football at Femal, and the baby wailed.

"Password?" Femal didn't know, couldn't figure out what he was talking about.

For the first time he showed real anger, digging the pistol into Elaine's ear. Her screams grew louder, the child holding her breath forever between panicked shouts, her face red, tiny little fists flailing around her face. Merle held her in one gnarled hand, the pistol in the other, his face suddenly ugly, his eyes chillingly bright. "Don't act like I'm stupid! Give me the fucking password for the boss's computer, *now*, bitch, cause I ain't gonna count to three."

She got it then, and Femal was about to shout the word at him when Mama's voice, strong and loud, said, "Hand that baby over to her mother right this minute, you no account white trash stupid motherfucker."

Como turned, slowly, and saw, at the same time Femal did, Mama standing there with the gun held steadily out in both hands, not even blinking, Mama still skinny and tiny, but now a force of nature, one solid and tough individual.

Mama said, "You don't, I'll blow your ass into the middle of next week."

Elaine's wailing was beyond sound, was now the frantic shouting of madness.

Femal edged toward them. If she could at least grab his gun hand, get the weapon away from the baby's head . . .

Como said, "Put the gun down, or I kill the kid."

"Go ahead on with your bad self, shoot her. Then I shoot you."

"The kid'll be *dead*, lady." Como not sounding so sure of himself now.

"But I be alive, my daughter and me. And you, well, I take care of you real slow. Won't kill you, though. I shoot your kneecaps off so you never walk again, then you elbows." Femal looked at her mother and saw a woman strange to her, a savage woman without mercy, with no kindness left in her, anywhere.

"Then I take a knife to you eyes and you tongue, you eardrums. I slice your pecker off last, and then what you be? A vegetable cain't even never play with hisself, cain't even kill hisself, sittin' in a wheelchair for the rest of your life wishing you'd'a listened to the little colored woman with the pistol." She stood stock still, the weapon never wavering. "Make your decision." Said resolutely, Mama taking aim.

"Take the kid—Jesus," Como pulled the weapon from

Elaine's head and Femal grabbed her, pushed at the pistol arm and began to run as Mama popped off one, two, three shots and Como was running, jumping, leaping through the doorway to the kitchen and a second later they heard the back door slam against the wall and the sound of feet pounding down the driveway.

Elaine was still screaming, right into Femal's ear as Femal shushed her, held her close, told her it was all right, everything was going to be all right, talking to the child in a voice that didn't sound too certain, watching Mama walk without hesitation into the kitchen, the weapon out in front of her in case Como was hiding in there somewhere. Femal heard the door close, heard the bolt slam home, then Mama was at the front door, turning the deadbolt.

Elaine was beginning to calm down, all cried out, sobbing mostly now, her little body shivering and shaking.

"It's all right, baby," Femal said, and Mama said, "Like hell it *is*! You best tell me about that goddamned password, and right now, girl," Mama saying it and Femal looking up, seeing Mama trembling now, holding her side tight with both hands, and Femal decided that it just wasn't the time to tell her not to curse in front of the baby.

"Sit down, Mama," Femal said, and her mother did.

Mama dropped the gun on her lap, looked at it blankly. "Don't even know if the damn thing got a safety or not."

"It was off. And you got him, Mama."

"They's blood all over the kitchen floor." Wasn't that just like her? Mama blaming herself for making a mess. Femal decided to tell her what she wanted to know, now, before the woman got a bucket and mop and started cleaning up the madman's blood.

"Mama? You know the man I work for, Darrin Favore? Well, the man you shot, the man who was going to k-i-l-l Elaine, works for him."

"Well hell fire, call the damn po-lice!"

"I can't do that, Mama."

"And why not?"

"Cause I stole from Darrin, Mama, stole a lot of his money."

Mama just looked at her for a moment, and Femal, filled with shame, had to lower her eyes.

"Didn't raise my girl to be no thief," Mama said. "That's what you turn into, you hang around with those kinds of peoples. You get the ways of the white mens."

"It was a lot of money, Mama."

"How damn much," Mama asked, and Femal had to look up now, had to see the look on Mama's face when she said, "Altogether, after the transfers tonight, about forty million dollars."

Her Mama hesitated, lips moving, repeating that amount, slowly. At last she said aloud, "Forty million?"

"That's right, Mama, money that he stole from other people."

Mama's voice was filled with terror, her eyes wide and panicked. "Child, where you gonna hide, where can you go after stealing that much money from a white man?"

Chapter 41

Charlie looked at the letter on the small counter in the kitchen of Merle Como's apartment. His car was parked in the alley, and it had taken him all of five seconds to break in, as the back door had been left unlocked.

The note was all in capitals, the words widely spaced, printed out precisely, as if the writer had taken care to get his message across clearly. The note said:

Dear Merle. The police were here looking into your window this night. I am not sure anymore that you can help me with my problems, and am starting to think that maybe you are full of the bullshit.

I have borrowed the twenty thousand dollars that I have found in your cereal boxes and under the ice cube trays in your refrigerator freezer. I am going to Miami to live with my family members who will be able to protect me.

It was signed, *PETER.*

The apartment was in shambles, had been recently

searched. Charlie hoped that it was this Peter person who had done it and not the police, who might still be hanging around outside, waiting for Merle to come home.

When Charlie spotted the devices on the glass table, though, he knew that it hadn't been the cops who had tossed the place, or else, he knew, they would have taken the four homemade bombs that were sitting there in plain sight.

Anything of value would have already been taken, and he silently thanked Peter for saving him the trouble of tearing the place apart. He'd give Darrin's place a thorough search and steal anything of value, for the kid, for Elaine, to give to her and Femal so they could go somewhere and start over again, but this wasn't about the money.

This was about Cat, who'd raised him.

Slowly, without touching them, Charlie bent forward at the waist and began to carefully study the devices.

Merle didn't know what to do, how to act. He'd never been shot before, never even been beat up except by his stepfather, and that was when Merle was a little kid and besides, the old man was dead now, his mother, too, there were no witnesses to his shame.

But now two women had beat him tonight, two nigger bitches, and one of them had shot him.

He drove home slowly, not about to take the chance of being stopped for speeding. He didn't know how badly he was hurt, but he didn't think he was dying. One bullet had lodged in his arm, he could *feel* it in there, hot and round. Another had nicked him low on the right side. He didn't know if that one was still inside him, although he didn't think that it was. He wasn't dizzy or lightheaded, he didn't think he was in shock, although he was losing a lot of blood. His shirt was soaked with it, the jacket he was wearing was solid red, and he could feel it seeping into his pants, under him and onto the leather seat of his uncle's car as he drove.

What had she shot him with, a little .22? How would he take care of this now? Uncle Dare was gonna have him a shit fit when he learned about this.

He parked in the alley behind his building and walked the short way to his building, staying in shadows. Ahead of him, a car was just turning out of the alley, its brake lights popping on, bright red in the moonless night. The car turned right, onto the street, and Merle, holding his right arm tightly, where it hurt the most, hurried through the freezing night, the cold welcome, making him alert.

He'd have Peter patch him up, tell him it was part of a gang war, tell him that he and his uncle needed Peter's help and as soon as this was over Peter would be one of them, a man of respect. First, though, Peter had to do them a service, had to go with Merle this night to a house on the North Side, help him kill a bunch of jig pud bitches who needed killing.

Peter would fall for it. He was too dumb not to.

Merle reached for his keys, his fingers red and slimy with blood, his teeth chattering now, got them and held them in his teeth as he reached for the rear screen door to his apartment, wondering how to play it. His right arm was nearly useless. He'd throw the door open, hold it with his backside so it didn't smack into the goddamned right hip that had been shot, then he'd unlock the wooden door with his keys.

He could do it. His only other option was to bang on the damn aluminum screen door and attract attention, waiting for that stupid Mexican to stop hiding under the bed and come see that it was him. That wouldn't be worth the effort.

Merle bit down on the keys and hoped he'd have his timing right; if that damn door hit his side, he'd scream for sure and wake up the entire neighborhood. He gripped the screen door handle with his right hand, threw it open and then the night was filled with light and he was lifted, picked right up and thrown backward, the door on top of him, flying through the air right with him, and he was still in the air when he heard the blast of the explosion.

Merle landed with a thud on the grass at the back of his apartment house, the door landing on top of him then bouncing away, hearing shouts and screams around him, unable to feel anything below his waist. There was no pain at all, not even in his shoulder or side, his entire body was numb, but mostly below the belt. With a determined effort he lifted his arms one at a time, held his fingers up real close to his face and wriggled them, pleased that they worked, although they were trembling something awful. He moved his jaws, clicked his teeth together. He could even tighten his chest, the muscles in his stomach. But from the waist down, he was dead. Paralyzed.

Merle said, "Oh, Jesus Christ in heaven." As he began to cry he heard a male voice next to his ear, filled with panic, say, "You poor kid, Christ, hang on, I already called an ambulance." The guy was doing something, tearing the belt off his bathrobe and fixing it to a part of Merle's lower body.

Merle was blacking in and out, biting his tongue to stay awake and alert. He was afraid that if he passed out, he would die.

Merle reached out, crying now, gripped the man's hand and squeezed it tight. He said, "Am I gonna die, am I dying?" and when he got no answer he said, "Do I got any feet left?"

The man said, "Mister, you ain't got hardly any *legs* left, that door over there gotta be the only thing that saved your life, took most of the blast. Shit, the house is on fire."

Merle said, "Jesus," again, crying, then, in spite of his best effort, he passed out on the lawn of his landlord's backyard.

•   •   •

Charlie waited until the lights went off in the house. He didn't want to face the man while he was awake and alert, not just yet. Before he did he had to be aware of where everything was in the house, every gun, every utensil that could be used as a weapon. Charlie himself had no assault weapon whatsoever; he was armed with just his wits, his knowledge of burglary, and the two remaining devices in the shopping bag at his side.

Favore was alone, he knew that much from watching the house. There was no car in the garage, no one guarding it, no guard around the house at all. The wife, where could she be? Probably with relatives. Charlie couldn't imagine anyone in grief turning to Darrin Favore for emotional sustenance. Favore was an emotional vampire, the type of person who drained you dry and still wanted more, wasn't happy until you were completely in his power. How could any woman stay with him? Did he have that much money?

For a split second he had to fight the idea of taking one of the devices over and putting it in Lina's car, or inside the door of her office at work. Simply being herself was enough punishment, although he sure would like to be able to take Lance away from her. Maybe, if he somehow got through this without getting killed or winding up back in prison, he would work at it, try and somehow get the kid to come and live with him. Raise him the way Cat had raised Charlie. He'd put a little more sense in Lance's head, though, not give him as much rope as Cat had given him.

At last the light went out and Charlie waited, prowling the place, acclimating himself to the grounds, crawling up to windows, aware of everything, what each room was, before making his move.

He went in through the basement window, jimmying the latch with a 25-cent pocket comb and pushing the thing in, dropping silently to the concrete and gently placing the bag on the floor beside him.

Should he wire the place and just take off? No, what

if the wife came home? It wasn't weight he was willing to carry. He wanted Favore, not anyone else. And he'd have to do it quick. There was no telling when his punk, Como, would come home. He'd get blown up and it wouldn't take long for somebody to get ahold of the boss, maybe even send some people over to protect him, if this slob was as big a shot in the mob as Charlie had heard.

He gave the basement a quick hunt, found nothing of value hidden in the washer or dryer, inside the sewer grate or the sub pump. Was about to take his devices and head upstairs when he saw an old, battered suitcase under a workbench and stopped, walked over to it and kneeled down, dragged the thing out of there and opened it up.

Then had to fight himself not to make any sound as he gazed at all that green money inside there.

Charlie made the call using his leased portable cellular, standing at the foot of the stairs, one of Favore's pistols in his right hand, the phone in his left. He dialed Favore's number.

The phone buzzed once, then again, then he heard Favore's voice angrily growl, "Yeah!"

"Darrin," Charlie said. "I took your money, punk, for killing Cat, and your sissy, Como, is dead, too. You're next, asshole." Charlie ended the call and dropped the phone into the suitcase with the money and the passports and waited a few seconds, knowing that Favore would not be able to resist running right down into the basement. He heard the double locks on the iron bedroom door snap back, and he saw the bedroom door open, and he stepped to the left, into the shadows as Favore came pounding down the stairs, in silk pajamas, passing Charlie by inches.

Charlie let him pass, then stepped out from behind him.

"How you doing, Darrin?" The first word wasn't out of his mouth when Darrin jumped, turning, gasping in fear.

Charlie waved the weapon at him. "Some door up there. What are you, paranoid?" Charlie smiled at him. "Don't move, don't talk, don't even fucking breathe."

Darrin stood staring at him, his eyes wide, drool running down his lower lip, onto his chin.

"Found your money," Charlie said. "Your passports, too."

"I've got more money, lots more of it, Charlie, millions."

"I tell you to talk?" Darrin fell silent and Charlie could almost hear the wheels turning behind his eyes. He smiled.

"I'll kill you if you say another word." Darrin nodded. He was trembling.

Charlie said, "The passports, I'm taking them over to a guy I know, a guy named Moretti. The money, that's for me. You, Darrin, for killing Cat, you deserve worse than I can give you. Moretti, now, that's another story. *He'll* take good care of you, I'll bet." Charlie paused, the gun rocksteady on Darrin's stomach, watching the man squirm and enjoying it.

"I'm gonna give you a choice. You can go into that bedroom and find another gun, do your own ass in, or you can get upstairs and lock that fire door behind you. Get dressed. Then start running, Darrin, see how far you can get before Moretti's boys catch up to you." He slowly backed away from the man, into the shadows, heading for the side sliding glass doors that led to the patio. "Either way you're dead. The first way is clean and quick, though, you know what I'm saying?" The last words spoken as Charlie, carrying the suitcase with the money, disappeared through the glass doors and into the darkness.

He waited in the car, saw the lights go on in the upstairs bedroom and wondered which decision the man would make, which way he'd go.

He'd bet that Favore would run. Would take the

chance of a long, slow death. Because he thought he was so smart, because he had that great education and thought that was all he'd ever need.

Charlie knew from experience that it wouldn't be anywhere near enough. The man would have to die, tonight, for what he'd done to Cat.

He was parked so that he could see the sliding glass door, and if Favore came through it he'd shoot him, as simple as that. Maybe shoot over his head, force him back inside and make him break for one of the other doors.

But Favore didn't try to go for the sliding glass door. Charlie saw the cab pull up, heard the horn honk, and he knew that Favore had made the wrong choice. He saw the outside light come on and saw the front door begin to open and right then the brilliant white light flashed and the door went off its hinges and into the house, glass flying everywhere. The cab, after a long second, took off from the curb with a squeal of rubber. The front of the house began to burn.

Charlie didn't waste time watching. He put the car in gear, but waited until he turned the corner before he turned his lights on. He grabbed the car phone and dialed the non-emergency police number and told them about the explosion, gave them Favore's address, and told the officer who answered to tell the responding units to be careful, it was a gang war, and those guys didn't play around, there might be other explosives in the house, say, attached to the back door . . .

Dick didn't get back from Gang Crimes South until after midnight, what with all the questions from the stupes at Internal Affairs, wanting to know if his "partner" had ever discussed chest pains or anything like that with him when they worked together.

At first he'd thought it was a setup, that they were trying to get him for O'Brian's death, but Simmons was right there, his sleeves rolled up in the hot office, his arms crossed, glaring at the IA guys and demanding at nearly every turn what exactly this had to do with Blandane, and after a little while Dick thought that it was going to be just fine, that they were only going through the motions, covering their asses and making sure that there were no loose ends to O'Brian's death that were likely to come back later and wrap themselves around the IA guys' necks.

Dick could relate to that, he didn't care for loose ends himself.

They would get through the autopsy and find out that the guy was a walking heart attack, was an accident waiting to happen. Dick didn't say anything out loud, but he was glad that the bastard had died, that he wouldn't be able to retire and suck off the public tit for thirty or forty years. He just didn't deserve it. Wasn't the department's motto To Serve and Protect? Whom did O'Brian ever serve but himself? And he certainly didn't protect anyone, unless you could call covering your own sad ass protecting something. Killing an unarmed man on the steps of a church wasn't the way to operate, even if the man *had* shot at you.

By the time Dick got back to North, Hurtah was gone. He'd explain things to him tomorrow, if Simmons didn't, first. What bothered him was the fact that he had wasted so much time, lost the night when he had felt so confident that he'd have something on Como before the end of the shift . . .

Which was why he'd come back. He'd get the computer report, and, if the watch was stolen, as he suspected, he'd take the thing home with him, confront Como with it first thing tomorrow afternoon, right after he checked in with Hurtah.

The report was sitting right there on the large desk that held the computer in the communications room, clipped to a sheet of paper with his name scribbled across the top.

Dick read it and the following report, then the following report, and the one after that, and he smiled, reached for the phone and dialed the number on the original sheet, and even though it was an hour later in Florida he right away got through to Miami Homicide, no problem.

At three A.M. he was sitting in a molded plastic chair outside the surgical recovery room at Mercy Hospital, patiently reading over his reports, the warrant, making sure he'd left no loopholes, committed no procedural errors.

"May I help you?" Dick started and looked up, saw a woman with bloody greens standing in front of him, haggard-looking, with blond hair pulled back in a ponytail. A tall woman who did not look happy to see him sitting there.

"As I told the nurse, I am waiting for Merle Como to be wheeled out of the recovery room."

"I'm Doctor Preston, his surgeon. He lost both legs above the knees, officer, and I don't think he'll be going anywhere tonight."

Dick looked up at her, wondering if he should stand, tower over her. He didn't think she'd be intimidated. Still, he wasn't sure he liked the way she was speaking to him. He decided to remain seated, as there was no use in further alienating the woman. He was within his rights, and she'd never understand, anyway, even if he yelled his business in her face.

He said, "This guy," turning a fax sheet with an old smiling face toward her, "won't be going anywhere, either. Not tonight, not tomorrow, not ever. His name's James Andrews and your patient in there killed him, beat him to death in an airport parking lot and stole his watch, his credit cards."

"He did?" The doctor's reaction surprised him. "I figured him for a political activist, I mean, the bomb and all."

"There's nothing political about this guy at all. Take my word for it. He was wearing the watch last night, and

I've got signed statements right here attesting to the fact that he used the credit cards yesterday morning in several different area stores. I've got the bartender's statement from the airport tavern, put them together. He's no political prisoner, doctor." Then, feeling the need to explain himself to her, she was, after all, half-smiling now, even though he'd raised his voice, he said, "You see, doctor, my boss gave me a job to do at three this afternoon, and I want it cleared up before I go to bed. Clamping the cuffs on this guy, in his room, unconscious or not, will complete that job."

"Does it make a difference? I mean, who'd know if you put them on him tonight or tomorrow?"

"I'll know." Dick felt a little pompous saying that, and quickly added, "Who else needs to?" He looked at her bloody uniform, screwed up his courage and took a chance. "Look, he'll be in there a while, and you've been working on him for a few hours. You want to clean up and get a cup of coffee, I'll tell you all about it?"

"No," the doctor said, and he felt his face fall.

"But . . ." She was biting her lower lip, making a decision. "I'm off tomorrow night, maybe we could get together . . . What was your name again?"

"Blandane, Dick Blandane."

She handed him a card, said, "My home number's on the back," and turned, walked rapidly away from him, stopped at the door and said, "The cuffs, they don't go on, right?" and Dick said, "Can I tell him he's under arrest?" and she smiled, which made him happy. He'd do that, make it legal, then there was one more thing he wanted to do before he called it a night and went home.

Chapter 42

Charlie drove over to Femal's house and left the car a couple of blocks away, as he figured that some mob guys would be paying her a visit as soon as they heard about the boss and he didn't want them getting a license number. He prowled the house, carefully, eyeing it, learning that they were either sleeping, which wasn't likely, or they weren't home.

He saw blood stains on the sidewalk leading to the street, and on the pavement running to the back door.

He went around back and climbed to the second-floor balcony, and looked through the window.

Saw an empty crib and drawers pulled out, a lot of baby clothing on the floor.

They had either skipped town or were hiding, either one being a good idea right about now.

He climbed down, was wiping his hands on his pants when he heard the voice behind him shout, "Freeze!"

• • •

Dick had gone back to the house, even though it was too late to knock on the door and ask his questions. He wanted to meet the two beat cops, Crier and his partner, in front of the place, have a talk with them, get them to save him some trouble and check their Department of Streets and Sanitation map, find out the name of the occupant from their water bill. All he planned to do was write the name down, tie up that one loose end, and then he'd go home.

The radio dispatcher told him that the two would report to the house as soon as they finished a disturbance call they were on, if he wanted to wait she'd send them by as soon as they were free, and the second he'd signed off he saw the man walking toward the North Side house, rapidly, and disappear around the back.

He'd seen a car turn a minute ago, onto a side street and disappear, and he didn't think anything of it, but now it bothered him, was this the driver? If it was, he wasn't up to anything good. Only hit men and thieves parked blocks away before they paid a visit.

Dick got out of the car and ran around the corner and down the alley, counted off the houses as he hurried along the gravel, stepping lightly. Saw the man, a figure on the second-floor balcony, looking through a window.

At the very least he had him for trespassing.

He used the man's own climbing sounds to cover the noise he made as he stepped into the yard, pulled his piece and walked up to him, waited for the man to climb all the way down before shouting for him to freeze.

Which was what the man did. Stood stock still and didn't even attempt to turn around, didn't do anything but give a little jump then stand motionless, slowly raising his hands and clasping them behind his head without being told. This wasn't his first pinch; he was a professional.

Dick slammed him against the side of the building and cuffed him, searched him, found no weapon, took out his wallet then spun him around, stepped back so the man could not kick out at him. He took out the man's driver's license and squinted at it in the darkness.

"What're you doing here, climbing around this time of night?" Dick looked at the license again. "Charles Lane."

"I got nothing to say, just read me my rights and take me in, officer."

"Nothing to say? The owner here a friend of yours? Can we knock on the door and wrap this up tonight, or what?" Dick spoke and watched the man's face, wanting to see some hope there, wanting the man thinking he could beat this before he dropped the bomb. But there was nothing, the guy didn't even flinch.

"You a friend of Merle Como's?" God, *that* got a reaction. Lane's face turned white and his face fell a little before he got it back, turned it into a cold, staring mask.

"How about his boss, Favore, he a friend of yours?"

"I got nothing to say."

Dick said, "I believe you," and took Lane's arm, directed him to the street, where the prowl car with the two officers inside was at the curb, idling.

"What you got there?" Crier said. He was sitting in the passenger seat and smiling at Dick, shaking his head. "We just spotted us a hot car parked a few blocks down, and you want us to play taxi for you, instead of sitting on it, is that it?"

"My calling you had nothing to do with this guy here, I just found him prowling the house." He opened the back door of the squad car and pushed Charlie's head down, helped him into the back seat. "Guy's name is Charles Lane, and I got him for trespassing, minimum. I'll check inside and see if there's maybe more we can lay on him. This the guy from last night, the guy was kicking Como when you pulled up?"

Crier said, "Naw, he even better than that. He the man reported to have stolen the car we just spotted," and smiled. "Good work, Blandane."

• • •

There had been no answer at the door and Dick had to call for a supervisor, he didn't have the authority to take this any further on his own.

What he did have the authority to do was to search the car that Lane had reportedly stolen.

"The man in our car, he *our* bust?" Crier wanted to know. His partner told Blandane that was only right.

They stood outside the car and watched as Dick searched it, stepped back and the joking stopped as Dick came out from under the front seat with the pistol that he'd found, held up by a pen through the trigger guard.

"Got an evidence bag?" he asked.

The suitcase in the trunk was a bigger surprise. He opened it carefully, started when he saw the money there, the telephone on top of a bunch of documents.

"Run the phone numbers, both the one off this portable and the one mounted in the car, call the cellular company if you have to, but find out who this guy called tonight. The money's gonna have to be counted and inventoried, it doesn't leave our sight before the night sergeant gets here."

"Yes, sir," Crier said, and he wasn't being sarcastic.

Charlie watched them from the back seat of the squad car. He felt nothing, just a numbness. He fought to keep his mind blank, his face the same. He would say nothing, but even with that, there was no way he could get out of this without doing some heavy time. If they checked the phone numbers he'd called, the party would be over.

The cuffs were cutting into his wrists, on too tight the way the cops always did you. He shifted in the seat, knowing he was going back to the joint for a while.

Or maybe not. What did they have? A call to Favore, a call to the cops. Could they pin anything on him? He could say he found the money and they couldn't prove that he hadn't.

The documents, though, those would hang him.

He had to think of something to tell a lawyer, and he had to stay strong. Not say a word until he was talking to a lawyer. These guys, he wouldn't even tell them his name.

He was Charlie Lane, and he'd killed for his brother. If he had to do time behind that, well, it would be an even trade.

He wondered where the woman and child were. Femal was a full grown woman, she had gotten herself into whatever trouble she might be in, but the kid, Cat's kid, she wasn't old enough to deserve anything but love. He could only wish that she was safe, and would remain so. Wherever she was.

Which was sleeping on her grandmother's lap, several miles above the sea.

The steward's name was Julian and he watched them, made a personal undertaking out of them because the old one, the skinny one, she didn't like white people, Julian could tell. She wasn't really mean or anything, just mistrustful, giving him looks whenever he'd walk by.

Which bothered him. His job was to win her over, it was his goal for this trip.

First class was nearly full, but the three of them had the first two seats of the plane, three generations of black women, it looked like, the old woman holding the beautiful sleeping baby, the daughter sleeping on her mother's arm, holding it with both hands as if for safety. The two adults sure looked beat. Even sleeping, he could tell that the daughter had had a rough day. Maybe she didn't like to travel. The grandmother though, she was acting as if it was her personal duty to stay awake, to keep an eye on the other two.

Sometimes old age did that to you, Julian thought. You knew the danger that was out there, the bigotry and evil. You'd faced it and survived it and now it was your turn to pass the wisdom down to your kin.

Julian didn't have a lot of kin, they'd disowned him when they'd learned he was gay and he always felt a little tug at his heart when he saw loving families traveling together, always went out of his way to try and make their trip more pleasurable.

As he did now, walking right up to the old woman who eyed him suspiciously, hugged the baby tighter to her breast. The child made a cooing sound, then settled in, safe.

Julian gave her his warmest smile and when he spoke he made sure it was in his softest whisper.

"Pardon me, ma'am, but would you like a bottle warmed? When that darling wakes up, she's going to be hungry."

"No, thank you," she said.

Julian lingered, looking down at the child. The woman had lightened her grip, had maybe figured out that he wasn't going to try and kidnap her.

He said, "She sure is beautiful," and that did it, the woman grinned at him, showing him gold teeth.

"She looks like her mother," the old woman said.

"No, ma'am," Julian said, "I think she sort of takes after her grandma," and that got a wave of a hand, a hushed chuckle.

"Oh, you go on with your bad self, talking like that." She was pleased, he could tell.

"It's a shame, though. She's way too young to enjoy Paris, the beauty that's there to see."

"That's not going to be a problem, her seeing Paris," the old woman told Julian. "We just stopping off there. Then we goin' on to Africa, and I believes we's going to be staying for a time."

ABOUT THE AUTHOR

EUGENE IZZI has lived in and around Chicago all his life. He is the acclaimed author of nine novels: *Tribal Secrets, Prowlers, Invasions, The Prime Roll, King of the Hustlers, The Eighth Victim, The Take, The Booster,* and *Bad Guys.* His next book from Bantam will be *Tony's Justice.*

THE WORLD OF EUGENE IZZI

"Eugene Izzi is a pro, one of the very best in the crime field," wrote Elmore Leonard after reading Izzi's ninth novel, TRIBAL SECRETS (published by Bantam Books in September 1992). Already hailed by *Chicago Magazine* as "a powerful and uncompromising writer," and heralded by fellow crime novelist Andrew Vachss as "the new master artist of crime fiction," Eugene Izzi has created a body of work in recent years that has garnered extraordinary reviews from across the nation.

Here, in selections from six of his novels, you can experience firsthand the remarkable talent of Eugene Izzi.

TRIBAL SECRETS

Raised on Chicago's mean streets by a father who has made a career out of killing for the mob, Babe Hill has fought long and hard to put his violent past behind him. And it looks as if he may have finally succeeded: his performance in a Sunday night Movie of the Week has made Babe Hill a star.

But success doesn't mean safety, and fame doesn't necessarily lead to happiness. Because when you've got millions of adoring fans, all it takes is one to make your life hell. Edna Rose doesn't care if Babe has a wife and kids. She knows that the sexy actor belongs to her—and she'll do anything to win him . . . anything.

Yet when Edna makes her move, she'll find she has unexpected competition. Babe's father has just ripped off his employers to the tune of one hundred grand, and now the mob means to make Babe pay for his father's sins. Suddenly everyone wants a piece of Babe, but it won't go down the way any of them expect. . . .

The first thing Tim said to him was, "Thirty-nine more, Babe, just thirty-nine more."

He looked like hell, his eyes heavy with dark bags under them. Babe wondered if he'd gotten any sleep. Tim set the machine, began walking on it for a total of five seconds before he pushed the Fast Accelerate button and kept hitting it until he was at six-minute miles, ten miles per hour, then Tim hit reset, began to run in earnest.

"Got an A on the psychology paper, on the interviews."

"With the kids?"

"Yeah. Put them in the room with the victims, one on one, let them see the people they'd hurt as humans instead of as honkies or niggers or just someone to get some dope money from. Eighty-three percent of the kids broke down, couldn't deal with it." Tim was running effortlessly, wasn't even sweating yet.

"I'm working on something else with them, if I can make the time. Want to put the more violent ones in a setting, maybe in the forest preserve, but just me and them, one at a time, with a baseball bat, some ground beef, and a skull."

"Where you get a skull?" The sweat was pouring off Babe now, and he was starting to gasp. He slowed it down some, noticed with a little perverse joy that Tim was starting to sweat a little, that he was breathing heavily. The joy left him when he realized that Tim hadn't slept in over twenty-four hours. He was bushed, and still in better shape than Babe was. Should he ask Tim about his father? Babe decided not to. If Tim wanted to discuss it, he'd bring it up. Babe hoped that he wouldn't. He might offend the best friend he had if he told him what he really thought.

Tim said, "You kidding me? I'm a cop. I can get all the skulls I need, discount."

"Then what?"

"These kids, their only perspective on violence comes from TV, from the movies. They see Stallone getting hit in the head with baseball bats, then kicked in the balls, then he gets up and kicks everybody's ass.

"I got a theory. I think if I fill the skull with beef, to represent the brain, then cover it with leather, for skin, then let them take a baseball bat to it, just for one whack—"

"Shit, it would explode the beef, drive skull bones into it."

"That's the point. I want to take the leather off and show them what they do to someone when they hit them in the head with a blunt object." Tim wiped his nose on his arm, took a deep breath and hacked, once.

"I want to personalize it for them, let them know that what they're doing isn't some cold, dispassionate act that has no consequence. I want to show them what they really do to someone, then let them meet the people they've mugged, see how it impacts on them."

"That's an undertaking, there."

"What else am I gonna spend my money on? I'm a veteran of Illinois, so I go to school free, and I don't have any kids, no wife. Anymore." Tim shrugged. There had been no bitterness in his voice. "I wish this damn thing went faster."

"You do that on purpose, to show me up?" Babe began to pedal harder, wondering where the other guys were. They didn't take it as personally as Babe and Tim did, had no vested interest in staying in shape.

"I do it to stay awake. Even at this pace, I'm liable to pass out, bust my skull on the damn handles."

"Have a heart attack maybe, and don't be waiting for me to give you any CPR."

"You don't know how?"

"I don't open-mouth kiss my wife, even, these days, with all the garbage in the air, infecting you."

"Watch those toilet seats, the shower stalls."

"Mosquitoes," Babe said, "they're carriers, too."

"Babe, I'm too damn tired to laugh."

A voice from behind him said, "He's just being nice. He'd laugh if you said something funny, Babe." This from Arlene, who was working the gym today. "Good thing you guys showed up, I was going nuts, staring at the walls."

"Making phone calls," Tim said, "at the members' expense."

Arlene was the assistant manager, thin and strong, with Chris Evert muscles. She ran the gym until the first of June then taught tennis lessons for the park district throughout the summer, when the gym was closed. She had a good sense of humor and backed Tim up whenever some clod would light up a cigarette in the place and he'd get an attitude.

"Good show the other night, Babe," she said now, "you gonna do the series?"

"Arlene, I just don't know."

She'd come from behind the counter to speak to them, and Babe knew that it was only because Tim had shown up; that she'd have never approached him if he'd been alone. Tim gave people strength just by his presence and the force of his personality. The phone rang and she bounced down the two stairs to the counter, picked it up but Babe couldn't hear her voice over the sound of the Exercycle's whirring, the noise of the treadmill.

"Babe?" Arlene hollered, "Hey, Babe, your wife's on the phone."

The gym was small, little more than a large house with an upstairs and a basement. The exercise room was cramped. There was a Universal machine with twelve stations, ruled by pulleys which Babe wasn't crazy about. He preferred free weights. There was the Exercycle next to the treadmill, which he rarely used unless there was too much snow on the ground to run the outdoor track. The locker rooms were downstairs and they had saunas, which Babe did use, enjoying the feel of the dry heat on his skin. The village maintained the place, hired the staff and charged a nominal fee for membership, and after the dinner hour the place was usually packed, but until then it was dead. Babe and Tim rarely had to wait for a machine.

It was the upstairs they cared about, anyway.

The village manager had let them strip the room, lay down plywood and canvas, cover the walls with gym mats. It was a bare room for which only the two of them had a key. They kept it clean and never entered wearing shoes, bitched when anyone would come up there to watch them.

It was where they sparred.

As soon as Babe hung up the phone, he went over and asked Tim if he'd mind cutting his run short, he could finish it later, there was someone coming to see him and he wanted that person to see him in action because maybe it would stop the guy from being too much of an asshole. Tim agreed without comment, and they carried their gym bags up the stairs, kicked off their gym shoes at the door, and stripped off their socks. Once inside they quickly wrapped their hands, reached into their bags and took out 16-ounce boxing gloves, with Velcro closures so they didn't have to fumble around and try to tie them with their teeth.

"No headgear today?" Tim said, and Babe just shook his head. Tim never wore it but Babe usually did. His face was his livelihood.

"You all right?"

Babe had been setting a three-minute timer against the wall when Tim asked the question, was bending down with one glove on and the other glove ready. He snapped the timer all the way over and shoved his hand into the glove, bounced toward Tim with his hands up, his elbows tucked into his side, partially crouching.

"I don't think so, Tim," Babe said, and attacked.

TONY'S JUSTICE

Get Tony Just. That's the word on Chicago's desperate streets. When the police won't touch it, when the private detectives want five hundred an hour, or the usual channels don't work, clients come to Tony because he can fix almost anything . . . or anybody. Except maybe himself.

He's a cop turned killer, who broke the law and served his time. Now, after years of bringing down child molesters and rapists, dope dealers and thieves, Tony's got a heart colder than the wind off Lake Michigan. He'll need it. Because his latest case isn't business—it's personal. It's Antek Bando, an ex-con like Tony, but whose soul wears even more ice than his, whose mind spews more nightmares than he can imagine, whose body deals—and takes—more murderous pain than

anything he's ever seen. He's got Tony scared, but more than that, he's got Tony mad. And when Tony wants justice, he'll seek it out and mete it out anyway he can . . .

Jack was in his own trunk, Tony behind the wheel of the car, Milt behind in Tony's car, following him. Tony had turned the brights off, stayed within the speed limit. Jack had been conscious for a while, Tony had heard him pounding on the trunk lid, and he'd raised his voice, told Jack if he did it again he would stop the car, would get out and punch holes in the exhaust system, see how long Jack lasted.

The pounding had stopped.

Before loading him into the trunk, Milt had stripped Jack of his watch and wallet, his pinkie ring, had taken the money from the wallet and thrown his credit cards into the wind. Out here, someone would find them and not look too hard for the owner. The watch and ring, the empty wallet, were in an alley garbage can. They'd be found, too.

Now Tony pulled the car onto the city access road to Wolf Lake, drove toward the frozen water's edge and stopped. Milt had pulled over before the turnoff. Tony waited until Milt walked up, then got out of the car, left it running. Walked to the back, tapped once on the trunk.

"Jack, you in there?"

"You're not cops!"

"Sure we are. And juries, too. And executioners."

"I'll get help, I swear to God I will, don't you understand I'm sick?"

"Thinking about it's sick," Tony said. "Doing it's evil. I ain't here to converse with you, Jack. Just to tell you to take a deep breath and hold it."

He walked around front and opened the car door, reached in and grabbed the gear shift, pulled it down into Drive and stepped back.

The car began to roll out onto the ice, the ice slowly breaking up in the shallow water, the front wheels hitting sand and digging in. Still, the car crept forward, breaking ice as it went, until the water hit the engine and killed it.

The rear wheels had made it all the way in, the front of the car being maybe ten feet out into Wolf Lake. From where Tony was standing and clear across the lake to Whiting, Indiana, this was as deep as the water got at this section of the lake, maybe three feet deep.

But Jack didn't know that.

The trunk would have maybe six inches of water in it, Jack feeling it in the blackness and thinking it was all over for him. Jack screaming now; harsh, brutal, throat-tearing screams that rent the night, shattered the winter's peace. He was probably thinking that an air pocket had slowed the car's descent, that he was minutes from death.

That was good. The thought of being with his Maker in a short while might help him change his ways.

If he was found before he died of exposure, or hunger.

Tony didn't much give a shit either way.

"You ready, Milt, or you want to stay around a while and watch?"

"It's fun, but it's too damn cold." Milt shook himself. "Man, Tony, I hate doing this shit, I really do. It scares me thinking that there's people like this in the world, it really does."

"Bet it scares them to find out that there's people like us in the world."

"Like *you*, Tony Justice, people like you. I'm just along for the ride."

"And the money."

"That, too. You want to drop me off at Falcon's? I left my car there."

"No," Tony said, "we got something else to do. There's some heads been disappearing from a pathology lab at the hospital, the chief of security wants me to find out who's taking them."

"Heads?!"

"Heads."

They had been talking at the water's edge, watching the car sway in the lake, listening to the muffled cries to God that Jack was now shouting. Now they began to walk back toward where Milt had left Tony's car.

"Heads?" Milt said again. "I ain't sure about that, Tony, after tonight. This gets too deep for me sometimes."

"There's five grand in it for us if we find the thief."

Milt nodded, pursed his lips as they reached the car. He got in the passenger seat, handed the keys to Tony as Tony slid in behind the wheel.

"Five grand? Shit, include me in."

"That's what I figured."

He started the car, slowly turned around, then turned right on Avenue O, heading for the expressway, the South Loop, and home.

"We start tonight?" Milt asked.

"Right after we get the hot plates off my car."

"You want to call the cops, tell them about Jack?"

Tony thought about it a minute, about the beastie's promise to make gentle love to what he thought was a seven-year-old boy. Begging God to help when he thought his baby-raping days were over.

It was nothing new to him; he lived in a city where flesh was bought and sold all day, every day, where a child's heart and kidneys and lungs could be had if the price was right and where there was no dearth of either buyers or sellers.

Still, in all the time that they had pulled the sting, half of them would find him turning the terrified freak in to the police, anonymously. This was the first time he had used that part of the lake, and he liked the idea, particularly for the guy Jack.

He also considered the fact that he'd had too many gay people in his life who were real and true men, who would have killed Jack if they'd heard him refer to himself as a homosexual. They knew better. The fools who let NASBA march in their gay rights parades didn't.

No, he didn't think he'd let the cops in on this one.

To Milt, though, he only said, "Fuck him."

KING OF THE HUSTLERS

Tone Nello is looking for a big score and he thinks he's found it, but Chicago's mean streets are filled with double crossers and this goes for the cops as well. While Tone is out working for the big job—others are out for his life.

Whenever anyone asked Tone what he did for a living he would say he was a salesman, and when they asked what he sold he would say, What do you need? Sometimes they'd laugh and put in an order, kiddingly, amazed later when he showed up with what they'd asked for and then, demanded payment. Sometimes they would shake their heads and walk away, puzzled, and sometimes they were insulted, figuring Tone was making fun of them. Tone figured that in the first place what he did was nobody's business. They could take it any way they wanted to. It was the truth.

He was a salesman and the world was his territory. As a

young kid they'd called him Anthony the Thief, and he'd enjoyed it until he got older and realized the dangers he faced—being in his line of work and advertising it. Later it had just turned into Tone. Or Nello. But mostly it was Tone.

Except for Aunt Amelia. To her, he would always be Anthony. She would never even call him Tony.

He loved to hustle. He could get anything and do anything and lived the philosophy that there was more money in shit than there was in gold. More often than not he worked with Bebbo because Bebbo was fun and easy to be with, but he couldn't tell Bebbo anything on the rare occasions that he wanted to open up because he knew that sooner or later Bebbo would use his words to prove some half-ass theory of his to Tone. Tone considered this an invasion of privacy.

He rarely felt down, and that was because he accepted, mostly, what he was and where he was going. Also because he didn't look at himself or his life too often or too deeply. Tone wasn't big on insight.

But he was doing it now, looking at himself and not liking what he saw.

They were in Frank Mancik's bar, not a neighborhood joint by any means but not a disco, either. Franky ran a tight ship. Patrons were encouraged to have fun but you didn't fight in Franky's joint because he would take a baseball bat to your head for showing him disrespect or for scaring the girls.

One of the things Tone liked the most about Franky's joint was the fact that girls came around there. On the North Side, where he usually did his drinking, there were women. Or females. Or significant others. Call one of the regulars in a North Side tavern a girl and she would be highly offended. In Franky's they were girls and liked it that way.

Bebbo was on, singing along as he danced with whoever was free, single and alone, the lyrics to "Mac the Knife" or some other fifties tune rolling off his tongue as if he'd written them. Throwing the girls up into the air and catching them, rock-and-rolling, jitterbugging, laughing a lot and making the girls laugh, too.

Tone was sitting at the bar nursing a beer and watching his friend and wondering what the hell was wrong with him. Wondering why he, too, wasn't out on the dance floor or doing the cigarette trick, making the ash go from one palm to the other. Wondering why he wasn't having fun.

Bebbo made it look so easy that other guys in the bar

always tried to do what he did and they always fell short, ended up looking like cheap imitations. This also made Bebbo look even more attractive to the girls when they saw how easily and naturally it came to him. This wasn't an act; it was him.

Tone felt a moment's resentment at his friend's antics, knew it would be sour grapes for him to think that Bebbo's behavior was childish, beneath a grown man. That would just be jealousy. Sometimes they would bounce off each other and have each other rolling on the floor laughing, but this wasn't to be one of those nights.

THE PRIME ROLL

Lano Branka has the magic touch. From the back-room betting parlors of Chicago to the glittering casinos of Atlantic City, Lano is raking in the bucks. But sometimes the tables turn, and lady luck turns the other way. And suddenly Lano comes up against a bookie who belongs to the Mob and then a union boss ends up dead.

Lano didn't even look at the gaming tables. He could hear Tough Tony yelling something at whoever the poor chump was rolling on the crap table, and little fat Hitler ordering the guy to quit fucking around, roll the dice or pass them. He wondered why Artie put up with the man. He knocked twice and walked on into Artie's office, cockily.

The thing that puzzled him was, their relationship had seemed to change for the better right when Lano's lucky streak began. Artie would talk to him more than he was used to, telling him things. Telling him about the prime roll and all that was supposed to go along with it. There were times, like earlier this evening when the Bulls covered, when Lano was sure he was on it; when the adrenaline was rushing and the blood was racing and his head was light. And there were other times when he was not so sure.

Such as now. Artie had told him that almost every professional gambler had one prime roll in his life, when everything went his way and he couldn't lose. One of the symptoms of it was a surge in ego; the gambler knew he just could not lose; it was as if God himself was rolling the dice. He could call what was going to come up before the dice hit the backboard. A feeling of serenity and all-knowing would fill the gambler, a warmth engulfing him with each throw of the dice, every flip of the cards. It was, Artie had told him, a nearly sexual feeling. Lano had never felt that, and didn't know if that was good or bad. He enjoyed the slight feeling of dread that filled him with every roll, and the rush of knowing that he'd beaten the odds. He'd told Artie over and over again that he didn't think he was on a prime roll, but whatever he was on, he wasn't complaining.

Now, as he closed the door behind him, he smiled widely. "Man chickened out, did he, Art?"

Artie smiled and nodded, rising and holding out his hand. "Good to see you, Lano. In this frame of mind, too."

"The fucking guy, his problem is, he gambles for money. He don't give a shit about anything else but trying to make a buck."

"That'll be his downfall." Artie sat down behind his desk and poured himself another shot of Fernet, offered the bottle to Lano, who shook his head. He never drank when he was working.

"You'll get the bets in for me?"

Artie didn't bother to answer him. He'd already said he would, and he wasn't in the habit of saying something more than once just to reassure people.

Lano said, "There's a horse in the tenth out at Balmoral. Bucking Bronco N. I want two dimes to win, two dimes to place."

"You give the bet to Elihue?" Artie said, and Lano nodded. Artie said, "I figured as much. Look."

Lano turned his head and looked at the camera pointed at the two men by the front entrance. Elihue was pleading his case with one of the roving handbooks, to no avail. The rule was, Elihue did no gambling on duty. Lano knew that Artie would say something to him for trying to break it. He saw Virgil grab the money angrily from Elihue's hand, thrust it into the face of the book, and point at his own chest. Virgil's face was a mask of intimidation and Lano could almost hear him saying, "You take the bet from *me,* motherfucker?" He watched the little bookie nodding again and again, writing something down in his black notebook, and as soon as the sweating man turned his back Elihue and Virgil slapped palms.

"Now, I won't place this bet myself," Artie was saying. "Can't, when I got the books out there taking them, and especially not when you're on a streak like this. What's the horse going off at?"

"Won his qualifying heat, then died last six times out. Program got him at twenty-to-one."

Artie grunted. "I had any sense, I'd book it myself. But my man out there, he just gave me an idea." He reached under his desk and pressed a button and Lano turned his head quickly to the screen, saw Elihue lose all of his infamous cool as the thing rang at his ear. Saw Elihue stare guiltily at the camera, then shrug fatalistically and begin walking toward the office. Artie grunted again and told Lano to keep his mouth shut.

INVASIONS

Frank Vale has spent the greater part of his life as a burglar of the city's most elaborate homes and its trickiest bank vaults. His brother Jimmy hasn't had it that easy. For the last nine years he's been in the state penitentiary. Tomorrow, Jimmy is getting freed and Frank wants to start a new life. But it's not that easy. They've got the chance for one last big job.

Jimmy walked down the third tier with his hands in his pockets because there were a bunch of black guys congregating on the catwalk a couple of cells away from the new kid's house. They knew him and would take his stance to mean he was carrying. To go the long way, around now that they'd spotted him would invite them to test him further, and he couldn't let that happen. He told himself that it was just another day. Another twenty-four-hour period to get through. He could start thinking about lessening the risk factor in his life tomorrow, when he was breathing free air for the first time since he was a teenager. Not now, though. He had to live today the way he'd lived the past 3,200 days. Fearlessly and unafraid of consequences. If these guys even *thought* they smelled fear on him—and fear had a smell all its own—they would pounce and he would lose and he'd wind up on Boot Hill with a "W" stamped on his marker.

The five black guys fell silent as he approached, and he made his mind as blank as his face, neither giving away a thing. He passed them, fought the urge to stiffen his shoulders as he waited for the sound of shuffling feet on the catwalk. He'd hear them coming and that would give him time to move before the shank struck. Or so he hoped.

Made it. Into the cell, and there the kid was, looking at him with large round eyes, authentic terror on his face. He was hiding something behind his thigh, sitting on the top bunk. When he saw it was a white man he relaxed, but not so an outsider would notice.

In a forced, flat voice, he said, "They're talking about me. What they're gonna do to me. Loud enough for me to hear them. The ugly one with the pantyhose stocking on his head lives here with me and he got plans." He lifted a piece of metal from behind his leg, hefted it, a good hunk, maybe a two-pounder, about a foot long. "I'm gonna kill them, they come in here." Jimmy liked him already, the kid hiding his terror and making plans, alone. The kid was working his lips, trying to keep from breaking.

Jimmy said, "They won't, you come with us, Bill. We can get you assigned to the fifth tier with me, down in a cell with one of our people. Any of these guys come near you, we kill them."

"I was just out drinking, Christ, celebrating graduation." He was whispering almost to himself. His voice now far-off and dreamy. His eyes were wet. He was a big kid, muscular, but his downfall was his face. He was too pretty to cut it and even if he whipped this bunch outside someone else would come calling with his gang. This guy had been cursed by his genes, by an accident of birth. What had been a blessing on the outside was a curse in here. The face that won him pussy in the outside world would turn him into one behind the walls.

"The cops, they started chasing me and I thought it was funny, trying to outrace them, and the squad, it comes right next to me and I went to run it off the road, you know, just like in the movies, but shit, it hit a telephone pole and the cop driving dies and *shit*! I don't know what to *do*."

"Keep it down, that's what. And keep it inside. No one in here gives a fuck about you but us. Don't tell anyone that story, ever. Anyone asks, tell them you killed a cop. You'll get by with our help."

"What do we do now?"

"We go out, walk right past them. The first one says something to you, level him with that pipe and keep swinging. They go over the side and we get up to five, you come into my house and throw the piece over the rail. Swear on Bibles we were together talking about women and heard some scuffling, some screaming, and nothing else. You got it?"

Bill nodded.

"Then let's go."

PROWLERS

Robert "Catfeet" Millard is a strong man in the mob—he's a master thief and a loyal one. When he finally gets busted, he knows he'll be taken care of when his time is up. The mob doesn't see it that way, however. Instead of the twenty-two grand he owed them when he went in, his bill is now a half mil—and they won't wait.

They didn't even let Catfeet draw breath as a free man. They were waiting for him at the bottom of the wide long stone staircase of the Criminal Courts Building at 26th & California. Mickey and another guy, what was his name? Larry, that was it. Fat strong bastard with a thick mustache who liked to be called Lar, the two of them drivers and bodyguards for Darrin Favore, who was the reason Catfeet had done this jail bit in the first place.

He walked down the stairs, fear strong inside him, trying to hide it as they noticed him and put on their tough guy glares. Catfeet did a little dance step down the last few steps, the way Cagney did at the end of *Yankee Doodle Dandy,* and was smiling as he stopped in front of them.

"Got a smoke?" He spoke to Mickey, who had a cigarette dangling out of his lips, the cold fall wind whipping the smoke away from his face. "I been smoking those damn Bull Durham roll-your-owns for a couple of years now, a Pall Mall would taste real fine."

They were going to see how far he wanted to take it, where he wanted to go. Catfeet knew this because Lar stepped back and crossed his arms and Mickey didn't say anything, just reached inside his heavy black chauffeur's coat, into his shirt pocket and pulled out a pack of Marlboros, shook one out past the edge of the pack and offered it to Catfeet who took it, ripped the filter off and stuck the other end into his mouth.

"How about a light?"

He felt a sense of power as Mickey put the smokes away and brought out his Zippo, some of the old self-confidence coming back to him. He'd go a little further, see how far he could push. He accepted the light with a grunt of thanks.

"You guys bring me a present? A fat envelope filled with thousand-dollar bills? I did twenty-eight months in there for your boss, never said a word to anyone."

Larry shook his head, made a spitting sound. Mickey

said, "We come to escort you home, to get the envelope from *you*."

"What envelope?"

"The one with the three and a half million inside it."

"That's what he thinks I owe him now?" Catfeet kept the fear out of his voice, but it was work. Favore could call it that way and make it stick, he had that kind of pull.

Catfeet took stock of the two sides of beef standing there in the cold, giving him the fisheye. Larry was stroking his mustache and sneering outright, a dummy who'd do as he was told and enjoy it. Mickey he knew pretty well from before, for years now. A jerk, or he wouldn't be able to put up with Favore for long, but a standup guy who knew how things worked.

So when he spoke he edged around so he could keep half an eye on Larry, but could look directly into Mickey's eyes, make this conversation one on one.

"You telling me he kept the meter running on the juice when I was inside? That what you're saying to me? I stand up and do time for Favore and he's not gonna forgive the juice?"

"It don't seem right to me, either. Feet, but that's the way it is."

"I ain't got that kind of money."

Catfeet heard Lar snort again and he ignored the man, kept his eyes locked with Mickey's.

"We're supposed to tell you—"

"Shit, let's tell him in the car. I'm freezing my balls off out here."

"What balls?" Catfeet said, and turned to face Lar, knowing now that he was safe. He knew where this conversation was heading, what they'd want him to do, and he wouldn't be able to do it if his head was busted or his fingers broken.

"You just better watch it, Millard. I don't take a lot of shit from the headbreakers and I sure ain't gonna take none from some punk of a thief."

To Mickey, Catfeet said, "Where's the car?"

Joseph Wambaugh

"Joseph Wambaugh's characters have altered America's view of police."
—*Time*

FUGITIVE NIGHTS

The fugitive is a man of the desert, wise in the ways of survival, and is willing to be violent to protect himself. Who he is and what his mission is become increasingly baffling to the police.

The trail of the fugitive will lead three mismatched people from remote desert canyons to the golden boulevards of Palm Springs, from funeral parlors to swank hotels to celebrity golf tournaments, from endless stakeouts to high-speed chases.

All of Joseph Wambaugh's special talents as a master storyteller are on display in *Fugitive Nights*. The result is one of his most skillful, baffling, entertaining, and suspenseful novels ever.

"Hilarious and chilling...Fugitive Nights had me wide-eyed and alert until the very end."—The New York Times Book Review

Don't Miss Any Of Joseph Wambaugh's Bestsellers